NANNY I WANT TO MATE

MIA KAYLA

Nanny I Want to Mate

Mia Kayla

Visit my website at http://www.authormiakayla.com/

Cover Designer: Jersey Girl Designs

Development Editor:

Kristy Deboer, authorkastalter@gmail.com

Megan Hand, meganhandwrites@gmail.com

Editor: Jovana Shirley, Unforeseen Editing, www.unforeseenediting.com

Proofreader: Judy Zweifel, www.judysproofreading.com

ISBN: 978-1-953370-01-3

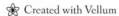 Created with Vellum

To my grandmother—Mamala,
This book is dedicated to you, the year you turned ninety
years young.
I love you above words, above measure. I am the woman
today because of you.

CHAPTER 1

CHARLES

I smelled weed. The strong, distinct stench of skunk. The scent would have been fine if I were still in college or out at a club or anywhere but here in my home, at the long dining room table, sitting opposite of the woman we were interviewing to be the nanny of my two small children.

She leaned back on the chair with one ankle crossed and rested on the opposite knee. Her hands settled behind her neck. She was so relaxed that I wondered if she'd fall asleep soon.

Our long-term nanny was leaving, and my brothers and I needed to find her replacement.

The brunette seated in front of me was dressed in a pressed suit, her makeup impeccable, which matched her stellar résumé. Everything was perfect, except for the fact that she reeked as though she were growing the plant in her purse.

Mason, my youngest brother, seated to the left of me, flipped to the next page of his portfolio. Erica Michelle Jones's name was neatly printed on the top tab. Mason had done a file on each candidate, complete with their résumé, background check, and list of questions he was going to ask. He had led the way in contacting the top nanny recruiting firms and gone through numerous résumés to pick the best of the best for his nieces.

Brad, the middle brother, sat to my right. The way his eyes were downturned and how he covered his mouth to hide the smile creeping up his face, I knew he was well aware of the smell emanating from the woman in front of us.

If Mason was aware of the stench, I would never guess it as he ticked off question after question on his detailed interview sheet.

Brad laughed and coughed to cover it. Given his playfulness, you would think he was the youngest out of us three. Nope. He was the most arrogant, and he suffered heavily from MCS—middle child syndrome—meaning he needed the most attention. When another cough-laugh fell from Brad's mouth, Mason shot him a look of disdain. I wouldn't doubt it if Brad was getting high from the fumes. I shook my head and then rubbed at my brow.

Mason smiled, shut the file folder, and stood to shake her hand. "We're highly impressed with your qualifications. We'll definitely be in touch."

When he pushed out from his chair, Brad and I followed suit.

And as soon as she left, Mason dropped to his seat and began writing detailed notes. "I think she's the best one we've interviewed so far."

I didn't have to say a word because Brad threw up his hands, laughing. "Are you serious? She smelled like she was born on a cannabis plant."

Mason's head shot up from the file folder, and he lifted an eyebrow.

"You didn't smell that?" Brad said, pointing to the door where Erica had just left.

"I wasn't really concerned with how she smelled. I was too busy interviewing her about her work history." Mason shook his head as though we were the crazy ones. "Maybe it's her perfume." His eyes were focused on his paper as he continued writing his notes.

I nearly laughed out loud but caught myself. *Didn't he know what that stank was?* Of course, Mason had never tried weed.

We were three brothers who had grown up in the same household, but we were different in every sense of the word.

Where Mason was meticulous and lived his life following a straight line, Brad was the opposite—rambunctious, playful, and one who would never settle down. Me, on the other hand? I'd been in one serious relationship since high school— the love of my life, the mother of my children. My life had been perfect until that split second when she left this world.

The smile slipped from my face. On cue, whenever Natalie filtered into my thoughts, my eyes would shut briefly, and I'd relive the moment she'd died, as though she were in the room with me. The memories were so vivid sometimes that they pulled me under to where I was immobilized.

I swallowed, pushing down the pain that always seemed to surface whenever my thoughts flickered toward the past.

"Daddy!" Mary, my almost four-year-old, skipped into the room. Her blonde curls bounced when she walked. She was the spitting image of her mother—the blonde in her hair, the blue in her eyes, the way her smile lit up the room.

Brad scooped her up in his arms before she got to me, nuzzling her neck and tickling her sides. "Sweet Mary. What did we tell you about coming in here while we're interviewing?"

Her giggles heightened. "Where's the babysitter?" She pushed out her lip and fluttered her sky-blue eyes at her uncle. "And what's that smell?" She inhaled deeply and then hopped out of his arms, lifting her nostrils in the air, like a puppy sniffing around at the dinner table. "I like it. It smells"—sniff—"kinda good."

Well, shit.

"Mary ..." I shared a knowing glance with Brad and tipped my chin toward the exit.

In the next second, Brad ushered Mary out the door. "Okay, out you go. We've got business to do."

He stalked toward Mason, reached for his paper, and wrote over his notes in big red letters, *Does drugs. Not qualified.*

"Hey!" Mason protested.

Brad turned to me. "Do you disagree? Do you believe she's qualified? I mean, this is a no-brainer. I don't care that she has her English degree from Stanford."

Both sets of eyes turned to my direction.

They always did.

As the head of the household and the oldest brother, as the CEO of our company—Brisken Printing Corporation—they always looked to me for the final word.

I shook my head. "No. She's not qualified."

She was more than not qualified. That woman would not be stepping in this house ever again.

Mason shut the file folder, and Brad sported a victorious grin.

I wished I felt some sort of victory. We were losing our

nanny who had been with us since my Natalie had passed. Finding a replacement was nearly impossible.

This was our third round of interviews, getting our candidates from well-known recruiting firms and passing *Mason's standard test*, which included an extensive background check and questionnaire, prior to interviews, with no luck thus far.

Sarah, my ten-year-old, walked in, followed by a woman dressed in the shortest black pleated skirt I'd ever seen. The damn thing was hiked up to just below her butt cheeks. Her green eyes perused the room before landing on Brad, and then her smile widened.

I refrained from rolling my eyes. I should be used to this by now—all the women who fawned over my brother—but there was a time and place for everything, and my patience was running thin with these candidates.

Brad showed no reaction. He was the brother who got the most attention from women. That was why we interviewed all his employees at our company—to make sure their first priority was the job and not landing my brother.

"I saw her wandering around the house," Sarah deadpanned, her tone showing her annoyance.

I had to wonder what I was in for with her, as she was already seeming to sprout that preteen attitude. Something that made me long for my wife even more.

The woman chomped on her gum and flipped her light-brown hair over her shoulder. "I'm interviewing for the nanny position."

Oh, great. I stifled a tired sigh.

She pointed a manicured red nail in Brad's direction. "Tell me you're the single dad." Her eyes wiggled in an exaggerated effect.

Brad's signature flirty smile surfaced but dimmed a

second later. "That would not be me." He saluted us and threw an arm around Sarah's shoulders. "I'm done here, guys. I trust Charles will make a sound decision for our girls." He pulled Sarah in close. "Uncle Brad is taking you and Mary out for ice cream."

Brad's gaze flickered my way for permission.

I wanted to go with them. Getting ice cream with my girls would be more fun than sitting here through another interview with a candidate I knew wasn't it. But Mason had worked hard to set up the interviews and go through the proper procedures in getting us the right person for the job.

My brothers were heavily invested in my girls. When my Natalie had died, I'd moved in with my parents so that they could help me raise the girls. When they passed not too long after that, due to a drunk driver–related car accident, both of my brothers moved into the house with me. Though they had their own places in the city, they both spent a few days a week here to spend time with the girls. They had helped me raise them from infancy to every momentous milestone in their lives. Brad had been the one to potty-train Mary while Mason had taught Sarah to read.

The woman sat down, all the while chomping on her gum. "He's such a handsome boy."

My eyebrows shot up. *Boy?*

"Your kid. The boy who found me in your kitchen."

A spark of fury shot through me as I glanced over at my beautiful daughter. Sarah's dark brown hair lay past her shoulders.

And this woman had mistaken her for a boy?

"Alright, we are out," Brad said. I nodded, because this was a lost cause already.

"Wait. We're not done here," Mason protested, but Brad was already out the door.

"I hope you don't mind, but I took a couple of cookies from that cookie jar on the table." She lifted her purse, flipped open the flap, and pulled out two cookies, the crumbs falling on the table. Then, she stuffed them back in.

My fury shifted to disgust. *Did this woman really just put two unwrapped cookies in her purse?*

Mason dropped his head, pinching the bridge of his nose.

The continuous smacking of her gum was grating on my nerves. I was about to dismiss her from this interview altogether, save Mason the misery of doing it, when she spoke first.

"So, before we formally start the interview, I have a few stipulations." She sat up taller and pushed her chest out, her cleavage almost falling out of her V-neck tank top. "I will need every weekend off along with every other Thursday and every first Monday of the month. I won't do bath time 'cause, yeah, that's kinda gross." She blew a bubble, popped it, and sucked it back into her mouth. "I don't cook but can microwave. I figure I'll be the one grocery shopping, so no worries on food there. And is the pay negotiable? Because it seems pretty low for a full-time, live-in nanny." She smacked on her gum. "Oh, and is there a maid? 'Cause I'm the nanny, not the maid."

Mason shot up from his chair so fast that it fell backward. "Get out." He breathed heavily through his nose, and his voice was barely controlled. He pointed to the door, and his jaw clenched. "Kindly get out of our house."

The woman pursed her lips, looking around as though she didn't understand the simple directions. "Uh, did you, like"—smacked gum—"want to reschedule or something, then?"

"Get out!" Mason's normally calm voice boomed and

echoed through our halls, making the woman jump to a standing position and scurry out.

When the door shut in the foyer, Mason rubbed at his forehead. "We'll never find someone." With both hands on the dining room table, his head hung, defeated.

I knew how many hours he'd spent going through numerous résumés and background checks, and I felt for him.

I patted his back, grateful that I had my brothers through this process. "We will. It'll just take some time. You know I appreciate all you're doing, right?"

He lifted his head and let out one long sigh. "They're my girls too. And I'm not stopping until we find the perfect person."

I nodded. "We'll continue interviews when I get back from Cape Cod."

I'd promised the girls one last trip before school started, and a promise made was a promise met in my book. What I'd learned through my experiences was that life was too short, and I'd be damned if my girls missed out.

Mason pointed to me. "Go get packed. Don't you leave tomorrow morning? Just remember, the only rule is, don't call us." He looked at me sternly. "Brad and I have work handled."

I sighed in resignation. They'd made me promise in front of the girls that I wouldn't open my laptop to check email or pick up my phone even if it was my secretary or anyone from work.

I tipped my chin, patted his back, and headed out the dining room to pack. It would be one of the last vacations that we took with Patty, our nanny.

I smiled because quality time with my girls was exactly what I craved.

CHAPTER 2

CHARLES

I tipped back my beer and rested against the beach chair, feeling the granules of sand beneath my toes.

Mary screamed for her older sister to chase her, but Sarah stayed, sitting cross-legged on the sand, pail and shovel in hand, going about her business and building her human-sized sand castle.

"Come on, Sarah! Play with me." The whine was heavy in Mary's voice.

I saw it coming from a mile away. Maybe, as their father, I should have stopped it, but this, their uninhibited fun, was what gave me joy.

Mary, a budding schemer, tiptoed up to Sarah and lifted a pail full of water. Then, she proceeded to dump it all on Sarah, the water ruining part of her creation, turning the sand castle to a plop of sand goo. Sarah, spluttering and about as raging mad as a ten-year-old could be, took off like a cheetah after Mary. The whole thing made me sigh with relief and a rare form of pure happiness that I only felt here and there since Natalie had passed.

"Ah!" Mary screamed, seeing her sister gain on her.

In the next second, Sarah toppled Mary and threw sand on top of her, getting it in her swimsuit.

A pang shot straight through my chest as I placed the beer down on the table next to me. If Natalie could only see this—our girls, growing up so fast.

If only ...

"Girls, girls, girls." Patty's voice boomed like thunder. She broke the girls apart and dusted the sand off their legs.

I chuckled at the scene in front of me.

When Mary started for Sarah again, Patty lifted her in her arms to keep her at bay.

The sixty-year-old woman had strength; I'd give her that.

"But, Nana," Mary implored, working her charm.

"Don't *Nana* me," Patty said, no nonsense. "You have to play nice with your sister."

She'd been with the girls for almost four years and functioned more like their strict grandmother than their nanny—thus the name *Nana*. Plus, since my girls didn't have any living grandparents around, Patty was the closest they were going to get to a nana.

Patty loved my girls like they were her own, and for that, I would be eternally grateful. When Natalie had died, my parents had hired Patty to assist us in helping raise the girls while I was at work. And when my parents had died a few years after, Patty had moved in with us permanently.

My phone vibrated on the table next to my beer, and I watched the light flash with a vendor's number. My fingers itched to pick it up, but I had promised the girls that I wouldn't work on this vacation. It was a promise I'd made to myself before we left for Cape Cod. And also one that Brad and Mason were making sure I kept.

Being the CEO of Brisken Printing Corp.—the largest printing company in the nation—I had endless responsibilities, but it wasn't anything that my brothers couldn't handle —Mason as CFO and Brad as VP.

I blew out a low breath, and regret settled deep in my gut as I thought of all the time I'd wasted on work before Natalie passed.

I wished we had taken that vacation to Europe that she'd always wanted. I'd promised her we'd go, but work always got in the way. A promise made was a promise kept. But back then, I thought we'd have eternity.

And then she was taken during childbirth, something no one could've prepared for. Her labor with Mary had been complicated. Natalie's blood pressure had been through the roof, and ...

I rubbed at my temple, pushing the memories of her lifeless body on the table out of my mind, and I forced my gaze back to my children. My biggest responsibility in life was raising those two lives that God had entrusted me with; therefore, I had to remind myself of that and focus on the present, the now.

When Natalie had died, people always said, "Be strong, for the girls."

And when a drunk driver had taken my parents a few years later, they would repeat their guiding words. "Be strong, for your brothers. You are the oldest. The CEO."

And I was.

I had been.

The only way I knew how to survive was just to push through.

So many people depended on me. Not only my girls and the family, but also the thousands of employees at Brisken. I had a duty to maintain with everyone. The reality of it all was that I just dealt. I didn't get bogged down with the details because if I thought about all the responsibility set on my shoulders, it'd stress me out.

Mary sauntered over with the biggest pout, and I couldn't help but smile. She was so sweet, really feisty, and mischievous as hell. But she owned my heart.

"Daddy! Sarah put sand in my butt," she relayed, disgruntled. "Now, I have it in my swimsuit. I bet I'll fart sand later." She crossed her arms over her chest.

In one big swoop, I pulled her close. "If I saw correctly, you doused her with water when she was playing quietly and minding her own business."

Her eyebrows pulled together, and right then, she looked like her mother—the blonde in her hair, the blue in her eyes.

Another pang. Harder this time.

My smile faltered but just a tad as she started making up more excuses.

"It was only a tiny sprinkle of water. Not that much. And it's only because she didn't want to play with me."

I touched a finger to her nose. "Do you want Daddy to play with you?"

"Yes! Yes! Yes!" She bounced on my knee and then hopped off. "Come chase me."

"How about I give you a head start?" I stood and rubbed my hands together for exaggerated effect, and then she took off into Patty's hands, who caught her mid-flight.

"Nana!"

"One second while I talk to your dad."

"No!" Mary complained.

Patty put her hands on her hips and gave Mary her no-nonsense look. "Mary Katherine Brisken."

Those three words had my baby cowering and pushing out her lip.

I couldn't blame her. I wouldn't want to be in trouble with Patty either.

"One second, okay?" Patty tipped Mary's chin with her forefinger and kissed her head. "And you play nice with your sister."

"Okay, Nana," Mary replied begrudgingly.

When Mary stalked toward Sarah's sand castle, Patty approached and sat down in the beach chair next to mine.

"Charles, how's it going so far? How's the search?" Concern was heavy in her eyes.

I exhaled deeply and rolled the beer bottle back and forth between my fingertips. "It could be going better. I'm sure this search has given Mason a few premature grays."

She laughed.

"How's your mother doing anyway?" I asked.

I knew how stressed out Patty was with her mother's health, and my brothers and I tried everything we could to make sure she took the time she needed to go home to Florida and be with her mother by adjusting my brothers' and my schedules.

"Well, I'm surprised she's lasted this long, but being ninety and still kicking is a pretty good sign. She's doing better since her stroke, but she's aging." The light in Patty's eyes dimmed.

"Patty, I'm sorry."

"She doesn't have that much time left, Charles." Her voice was soft, fragile even.

"I know."

I'd lost both parents, so I knew the feeling. I'd mastered losing people. What I hadn't mastered was the pain. I was so used to losing people that I couldn't afford to lose any more. It had taken me years to stop putting Mary and Sarah in my own little self-made bubble, to stop going to every single playdate, to stop watching them fall asleep.

I took another long pull of my beer and focused on the waves rushing to the shore. That was much better than looking into Patty's sorrowful eyes, which mirrored my heartache.

"I'm going to take care of her," Patty said with a nod and a little more sadness since I knew she was going to miss the girls.

I nodded. "I just wish you weren't leaving."

Day by day, the hope that we would find someone as capable as Patty was dwindling and turning into desperation. In the moment of silence that spanned between us, I relived the nightmare of interviews that we'd already gone through—the hippie chick who had shown us all her herbs to treat the kids' ailments and the drill sergeant who had told us her ways of disciplining the children, which I was pretty sure were all illegal.

Damn it. A worry threatened to choke me, and panic filled my insides. We were never going to find someone capable.

I cleared my throat. "What if we moved her here? Your mom."

I'd suggested this earlier to Patty, but she'd shut me down.

"It's not possible. I have to go back." Her voice was resolute, her words final.

My breathing sped up as though I'd been knocked in the face with the bottle, but really, it was her words. "It is possible though. I have the means to make it happen."

If tears could compel this woman to stay, I would force tears down my face like a little baby, but I had no idea how to even cry. My body had been built to keep myself intact, my emotions in check.

"I have no idea how to raise these girls alone." My body shot up from the seat, and I paced the short distance in front of my chair. "I can't do this without you. What does she need? Let us set Eleanor up here. I'll pay for all medical expenses, living expenses. All of it."

"Charles Emmanuel Brisken." She used the exact tone she'd used on Mary only moments ago. She patted the seat that I had evacuated. "Sit down."

My breathing quickened, as though I'd run a race, though I was standing perfectly still. "Patty, you can't leave us." I blew out a breath.

I had my brothers, but it was different. I didn't trust many people with my girls, but I trusted Patty. My brothers and I knew her. The girls knew her. Above that, we all loved her.

"Charles, please take a seat," she said patiently.

I fell to my seat, but I wasn't ready to admit defeat.

Her jaw tightened, and she angled her knees parallel to mine. "I've been thinking about this for a while now. It hasn't been easy, but she doesn't have that long, and it isn't right that someone else is taking care of her. She'll be transferred to a nursing home that has care round the clock, and I'll be there with her every day."

"Move Eleanor here." Desperation was heavy in my tone. I couldn't help it. "We have a ton of room. You want privacy? I'll build you another wing. Forget the nursing home. I'll hire in-home care." I rubbed at my temple, the panic rising to my throat, threatening to choke me.

"Charles, I can't uproot her from Florida."

"Patty ..." I was six-two, stocky like a football player, and the CEO of a Fortune 500 company. I didn't beg. Begging was not in my vocabulary, but now was a whole different story. "I'll triple your salary."

Patty gave me a look, one of those stern looks that she only gave the children. "You know you pay me more than enough. It's not about the money. I have to do this."

And as I stared into her eyes that held so much wisdom, I knew she had already made her decision. There was nothing I could say or do to change her mind. In the deepest part of me, even though I didn't want to see it, I knew it was the right decision for her—to take care of her family— because that was the decision I would make.

I dropped my head and ran both hands through my hair. "I ... I can't possibly do this alone." I breathed deeply through my nose and exhaled a shaky breath, my whole body trembling now. "I just ... can't."

"Look at me," she said harshly.

Instead, I closed my eyes tightly because in about two more seconds, I was about to lose it.

Our life was stable now. We'd had years of instability because tragedy hit us year after year, but now ... things had finally subsided, evened out. Routines had been established. This would be another blow, another hiccup to the girls' everyday lives, to my everyday life, to all of our normal.

I couldn't remember the last time I'd broken down. One of my greatest strengths was to keep my composure in the hardest of times because so many people depended on me. But today, as time dwindled down and Patty's end date with us quickly approached, I panicked.

Leading a multimillion-dollar company did not make me nervous. But this—raising my girls by myself—made me so nervous that I wanted to throw up. Maybe if I'd had boys, I could have managed, but girls? I exhaled a shaky breath. *What did three men know about raising girls?*

"Charles ..." She knocked on the table. "I'm waiting."

I lifted my head to see Patty smiling at me.

"I'm glad you're laughing at my misfortune."

"If I thought for one second"—she pursed her lips—"that you weren't capable, I wouldn't leave you. I wanted to leave a year ago when my mother really got sick, but I couldn't then, and you know why."

"And I appreciate it, Patty." I searched the heavens for some sort of sign from my angel.

God, did I miss her. Especially in moments like this.

"You know Natalie would be proud of you. You know that, don't you? To do all of this by yourself and raise those beautiful girls."

I sank into my chair, and my eyebrows pulled together. "That's the thing. I'm not doing this by myself. You've been assisting me throughout it all. Since Natalie passed away, since my parents hired you on, you've been there."

With one more attempt at making Patty stay, I picked up my beer bottle, dipped my finger in the bottle, and applied it to the bottom of my eyes. "I'm crying here, begging you to stay."

I turned to face her, and she covered her mouth in laughter.

"Your desperation is showing now, Charles. You're cracking jokes."

My eyebrows pulled together. "I crack jokes." *Didn't I?* Maybe I wasn't the best at it. I needed to get a joke book.

Sixty years of wisdom pushed through her eyes. "Charles, you'll be fine for one reason alone. You love those little angels with all your heart, and you only want the best for them."

I nodded, the panic still making things fuzzy. That was

the truth I knew and lived by—wanting the best for my children.

I glanced at my daughters fighting in the sand. Mary had toppled over Sarah and was burying her.

My eyes met Patty's, and we both laughed.

"Did you say angels?"

Her smile stretched across her face. "Yes, most definitely. Angels when they are asleep."

When she let out a deep chuckle, I slumped against the beach chair and ran one hand down my face. I'd miss this lady, not only because I needed her to help with the girls, but also because she reminded me so much of the mother that I had lost.

"Patty, don't go." It was my last desperate plea, but I knew it was all for nothing.

She needed to do what was best for her family. Out of everyone, I understood that the most.

"Don't worry, Charles," she urged with empathy. She sat back and sighed, and then she eyed me for a minute, finally saying, "I think I have someone who can fill the spot. Someone I would trust with the girls, someone I would trust with my life."

My back straightened in the chair because this was the first time Patty had mentioned it—a direct referral.

"Who is it?" I asked with wide eyes, wondering why she'd been holding out on me all this time.

Patty's smile widened. "I'll give you more information once I talk to her. If she says yes, then I have no doubt you and the girls will be in good hands."

That ugly panic finally started to subside. "Can I bribe this person with a new car? Higher pay she can't refuse? A vacation to Fiji once a year?" I laughed, only half-kidding.

The humor vanished from Patty's features. "It's not like

that, Charles. Money will not be the determining factor in this person's decision in taking the job. And if by chance she decides to take the position, there will be a slew of stipulations that is attached with her coming on board." She patted my leg. "But we'll cross that bridge when we get to it."

I frowned at her. *Stipulations?* I wondered what they could possibly be.

CHAPTER 3

Becky

I rubbed at my throat, swallowing air because I could. Because I remembered a time when I couldn't. Where darkness surrounded me and I couldn't breathe.

My eyes shut, and I gritted my teeth.

I pushed those memories back down, to a place I refused to revisit—my past.

That's not my life anymore.

A movie on the television had triggered the memory. It was a movie that Eleanor, the ninety-year-old woman I was taking care of, had wanted to watch. Eventually, she had fallen asleep, but I hadn't turned off the television.

I didn't like violent movies because it hit too close to home. I couldn't avoid the memories in my nightmares, but I had a choice to avoid them now.

I inhaled deeply and forced myself to the present. Automatically, I stood and paced the room, back and forth and back and forth again, watching Eleanor sleep. Her bed was situated in the great room by the kitchen, so I'd have everything I needed to watch her. Her lips were slightly ajar, and she seemed peaceful in her slumber, forcing the corner of my mouth to tip upward.

I walked toward her bed and pulled the covers over her arms, my fingertips lightly brushing against her skin. My heart ached as I noted her deterioration. She'd always been independent since I'd met her but not in the past few months.

She could sit up but couldn't eat by herself anymore. I had to spoon-feed her. But her mind was alert. It was in her nonverbal cues that told me she was okay, her little smiles and the evident frown and the tip of her chin when she was being stubborn—and ninety-year-old Eleanor was more stubborn than a child.

There was no denying her body was ailing. She was unable to get out of bed nowadays, and Patty, her daughter, had made the hardest decision. She'd be transferred to a nursing facility, which had round-the-clock care available for her. Currently I was at their home caring for her.

I had done everything in my ability to keep Eleanor comfortable here. I didn't mind changing her and giving her the meds. But ultimately, Patty was leaving her nannying job because she wanted to spend whatever time her mother had left on this earth with her.

And I got that because they were close.

Eleanor and Patty were the family I'd never really had. This never felt like a job because from day one, Patty had invited me to eat with her and filled me in on her childhood, on how Eleanor was the best and most patient mom.

She'd told me how her parents had fallen in love—a love made for romance books, a love that was everlasting, a love that I'd never known.

Patty's stories were what I craved because I'd had an untraditional childhood. I'd never met my father, and my mother had been in and out of jail. I'd been sent to foster care, where I bounced in and out of homes until I was fifteen. Then, I'd run away, and I'd been fending for myself ever since.

So, this—this life I'd built with the people I cared for—was my family.

The doorknob shaking had me jumping up to a standing position and my heartbeat picking up in speed.

All my muscles tensed. My anxiety spiked, and my heartbeat pounded in my ears.

But then Patty walked in, pulling her suitcase behind her.

I let out a long sigh of relief.

When would my nerves ease up?

When would my life get back to normal?

Never, the tiny voice said.

Because since I had been born, my life had been anything but normal.

"Hey." My heart rate stabilized as I assisted her, taking a bag from her shoulder. "I wasn't expecting you this weekend."

"Yeah, Charles gave me the weekend off to settle things."

I made my way to the living room, following her in through the small two-bedroom ranch.

"I hope it won't be too long, Becky. They are looking for my replacement, but you know their love for the girls is endless, so they want to find the perfect match."

I smiled. I lived through Patty's stories when she came home. About the family she cared for. I felt like I already knew them sometimes. As I didn't have a family of my own, it was refreshing to hear her stories about her sweet Mary and Sarah.

"How's Mama doing?" Patty approached the hospital bed and ran her hand down her mother's arm.

"Good. I changed her bedpan this morning. The nurse came in earlier to check her stats, and she's fine." I pulled Eleanor's blanket higher, up to her chin. "She makes me laugh. Today, she wanted me to brush her dentures with a different toothpaste, not the normal one, but the whitening toothpaste." A laugh escaped my lips. "The girl doesn't even wear them anymore."

Patty smiled, staring at her mother and shaking her head. "You know she's messing with you, right?"

I nodded. "Yeah, I know."

Eleanor sure was an entertainer.

When Patty wasn't here, Eleanor wanted to show me albums upon albums of her family, which included her deceased husband, Henry.

Their lives had been filled with happiness and vacations and endless laughter, something I'd never had while growing up, something that I was jealous of.

I fidgeted with the end of my shirt. "I've started looking for a job already, so you don't have to worry about me."

Patty turned to face me, her smile slipping. "Where will you be heading?" Concern was heavy in her eyes.

Patty knew I had a past, but she didn't pry. That was the stipulation of me coming on board—that she wouldn't ask me about my past. In return, I would take care of her mother and move on to a less stressful future.

I swallowed. I hadn't planned my next course of action, but I couldn't stay here long, couldn't be too comfortable. It was time to leave, to pick up and move anywhere. I only stayed here longer than I'd anticipated because of my fondness for Eleanor and Patty. Plus, I was careful—really careful. I rarely went out, only for walks, and I always ordered our groceries for delivery. Honestly, it was the perfect job for someone who didn't want to be found—someone like me.

I rustled a hand through my long blonde locks. "I don't know. Maybe somewhere colder. North." I had money saved, but it would only last me so long. I needed a job that could pay me under the table. Something like this. "If you have any prospects," I hinted, trying to hide my desperation, "any elderly person who needs care."

That was my expertise. I wasn't grossed out easily, and I wasn't a nurse, but in my former life—one where I could afford a college education, one where I wasn't running—I would have been a nurse. I enjoyed taking care of people who couldn't take care of themselves. Maybe it had been caused by my past, of no one taking care of me, growing up.

Carl, an adult who was severely disabled, had been my first job that didn't include waitressing or working at the grocery store. Carl was the first job I took that helped me disappear from the face of the earth. It had happened by pure accident, and even taking on the job as the caregiver for Eleanor had happened by pure accident.

I was so grateful, but I was finding myself in need again. If only I could have the same luck ...

Patty eyed me, tipping her chin toward the table at the far end of the room. "Go sit. Let me get some coffee going."

"Oh, I'll do it." I was already heading toward the kitchen when she waved me off.

"No. You sit. I've been on a plane and in a car half the day. I need to move and get my steps in." She checked her Fitbit, noting her number of steps.

After the pot of coffee brewed, she poured the liquid in a mug and walked over to the couch with two steaming cups.

She leveled me with a stare after handing me my cup. "I know there are things going on with you."

My whole body tensed. Patty never asked me about my former life, a life that I wanted to forget. She knew the rules, but the concerned look in her eye told me that this time was different. If she asked me about my past, I wouldn't be able to tell her. Mostly because I didn't want anyone else involved in my mess.

She placed one soft hand on mine on the table. "Don't worry. I'm not going to pry. I don't know your past. But I know you now." She patted my hand twice, an affectionate look in her eye. "And I know you are a good person. A person who has taken exceptional care of my mother these past few years, even staying with her and lying by her at the hospital. Do you have plans for where you're going to go? I need to know you're going to be okay."

My eyes peered over to Eleanor in her bed, and the corner of my lips tipped upward. She was my confidant in all things. She'd suffered a stroke a few months ago, which had deteriorated her health. I'd refused to be away from her when she was at the hospital, staying right by her bed until the doctors decided that she could be cared for at home.

My eyes focused on the lines etched on the table as I gripped the heart-shaped pendant they'd given me. "I'll be okay. I just can't ..." *I just can't tell you where I'm going because I don't know what my next steps are.*

But one thing I knew was that I was a survivor. I'd do what I had to do to survive.

Patty ducked her head so that I had to meet her eyes. "I want to help you find a new job." She tucked an escaping hair behind my ear. "I do. Because you helped me and because I know you have a good heart."

Her words hit me like a truck; her kindness was overwhelming. I nodded through tear-filled eyes, knowing I'd miss this family—my unconventional family.

She nodded resolutely after watching me a moment, as if it was settled. "I will get you that job you need. But it will be in Illinois. If you are willing."

CHAPTER 4

CHARLES

I snuck out of Vivian's bed, careful not to wake her, but as soon as I stood, she stirred and opened her eyes. She lifted her head from the pillow, and her eyes bore into mine. Her sleek black hair fell over her shoulders, and she pushed herself to a sitting position.

"Charles? Leaving already?" Her glance slid my way, raking boldly over me.

I nodded and slipped on my boxers and slacks. "Yes. Sorry, I have to get back home."

"Home. A home is not a house; it's the people you choose to share it with." Natalie's words. Not mine.

And although I had the girls I loved beyond comprehension, my home since Nat's death had been incomplete. It was something that I'd come to terms with.

"Charles," she uttered, her voice silky.

I had blanked out on Vivian again.

I turned toward her, my face apologetic. She knew what our relationship was. I didn't lie and pretend to be someone I wasn't. I had been an empty shell of my former self since

Natalie had passed. That was all I could give Vivian. It was all I had.

"I'm sorry. My mind has been in other places."

All the stress from looking for a replacement for Patty was weighing me down. I'd been home for almost a week now, and there were still no prospects remotely qualified to fill Patty's position.

She smiled suggestively. "Your mind and other things were fine thirty minutes ago."

She tore off the covers and exposed herself. I turned away.

It had taken two whole years for me to give in to Vivian's flirtation, yet it didn't let up the guilt. How could I be cheating when my wife was already dead?

In the next second, her hands were around me, and her lips were against my neck. "Stay, Charles. I'll make it worth it. I promise."

I extracted her hands and peered down at her. Vivian was stunningly beautiful with her light-olive skin and silky, straight jet-black hair that rested just above her waist.

"You know I can't. I have to get back to the girls."

Her calm, put-together demeanor faltered, and I exhaled deeply. I didn't want to give her hope, hope for a future between us that would never come.

"Vivian, maybe it's time that we—"

She went on her toes and silenced me with her lips. "Enough. We've discussed this. I'm okay with this arrangement, Charles. I know this is all you can give me right now."

I stared down at her, my eyes firm. "This is a permanent situation for me. This is all I can give you ever, and you deserve more than what this is. You deserve a future with a guy who can stay the night. Vivian, you deserve dinner and a movie and not a couple of hours of sex every other week."

Her hands trailed up my chest, slowly running up and down my nipple. "I look forward to our sex sessions every other week."

I took her hands in mine, and my chest seized. I knew if I gave her an inch, she'd take it. Problem was, there was nothing in me left to give.

"That's the thing. You should look forward to more than that."

"I'm not looking for anything more, Charles." She raised a fine, arched eyebrow. "I'm not the marrying or children type. You know this about me. And right now, this is all I have time for too."

Beautiful yet cutthroat, Vivian looked like a woman but was internally built like a man. She was a partner at the law firm that we used. She wasn't the lawyer we dealt with because I wasn't going to complicate my life any further.

Like me, her time was limited, but the difference between us was that I chose to make time for my family.

"I don't want to be that guy who gives you false hope. I've told you time and time again, Viv, that you have so much to offer."

"Enough," she said, her tone sharp yet playful. "You've always been honest with me. I'm an adult, Charles, and this is what I want." She reached for the button on my slacks. "I want another hour, and that's all."

Her lips met mine, and I flinched. The thing with Vivian worked because in the moments I was with her, I disconnected my heart from my body. Because that heart— the organ that pumped blood to every part of my body— belonged to someone else. And that someone else was no longer alive.

———

The next morning, I walked into the kitchen and found Brad sitting at the kitchen table. He was a disheveled, hungover mess. His hair was not styled to his normal perfection, and his eyes were bloodshot. But he was dressed and all ready for work. This was nothing new, as this was his lifestyle that I was used to. As long as he showed up to work and did his job as VP and was present when the girls needed him, I didn't care what he did afterward.

One day, someone would knock him on his ass. Hopefully, a woman who would tame his wild ways.

He stared up at me and waved a weak hand. "Hey. Where were you last night? You weren't home when I left, which was pretty late."

I swallowed and walked toward the coffee machine. "Vivian's," I said the word curtly, brooking no further comment.

I didn't know why I felt guilty. We were all grown men. Some would judge his lifestyle more than my life choices. Still, I didn't want to live this life. I'd tried to break it off with Vivian multiple times because I didn't like how our relationship felt—like she was my dirty little secret.

I judged my moral compass based on my children—whether they would be proud of me. Would they be proud that their father was leaving the house to have sex with a woman he wasn't involved with seriously?

No, they wouldn't.

But I admitted, I had needs, and I was a weak man. It didn't make it easier that Vivian was a proponent of our convenient relationship.

"You need to stop feeling guilty," Brad said, reading my mind. "You're not doing anything wrong."

I ignored his comment. I didn't judge Brad with his life choices. He never brought anyone home to meet the girls.

That was an unspoken rule, and I knew he loved the girls like they were his own, so he wouldn't anyway. He could live his life how he wanted to live his life ... but me ... I had children. Two girls. Without a mother. I needed to hold myself to a higher standard.

"Drink some water. Sober up before the girls get up," I said.

"Nice to see you still hungover on a Monday morning," Mason shot out as he strolled in, all ready for work in his crisp, pressed navy-blue suit, holding his portfolio. "Where did you go?"

Brad groaned in his misery. "Bar, dinner, and then back to Kelly's house."

"On a Sunday night?" Mason said, indignant. "And who the hell is Kelly?"

"My new girlfriend." Brad rubbed at his head, squinting as though it hurt to open his eyes.

"You can't call the new girl you just met at a bar your girlfriend." Mason made a gagging noise in the back of his throat, as though he were going to throw up. "Thank God STDs are not airborne."

Brad rubbed at his temple. "Shh. Quiet." He rested his head against his hands. "Anyway, what's on the agenda for today?"

Mason threw Brad a look before his head dipped down to his detailed schedule, the one he printed out every morning just for himself. "Sonia will give you your schedule when you get to work. But for me, besides today's ten o'clock with the new supplier and our quarterly meeting with the managers, I've got nothing assigned. The agency just sent me more nanny résumés. I have to go through them, so we can set up more interviews this weekend."

Brad groaned again but for a whole different reason. I wanted to join him. I was beyond frustrated.

Patty had returned from seeing her mother, but she hadn't mentioned anything regarding her referral. If she didn't by today, I was going to because my patience was all dried up.

Mason shut his portfolio, taking his regular seat at the table. "I think we're getting close though. To finding the perfect nanny. Not to worry. I'm a great people-reader."

Brad lifted his head and sported a heavy smirk. He threw me a look, and I discreetly shook my head.

Hold your tongue, brother. It's a lost cause.

"Little bro"—Brad's tone oozed with a light humor —"good people-reader? I'd have to question that, given your choice in women."

The smile slipped from Mason's face. "Shut up, and that's why you'll be single for life. You'll never have what Janice and I have."

Brad flinched, but in the next second, he shot back, "Yeah, if all I could get was a gold digger, then I'd rather be single for the rest of my life."

"Gold digger?" Mary sauntered in, surprisingly all dressed in her uniform, holding her favorite wand in her arms. "I want to be a gold digger."

I smirked, shaking my head.

I had to hand it to Mary for breaking up all the tension in the room.

Brad sobered up as though our mother had walked into the room. He pushed back his hair, scooped her up, and kissed her full, round cheeks. "You'll never be a gold digger."

"But I want to. I have my own shovel in the garage.

Where would we go digging for gold?" Her blue eyes were wide and so damn beautiful, just like her mother's.

Mason laughed beside Brad. "Well, there are public mining areas. I'll have to look it up."

She pointed her wand at Mason. "You do that." With her wand, she tapped the paper. "Are we going to look for my babysitter today? Because Teddy Monster is ready to ask the questions." Her smile widened. "And I set up an obstacle course she'll have to go through."

Mason and I shared an amused glance. An obstacle course? Only my daughter. If they could pass the Mary test, then they were hired.

Mason touched the tip of her nose. "Not today, but this weekend."

Brad set Mary on her feet and took off out of the room. "Why can't we move Patty's mom here again?" he said, his voice defeated.

I wasn't about to answer his recurring question. He already knew why.

Brad tipped back his chin, his stare wandering over to the door where Mary had exited. "We've been searching for weeks, and we haven't found any person remotely qualified to watch our girls."

"Fourth time's a charm; I'm sure of it," Mason said, though I could tell even his optimism was waning.

"I think the saying is, *Third time's a charm*, and we are way past that," Brad said.

Patty strolled in, showered and ready to start the day. She threw a glance our way and smiled. "Why such the sullen faces, boys?"

Brad groaned again. He walked to Patty, reached for her hand, and got on his knees, as though he were about to propose.

Patty threw back her head and laughed. "I think you're a little young for me. This would be taking *robbing the cradle* to a whole other level."

I chuckled. *Brad and his theatrics.*

He pouted. "No ... stay, Patty. This is me begging you to stay."

She sighed, amused. "Get up, Bradley."

"Come on, Patty. We need you." He took her other hand. "We're a bunch of men, raising girls. I don't want to even think about hormones and PMS and all those things girls go through. Who is going to answer their questions?"

She tugged him up then and patted his cheek. "Sit down. Let me get breakfast ready and then the girls off to school, and we'll talk about my replacement."

I perked up, wondering if she was finally going to give us this secret candidate she'd been holding on to.

"That's the thing; we've looked and interviewed, and every single one has failed." Brad firmed up his shoulders.

By the look on his face, I knew he was never giving up. It was one of his greatest qualities—determination.

Patty threw me a glance, and I shrugged because he wasn't lying there.

"Patty, there was one who smelled like weed," Brad said, disgusted. "Mary said she liked her perfume, which is a little scary. My niece was getting high on the fumes. Now, is that what you want to leave your girls—the girls you love, our innocent Mary and Sarah—to?" His stare was fixed on hers, challenging her.

I had to give it to Brad; he wasn't letting up.

Patty sighed, and her shoulders slumped.

"Let's just say, no one can compare to you," I said.

"Well"—she tipped her chin—"that is true. But I think I

have a solution. I will not leave my girls to a weed-smoking nanny, all right?"

Brad nodded, looking every bit the winner in this match. "Okay, I'm glad you came to your senses. I'll make the arrangements to have Eleanor moved here today."

Brad got out his phone—about to call his secretary, Sonia, most likely—but Patty was quick to pluck the cell out of his hands.

She laughed and then lightly slapped Brad's shoulder. "I have to get the girls ready. I'll be back, and then we can talk about my replacement. I think I have the answer to our problem."

CHAPTER 5

CHARLES

After dropping off the girls, I met Brad, Mason, and Patty in the boardroom at Brisken Printing Corporation. We had to be at work for a morning meeting, so I'd suggested that Patty drive to the office, so we could have our discussion and still meet at the scheduled time with our vendors.

Patty had a solution, and we were all ears. After three rounds of nanny interviews, we had nothing, and I doubted that the fourth round would be any better.

Sonia, Brad's secretary, strolled in and placed a new pot of coffee and some cookies at the center of the table. "Here's the creamer and sugar."

She adjusted it on the tray and began to walk out when Brad called out to her, "Hey, where's the hazelnut creamer I like?"

Brad didn't take flavored creamer with his coffee. He was baiting her, which was what he did best.

Sonia turned, pushed her glasses further up her nose, stared at him, blinked a few times, unaffected, and then about-faced and walked straight out of the room, as though he hadn't said a word.

I kept my face steady, but Mason busted out in full-blown laughter beside me. "And that's why we hired her ... because she doesn't take your shit."

Which was exactly so. Brad had gone through a phase of dating all his secretaries, who in turn had quit when it didn't work out because of his playboyish ways, which disrupted our flow of business.

Now, Mason and I were in charge of hiring anyone on Brad's team. Sonia had been the most recent hire on Brad's team. She took care of his schedule, kept him in check, and most importantly, didn't fall for his womanizing antics. She had a boyfriend, which was an added plus. Not like significant others had deterred the other secretaries, but this was Sonia. Sonia was different. She had self-respect and an aversion to Brad's charms.

Brad leaned back and tipped his chin. "Sonia loves me. She just doesn't know it yet," he joked.

Patty sat back and sipped her coffee, eyeing him with this all-knowing look I'd seen too many times before. "Maybe she is exactly what you need to change your ways."

Brad lifted an eyebrow, smiling, giddy even, and Mason pointed a shaky finger at him. "Don't even try it. Don't ruin a good thing, okay? We have this company running like a well-oiled machine since we hired her. We don't need you trying to screw your secretary. *Again.* Break her heart. *Again.* And have her quit. *Again.*"

Watching Mason's kick-ass face, I knew this could escalate quickly. I tapped my knuckles on the table. "Focus. We all have a meeting at ten." I turned toward Patty. "So, you said you have a solution, a possible replacement?"

I quietly prayed this was a viable candidate. Though I

trusted Patty with my life—because my girls were my life—I still wondered if whatever she was about to say would truly be a solution. I had become so doubtful that I even doubted Patty.

"I do." Her confident gaze landed on each of us. "Becky is currently the caretaker of my mother. She has the gentlest soul. Very kind. Very patient. Very loving."

I rested my elbows on the boardroom table, watching Patty light up, just talking about this woman, whom I'd heard about numerous times before.

"I've taken her in like my pseudo daughter. Seriously. I wish I could keep her with me, but it doesn't make sense for me to pay her when my mother will be at the nursing home for round-the-clock care and I'll be there with her." Patty's smile widened, and her eyes lit up with an inner glow. "She's young, and she needs to be somewhere else other than in a house with old people."

"How young are we talking about?" Brad asked, a little too interested.

Mason kicked him under the table, and Brad jumped. "What? And please. I'm not that dumb that I'd bang the nanny watching my girls. That's where I draw the line. I'm not going to do that, no matter how hot she is." He smirked. "Is she hot?"

Patty nodded. "Yes, she's very attractive."

Brad wiggled his eyebrows in an exaggerated effect.

"How long have you known her?" I reached for the coffee in the center of the table and poured myself a cup.

"Well, she cared for my best friend's son, who was disabled, until he died. That was for a few years. And then she's cared for my mama ever since."

"Where is she originally from? Does she have experience with kids? Does she have a family of her own? Do you have her résumé handy?" Mason spat out the questions in rapid succession, and I rubbed at my forehead.

"So ..." There was a long, pregnant pause as she stared at all of us. "Regarding her background, I have to say I don't know too much about her past." She raised a finger, not missing a beat. "But I trust her wholeheartedly. I trust her with my mother. I would trust her with those girls too, and you know I love those girls."

Brad slammed a palm against the table. "Sold."

Mason's eyebrows flew to his hairline. "Wait a second here. We haven't run a background check yet. What's her full name and social security?"

Patty leveled him with a stare and shook her head. "It's not like that, Mason. You won't be able to run a background check on her, and she only accepts cash."

Stipulations, Patty had said. This was it.

He blinked and then double-blinked at her, as though he didn't understand or that was the wrong answer. He tilted his head, assessing her, and then slowly said, "No. Sorry, that won't do." Mason did a slow shake of his head. "I mean, really? Trust a person we hardly know anything about, living in our house, watching our girls, one we can't even do a background check on?"

Brad pointed to Patty. "Patty basically vouched for her. That's like Mom vouching for her. How's this any different than Mom going with Auntie Carol's recommendation of Patty? She didn't run a background check. Right?"

That was true.

They both looked at me.

They always looked to me for the final answer.

I had the final say for every big decision at Brisken Printing Corporation and in all things family-related. I'd planned our last takeover, our last merger. I'd planned our parents' funeral, had the final decision on the flowers and the venue and the food at the reception. I had the final say in all things.

My gut told me to trust Patty. My mother and father had hired Patty on a recommendation, and given the way Patty talked about Becky, I knew she trusted this woman. If Patty trusted this woman with her mother and even our girls, it was worth meeting her.

But I couldn't give in just yet. A small smile formed at my idea. "I think we should put her through the Mary test."

CHAPTER 6

Becky

The Brisken men had asked me to fly up to Chicago, but I couldn't. I couldn't risk it. So, I had agreed to take a bus all the way from Florida to Chicago.

Patty picked me up from the bus station, and I was mute the whole ride in their car, wringing my hands in my lap.

"You'll do fine, Becky," Patty said soothingly. "I've talked you up. Plus, all you have to do is be yourself."

"Thanks, Patty."

Word of mouth was how I'd gotten out of my situation. It was how I'd lived the last few years of my life. I needed this job. I didn't have a huge network of people to find me another job or a résumé that I could give out.

I blew out a breath and stared at the back-to-back traffic in front of us. Big city. Another opportunity. New life. I placed heavy palms on my knees, forcing them to stop shaking. I'd never lived in a big city. My life before had consisted of rural farms and eating at the local sub shop connected to our gas station.

I needed this.

Patty had briefed me on the family. Some information I'd already known because when she came home to visit Eleanor and gushed about the girls, I would eat her stories up like it was my favorite meal. I drank up her day-to-day mishaps with Miss Mary and deep conversations with Sarah. I lived through their excursions and vacations and daily activities.

Yes, I was nervous, but a big part of me was excited to meet them because it felt as though I knew them already.

She waved to a guard, and he opened the gates to a well-manicured, elite subdivision. We drove up a winding road that led to a palatial mansion that had my jaw dropping to the ground. Lights highlighted the pillars of the mansion that framed the door, and the window-height shrubbery etched against the building was like lines against a painting.

"It's just a house," Patty said, noting my shocked reaction. "What makes a home is the people in the house. And I have no doubt you'll grow to love these people."

I bit my bottom lip. "Patty, I'm nervous."

She placed the car in park and put a tender hand on top of mine. "You'll do fine. Promise."

I wished I were as sure as she was in me.

"Can you tell me what to expect? I don't remember the last time I've been on an interview. I think it was at my last paycheck job at the Piggly Wiggly."

Patty laughed. "So, yes, you will have an interview with all of them because Mason—he's the youngest of the Brisken men—is the most meticulous with things like this. He'll want a formal interview. But I imagine it'll be normal questions and be a little laid-back. I've told them not to pry into things that they shouldn't."

"Okay." My shoulders relaxed just a tad.

I pushed up the sleeves of my light-pink V-neck ribbed sweater. I pressed a sweaty palm down my dark-washed jeans and pulled my long blonde ponytail over my shoulder. I had worn my best attire today. I would have worn black dress pants if I had any. I knew that first impressions mattered, and I wanted to make a good first impression.

"The hardest test you'll have today is the kid test." There was a funny look on Patty's face.

My brows flew to my hairline. "Kid test?"

"Yes. Sarah will go along with what her uncles and dad tell her. She's sensible, and she listens to authority and will trust that the people who love her will make the right decisions." She breathed out one long sigh. "Mary ... sweet Mary, is a whole other story. She's making this particularly hard—their search for my replacement. I think, in her mind, if they don't find another nanny, I won't leave, but we all know that's not the case."

"Gotcha." I gave a shaky nod. "Impress sweet Mary who isn't so sweet." I bit at my pinkie nail and forced a breath out.

I can do this. I can do this. Maybe if I believed the mantra in my head, I could do this.

Patty shook her head. "She's sweet when she likes you, and there is no doubt she'll love you. Mary has this innate gift on how to read people, their intentions and their heart." She tipped my chin with the lightness of her fingertips. "And you, Becky, have the kindest of hearts."

The mansion door opened and shut and then opened again. For a brief second, a mini human peered out, and I saw a flash of blonde hair and electric-blue eyes. My eyes blinked wide. She was stunning.

The door shut again, and Patty stepped out of the car.

"And that will be my Mary. We'd better go. She's expecting us."

With one big breath, I straightened and pushed back my shoulders, exuding confidence I didn't really have.

Patty's voice resounded in my head, and I made it my mantra. *Be yourself. Be yourself. Be yourself.*

I swallowed hard.

What if it wasn't good enough?

━━━

When I entered the house, the three Brisken men—who were all tall and alarmingly good looking with dark brown hair and chocolate-brown eyes—stood in the foyer to meet me. I had to pause and blink, almost pinching myself as I took the three brothers in.

I swore I'd stepped into a magazine featuring the rich and famous.

"Hi. I'm Mason." He offered his hand and I shook it firmly.

"I'm Becky," I said.

"Let me take your bags." He lifted my bags out of my hands like they were air.

Mason had a runner's build. He wore a pressed polo shirt, meant for work, and slacks that were creased as though they were newly ironed.

He was assessing me already with his eyes, trying to get a good read on me. I teetered in my gym shoes and tried to rein in my nerves. Patty had briefed me on each of their personalities. Before he even introduced himself, I would have guessed he was Mason.

Another Brisken brother stepped forward, this one with a mischievous, boyish grin, as though he had a secret, and he had buckets of charm oozing out of him, simply standing there. "And I'm—"

"Brad," I said, smiling, finishing his sentence.

He laughed, taking my hand. "How did you know? Patty has been talking about me," he guessed. "Is it my stunning good looks? My award-winning smile?" He rubbed at his jaw in an overly exaggerated way, and I laughed.

"She talks about you guys all the time when she comes home." I motioned to everyone.

He nodded and then leaned in, getting eye-level with me. "Just know, I'm not into dating nannies, so don't get any ideas." Despite his words, he gave me a flirtatious once-over. "Though I do think you're quite a looker." He nudged Patty's shoulder. "You were right, Pats."

I tipped my chin, my eyes light. "But if you aren't into nannies, is all the talk about what's happening between you and Patty just gossip, then?"

He smirked. "I already got down on one knee. Ask her."

Patty simply shook her head, as though she was used to Brad's jokes.

My eyes took in the only man left that I hadn't been introduced to—the father of the girls, the one who most likely had the final say. He was built like a football player, broad shoulders, arms as big as boulders. His face was ruggedly handsome, and his profile was sharp and confident and spoke of power.

My nerves spiked again, and I took a calming breath before stepping toward him. "And you must be Charles."

When I placed my hand in his, I had a strong awareness of my heart beating too loudly in my ears. I blamed it on the fact that he was the girls' father, so I had to impress him the most.

His eyes were a stunning brown, reminding me of

molten chocolate. The other brothers had dark chocolate eyes, too, but something in Charles's irises
stilled me.

Where Brad oozed charm, Charles exuded strength. It
wasn't in the broadness of his shoulders or his over-six-foot
height. It was the depth behind his eyes, a strength that I
was familiar with—living through a life that hadn't been so
kind.

"I am. Becky, it's nice to finally meet you."

My heart stutter-stopped in my chest, and when he
spoke, it felt as though I'd been pumped with a hundred
shots of adrenaline.

I didn't know if it was anxiety for the interview that had
my palms sweating or because Charles was insanely
attractive.

Charles

When she placed her hand in mine, I noticed how soft
her fingers were, how fragile, how gentle her hand was, but
that was nothing compared to her stunning green eyes, the
color of emeralds. Her delicate outward appearance was
contradictory to what I read behind her eyes—a strength
and power behind her stare.

I cleared my throat, noting we were standing there a few
seconds too long, our hands locked, and I hadn't said more
than two words.

"It's nice to meet you," I said, dropping my hand from
hers. "Patty has told us a lot about you."

One thing Patty had said spot-on was that Becky was
attractive, not in an over-the-top way, but in the lightness in
her features—her dirty-blonde hair, the shape of her face
and her button nose.

She had this shiny, shimmery stuff on her lips, almost the color of a warm peach.

I swallowed.

Hard.

I tore my gaze back up to meet her eyes and blew out a steady breath. Something about her beauty struck me stupid and speechless. I was shocked at my instant attraction to her. It wasn't that I didn't appreciate the beauty of the women around me, in the office or walking downtown for lunch, but I was never one to take a second glance.

Her face was delicately carved, her mouth small, her lips full. It was in the simplicity of her beauty that I couldn't take my eyes off of her.

Mason placed her bags by the stairs. "Patty can show you to your room, but do you want to get started with the interview first?"

Brad groaned and rolled his eyes. "Can you let the girl sit or relax or even take a piss after her long bus ride?"

"The girls are waiting," Mason snapped at our brother, and then he averted his stare because I shot him a look of warning. "Unless you want to rest for a bit, and I under-stand that too. I'll leave it up to you."

"No, it's fine." Her voice shook with a nervousness that I could easily pick up on. "We can get the tough part out of the way."

She wiped her hands on the front of her jeans, and my immediate reaction was to lean into her and tell her not to be nervous.

When she smiled, it lit up her whole face, and it light-ened my insides.

I scratched at my day-old stubble, wishing I had shaved today. And suddenly, I felt underdressed as I glanced down at my jeans and fitted shirt. I should have worn something more professional even though we were having the interview at home.

Becky followed Mason and Brad to our dining room, where Mary had set up a station of stuffed animals on the long glass table and where Sarah sat right beside her with her journal.

"Girls," Patty began, motioning to Becky beside her, "this is Becky, my friend."

Patty beckoned the girls over, and after they approached, they each shook Becky's hand.

The way Becky's face lit up had me inching forward. Her smile was infectious, and I found the corner of my mouth tugging upward.

"Patty has told me tons about you girls." She ducked down, placing her hands on her knees, getting into the girls' line of sight, shrinking to their mini sizes. "That you, Mary, love everything slime and Play-Doh, that you especially love making food from it."

Then, she turned to my overly cautious Sarah. With one look, I could tell my daughter was already assessing her.

"And you love Minecraft, Legos, and journaling."

"I do like building things," Sarah responded, sporting a cautious smile.

"And I also like to play doctor," Mary piped up, getting in Becky's face, obviously wanting all the attention back on her.

"That's amazing, Mary. I love taking care of people, so I consider myself a pseudo doctor of sorts." She winked.

I took in their interaction, which was natural, different from this past weekend, where the interaction between the kids and potential nannies had seemed forced, rehearsed.

For the first time since this whole *finding a new nanny* debacle had started, a sliver of hope pushed through.

When Mary took Becky's hand in hers, I knew that she'd already won my daughter. But Sarah's quiet demeanor told me she wasn't exactly sold yet.

Patty motioned to the seats at the dining table. "Let's get started, shall we? Piggy and Teddy Monster and Pooh want to ask you questions, Miss Becky."

Mary sat at the head of the table, sitting on her knees so she was taller. She hadn't done this with the other candidates, as their interviews had been more formal. But she'd voiced her opinion about interviewing Becky. Mason, of course, was against it, but Brad always—sometimes excessively—accommodated every little wish of Mary's.

Becky sat right by Mary as we all took our seats. I was opposite of Becky. Brad was beside me and then Mason. Somehow, we always ended up sitting in birth order, as though we subconsciously knew our place.

Mary raised her fluffy pink stuffed pig. "Piggy wants to know what you know how to cook and what you'll be feeding us."

"Well, funny enough, cooking is one of my specialties." Becky smiled.

The corner of my lips tipped up. My eyes flickered to her shimmering lips again, and I shifted in my seat, an unease filling my chest because ...

Shit, I am checking out the nanny.

"What do you like to cook?" To my surprise, the question fell from my mouth.

Everyone's eyes turned toward me. The last few interviews, I hadn't said a word, mostly because Mason and Brad led them all. I had simply observed.

I cleared my throat. "The girls don't have allergies, so that's a good thing. I know there are a ton of kids at their school who have allergies, and that's tough, so I'm glad our girls don't have any." And now, I was rambling, and I didn't ramble normally.

All eyes were on me still, as though I'd grown an extra set of ears.

I tipped my chin toward Mason. "Mason is pretty strict with their diet, so I don't have to be. Do you want to go through your restrictions?" I adjusted the collar of my shirt, feeling heat creeping up my neck.

Is it hot in here? Yeah, it is hot in here.

I stood and looked at the thermostat. *Nope, a pleasant seventy degrees.*

I took my seat as Mason plucked out a list of approved foods from his portfolio and passed it to Becky. "Yes. So, I just make sure they get in more protein than carbs. I minimize their sugars, and there are no preservatives or sugary drinks in the house. Fresh-squeezed orange juice is okay."

Becky fumbled for something in her purse. "Okay. Maybe I should take notes."

Brad shook his head. "Don't worry, Becky. As long as they are not starving or dehydrated, you're straight. Don't bother with Mason. He was dropped on his head multiple times when he was younger." His mouth quirked up in humor.

Mason threw him a look, and I knew in about two seconds, they'd be at each other's throats again, so I changed the subject quickly. "Sarah, do you have any questions?"

She blinked up at me and slowly shook her head, chewing on her bottom lip.

My eldest internalized a lot, and it took great effort on my part to get to the bottom of what she was actually feeling. I made a mental note to take her out later for a daddy-daughter date.

Nat had always been attuned to Sarah, knowing if

something was bothering her before it got out of control. I had to remind myself to be focused and present and to be aware, and I usually was with Sarah. I'd have to know more of her thoughts later when I spoke to her.

"Okay, girls, you guys can leave and let us handle it from here," I said, pointing to the door.

Patty ushered the girls out, and after they left, Mason started his regular questions that he had for every candidate.

"So, Becky, can you tell us a little about yourself and your past work experience?"

She visibly swallowed, and Patty shot Mason a look.

It was an easy enough question, but what Patty had told us earlier, I knew we shouldn't be pushing too hard.

Becky wrung her hands on top of the table. "Well ... let's see. I'm a certified nursing assistant. I got my certificate online and went to nursing school for a bit but didn't finish because of life."

Curiosity nibbled at my insides, and I rested my forearms at the edge of the table. I shouldn't wonder what life event had gotten in the way of her getting her degree, but I couldn't stop myself from wondering.

"I took care of Carl from when he was twenty to twenty-three." Her eyes flickered toward the table and then up to meet our eyes. "Until he died. He was an unbelievably loving and gentle soul." She swallowed and bit on her bottom lip. "And then I've been taking care of Eleanor ever since. I know her body is deteriorating, but her mind, it's sharp. I mean, she suffered from a stroke and lost her ability to talk, but she can beat me at Scrabble still."

Patty laughed. "That woman and her word-building skills is amazing."

"So, any boyfriend, husband, kids?" Mason said.

We all turned to him.

Becky's facial features dropped. It was the first time the permanent smile on her face had slipped since she'd stepped into the house. "Well, no boyfriend, no husband ..." There was a long pause, and I had seen a flash of pain flicker through her eyes, but it was gone a second later. "No kids either."

They hadn't noticed it because they hadn't experienced the pain that I had. But I swore it had been there.

Brad grabbed the sheet of paper, where the questions were listed, and flipped it over to the blank side. "My turn." He was winging his turn. "Favorite Disney film?"

As the questions continued, I watched her every reaction. I knew her nervous tells—the wringing of her hands, the biting of her bottom lip.

And with each question, that niblet of curiosity grew.

One thing I excelled at was being a good people-reader. I had to be. I was the head of the largest printing corporation in the nation. I'd guarantee that all CEOs had the same strengths, one of them being the bullshit-reader. I had to make multimillion-dollar decisions for Brisken Printing Corp., so there was no way I could mess around when my family and the multiple families that I employed depended on my sound decisions.

As I sat back and took in Becky and all that she was, there were three things I noticed that counted.

1. She was nervous.

2. She was a genuine, trusting person, like Patty had indicated.

3. She had a past. One that she wanted buried deep and kept there.

CHAPTER 7

CHARLES

Thirty minutes later, the interview was over, and Patty and Becky were outside, playing with the girls, while my brothers and I were still congregated in the dining room.

I sat down as Mason paced the room. Brad had kicked up his feet and placed them on the other chair, getting delight out of Mason freaking out.

"I don't like it. She seems like a nice woman, but seriously, we know nothing about her. She can't provide us with a social security number and ..." He paused. "I can't properly run a background check on her because we don't know where she's originally from. And do you know how many Becky Summers are out there? And is her name Becky or Rebecca?" He scratched at his temple and placed one heavy hand on his hip.

Brad threw his feet off the chair. "Why the hell did you run a background check on her when Patty specifically said that she wouldn't be up for it?"

Mason threw both hands up like Brad was crazy.

"Because it's Mary and Sarah, and I told you, I couldn't properly run one."

Brad scoffed, exasperated. "What do you think is going to happen? That Becky is going to kidnap the girls and hold them for ransom?"

Mason slapped his head. "That scenario didn't even cross my mind, but shit, it might ..."

A muscle jumped at Brad's jaw. "Listen, she took care of that disabled man for years for Patty's best friend and then Patty's mom after that. You can't get a better rec than that from Patty." Brad turned to face me. "So, big bro, ultimately, this is your decision."

I steepled my fingers together and leaned back in my chair. I'd already made up my mind, and I sensed Brad already knew that; otherwise, he wouldn't be giving me that victorious grin.

My decision was based on the fact that Patty trusted her, Mary liked her, and at the moment, I had no other options, given Patty was leaving.

Plus, my people radar told me that Becky was a good, kindhearted woman.

"I think we should give her a shot."

Mason lifted both hands to the ceiling as his mouth slipped agape. His voice was almost whiny. "Charles, come on. Let's talk about this."

I swore my parents had spoiled him so much, being the youngest, that he'd perfected the whine, even as an adult.

Relief flooded my insides. By the look on Brad's face, I knew he felt the same.

Brad stood and then patted me on the back. "I'll round up the troops and tell them to get ready for dinner."

We were going to the girls' favorite Italian restaurant

today to celebrate Patty and the little time we had left with her.

I nodded and then forced my attention to Mason as I stood. He was breathing hard, face red, like he always did when he truly believed he was in the right. His heart was in a good place, and no one, not even Brad, could fault him for that.

I walked over and placed my hands on his shoulders. "Just listen," I said, knowing he was going to list his twenty reasons again on why we should be cautious in hiring Becky. "We could interview hundreds of candidates, and they could all look good on paper, but at the end of the day, they could be horrible people."

The fierce determination in his eyes softened then, so I continued, "This comes down to one thing—trust. And I trust Patty. Plain and simple." I squeezed his shoulder. "Patty loves our girls like they are her own. She trusts Becky with her mother's life and even our girls. Patty has fully vouched for her."

"But—" He started to argue, stubborn ass that he was.

With a firm shake of my head, I said, "No buts. We're giving Becky a shot. It's not a permanent solution, so we have every right to change our minds. But in the meantime, we will be nice to her and allow her to do her job. Okay?" I lifted an eyebrow. "Mason?"

He blew out a breath and nodded, his eyes downturned. "Okay."

I snaked an arm around his shoulders and ushered him out the door. "Now, let's get some dinner."

Becky

"You're hired," Charles said.

My eyes widened before my hand flew to my mouth, and I gripped his forearm with both hands. "Thank you!" Then, I flushed red because I had in fact almost jumped on him.

In my defense, he was the one who had relayed the news, and he was the closest person to me at that exact moment. I would have happy-attacked Brad, Mason, or even Patty if they'd told me the news.

I wanted to blame embarrassment for the heat that rushed my body, not the feel of his strong forearm underneath my fingertips. It could have been my imagination, but I swore his cheeks had reddened.

I backed away slowly and took in everyone's eyes on us —particularly his brothers' eyes, which were on Charles.

Charles cleared his throat and tipped his chin. "You're ... you're welcome, Becky," he stuttered, averting his gaze and motioning to the door. He plucked out his wallet. "You'll need this. It's a credit card for the expenditures for the girls. It has a very high credit line, so don't go disappearing with it."

I took the card from him and stared at it. I didn't know if this was a joke or if he was serious because his face was serious.

He turned to Patty then. "Patty, please give Becky the phone we gave you before you go."

"Will do," Patty replied, a small smirk playing on her lips.

"We should go now." He stuffed his hands in his pockets and then tugged out his keys. "Um ... we have dinner reservations." He pulled at his collar and then adjusted his shirt.

As everyone filed out, I squeezed Patty's hand beside

me. "Thank you, Patty!" Then, I hugged her because I was beyond excited and relieved.

There was no doubt I would love it here by the stories Patty had told me and the vibe I was getting from the family. This would be a change, no doubt. I was used to caring for adults, but I imagined that the children would bring a different kind of joy.

When Patty patted my back, I whispered, "That was awkward, huh?"

She pulled back, smiling. "Not awkward. Just funny." Then, she hooked my arm in hers. "And I'm so happy. This puts me at ease. You here, taking care of my girls."

━━━

Thirty minutes later, we pulled in front of a swanky Italian restaurant. Patty and I rode with Charles while the girls rode with their uncles. I knew it was an upscale place, given the amount of cars waiting for valet service, the ambience, and even the patrons standing by to get inside—women in their cute dresses and men in business-casual wear at their sides.

I tugged at my sweater and pulled my ponytail to my side. I wished I'd changed my clothes, but I didn't own anything fancy. Plus, the men hadn't changed and were in casual attire. Still, I couldn't help but feel a tad bit under-dressed and out of place.

In big, bold letters, *Café Italia* was written against the awning above the restaurant. I'd never been to a fancy restaurant. There was never an opportunity to go. The fanciest restaurant I'd ever been to was at the casino buffet, and that was a comped meal.

A valet attendant opened the back door to Charles's Range Rover, and I stepped out of the car.

Brad and Mason had driven in a separate car and were right behind us, and I followed the clan.

Everyone's eyes flipped up to Charles as he led us past the people waiting outside, past the double doors, to the inside, where a sophisticated woman with a red bob holding menus greeted us.

I tugged at Patty's arm. "Patty, I'm not sure I can afford a meal here."

She linked my arm through hers. "Don't worry. Charles takes care of everything."

I smiled awkwardly, all teeth showing this time. "Are you sure?"

"Yes, honey. You're officially employed by the Brisken household."

My attention was forced to the front—to this tall woman with Pantene-sleek chestnut-brown hair in a fitted dress.

"Good evening, Mr. Brisken. Your table is ready. Please follow me."

I forced myself to stop fidgeting and concentrated on pushing one foot in front of the other. I couldn't help it. I was a bucket of nerves and totally out of my element in a fancy restaurant in my casual clothing.

As we were escorted to our table, I observed everyone noticing the Brisken men. I couldn't blame them. They were gorgeous. I mean, when three tall, model-looking, dark-haired, brown-eyed men strolled into Café Italia, everyone—men and women, old and young—openly gawked as we walked past tables to the back of the restaurant.

Maybe they were staring because Brad carrying Mary or Sarah was knowingly making Mason laugh so loud that it was making everyone turn, but my money was on the fact that this family looked as though they had stepped out of a Gap commercial.

Seriously.

But although the men were stunning in their separate and unique ways, Charles stood out to me. Because his beauty was like that of a god you couldn't touch. Strong, fierce, powerful.

He didn't talk often, but when he did, he spoke with authority and strength. Undoubtedly, he'd been groomed for and grown into his position as the CEO of Brisken Printing Corp.

We were led into a private room in the back of the restaurant, which had one long table for twelve people. Appetizers were already set on the table, and when I sat down, two waiters entered, dressed in black button-down shirts and black slacks.

"Sir, would you like your regular drinks and meals today?" he asked, addressing Charles at the head of the table.

"Yes, but we also have a new guest." Charles motioned to me, and I smiled shakily.

I wasn't used to attention being called to me. I was used to being in the shadows. To living in the shadows, out of necessity. Just the thought of coming into the light was making me shiver. As soon as that thought pushed through, automatically, my eyes scanned the room, the vicinity, and I zoned in on the exit, like I always did when I entered an unfamiliar area.

"Becky, what would you like to drink?" Charles asked with an air of kindness.

"Just water, please," I croaked out, apparently having lost my voice in the process of all the attention.

His brows knit together. "You sure?"

"Yes." I nodded curtly, so he wouldn't doubt me.

The waiter took out a pad from his back pocket. "And for the meals?"

"Please order our regulars too. Becky?" Charles asked. "Take your time, looking over the menu."

I swallowed. "I guess you guys come here often." I flipped open the menu and scanned it quickly. I'd never been in this position, having to choose from my pick of fancy meals. It was fun and also unnerving.

"It's our favorite restaurant," Sarah said, taking a cheese stick from the middle of the table.

I ducked my head into the menu in front of me, feeling everyone's eyes on me. Silence ensued, which made my ears feel impossibly hot.

I lifted my head. "Suggestions, anyone?"

"I like the mac and cheese here," Mary answered, bouncing on her booster seat.

"I always get the chicken parm, gluten-free pasta, with a side of vegetables. The chicken is baked, not fried," Mason added.

Brad pointed to me. "Whatever you do, don't pick that."

"Try the steak, Becky. It's good," Charles added. "The steak here is tender with just the right amount of fat. A little amount of fat is good on steak because it adds to the juiciness. The little specs of fat found inside of the muscle is called marbling."

The brothers' eyes swung Charles's way. Mason's mouth slipped ajar, and Brad covered his mouth to contain a laugh.

"What?" Charles shot out.

I didn't understand what was so funny.

Brad tried to dim his amusement. "I didn't know you were such a steak expert."

"I ..." Charles's eyes flickered my way, then to his brothers', and then to the girls. "I learned it from watching all those cooking shows with the girls."

"Dad picks up on the most interesting information," Sarah added. "I don't even remember that fact."

I smiled.

"Okay." I shut my menu. "I'll have a steak, medium."

As our food was being prepared, I took in the interaction of the family—how over-the-top goofy Brad was; how Mason was the opposite in his demeanor, taking jabs at Brad when he could; how Charles sat back, simply taking in everything in his silent strength, which was overpowering.

Normally, a person of his stature and height would intimidate me, but there was a tenderness in his gaze as he dealt with his children that eased me and melted my heart into a puddle of goo.

I knew his wife had died during childbirth, which must have been traumatic for him, but I wondered if he was still heartbroken and if that was why he hadn't remarried.

The moment that thought filtered through, I straightened and shook my head. I knew nothing about his life. He could very well be on the way to marriage with a girlfriend he'd been dating.

I bit my lip and told myself to stop wondering about my new handsome boss because that could lead to very dangerous things—one being unemployment.

When Brad and Mason bickered or Mary and Sarah started up to annoy each other, Charles silenced them with a few words. When he spoke, there was an authority in his tone that made everyone listen.

"Daddy," Mary whined, "where's the food? I'm hungry."

Charles tipped up Mary's chin. "Soon."

"I can't believe the service right now. Usually, it's impeccable but not today," Mason added. "We've been waiting over an hour for our food. This is a little bit ridiculous."

"Mason, dear"—Patty patted his hand on top of the table—"patience. And it seems like it's a busier night than normal."

My eyes made it around the room, to the packed restaurant beyond the glass doors. Every table was occupied.

A good while later, the two waiters held two large, circular trays as they entered. When they placed our plates in front of us, my mouth watered as the spices from the steak filtered through my senses.

It had been a good long while since I'd had a steak, and I couldn't remember the last time I'd had a steak at a restaurant.

When my knife cut into the juicy, tender meat, I frowned. The meat was practically breathing, red and medium rare, if that. I had asked for it to be medium.

"Yeah, that won't do. I think it's still half-alive," Brad peeped up beside me.

"It's fine." I could eat the potatoes and vegetables, but boy, did I want a steak. I didn't want to make a fuss.

Charles's eyes flitted my way and back to my steak. The muscle in his jaw twitched, but he stayed quiet.

When the waiter came to drop off more food, Charles lifted a finger to get his attention. He motioned to my plate. "Her steak is rare. She ordered it medium."

The poor waiter lowered his gaze, already grabbing the plate. "I'll have it up to the kitchen in no time."

"When can we expect it back?" Charles asked.

The waiter shrugged and teetered back on his heels. "Honestly, sir, we're kind of backed up. I'd say, ten or fifteen minutes."

With a shake of his head, he said, "That won't do. Set it down."

The waiter grimaced. "Are you sure?"

Charles pointed to the table. "Set it down."

The waiter did as he had been told, most likely at the seriousness in Charles's voice.

"Becky, you can have my steak."

I shook my head. "No, it's fine. I'm fine."

When he reached for my plate, I took the other side. We both stood, the table between us, playing tug-of-war on a plate of raw steak.

"Just eat mine. It's a perfect medium."

"No, really, I can deal. That's your steak." My face warmed. I hated everyone's eyes on me. I did better in the corner, unnoticed.

"Becky ..." The tone he used was one he'd used on the waiter and the children, but one thing I did not do was bow down when I was being pressured.

"Charles, it's fine," I said, equally as curt. I was feeling the heat of everyone's gaze on us and trying not to let it get to me.

"Children, there is no need to fight in this fine establishment," Brad said, reaching for the plate between us, plucking it out of our hands, and replacing mine with Charles's. "Now, we can all eat."

My face flushed even deeper, my whole body feeling like it was sweating. "It's really okay, Brad," I said.

He gave me a pointed look as I sat down. "Don't even try it. No one can win against Charles. Not me. Not Mason.

Not the girls. Not at a game of basketball, not at a game of Mario Kart, not in the boardroom, and I doubt on a plate of steak. So, yeah ... it's a lost cause. Just enjoy your food."

As soon as Charles sat down, my eyes flickered up to meet his, defeat and a bit of gratitude rushing through me. "Thank you." I tipped my chin toward his plate. "Aren't you going to send that back to the kitchen?"

"It's fine." He cut up Mary's chicken strips next to him. "I don't want to make the girls wait any longer. Plus, we always eat together."

The look on his face told me I shouldn't try to push it. I wasn't used to people taking care of me in this way. I was used to fending for myself. "Thank you," I repeated.

"You're welcome." He nodded, a tiny tip of a smile to his mouth. "Now, Mary, can you please say grace?"

Mary smiled big and wide. "God is good. Thank you for food."

The table laughed.

"All right, let's dig in," Brad said, already twirling his fork in his fettuccine.

I bit my lip for a second, watching everyone else eat before I tried the first bite of my steak. And it was absolutely divine. My mouth was in heaven as the meat melted against my tongue. I almost sighed out loud; it was so good. I could have hugged Charles for giving up his dinner for me.

"So, now that you have Becky working for you ..." Patty's voice trailed off as she cut up Sarah's chicken beside her. "I'm requesting an early leave—this Sunday."

Charles sat up straighter in his seat.

Brad's eyebrows furrowed. "Come on, Patty ..."

Mason visibly frowned. "Why so soon?"

Her eyes crinkled as she spoke, "My job here is complete. Mission accomplished, as Sarah would say." She patted my hand on the table. "And now, Becky is here. I'm at ease, leaving. You guys have everything you need now."

My heartbeat picked up in speed, and I blew out a breath. All my belongings could be packed up within two suitcases. Given my circumstances, I didn't keep anything with me that wouldn't allow me to leave quickly if I had to.

I'd been with Patty for so long that I couldn't help the nervous butterflies that took flight in the pit of my stomach, moving on to my new family without her. Though I was excited to start anew, caring for the children, I couldn't help the feeling of apprehension from pushing through. I knew nothing about Chicago, the big city, or how to care for children. I'd thought there would be a transition period, a time where I would slide into the job with Patty beside me.

I guessed that was not happening.

The gnawing nervousness had my stomach flipping and flopping, and my steak didn't taste as good as it originally had.

CHAPTER 8

Becky

The next few days flew by, and before we knew it, the dreaded Sunday arrived. Mary and Sarah cried all day, understandably so, as Patty was the woman who had loved them and assisted in raising them for the last four years.

The girls were by Patty, hugging her fiercely on the couch, their delicate arms wrapped around her small frame. I took it upon myself to make sure that all her bags and boxes were labeled properly.

Patty had been with the Brisken family for years, so it only made sense that she had accumulated so many personal mementos from their time together.

On my hands and knees, I labeled the fourth and last box. Charles had paid extra to ensure that all of Patty's belongings would go all at once.

When I had initially helped Patty pack, I'd realized how intertwined she was in their family. Homemade presents from the girls. Paintings they'd made together. She was in almost every family photo and had gone on a handful of family vacations with them—the Bahamas, Disney, Universal.

I couldn't help but gawk at some of these photos, three well-built, shirtless men on the beach with these two young girls. Talk about chick magnets. There was no denying the bystanders in the picture openly ogling in the background. But it was Charles that stuck out to me.

From me gripping his forearm, to our steak incident, to my first night here when he'd brought my belongings up to my room, and right after when I'd watched him tuck in the girls, I couldn't stop thinking about him, even when he wasn't in the room.

I told myself I needed to get a grip, but tell me what woman wouldn't be attracted to a man who had the strength and build of Zeus and the gentlest of hearts?

I could be attracted to him—that wasn't a sin—but I'd vowed after my last relationship to never share my feelings and life with another man ever again.

Last night, I'd gotten the girls ready with Patty, trying to memorize the routine, and I'd walked in on Charles reading Mary a bedtime story. My heart had melted as Charles lay on her tiny bed beside her, his voice soft and sweet, opposite of his normal commanding tone.

"She all packed?" Charles's tone had my body warming again. His voice had a trigger to my internal thermostat that I couldn't control. The only thing that helped was not looking at him directly.

"Yep, all packed." I stood still, averting my stare from his face, and then I crouched down to lift up the box, but Charles beat me to it.

"I'll get that."

Our eyes locked, and my breath caught in my throat.

"Thanks." My voice was barely above a whisper.

His lips tipped up but only slightly. It was as though it were a crime to smile or more so that his smiles were reserved and he saved them only for special occasions.

"Raised as gentlemen. Our mother taught us well," Brad said, sliding next to me.

Mason growled behind him, "Quit flirting, and get these boxes and suitcases in the van." He was dragging two suitcases behind him.

"I'm not flirting." Brad's smile slipped. "No offense, Miss Becky, you are beautiful, but I draw the line at dating the nanny since you are basically going to be like family, and that's incest." He made a pretend face of disgust.

"Wish you'd draw the line at dating your secretaries." Mason threw him a look before he disappeared outside.

"I haven't dated Sonia ..." Brad called out to Mason. There was a long pause, as though it was supposed to be ended with *yet*.

I could hear Mason outside. "Yeah, the first one you haven't dated. Let's keep it that way, shall we?"

Brad grunted and then proceeded to drag a box out the door.

Charles walked into the house, hands on his hips, which stretched the white shirt over his broad shoulders.

I tore my gaze away before I started salivating all over the floor.

Becky, get a grip.

I bit my cheeks to force myself to focus. This was my boss, the one who paid me. He should be the very last on the list to ogle.

"We're about ready. Van is loaded. Let's be in the car in five minutes." He headed over to the living room, where Mary and Sarah had a tight vise grip around Patty.

She was whispering something in their ears, which made the girls cry harder.

The frown on Charles's face was evident. He stood there, shoulders lax, staring at their interaction. I watched the expanse of his chest, but there was no exhale, as though he was holding his breath.

After a beat, he cleared his throat, standing under the doorframe. "The driver is here. We're leaving in a few." His voice was softer now, sadder even. "Mary, sweetie ... make sure you use the bathroom before we go, okay?"

There was no answer from the girls; only soft sobs escaped their lips.

After a few seconds, he turned. "I'll wait for you guys in the car." His eyes met mine briefly before he headed out the door.

Charles had rented a van, driver included, so that all seven of us, along with the boxes and suitcases, could ride and bid farewell to Patty.

Sarah, Mary, and Patty were all in the third row, and I was sandwiched between Brad and Mason in the second row as the driver took off from the Brisken estate.

Charles sat on the passenger seat in the front, on silent mode.

Mary's cheek was attached to Patty's shirt, and after thirty minutes into our car ride, her cries ceased, and she fell asleep on Patty.

My heart clenched as I thought of the distance between us, at the loss of this woman who'd been a mother figure to me for years. I would miss her dearly.

"We'll miss you, Patty," Mason said, turning to face her. "We need an update on Eleanor, and if you need help with anything, with her move ... let us know."

"We'll especially miss your apple pancakes. Make sure you leave Becky the recipe," Brad added.

Patty chuckled. "I have. Becky is up-to-date with all the recipes, the girls, and your schedules. She has a photographic memory, that one." Patty patted me on the shoulder from behind.

"Is that so?" Brad said, turning to face me. "How good are you with counting cards? Have you ever been to the casino?"

"Ignore him," Mason said beside me.

I simply smiled. "In my former life, I used to live at the casino." I bit my cheek as soon as the words flew out. I couldn't believe I'd said that.

Mason stiffened beside me, and I swallowed, wondering why I'd been so forthcoming.

"Oh, we want to hear stories." Brad grinned.

Charles peered behind him, at me, and I held my breath.

Clearing my throat, I said in my defense, "That was a long, long time ago. Years. Nowadays, I'm all about making money, not giving it to the slot machine." Or more accurately, the tables.

I pulled at the collar of my sweater and shifted in my seat. I wanted to slap my own head for letting those words slip.

"Were you any good?" Brad asked, genuinely curious. "In your rebellious younger years?"

I averted my stare, looking straight ahead of me. I needed to be more careful. I needed to watch what I said in front of these men. I added with caution, "My ex-boyfriend was good at gambling. If there is such a thing." Too good, which was why he had been banned. A person could only go through a never-ending winning streak for so long until cameras and people caught on. He'd gotten away with thousands before it stopped. "I kinda just watched." I bit my tongue from speaking further.

Liar. I had been his wingwoman. For a long while, it was the way we'd made rent, bought groceries. The memories flooded me with shame. I closed my eyes briefly and pushed back the guilt and all thoughts associated with my past. I pushed them deep down to the recesses of my brain that I never revisited.

When we pulled into the departure terminal, I released a heavy sigh, thankful the attention was off of me because as we approached the American Airlines sign, the car went eerily silent.

When the driver pulled up to the curb, Charles got out of the car. My eyes followed him walking out to help the driver unload the boxes from the back.

Mason and Brad turned to Patty, extending their hands. She gripped them fiercely, and their eyes locked for a few good long seconds.

"Promise me you'll visit, okay?" Mason said quietly.

She nodded. "I will. And we have Mickey right next door, so you'll have to visit me too."

Her frail hands tightened over theirs. "You are good men. I don't have to tell you to take care of my girls because they were your girls before they were mine." Her voice cracked at the end. "You both will make some fine husbands one day. I just hope you find women worthy of your love." She gave their hands a maternal pat before releasing them and throwing her arm around Sarah and the sleeping Mary in her lap.

Brad laughed. "Notice how she said that she hopes *we both*"—he motioned between Mason and himself—"find women worthy of our love."

"Shut up," Mason said, rolling his eyes.

Though I was new, I caught on quickly. It wasn't a secret that Mason had been in a long-term relationship with a woman. I had yet to meet Janice, but from what I'd heard, I wasn't missing anything. No one, not the girls or the brothers or Patty, liked Janice. A part of me was curious about her, therefore wanting to meet her, yet I was a little nervous that she'd be a total witch.

The double doors opened, and Charles motioned for us to get out of the car.

Brad stepped out first, and when I scooted to the edge, Charles extended his hand. I tried to ignore the shock of warmth that traveled down my arm when my fingers met his or the way my heart raced, but it was undeniable, how my body reacted to him.

Once again, I tore my gaze away and focused on the ground. Sarah exited the car and flew into Mason's arms, already in a fit of tears. He picked her up, hugging her close to him, as though she were a toddler. It was so dear that I almost teared up myself. I wondered if she knew how lucky she was to have people who cared so much for her that they were there to comfort her when someone was leaving her. A sharp pang hit me square in the chest as I thought of my lack of caring people, growing up. I shoved it away as I normally did and reminded myself to be in the present. A present I was extremely grateful for.

Patty kissed Mary's forehead over and over, getting the little one to stir awake.

When her puffy eyes opened, she took in her surroundings and began to wail, "Don't go. I promise to be good, Nana. I promise I'll be so good. I promise."

My heart seized as I saw her break down. I barely knew them, and already, their pain was tearing me apart.

It was a full-on tear-fest.

As soon as Charles had to peel poor Mary off of Patty, I bit back tears.

I will not cry. I will not cry.

But it was too late.

I blew out a few shallow breaths as everything started to hit me.

Patty stepped out of the car. "Stop." She placed one palm on my face, gently wiping away my tears. "Don't cry."

My arms wrapped tightly around her, and my head went to the crook of her neck. I owed Patty my life. She'd taken me in like her own daughter, trusted me to care for her mother, given me my livelihood, and now had found me this job. I was forever indebted to this woman.

"It's not like I won't visit. I have to see all my girls, you included."

"Thank you, Patty. You'll never know how much I appreciate you."

"Just take care of my girls," she whispered so softly that I barely heard her. "And take care of Charles. Out of all the men, he needs the most care." There was a pointed meaning to her words.

I blinked back my tears, and when I pulled back, she patted my cheek.

Charles handed a distraught Mary to Brad before stepping into Patty's embrace, lifting her in a fierce hug where her feet dangled from the ground, and then he kissed her cheek in the sweetest way.

After placing her on her feet, he leaned into her, getting in her line of sight. "You're family ... you hear that, Patty?" He placed one fist on his chest and one on her shoulder, peering down at the much shorter woman. "I owe you so much. You've loved my girls, our family ... and I am just so grateful that you came into our lives." His voice choked with emotion. "Whatever you need, whenever you need it, it doesn't matter what it is, you come to us, okay?" He brought her in again, patting her back. "If there is one thing you've learned about us, it is that we take care of family, no matter what the cost. And you, Patty, are family."

I took a few healthy steps away, giving everyone time to say their good-byes.

Truth be told, if I heard Brad and Mason and Sarah's proclamation of love and gratitude and their sad hugs, I'd be a goner, in a bucket of tears again.

When Brad encased Patty in a hug and shook her as though she were a tiny doll, Charles walked toward the far end of the van.

I watched him a good distance away. He turned the opposite direction, his back toward us. He pinched his nose, his chin dropping to his chest. After a long beat, he placed both hands on his hips and lifted his eyes to the open blue sky, as though searching for an answer written in the clouds.

He turned around, and I purposely focused my eyes on the group congregated around Patty. It was either that or admit that I'd secretly eyed him when he wasn't looking.

Suddenly, Charles made his way toward me. The lines of his jaw were tight, his shoulders raised, back straight, as though he was disconnected from what he was watching in front of me, though I felt how distraught he was, as it was coming from him in waves. It was in his eyes, which held such sadness.

I didn't know what came over me or where all my courage came from, but I reached down and gripped his hand, giving it a gentle squeeze. "Everything will be okay. I promise it will be," I whispered. Because I had promised

Patty it would be, that I would care for these children like they were my own.

He surprised me by intertwining our fingers in the most intimate of holds, though his gaze stayed on the group. "I know it will be. It has to. Because that's my job—to make sure it is okay." And I felt the weight of his responsibility in his voice.

At that, I held on tighter, hoping he could feel my own determination and little bit of strength there. I hated how he'd been dealt such bad cards in life, but he had to know, at least for the moment, that he didn't have to go through this alone.

Just then, his gaze swung over to me, and I swore I had seen a ghost of a smile.

Or maybe it was just wishful thinking, but either way, my heart flipped and flopped.

CHAPTER 9

CHARLES

Becky was great with the girls when we came back from the airport. She played Barbie with Mary for at least an hour and built some sort of fortress with Sarah in an online forum.

After dinner, everyone was emotionally and physically exhausted from the long day of bidding Patty good-bye. Becky was getting the girls ready for bed, and I was cleaning the kitchen when Brad and Mason strolled in.

"Hey ..." Mason said, approaching with his Cartier messenger bag over his shoulder. "I'm heading to Janice's tonight, if that's okay. It's been a few nights since I've seen her."

Brad scratched the top of his head. "Yeah. I wanted to go to the city tonight, too, and check on my place."

I lifted my head from the sink, leveling them with a stare. "You don't need my permission to leave."

They ignored the statement.

"Do you want me to stay to help with the morning routine tomorrow?" Brad asked. "Because I can just go to the city tomorrow night." He shared a secret glance with Mason, and it annoyed the hell out of me because this was what they did—worry about me when I was perfectly fine.

I crossed my arms over my chest. "No. We have Becky. She'll be in charge of the morning routine, and I'll be here, so ..." I turned back to the sink of dishes and focused on rinsing them and placing them in the dishwasher.

"It's fine. I'll stay," Brad said, which made me slam the dishwasher shut.

Maybe it was unfair. They were simply concerned and looking out for me. But I was used to change. If anything, change was all I knew.

"Listen, I'm going to be okay tomorrow." Plus Becky was here to assist with the girls.

When had I ever broken down? Okay, that one time—when Natalie had first died—but the boys hadn't witnessed it, only my mother. I'd promised myself that it wouldn't ever happen again, and it hadn't. Maybe my mother had told them. I wouldn't put it past her since we were so close.

"It will be fine," I said slowly, so they would believe me and take the hint.

This was the thing about my brothers—they were always here. When our parents had died, they had moved in to help me raise the girls. What men in their mid-twenties uprooted their lives to raise two young girls? They had. They moved around their schedules, and at the very beginning, one of them was always here in the mornings to drop the girls at school, to help Patty get them ready. Both of them had been here at every milestone, attending most of their school concerts and events.

They made sure that they were present, and the girls didn't feel any lack of support. And I appreciated them, truly ... but a big part of me felt as though I was taking away a part of their lives. The guilt was overwhelming at times. It was a natural feeling I lived with; it surrounded me, and I'd accepted the fact that it would always be there.

I didn't need to tell them how I felt because they knew, and they disagreed, still wanting to be ever present in the girls' lives.

"Promise. If I need you guys, I'll call." I threw them a small smile for good measure.

My stare bounced back and forth between them, and after a beat, Brad nodded. "Okay, I'll say good night to the girls and pack up my stuff."

"All right then. I'll see you tomorrow night for dinner." Mason patted my back, and Brad saluted me as he strolled to the foyer.

My hands fell to the edge of the sink, and I let my head hang. Patty gone would be an adjustment, but it'd be fine, right?

It had to be.

CHAPTER 10

Becky

Darkness surrounds me, and the rush of pressure in my ears is so overwhelming that I think my eardrums will burst.

My heart pounds, louder, faster, harder. I hear the thumps of my chest in my ears.

But what is overwhelming is the pressure. The intense pressure above me. Below me. All around me.

The worst is ... I couldn't breathe.

Could not get air into my lungs.

Could. Not. Breathe.

I lose focus.

Everything blacks out around me.

And I am floating into space, but this space feels warm and, for the first time, safe, so I welcome this space in the blackness because in the dark, in this area, there is no pain.

I let it take me. Take me under. And I know the moment the air from my lungs slowly leaves my body until I have no more air to breathe.

But then ... I am jolted back to reality, struck by an

impact, an unbearable pain that reminds me that this hell is my life.

Suddenly, I jerked upright on my bed, sweating profusely, breathing heavily.

My hands flew to my chest, hugging myself, keeping myself together. I took in my surroundings—the pale yellow walls, the neutral curtains—and I exhaled deeply, one big sigh of relief. This was my new room, my new employment. This wasn't the hell I used to live in.

I inhaled deeply, taking breaths in big, overwhelming gulps.

I'm alive.

Please. I hope I didn't scream this time.

I pushed the covers off of me, slipped on my slippers, and headed downstairs, needing a drink of water.

I hadn't been in the Brisken household long, but I had already memorized my surroundings. That was how I'd trained myself—to know where I was at all times and to know where the exits were.

I lightly walked through the foyer, down the hall, and into the kitchen. The floors creaked with age, but I was light on my toes.

I flipped on the light to get a glass in the cupboard and opened the fridge to get some water. My eyes caught a shadow in my peripheral view. And then I screamed.

The glass dropped to the floor and shattered.

Charles was up from the chair at the kitchen table and next to me in a nanosecond, bending down to pick up the big pieces of glass.

"I didn't mean to scare you," Charles said.

After catching my breath, I met his eyes. "I didn't

expect you there." Of course not. He'd been sitting in the dark.

He laughed. "I'm sorry." Then, he answered my question with a nod of his chin. He picked up a another piece of glass and threw it in the trash. "Don't move. I'll get the broom."

I stood, feeling a sharp pinch on my big toe. "Mother-pluckers." I hopped on one foot, realizing I had stepped on a shard of glass.

"I said, stay still." Charles's voice boomed.

I flinched, cowering into myself. I hated that it was an automatic reaction, that my body had been taught through the years to fear a man like that. He stilled, his eyes widening just a tad. When I tore my gaze from him, he walked toward the closet.

He came back in with a broom, sweeping all the tiny pieces of glass away. I bent my leg and pulled out the piece of glass from my toe, and tiny droplets of blood rushed to the surface.

"Do you have a Band-Aid?" I asked, applying pressure to my big toe.

A moment later, I yelped because steady arms went under my knees, and I was off the floor. My arms wrapped around his neck, and I felt his strong shoulders pressed against my body. I swallowed. This man must live at the gym. My pulse picked up in speed at the nearness of him.

He placed me on top of the kitchen table and averted his eyes. "I didn't want you stepping on any more glass. I'll need to clean up that area later." He walked toward a set of drawers by the coffee machine and pulled out a first aid kit. After placing it on the table, he opened an alcohol wipe, sat on the chair, and lifted my foot.

"I can do that." My voice shook, and panic settled in my gut.

Only then did his eyes meet mine, a deep chestnut brown to my green ones. "It's fine. I'm used to this. Mary is a stunt devil but also the biggest baby. I have to bandage her small paper cuts." He lifted the bottom of my pajama pants, and his eyes flashed to mine.

I pulled my foot back, my knee to my chest.

"What happened to your ankle?" His voice heightened.

I swallowed hard and couldn't meet his gaze. "I was a daredevil in my younger years. Bicycle accident." The lie came out naturally, flowing from my lips, as I'd repeated the story a million times before.

I lifted my head and offered a small smile. He didn't return it.

Once again, he gently lifted my ankle and met my eyes. "May I?"

I bit at my thumbnail, feeling sheepish all of a sudden. "Sure."

When he swiped at my toe with the alcohol wipe, I held my breath. The action was slow and deliberate. His strong hands were tender against my skin, and everywhere he touched felt intimate in a way. I bit my bottom lip, watching him as warmth spread throughout my body.

After he tore open a bandage and wrapped it around my toe, he stood.

In front of me, between my legs.

My heart lurched madly at his close proximity.

His chest was a massive wall, his shoulders big as boulders, and he was stunning, his hair a disheveled mess, understandably so since—I assumed—he'd rolled out of bed. But his attractiveness wasn't in the darkness of his hair or the strength of his body in front of me. It was in the gentleness in his demeanor, in his touch.

He was a walking anomaly. His body was built like a football player, his persona as big as a god, but he was warm, kind, quiet.

His eyes flashed to my mouth, and I swore it was as though the air had been vacuumed out of the room. My heart was in my throat. I hadn't been this close to a man in years.

Without warning, my nipples pebbled under my shirt. *Shit!* And of course, I wasn't wearing a bra.

His eyes flickered down to my breasts, and he let out a shaky breath. Stepping back, he cleared his throat, running a hand through his hair, and then he turned around and walked straight to the fridge, as though he was embarrassed that I'd caught him staring when I should be the one embarrassed.

"Let me get you a glass of water, and then I'll clean up this floor."

I hopped off the table. "I can get it."

"No." He turned to face me, clenching his jaw. His stern tone had me stilling in my spot.

"Please ... just sit down, Becky. I don't want you to hurt yourself again."

I stood there, still and stoic, blinking at him. I had a feeling this man hardly used the word *please*. So, I sat down. Like a child being told. And for some reason, even though I'd fended for myself for most of my life, I obeyed. And for another reason completely unknown to me ... I liked it.

Charles

One thing that I knew about myself was that I wasn't a

liar. I didn't lie to others, and I most definitely did not lie to myself. When Natalie had died, I hadn't told myself that everything was going to be fine. I had known in my gut that things would never be fine, but I'd straightened my shoulders and told myself I had two girls to raise and had people who depended on me.

I'd decided life was shit, but the truth was, I had the business and little lives to take care of.

So, now, I wasn't about to lie and tell myself that I wasn't attracted to Becky—because I was. She was breathtakingly beautiful but in a quiet way. She didn't want to be noticed, but I noticed. I noticed everything about her.

When I handed her the glass of water, my eyes betrayed me and flickered to her well-endowed chest. Again. Fuck, I was a terrible human being. The absolute worst cliché that a man could ever be—attracted to his nanny.

I tore my gaze away, grunted, and headed to get the mop.

"I can do it, Charles."

I shook my head. "No, it's fine. I just want this taken care of because the girls will be down here in the morning, and I don't want little pieces of glass everywhere."

She sat in silence, and I worked in silence. It took a few minutes to get everything wiped and dried, and I joined Becky at the table with my own glass of water.

"Do you always do that? Sit in the dark?" she asked again.

"Sometimes," I said, focusing on the condensation on the glass.

What I wouldn't tell her was that, most nights, I was down here, in the dark. Because I couldn't stand being in my room alone, without Nat. I used to be the man who slept soundly every night. Natalie used to complain that as soon as my head hit the pillow, I was snoring. I was no longer that man. I hardly slept anymore. I was used to functioning on little to no sleep, mostly because I'd relive that horrid night over and over again.

"Why?" Her eyebrows quirked.

"I have trouble sleeping," I said honestly—too honestly.

"Me too."

There was a tenseness in her voice that had me locking my eyes with her. They were the prettiest green color I'd ever seen. I found myself wanting to drown in them.

"Why?" I asked. More curious than I should've been.

She shook her head, focusing on the table now.

I knew not to push too hard. I knew she had a past, and what I needed to focus on was the fact that she was our nanny—and not look at her breasts. What an honorable employer would do was get up, say good night, and let her get on her way, but I was a damn nosy employer. I had a curiosity so strong, it was hard to swallow this damn water I kept drinking.

I knew how this worked.

Tit for tat.

I was in business after all.

So, I offered, "I can't sleep because of the nightmares." My voice didn't sound like my own; it was soft, distant, disconnected.

She peered up at me because I'd gotten her attention.

I hadn't told anyone but my therapist that I still had nightmares of Natalie dying on the hospital bed. I still pictured her elated face as the nurse set a crying Mary in her arms, moments before she coded blue and they rushed me out of the room. Her blood pressure had skyrocketed. She'd had preeclampsia and ...

Becky's voice was careful, curious, just like I was. "Do these nightmares come every night?"

I let out one slow breath. I didn't want to give too much, reveal too much truth, truth that I didn't want others to see —that I really wasn't okay.

My brothers continued to worry about me, and I didn't need to add anything else to their plates. To everyone, to the world, my life, even after my deceased wife, was perfect. They just didn't know that, every day, I walked through life, not seeing, only going through the motions. I wouldn't consider this living, just being.

I stared at her for a few seconds before letting a little more out. "Not every night. But most nights." I took a sip of water, waiting for her to give me something ... anything. More ...

Because I wanted to know her more. It had only been days since I'd met her, but the need to know her surpassed my need to keep my nightmares a secret. A truth that shocked the hell out of me.

After a deep breath, she whispered into the air, "I have nightmares too."

We were both silent for a beat, knowing we were sharing intimate details now, breaking the seal of the nanny-employer relationship. She could probably guess what mine were about. I found it unfair that my life could be read in a newspaper or on the internet, being the CEO of a high-profile company, and I knew nothing about what kept her up at night.

I needed to know, so I kept going, giving snippets of what haunted me, snippets I never let anyone else see. "Sometimes, I get a break. The longest has been a week, and then I think the nightmares are over ... but they come back

clearer." More frightening. So vivid that I wake up sometimes in a cold sweat, screaming out for Nat.

Becky held her glass tighter, her gaze dropping to the
table.

"You're lucky." She stood. "My nightmares never give
me a break." She walked to the dishwasher and placed her
glass in the top drawer, already done with the conversation.
"Good night, Charles. Thank you." She lifted her foot and
wiggled her bandaged big toe.

"Good night." I guessed that was all I was going to get,
but if her nightmares never ceased, maybe she'd be down
here tomorrow night.

My shoulders eased, and as pathetic as it seemed, I was
relieved she had nightmares too. Because tonight was the
first time since Natalie had died that I felt less alone.

CHAPTER 11

Becky

The next morning, I was up early before the girls to make breakfast and pack their lunch. Patty had given me a schedule of when the girls got up and what time they had to be out of the house, so they weren't late for school. I'd functioned on schedules with Eleanor and her meds, so Patty's detailed directions had put me at ease.

When I stepped downstairs, Charles was already there, standing by the coffee machine, dressed in a dark navy-blue suit, all ready for work.

I staggered to a stop and stole a moment to take him in, as his back was toward me, his head downturned, watching the coffee brew.

It seemed as though it had only been hours since I'd last seen him. I doubted he ever slept if he had frequent nightmares. I didn't like that the similarity bonded us, but it did.

A deep cough escaped him, a very dry cough, and it startled me from my stalking-fest.

I approached slowly. "Are you getting sick?"

He turned to face me, his eyes widening. For once, I'd

startled him. "No. There's no time to get sick." He poured himself a cup and reached for another mug. "Coffee?"

"Yes, please. Just black." I leaned against the counter.

He stared at me for a second too long before pouring me a cup. "I've never met a woman who liked her coffee just black."

"Black like my soul." I smiled, reaching for my cup as he handed it to me.

He laughed. It was a quick chuckle, but I drank it all up because even after knowing him for only a week or so, I'd only heard it a couple of times.

I sipped from the cup and smiled. "Usually, sickness doesn't pick a time." I lifted a finger. "Actually, it picks the worst time to take you down."

He nodded his head. "Yeah, which is why I take a ton of vitamins. There isn't a cold I haven't killed yet in a few days, tops."

"Lucky." I made my way to the fridge, self-conscious as he leaned against the counter, ankles crossed, just staring at me.

This time, I wore a gray sweatshirt over my white tee. I wasn't making the same mistake that I'd done last night.

"Sarah is up," I said, matter-of-fact.

"Yeah, she's usually up before her alarm. She's my organized child. Mary ..." He shook his head and took another sip of his coffee. "Good luck waking that kid up. She's a whiner until we're almost out the door."

I laughed. "I have to look at their schedules to see what time they get out of school."

"Three thirty."

I knew from what Patty had said, as it was a private school, they didn't have bus service, and I'd be picking them up daily.

"I'll be in the carpool line at three." That was a great amount of time at home. I mean, besides the girls' laundry and getting dinner ready, there wasn't much to do. "I know that Patty said you didn't like her tidying up, but I like doing stuff like that, and there is so much time in the day, so ..." I smiled before I took another sip of coffee.

"No," Charles said, his answer firm with a rich timbre of his voice. It wasn't even a soft no. It was a hard *no means no*. "We have a cleaning lady. Your main priority is taking care of the kids, helping them with their homework, doing activities with them." His fingers tapped against his mug. "You're up early, and you most likely won't sleep before ten. After dinner and homework and baths and getting ready for the next day, it's a lot."

I blinked at him, tightly holding my hot mug. "But I won't even know what to do with myself." Maybe it was embarrassing to admit, but I had no life beyond my job. And I preferred it that way because keeping myself busy with my job kept my mind wandering into the past, to memories I never wanted to revisit. Plus, my job kept me inside, avoiding the possibility of being found.

"Relax," he said, his voice gentler this time. "When they're home, you'll be busy." He lifted his eyebrows to bring his point home.

I placed my coffee cup against my lips, taking a sip. "Honestly, there is only so much TV I can watch."

He studied me for a second, unnerving me. "Have you ever thought about finishing your nursing degree?" His voice was soft, cautious even. He placed his coffee cup on the counter.

Just the thought sparked me with excitement. Had I *thought* of it? I'd dreamt about it. I knew I was going to eventually get my nursing degree because I wanted something of my own. I didn't own a house or a car, but I wanted a degree. And when I did get it, no one could take that away from me.

"I want to," I said vaguely.

At my response, his face lit up. "You should. You could take some classes at the local community college. You'll have from after they leave till three to take classes. And I'm sure they offer online courses too."

I gulped, touched by his kindness. He barely knew me, and he wanted good things for me. The sentiment was overly kind, and a rush of energy surged through me at the thought.

"Thank you." I placed my hand on his forearm, grateful. With the raise that I'd received from watching Eleanor to now watching the girls and the fact that rent was free, I could afford the credits at a local community college.

His eyes flickered to where we were connected, and a moment later, he pressed a hand on top of mine. "You should really think about it. We can make it work around here."

Our eyes locked for a few long seconds, and the natural, comfortable feeling I felt around him shifted into something else, something deeper, more intense. I had to turn away from him and place my own mug on the counter.

"Thank you," I repeated. My heartbeat picked up in my chest, and my cheeks warmed.

To distract myself, I opened the fridge and got some eggs out, clearing my throat. "So, per Patty, Mary likes scrambled, and Sarah like her eggs sunny-side up. How do you like your eggs?"

"I don't eat," he deadpanned.

"At all?" I playfully widened my eyes. "How'd you gain all that muscle, then?"

The side of his mouth tipped upward. Goodness, was it cute. Why couldn't I get a full-on smile? I was sure when his smile surfaced, it was wonderful, like the sun shining through the clouds after the rain.

"I mean"—he shrugged—"I don't normally eat breakfast. If I do, it's not a big one. I just grab another coffee when I'm near the office."

I flicked my hair over my shoulder as I grabbed a bowl to scramble Mary's eggs. "You should know that breakfast is the most important part of the day."

I passed him the carton of eggs, and he placed it on the kitchen island. Then, I passed him the bacon. His fingers brushed mine as he took it and set it on the island.

"Did your mom tell you that? That's something my mom always said when she was making us breakfast."

I blinked up at him, my smile slipping. Any mention of my mom sent me to a place in my past that I didn't like to go. My voice was low, almost hoarse. "My mom ... yeah, I don't like to think about her often." The last time I had seen her was years ago. "She"—I went to the fridge again, getting out the orange juice—"wasn't a very good mother." I stared at the bowl of fruit, at the salad, at the milk and swallowed hard.

"Becky, I'm—"

I held up a hand and smiled that forced smile that always seemed to pop up as a coping mechanism. The one that said everything was okay when it really wasn't.

"Don't be sorry. My life is so much better now that she's not in it." I sucked in a hard breath and I flicked my hair over my shoulder as I grabbed a bowl to scramble Mary's eggs. "I didn't even check for the lunchmeat. Patty mentioned that Mary only eats ham," I said, changing the subject so quick that I probably gave him whiplash.

I heard the fridge open, and a moment later, ham was on the kitchen island.

"Yeah, Mary is addicted to ham. We have to have it in the house at all times. She even likes it in her eggs."

I chanced a glance at him and read curiosity in his eyes, but I was so thankful that he didn't press me further. I didn't have any friends for that very reason. They would want to know everything about me, which included my past and that was off-limits.

He moved to the other counter, grabbing a loaf of bread. "I liked to tag-team with Patty in the morning when I could. I hope that's okay."

"This is your house. Of course it's okay." I moved around him and got a pan from the cupboard.

"Becky ..."

At the sound of my name on his lips, I turned to face him, pan in hand.

"I want you to feel like this is your house too. I want you to move freely around this house as you would your own house. That's what I told Patty when she moved in with us that very first day. And I want you to be open with me— about the kids and about you, what is bothering you, about how we can make this transition easier for all of us."

I stared. Because I couldn't say anything. No one had ever really wanted to take care of me like that. Put me at ease, make me feel at home. Not a man anyway. Never in my life.

When I didn't answer, he tipped his chin. "Can you do that?"

I nodded. "I think so."

He proceeded to pack on the mayo and ham as he made the girls' sandwiches.

"Patty wasn't kidding. You're a very hands-on dad."

His eyes met mine briefly before focusing on his task at hand. "I try to be. I don't want them to feel like they're missing anything by not having their ..." His voice trailed off, and he paused for a second before packing the sandwiches into brown paper bags. Then, he proceeded to the pantry to get some chips. "It's the one job I can't fail at."

Now, *that* I understood better than he'd ever know.

CHAPTER 12

CHARLES

The last time I had gotten a call from school, Sarah had sprained her ankle. So, when the principal called me to tell me that Sarah had gotten in trouble, I was driving ninety on the highway, rushing to the school.

I had called Becky, but she hadn't answered. When I'd told Brad and Mason that I was leaving work early to head to the school, they had wanted to come with me, overly concerned for the kids, but I'd flat-out told them no.

Adrenaline pumped in me as I turned into the parking lot, my heart beating a mile a minute. Sweat beads lined the back of my neck as I jumped out of my car, got to the entrance, and rang the buzzer for them to let me in.

When the door buzzed, I yanked it open and didn't stop my quickened stride as I made it to the principal's office. I stopped mid-step, hearing Becky's heightened voice beyond the principal's door, which was slightly ajar.

"So, there are no repercussions for the other girl? None whatsoever?" Becky's back was toward me, her hands fisted by her sides.

I walked straight into Carol, the principal's office without acknowledging the secretary, noting Sarah was sitting in the chair in front of her desk.

"That's straight-up bullying, and this is bullshit. You can't reprimand Sarah for sticking up for herself."

"What's going on here?"

My voice had everyone—Becky, Carol, and Sarah—turning in my direction.

"Charles ..." Carol stood from behind her desk and adjusted her red suit jacket. "Sarah got into a fight this morning with Jennifer O'Neal."

My eyes flickered to Sarah before landing back on the principal.

Becky took a menacing step toward the principal. "You can't start the narrative like that!" Her eyes were blazing fire, the green popping. She flipped toward me. "Charles." She tilted her head and clenched her teeth in a sarcastic smile. "Let me start the real narrative here. Jennifer O'Neal decided to pick on Sarah's half-ponytail today and make fun of the fact that it wasn't perfect, but it was *okay* because she didn't have a mom to fix her hair." She threw up both hands and then turned her attention back to Carol. "Let's just tell it how it really is, right? And why isn't Jennifer O'Neal in here, getting reprimanded, huh? Why is she not in here? I think her parents should get a call, too, because she's a bully."

Carol pulled at her suit jacket and placed a hand on her lip, leaning in. "Jennifer wasn't the violent one in this situation."

I breathed through the next seconds, searching Sarah's face but she wouldn't meet my eyes.

Becky screeched, "Violent? She pushed the kid who

was getting in her face. I would have done more than push her. Unbelievable. You're ..."

Before Becky got out her next words, I lightly took her forearm and ushered her behind me.

"Is that what happened, Carol?" I asked, eyes devoid of any true emotion, wanting the facts.

"Well, yes." She addressed me with a quiet firmness, "According to Jennifer, she said something about Sarah's hair but did not in fact mention her mother. That's why she's not in here." She had the decency to look somewhat apologetic. "But she will be talked to. Separately."

"Really?" Becky said with doubt. "So, Sarah shoved the girl because she'd mentioned something about her hair. Really? Charles, do you believe that? Come on now."

"Becky," I said, my voice meaning to calm her down, but looking at the fire behind her eyes, I wondered if it was possible to calm her.

"You know how kids are, Charles," Carol contested.

My eyebrows pulled together, and all my muscles tensed. "I know how kids can get, but I know how *my* kids are. And my kids are not violent unless provoked." Well, one of my kids really. Mary was violent when she threw her tantrums, but I was working on that. I tipped my chin to Sarah. "Let's go. I'm taking you out of school early. Becky, please grab Mary, too, and I'll meet you in the front. I'm going to talk to Carol for a bit."

Becky lifted her nose, her eyes still narrowed at Carol. She slipped a protective arm over Sarah's shoulders and ushered her outside.

When the door shut, Carol sat down, but I stayed standing. This was going to be short and to the point. "I suggest you set up a meeting with Brandon and Ellie O'Neal. I want to be involved in the meeting. Make it for sometime within the next few days."

"That won't be necessary. I will speak with them direct-ly," she said, a hint of alarm in her eyes.

I paused and stared at her, giving her a moment to shift in her seat. "It is of the utmost importance that I meet with them." I paused again, and she adjusted the collar of her shirt. "You see, I know that the O'Neals are generous contributors to this school. But ... so am I. I don't have to remind you who single-handedly funded the gym." I tilted my head. I didn't know the figures exactly, but I was pretty damn sure that out of all the parents of this elite private school, I gave the most. "I've been here a long time, Carol, and I love this school, but I will not have my daughter being bullied."

"Charles ..." she stammered.

"No." My voice was cutthroat. "I won't tolerate it. I suggest you schedule a meeting with Jennifer's parents today." The *or else* at the end of the sentence was implied. "I'll wait for your call before the end of the day. Thanks." I unbuttoned my suit jacket, turned to leave, and exited the school to find—oddly enough—a laughing group of three.

As soon as they saw me, they sobered up, and their laughter ceased.

"Don't stop on my account." I tried not to smile at them, not sure if this was a smiling situation just yet.

"Daddy!" Mary rushed toward me, jumping into my arms. "You took us out of school today? What's the occa-sion? Can we get ice cream?"

"Maybe later." After pressing a quick kiss to her cheek, I set her on her feet. I needed to talk to Sarah.

"I heard Sarah beat up a girl," Mary exclaimed proudly.

"I didn't beat her up. I shoved her," Sarah deadpanned,

annoyed and looking a little like a dog with its tail between its legs.

Her eyes still wouldn't meet mine, and I knew she was embarrassed. Sarah was not a crier. I chalked it up to the fact that she'd cried all her tears when her mother died. But I could sense her anxiety rolling off of her.

"Becky, can you take Mary home? I'll drive with Sarah."

Becky teetered on her heels, and a part of me knew she didn't want to leave Sarah alone right now.

"It's fine. I'll just be a little bit," I said.

"Okay." She headed to the car—a BMW SUV that was her designated vehicle while she stayed with us.

Slipping my hand through Sarah's, I walked us toward my vehicle. Her eyes were downturned, her shoulders slouched. I decided to have this conversation now, not wanting to drag it out any longer.

"Hey," I said, sitting down at the nearest bench.

In small script letters on a plaque in front of the bench, it read, *In memory of Clara and John Tippins*. There was a bench similar to this at the playground behind this school ... dedicated to Natalie. I never wanted Natalie to be simply a memory, forgotten. The bench at the playground, our pictures all around our house, the brick at Wrigley Field, the plaque at the children's hospital where Natalie had volunteered when Sarah was at school. I wanted good reminders of her everywhere—not only for myself, but also for the girls. What I didn't want was an entitled little brat reminding Sarah of what she'd lost.

"What happened?" I asked, my tone tense but not because I was upset with her.

Sarah cowered into herself, both hands wrapped around her stomach.

"Hey." I angled myself to where she'd be forced to look

up at me. Then, I smiled. "Whatever you did, whatever happened, just tell me the truth, and I won't be angry. You know this."

She released a breath and fisted her hands in front of her. "I was roughhousing with Kristen. We were chasing each other and playing on the monkey bars. My hair got stuck on Kristen's uniform. We were fine and laughing and stuff, but when I got unstuck, my ponytail was messed up, and Jennifer ..." Sarah's voice lowered. "She's just a bully, Dad. Just like Becky said."

No surprise there, given I knew her parents a bit. The father was a trust-fund baby who had a lot of online businesses but was never consistent in one thing. The mother served on the PTA, strictly to control the outcome and votes of the meetings.

"What did she say exactly?"

Dark brown eyes identical to mine flicked up to me. "Just mean stuff. You know ... the stuff insecure people say to put others down because they want to make themselves feel better."

I laughed. Not 'cause it was funny. But because my girl was wise beyond her years.

Sarah's eyes narrowed. "I'm not going to let her talk to me like that, Dad. I'm not going to let her or anyone say things about Mom and use the fact that she's not here against me, so I shoved her." Her voice lowered to a tone where I almost didn't hear her. "I don't need someone to remind me that she isn't here anymore because I remember every day, all by myself." Her gaze dipped lower, and her bottom lip trembled. Her emotions poured out of her in waves, and I felt her immense sense of loss.

My chest concaved, and I reached for her, pulling her into my lap. "You're the bravest kid I know, you know that?"

"I'm sorry," she finally said, her voice shaky. "I guess I'm not sorry for shoving her, but I'm sorry that you had to miss work for this."

"Sarah ..." I tipped her chin with my fingertips. "Do you think I'd rather be at work than here with you right now?" I lightly guided her off my lap and stood. "Don't apologize for sticking up to a bully." Because Sarah and Becky were right; in every sense of the word, Jennifer was a bully. "I'm going to talk to her and her parents."

"Dad, you don't have to," Sarah whined.

"Oh, but I will. I'm just going to have a conversation with them."

Sarah scrunched up her face. "A few choice words? You're scary with your conversations."

I fully intended to make my point known, but I wasn't going to elaborate with Sarah any further. "It'll be fine, but first things first. Let's pick up Mary and Becky. Wouldn't want to waste this school-work ditch day."

The blinding smile on Sarah's face lightened my insides. "School-work ditch day. We haven't done this since Mom was alive."

The pang hit me square in the chest. "I know. You should get in trouble more often." I took her hand and led us to the car, all the while thinking, *I wish I had taken more school-work ditch days when Natalie was alive.*

CHAPTER 13

Becky

You'd think ice cream would have calmed me down. But it didn't. Sarah's sullen face when I'd walked into the principal's office made me want to scoop her up, take her into the car, and have a few not-so-kind words with Jennifer O'Neal.

I didn't even know the kid, but I already pictured her in my head. Entitled and bratty without a filter. Most likely, her parents got her whatever she wanted. You could be rich and get everything you wanted and still be brought up with the highest integrity. This girl had not been.

I chomped on my ice cream, knowing full well that I was going to get a brain freeze in a hot second.

"Chocolate and cookie dough!" Mary lifted her cone, waving it in the air like a sword. "My favorite."

"Mary, watch your ice cream," I warned. "You won't be happy if that falls to the ground."

Her eyes widened before she brought it down and licked at the dribbles slipping down the sides. "So yummy!"

I appreciated her enthusiasm, but it didn't break me from my mood, especially since Sarah had been so quiet over the last thirty minutes. She was normally a quiet child, I'd noticed, more introverted, but I knew she was thinking about what had happened earlier.

Charles noticed, too, because he surprised her by sticking his spoon into her cone.

"Dad!" she protested, smiling.

"Well, you're over there pouting, while your ice cream is melting everywhere."

He wasn't lying there.

Sarah licked the sides, cleaning up the chocolate dripping onto her fingertips.

Charles sighed. "What's the matter, Sarah? I told you everything is going to be fine. If you're worried about Jennifer bothering you tomorrow, it won't happen. I'm expecting a call today, and I'll make sure people are put in their places."

And this was why I was really starting to adore Charles, even in the short period of time that I'd known him. His love and need for his kids to be safe and happy knew no bounds.

"I'm not scared of her, Dad." Sarah's tone turned incredulous.

"I didn't say you were. I'm just wondering why you're not enjoying your ice cream." He turned to me then. "And you too. What's up with the pout? I'm going to have to help you with yours soon too."

I laughed because how could I not?

"Why can't everyone just relax on school-work ditch day?"

"I'm sorry." Sarah sighed. "It's just ... when I think of Jennifer, I get so mad. Ugh!"

"Me too, Sarah. Me too." I lifted my hand, and she slapped it in a high five.

Charles threw me a *real mature* look, but the aggravation I felt made me act petty.

"She doesn't know how it feels to have your mom gone. So, for her to say that ..." Sarah's voice trailed off, and my stomach tightened.

I chomped more of my ice cream, thinking of how mean kids could be.

I'd experienced bullying at the highest level, kids making fun of my clothes because I couldn't afford the latest trends, kids making fun of my druggie mom and her vices. Words did more damage than any physical punch could do. The group of girls who used to pick on me had uttered words to cut me down, only to build themselves up. As long as I had been the butt of their jokes, they'd remained the popular ones.

"She's a jerk, okay? Plain and simple." I leaned into the table, resting my elbows on the top "A bully will take every opportunity to try to take you down. Who knows why, but don't let them. You have to think of the positives—that your mom was one hundred percent awesome and present in your life when she was here. You're lucky, Sarah ..." I said, taking a long moment to pause. I never liked sharing pieces of my past. Reliving my past kept me from moving on. But with Sarah, I felt a connection to her in this instant, so I allowed myself to share. " 'Cause not everyone has a mom like you did. I'll let you in on a little tidbit about me." I leaned in closer, locking my eyes with her. "Your mother was more of a mother to you in the short time she was on this earth than my mom ever was. Just for the fact that she was present and here and loving you."

Sarah visibly frowned. "Why? What happened to your mom?"

I didn't want to trouble this sweet girl with my past. A

lot of my history was incomprehensible—and too much emotional baggage for one child. I also didn't want to reveal too much. Plus, no one needed to know about my messed-up history because if they did, people would dig into things I never wanted to discuss.

As I stared into Sarah's eyes, I truly wanted her to know how lucky she was and to focus on the positives. The contrast of our mothers definitely showcased that, so I decided to share a little more of myself.

"Circumstances made her"—I didn't know how to phrase my sentence without sounding bitter—"unavailable." I almost coughed out a laugh. "She was always working." *Selling on the side* was the real truth of it.

Sarah got up from her chair, surprising me, and when her arms wrapped around me, I stilled, aware of the flood of warmth in the center of my chest. "I'm sorry your mom wasn't there for you. And you're right; I'm not going to let what she said get me down." Her arms tightened around me. "Thanks for sticking up for me today. It means a lot."

Holy moly, wow. My free arm slowly wound around her back, bringing her closer. I tipped my chin, resting it on top of her head, taking in the scent of her apple shampoo.

From my periphery, I could see Charles was staring at us—this look of wonder, awe even.

My cheek pressed against the softness of her hair, and I let out a low breath. "I say, we go to her house and TP it or wear a scary mask and stalk her outside her window." My tone was light, but crap, I meant every word.

The giggle that fell from Sarah's lips lightened my insides.

"Before this conversation falls to the dark side, let's go." Charles tipped his chin toward the door. "We can head to the park or go home and watch a movie."

"Or we can go to Jennifer O'Neal's house," Sarah piped up, wiggling out of my hands. Her eyes shone with an inner glow, a calm that hadn't been there earlier, and I was glad that some of that ease had to do with me.

I stood first, ready to leave and move on from the Jennifer O'Neal debacle. Sarah followed, linking her arm through mine, and my heart damn near exploded.

We ended up at the park, Charles and me sitting on a bench, watching the girls on the swings. The light breeze and early fall sun warmed me all over. I didn't remember going to the park much when I was younger. I remembered watching a lot of television, being home a lot, and learning how to use the microwave at a very young age.

So, watching the girls jump from the swing and run from the monkey bars to the slide to do their self-made obstacle course gave me joy.

Charles bumped his shoulder against mine, breaking me from my thoughts. "Hey."

I smiled up at him. "Hey."

"Have you ever nannied before for kids? I mean, you mentioned that you watched that older kid before Patty's mom, but have you ever watched younger kids, or were you around them a lot?"

I shook my head. "No. Why?"

His eyes flickered back to the girls, and a light smile touched his lips. "You could have fooled me. You handled that so well back there. Well, at the ice cream place. At the school ..." He glanced down and let out a low laugh. "You have a temper on you, Miss Becky."

I couldn't deny that. After you'd been pushed and

shoved and pushed some more for so long, you eventually snapped.

Just reliving the day and seeing Sarah's sullen face when I had walked into the principal's office tore at my insides. "I'm used to people like Jennifer. I've encountered them all my life—when I was younger and"—I took a long pause—"even when I was older." My eyes moved to the girls. "I remember feeling helpless and angry. Just seeing Sarah sitting there, feeling as though she was guilty for something other than sticking up for herself, made me so ..." I searched the air, trying to look for a word that would describe my anger and agitation and frustration at the principal for not even reprimanding the other kid. I came up short. "Mad!"

He laughed again and placed his hand on my arm. "I'm jealous, quite honestly."

"Of my anger management issues?"

Humor danced in his eyes. "No. Of your ability to just connect with Sarah that way."

"What way?"

"In a way that Natalie connected with her, in a way that sometimes Mason can connect with her. What she's missing is that motherly touch." His eyes teetered back to the girls, the smile slipping from his face.

I smirked. "Are you saying Mason has that motherly touch?"

We both laughed, and I savored the deep sound of his voice, a real, honest-to-goodness laugh.

Charles kicked the mulch on the ground, his stare firmly planted on his children on the swings. "Natalie always had a way of digging under the surface. As you know, Sarah is an introverted kid. She analyzes things a lot. Sometimes, I try to talk to her when I know something is bothering her, but she clams up." He rubbed one hand against his jaw. "I wish I could click with her in a way that you did today. Where she'd just open up to me." He shifted and pulled out his phone from his suit pocket. "Look at this. You can't say I'm not trying." His finger swiped at the screen, and he opened up the Kindle reading app.

How to Be a Cool Dad.

I couldn't help it. I laughed out loud. Not a full-on belly laugh, but a good chuckle.

"What?" he said, sheepish. "I'm trying."

I grabbed his phone out of his hand. "Let me see this." As I scrolled through the chapters, I saw there was everything from kid conversation starters to dad jokes. "Seriously?" My finger swiped at the screen as I read fast. "Let us see here." Good gosh, some of these were bad. "Okay, how do you get a squirrel to like you?"

Charles's eyebrows pulled together. "I don't know."

"Act like a nut." I shook my head. That was bad, but it got worse. "Okay, next one. Why don't eggs tell jokes?"

A laugh fell out of Charles's mouth.

"They'd crack each other up." I shook my head.

He reached for the phone, and he continued to scroll. "Did you hear the rumor about butter?"

"Oh gosh. No, what?"

"Well, I'm going to spread it." He shook his head, grimacing and laughing at the same time.

Now, I had a case of the giggles. As he continued with the most horrendous jokes, we both laughed so hard that the kids came over and wanted to join in the fun.

"I wanna play," Mary said.

"What are you guys up to?" Sarah said, sitting by her father.

Charles angled his phone away from her. "I've got a great joke about construction ..."

The girls' eyes widened as they waited for the punch line that I knew would be bad.

He finished with, "But I'm working on it."

The girls' faces were blank, and Charles and I started cracking up.

"Is that supposed to be a joke, Dad?" Sarah tilted her head, thoroughly confused.

Charles nodded and lifted a finger. "I've got another one." He pressed the screen on his phone. "If a child refuses to sleep during nap time, are they guilty of resisting a rest?"

Good Lawd this was horrid, but I couldn't stop laughing.

Mary hopped on my lap, wrapping her arms around her center.

"Where's the end of it?" Sarah asked.

Charles rubbed at his eyes. "That's it. That's the end of it. They're guilty of resisting *a rest*. Get it?"

Sarah scrunched her nose. "Dad, you're weird."

"I can't argue that," he said, standing up and sobering a little. "Enough dad jokes. But don't be surprised if I bust out with more later."

Sarah jokingly rolled her eyes. "Please don't, Daddy."

Charles

After ice cream, I grabbed a pizza, and we headed back home to eat dinner and watch a movie. As I sat on the floor, my back against the couch, with Mary on my lap, I couldn't help but savor the feeling of normalcy that I hadn't had in years. Movie night.

When was the last time we had an honest-to-goodness movie night?

The marathon of princess movies just started, and there was no doubt in my mind that it would only end with the girls asleep on the floor and me carrying them up to their rooms.

Becky's shoulder was against mine, as she was sandwiched between me and Sarah.

Mary let out a peal of laughter as Sebastian the crab belted out his song. It reminded me of so many years ago—with Sarah on my lap, my one hand on Nat's stomach, Mary still forming in her belly.

A sharp pang hit me directly in the chest. I missed those times—the silent, simple moments that I had been able to enjoy with my family, where we were seated on a cushion of pillows on the floor. We never did sit on the couch like normal people. We would all be laid out on the floor, comfortable, how my family had always watched movies.

My gaze moved to my right, noting Becky's smile, wide and genuine as Princess Ariel sang on the screen. Where Mary was snuggled against me, resting her head against my chest, Sarah was seated right next to Becky, shoulder to shoulder, their expressions similar and their eyes glued to the television.

I missed having this with someone—that comfortableness of enjoying each other's company in the everyday moments. Having someone by me, with the girls.

I craved this familiarity with someone else, this closeness. And I just now realized how much I wanted it again.

I shook my head from the thoughts. I could absolutely not have that closeness with Becky—our nanny. We needed her. I did not need to complicate our relationship, our lives.

The analytical side of me ticked off reasons as to why it

wouldn't work—one being that Becky was my kids' new constant. I couldn't even attempt to have something between us because if it didn't work out, we'd have to find a new nanny. I doubted Patty had another referral on her list; plus, I refused to go through another agency.

More than that, Becky just fit with us. And I didn't want to even think of having to let her go because of my carelessness. That wouldn't be fair to her or the girls.

The lights were dimmed, and the only light shining was from the flickers coming from the television. There was electricity in the air, heightened by the darkness, and I couldn't help but watch her—against my better judgment and that internal argument I'd just had with myself—as she enjoyed the movie.

I noticed everything about Becky. Her neck was slim and pale. I studied the lines of her jaw, the height of her cheekbones. The way her eyes crinkled when she smiled.

I tore my gaze away, trying to focus on the television, but my stare always managed to return to her. Loose blonde tendrils softened her face, making her look almost childlike. Her facial structure was delicately carved, her mouth full, temptingly curved into a smile. Her lips sexy.

I scratched at my brow, feeling like a pervert now as I wondered how she tasted, how those sweet lips—

Shit. Shit. I had to snap out of it.

I coughed. And coughed again as I shifted to stand. "I'm going to get some water. Anybody want anything?"

"No, thanks, Daddy," Sarah said.

Becky's green eyes met mine as she smiled. A smile I could easily become addicted to. "We're out of popcorn. I can pop some and get the drinks."

It took a moment for me to breathe and turn in the other direction.

My lips tipped up into a forced smile, so forced that it felt unnatural. "It's fine. I'll do it."

My feet padded through the plush carpet of our family room to the kitchen, and I rested my arms against the kitchen island as I stared out the window to our backyard—the inground swimming pool, the girls' tree house.

There was no doubt I was attracted to Becky. Problem was, I wasn't only attracted to her beauty. I also loved seeing how she was with the kids. It reminded me so much of Nat's natural, caring aura. That was dangerous because being attracted to her was one thing, but wanting more from her was another, and little by little, I was starting to want what I'd had with Natalie but with someone else—someone who wasn't Nat.

Guilt settled in my gut. It was not the same guilt that I felt with Vivian, as though she was a dark little secret that I was ashamed of.

No, this ... this felt different. As though it was some sort of guilt that I needed to confess, not just a dirty feeling. This felt like I was breaking the ultimate rule—wanting to share a piece of my life with someone else.

I let my head hang, breathing slowly through my nose and out of my mouth. "This is crazy," I uttered the words that were screaming in my head.

There was only one way to settle this. It was the only way I ever settled things when it felt like life was a little out of control.

I had to talk to Nat.

And to do that, I had to visit her.

CHAPTER 14

CHARLES

I'd been here every month since my Nat passed, sitting cross-legged on the grass, staring at her headstone and wishing and dreaming this weren't my reality. But it was.

Natalie Mary Brisken. Beloved mother, wife, and friend. Best friend.

Because that was what she was to me—my best friend. We'd been best friends first throughout high school. She'd been my confidant in all things. I'd known I wanted to be with her forever the moment her asshole of a boyfriend had broken her heart because I wanted to be the guy to put it back together and make sure it never happened again.

And that was how our love story had begun.

But this wasn't how I wanted our love story to end—my life without you in it.

My fingers brushed against her headstone, and my heart seized. I'd pictured us growing old together, watching our kids grow up and then eventually our grandkids.

When she had been pregnant with Mary, our life was complete. We'd had Sarah already, and another child would only add to our bubble of happiness. I was at the top of my game, newly transitioned into CEO as my father was stepping down. Everything was perfect.

Until what was supposed to be another joyous time in our life had turned into tragedy.

I breathed through my next words. "I know you know what's happening before I even say it." It was hard to put into words what I was feeling in my heart—or more so, what was going on in my head. So, I diverted to easier topics, to what I could easily talk about.

"So, Sarah is doing well. She started reading this fantasy author. Mason did research, and he doesn't think it's age appropriate. I agreed with him on that one." I laughed because everyone needed a Mason in their family. He was the book, food, and television police. "It's young adult, but there is ... yeah ... I haven't had the sex talk with her yet. I was hoping that you could do it for me when the time came to it ..." My voice softened, and my chest tightened again.

My lips turned downward. Big talks, huge milestones that were celebrated—they were just reminders that Nat was gone.

"I miss you, babe." My fingers reached for the grass, pulling them out from the roots. A huge lump formed in the back of my throat, and I tried to swallow down the pain. "We have a new nanny ..." I let my words trail off. "A highly recommended person from Patty." My fingers pulled at more grass, uprooting it from the soil. "I don't even know why I'm here. I mean, obviously to visit you." A low laugh escaped my lips.

I could already picture her blue eyes blazing back at me as she said, *Charles. Get to the point. Get it all out. It'll make you feel better.*

I sighed. I never beat around the bush. Not when it

came to work, not when it came to my brothers, but I was always afraid to upset Nat. Whatever that was—afraid to tell her I'd gotten into a fender bender when Sarah was in the car, afraid to tell her I had to work late or cancel our vacation because of work.

Now, that same feeling bubbled to the surface.

I was always the most vulnerable with Nat—when she had been alive and now. With her, I was my truest, rawest form, and I missed that because everywhere else in my life, I had to be strong—for the company, for my family. But with Nat, she was always my strength, the strong one in our relationship. She always knew what I needed before I did. When I'd had a bad day at work and when I was down, she'd wrap her arms around me and kiss the hollow of my neck. She'd tell me how wonderful I was, make me my favorite dessert, give me a massage. She was my daily dose of sunshine in a stressful day.

I stared at her tombstone, knowing she heard me— because she always seemed to answer my requests, big or small.

Tell me about Becky.

I could almost hear the words in my head, as though it had been whispered. Part of me wondered if it was my subconscious conjuring up what Natalie would say.

Charles. Just spill it.

I laughed again, picturing her face, the tilt of her head, her raised eyebrows, as if to tell me, *What already? Tell me.*

I closed my eyes tightly, seeing only darkness behind my lids. *Where is all this shame coming from?* I hadn't made a pass toward Becky.

Not yet, the voice said.

Through the darkness, Natalie's face came into view, her smile blinding, a warm peace washing over me.

"I think I'm attracted to her," I finally said, in a hushed tone.

I'd told Natalie about Vivian before, in passing, as though I were in a confessional and she were a priest.

This felt different. As though I was seeking advice.

"It's more than attraction actually." I rubbed at my brow, searching her headstone for something, anything. I didn't know. A sign maybe.

"I think ... I think I'm beginning to like her. She's great with the kids, caring and sweet and thoughtful. Protective even though they aren't hers." I let out a long sigh, admitting it more fully. "I like her." *Shit. This is real.* More real than I'd thought. Plus, I knew the feeling; it wasn't as intense of a love that I'd had for Natalie, but it didn't mean it couldn't get there. "I don't even know why I'm sitting here, telling you all this."

I was lying. I knew full well why I was here, telling Natalie. I wanted her approval. Her blessing.

It's okay.

The voice was stronger this time. As though I'd heard it right next to me.

My head popped up to see a woman, an older woman, maybe in her late fifties, early sixties. She was kneeling down next to a tombstone two away from Natalie's. She was laughing, silent but notable.

"It's okay," she repeated, louder this time.

I blew out a breath. At least I wasn't going crazy.

"I know it's okay. That everything is going to be okay," she said more firmly.

I blinked, moving from my knees to a crouched position, wondering if this was the direct sign that I had been looking for because as the woman stared at the tombstone, it was as though her words were being spoken directly to me.

"Everything is going to be okay," she repeated. "I know you'll send me an angel. You always do. You were my angel on earth, and now that you're not here anymore, you'll send me an angel, exactly what I need. And then I'll know I'm taken care of."

The woman touched the tombstone and stood, and before she turned to walk away, she caught sight of me staring back at her. She smiled as her grayish hair rustled against the wind. "Everything will be okay."

I shifted on the ground, getting up to stand, and smiled back even though this eeriness rushed through me. Something about this woman ... it was like she knew me. Knew my troubles.

I watched her walk past the trees, past more headstones, and get into her car. Then, I dropped to my knees again, and I touched the words on Natalie's headstone.

Beloved mother, wife, and friend.

"Baby, please ... send us an angel too. Because I need help with myself, with these girls, with big decisions that I'm not sure how to make." I paused, feeling deep emotions hit me directly in the chest. "Nat ... can you do that for me, please?" My vision blurred, and the heaviness in my chest spread everywhere. I missed her so much that it hurt every part of me. I went on my knees, leaning closer to the headstone. "I know you're looking out for us. You always do." I pressed two fingers to my lips and then to the carved word *wife*. "I love you, baby. Forever and ever. Until we meet again."

⸻

I sat at the kitchen table in the pitch-dark. Who knew what time it was? Three in the morning maybe. We'd been in our regular schedule for the past few weeks, and the girls had adjusted fully to Patty being gone and Becky being in charge.

Earlier, I swore I'd heard Becky scream, which was why I'd gone down to the kitchen, waiting and hoping she'd get a glass of water but she hadn't.

It was cruel in a way—that people had to handle their nightmares alone in their heads.

Meeting her down here, in the dark, that night she'd cut her toe had made me feel better. For the first time in a long time, I hadn't felt alone—as though she understood me as we bonded from the nightmares of our past.

The house was fully asleep, and you'd only realize it was a scream if you were awake at such a god-awful time, which I was.

Yesterday, I'd heard her. I swore it hadn't been my imagination. I'd stood by her door, all of me wanting to go in and hold her, which was absurd and obviously could never happen.

I wanted to hold her because I understood about nightmares, how real they were, how when you were stuck in one, it felt as though you were never, ever going to get out. It was like reliving the worst moment of your life over and over again, and that was why, at times, I was afraid to close my eyes.

Only when I was bone tired did I reluctantly fall asleep, against my will, only to wonder if this was going to be another night that I was going to wake up in a cold sweat.

Suddenly, I heard footsteps padding down the stairs, and I sat straighter in my chair. When she flipped on the lights, her eyes eventually spotted me at the table.

"I ... I don't want to be scared again." Her voice shook,

and her arms were wrapped around her waist, as though she were holding herself together.

I didn't know if she meant me scaring her or the nightmare.

Her hair was in a sexy bun on the top of her head, and she wore a gray sweatshirt that was way too big for her frame and plaid pajama pants.

"Another nightmare," I guessed, not really asking because I already knew.

She nodded.

Immediately, I stood, walking to the fridge. "Sit. I'll get you a glass of water."

I sat opposite her at the table, passing the glass to her.

When she placed the glass against her lips, I noticed her fingers were trembling.

There was an innate need in me to comfort her. Maybe it was because that was what I was used to doing—comforting people, tending to people, making sure everyone was okay.

But this need was stronger ... and it took all the energy in me to keep steady and not reach for her, so I gripped my own glass, my fingers threatening to break it.

Her eyes were glued to the table. "It's the same dream every night."

My fingers tapped against the glass as I held my breath, waiting. I kept my mouth shut, not wanting to push her, but needing to know what haunted her every night.

Her eyebrows pulled together, and her stare turned distant, empty even. It was as though she was reliving a memory, the same way I did in my nightmares.

"I'm drowning. I can't breathe." A shudder escaped her as she continued, "And the thing is ..."

Her expression turned slack, and the hollowness in her

tone ate at my insides. Whatever was going through her head in that moment was unbearable; I could tell because I'd lived through the same pain. Maybe the cause of that pain wasn't the same, but the end result was the same—heartache, anguish, despair.

"And it's only a nightmare 'cause I can't die. As hard as I try to give in to the darkness ... it won't take me."

Her words haunted me and the whoosh of air from my lungs was audible. This time, I couldn't help it, as my will wasn't strong enough, and I reached over and placed a hand on hers.

She laughed then, shaking that unbearable wretchedness she'd felt away, as though it never truly existed. "It sounds stupid, right?" She lifted her eyes to mine. "But the suffering is too intense that I just want death to take me under. It makes no sense. It's just a dream." Her eyes flittered to something over my shoulder. "I think it just keeps happening because I can't swim."

I didn't answer because something inside of me, that gift I had of reading people, told me that this recurring nightmare went deeper than what she was leading me to believe.

"You can't swim?" I knew how this worked. I knew the power of deflection, of asking a different question to get to the bottom of what you really wanted to know.

She shook her head, and my thumb moved in lazy circles on top of her fist.

"I can't. I almost drowned, and that's why I'm deathly afraid of water." She took a sip of her drink. "If I never had to take a shower, I wouldn't."

I registered the lightness in her tone, the words she'd uttered that was meant as a joke but I didn't laugh. I wanted to know more. I needed to know more. "When did it happen? When you were a kid?"

Her eyes flipped to mine, her smile slipping, most likely at the seriousness of my tone. She shook her head, pulling her hand from under mine. "When I was twenty-one."

The change in her demeanor told me I shouldn't ask any further questions, so I gave a little. A little of myself.

"My nightmare is from the day Nat died, which weirdly was supposed to be one of the best days of my life—because it was the day Mary was born." My heartbeat picked up in my chest. It always did when I spoke about Nat and the tragedy that had taken her life. I never spoke about her death to the kids, to my brothers. I wanted my girls and everyone around me to remember how she'd lived, not how she'd died.

"I'm sorry, Charles. I know that must have been hard." Sympathy shone through her eyes. "And to live through it again in your nightmares."

My eyes focused back on my glass, half-empty now. "But I get it—you wanting to just give in to the darkness."

There were times that I just wanted to lie in bed, take a sabbatical from work, from life. No one would fault me from wanting to. But I didn't. I couldn't. Not when the weight of the company and my girls' lives were on my shoulders.

"Because it's easier ... it's easier to give in to the darkness than wake up." Her voice was so quiet, as though she were only speaking to herself.

In that moment of silence, where my brown eyes locked with her sparkling green ones, I felt close to her. I hadn't felt a closeness like this with anyone in a long time. I understood her on an intimate level because those were the same exact words I'd almost said before she said it first—that sometimes, it would be easier to just let the darkness swallow you whole.

CHAPTER 15

Becky

During the weekdays, we fell into the motions of almost domestic bliss, where I made breakfast and he made the girls' lunches. The other men of the house would file downstairs just as Mary and Sarah were at the table, and we'd have breakfast together, as a family.

Brad and Mason weren't there often, but they were there enough that when one was missing, it was noticed.

I enjoyed my busy day, but what I looked forward to the most was the evenings ... when the house was dark and I'd tiptoe downstairs and Charles would be waiting for me with my glass of water already on my side of the table.

We'd been doing this for the past week. It was like our secret time together, kinda like a date but not really.

Was it crazy that I looked forward to us talking this way, meeting this way, connecting in the darkness?

I slipped into my regular spot, and tonight, there was a ghost of a smile on his face. It was refreshing, and it put me at ease.

"What?" Now, I was smiling like an idiot.

"It's like we're sneaking out like teenagers, but we're really sneaking downstairs to get water."

"Yeah." I laughed softly so as not to wake anyone else. "It feels forbidden in the same way, but there is no way we can get in trouble with parents."

"Did you do that?" he asked, his voice light. "Sneak out of the house?"

My gaze dropped to the table. "No." I placed the glass to my lips and took a gulp. "If I was missing, no one would look for me. I've been on my own since I was fifteen."

He rubbed at his brow. "You said you were in and out of the foster system."

I'd given him little tidbits on our evening dates, but I'd never given him the whole story. "I was. But I didn't stay in the system." My fingers tapped against the glass. "Let's just say, my last foster home was a bad experience. Tim ... yeah ... he was a handsy guy."

The muscle in his jaw twitched, and his one hand formed a fist on the table.

I shook my head. "It never got that far, but I could imagine it would have if I hadn't left."

His whole body stiffened, and it was as though he weren't breathing.

"Charles ... I'm okay." I placed a hand on his, my thumb massaging the top of his fist. "The things that have happened in my life have made me who I am today—strong, resilient, a fighter."

His stare flickered to where we were connected and then back up to meet my eyes. "You're the bravest woman I know."

If only those words were true. If I were brave, I wouldn't have run. If I were brave, I would have stayed and fought, and that motherfucker would be in jail.

My gaze went to my glass as I played with a bead of condensation. "I wish I saw myself how you see me."

The corner of his mouth tipped up. "And I wish I saw myself how you see me."

I couldn't help but smile at that. We were so alike that it was eerie. The difficulty, the tragedy, feeling all alone in the world yet having to be your own strength and getting through it, no matter what.

"Charles Brisken," I said with a tip of my chin, "I see you how everyone in the world sees you. I see a man who has been through a lot, a man who has seen tragedy that would take the strongest of men down. But you ... you stood up and have been fighting since day one. You have the most integrity and strength in any man that I've ever met or even heard of. So, take it, own it, and believe it because it's true."

He released a full-on breath, and the smile I rarely saw surfaced. "You are good for my ego, Becky."

"Daddy ..." Sarah called from upstairs, and we both jolted from our chairs and rushed to the bottom of the stairs.

A wailing Mary echoed from the second floor.

"Mary wet her bed."

A second later, Brad appeared at the top of the stairs, holding a crying Mary. One eyebrow quirked up as he took us both in, and he held this expression as though we'd been caught sneaking out—together.

My first foot was on the stairs when Brad held up a hand. "Becky, it's fine. Mason is already changing and disinfecting her bed. I'm going to get her changed." He snaked one hand around Sarah's shoulders, already guiding her to her room. "You guys just ... do whatever you guys were doing." He coughed at the end to cover up a laugh.

"We were getting water," Charles said matter-of-factly, already making his way upstairs.

I followed right behind him.

Brad was almost to Mary's room when he said under his breath, "Is that what we're calling it now ... getting water?"

My cheeks warmed at his words.

Charles grunted and took a sleepy, wet Mary from Brad's arms. "I'll change her. She'll sleep with me tonight."

We watched Charles walk to the far end of the hall and shut the door to his master bedroom.

The side of Brad's mouth tipped up, and he pointed to me. "And you. Don't get any ideas." His voice was playful, typical Brad. "We will not be getting water together. Ever."

I laughed because out of all the Brisken men, I swore it was Brad who'd been dropped on his head at a young age.

"Can we get coffee though?" I joked.

He furrowed his eyebrows. "I don't even know what that means." He scratched the back of his neck and tilted his head, assessing me. "If coffee is anything like getting water, then no. But if you mean *coffee*, coffee, like straight-up coffee, then yeah."

I yawned and half-laughed, turning to walk toward my wing of the house. "Good night, Brad."

Charles

Mary was in the grocery cart while I pushed it down the aisle. Becky had two grocery lists in her hand—hers and then there was Mason's with his organic and gluten-free items.

I'd fallen into this routine with Becky—a comfortable, more than enjoyable routine. It was almost as though we were a family, married. The only difference was, we weren't together.

I really hadn't changed the routine we'd had with Patty.

I had always helped get the girls' breakfast and lunches ready in the morning. But there had been a big difference with Patty, the big difference being that I hadn't been attracted to my former nanny.

I had never really gone grocery shopping with Patty, but here I was, pushing the cart behind Becky, like she was the mother of my child.

Remember when I'd said I didn't lie to myself? Truth was, this was an unhealthy habit that would end badly.

I'd told myself time and time again, as long as I didn't cross that line, we'd be fine. But our late-night dates at the dinner table over water and the light brushes of our arms as we prepared the girls' lunches every morning were barely walking that fine line.

I couldn't help it. I craved it, this closeness with another human being that wasn't simply sex, but something more, sweeter ... intimate.

She placed a hand on my arm, getting my attention. That gentle gesture had me leaning toward her, taking in the intoxicating smell of her shampoo.

"Brown rice pasta is okay, right? That's gluten-free." She lifted the box toward me, quirking an eyebrow.

Mary grabbed it, already placing it in the cart. "Yep. I love pasta."

I nodded, answering her question, "That's fine, Becky."

Her hand remained on my arm as we moved farther down the aisle. A stronger man would have moved away, but I'd learned that, with Becky, any self-control I had would continually get tested.

"You said we could get cookies." Mary peered up at me with an evident pout and expectation in her eyes.

"It's the next aisle over. A promise is a promise." I touched the tip of her nose with my fingertip.

"But I want to go to that aisle now." She crossed her arms over her chest, pushing out her pouting lip.

"Charles ..."

I heard my name being called from a distance, but before I turned around, I already knew who that voice belonged to.

Vivian.

I turned and swallowed, watching her walk stealthily in her four-inch heels. She must have been coming from work because she was in a fitted black skirt suit.

My whole body stiffened as she approached.

The smile on her blood-red lips diminished as she took Becky in.

Becky pulled away from me, dropping her hand that she'd just had on my arm to her side.

"Hey." Vivian's voice oozed a sophistication few women had, bred from an elite family, learned and practiced at an Ivy League school.

"Hey, Vivian."

She had called a few times, but I'd been ignoring her calls, and she never left messages.

It'd been almost a month since I'd seen her, and one thing I wasn't lying to myself about was that I wasn't interested in seeing her anymore. I should have broken up with her properly, but my mind had been preoccupied.

"It's been a while," Vivian said, her words laced with curiosity.

"Yeah. I've been—"

"Busy," she finished my sentence, her eyes flickering toward Becky. "And you must be Miss Mary."

She stepped toward the cart and ruffled Mary's hair. In turn, Mary's frown deepened.

"Mary, say hi," I tried to coax her.

"Hi." She turned her frown to me. "I want my cookies, Daddy." She wiggled in the cart, patience running thin.

"And we will get them," I answered her.

Vivian extended a manicured hand to Becky. "And you are ..."

Becky smiled politely, shaking her hand. "I'm Becky."

"Nice to meet you." She paused, examining Becky with a look of disdain from her blonde hair pulled high into a ponytail to her long-sleeved gray crew shirt, to her jeans, to her gym shoes. "So, you must be Charles's ..."

"Nanny," Becky said, her tone defensive and sharp. "I'm the girls' new nanny."

"Oh." Vivian nodded, her arms lightly crossed against her chest. She pointed to me first and then to Becky. "So, you two are ..."

I gripped Vivian's elbow and pulled her farther down the aisle, momentarily leaving Becky and Mary. This was so out of Vivian's character—catty, jealous. It wasn't in her.

"What's going on here, Viv?" I kept my voice discreet.

She swallowed and reeled back. "No, Charles." She pushed a finger into my chest, getting into my face. "Do not put this on me. I know what this is and have never pretended it to be anything more. You are not one to bull-shit me. Until now."

I blinked. "Bullshit?"

"Is this how we're going to end? No phone call? No conversation? Ghosted like we're in high school?" She tsked. "I thought you were better than that. I can handle the truth." She placed one heavy hand on her chest. "Of all women, you know I can handle the truth very damn well. All I need is a little respect and straight-up honesty."

I exhaled a heavy sigh. She was right. I wanted to tell her I had been preoccupied with other things—Patty leaving, Becky settling in. I had meant to call her back. I wasn't afraid of confrontation. In my line of business, confrontation happened daily. I'd hurt her when that was the last thing I'd wanted to do.

She shook her head condescendingly. "I wasn't important enough to call. That's what it comes down to."

"Vivian ..."

When I gripped her wrist, her eyes narrowed, and she shrugged me off.

"I know we're just fuck buddies." Her tone was low and menacing. "But the least you could have done was called me to tell me that you were now fucking the nanny instead." She spat out the words, hard and low, as though she wanted them to hit me.

My eyes narrowed. "I'm not—"

"Shut up, Charles. If you're not now, you will be soon. I see the way you look at her. I'm not stupid." She straightened and adjusted her suit jacket. After pushing her hair back, she composed herself, stone-faced but pleasant, as though seconds ago hadn't just happened. "Have a nice life, Charles."

"Vivian, I'm sorry. I never meant—"

"Shut up, Charles. It's a little too late for any of that."

I blew out a breath and ran both hands through my hair, watching her walk away.

That had needed to end a long time ago. I had known it'd eventually end, but I hadn't expected it to end this badly.

CHAPTER 16

Becky

After the grocery store, we drove home in silence. The only sounds in the car were of Mary singing "Old MacDonald" and her happily chomping on her cookies like the cookie-monster champ she was.

I hadn't asked Charles about Vivian. I had no right to his past or his current life that had to do with anything other than the kids. What he did with whoever he did it with was not my concern.

But, boy, had my heart sunk when I saw her. She was beautiful with her Pantene-slick, dark hair, her olive skin, and tall, slim figure that only belonged to models. And when Charles leaned into her and placed his hand on her wrist, I couldn't take any more. I'd about-faced and walked Mary toward the other aisle to get cookies. I didn't know why I had assumed Charles was single.

Maybe it was because, for the past few weeks, when he wasn't at work, he was home with the girls.

He didn't have people calling him other than his secretary and his brothers.

For the most part, his life was chill, laid-back, and routine.

But I should have known better. He was a good-looking man, who exhibited strength and a force like a god. Above that, he had a kind heart. Every sane, single woman in the vicinity was probably calling on him, and I didn't even know it.

He didn't owe me an explanation, and I wasn't going to ask. So, I hadn't expected him to shut the fridge after we emptied the groceries and corner me. His hand was heavy on the stainless steel as he towered over me, my back against the fridge.

He was so close that I could smell the mint on his lips, and his chest was only inches from my face.

"Vivian is someone I used to have relations with, but that's done. It wasn't anything serious, and it's over."

I pressed a hand to his chest to stop him from speaking further. "Charles, you don't owe me an explanation."

His heartbeat picked up speed underneath my palm, and the heat from his body radiated off of him in waves. "I know." He held my gaze, and then his stare flickered to my lips. "But this is me. I don't have the mental energy to let things fester, and not telling you bothered me all the way here."

He was so damn beautiful; it hurt to look up at him. My next words came out as a breathless whisper. "But why?"

He let out a shaky breath, and his eyebrows furrowed, as though my question confused him. "I ... I don't know why." He sounded lost, his voice soft, vulnerable even.

When someone cleared their throat, we peered up.

It was Brad, smirking, walking in with Mary. He raised both hands. "You guys getting water? Okaaayyy," he drawled out.

He turned and was about to walk out of the room when Mary charged toward us, encompassing both of us in an embrace, forcing me and Charles even closer together. "Bubble of love," she squealed.

My eyes met Charles's, and he picked up Mary and squeezed her into him. "Two or more people in a hug is a love bubble," Charles said almost apologetically, answering my unasked question. After he placed her on her feet, he patted her back. "Go get washed up. Dinner will be ready soon."

We'd picked up a pizza on our way back because Mary had begged for it, so luckily, it was ready on the kitchen island.

I still didn't know what had transpired at the fridge, but all I knew was that my cheeks were on fire, and I most likely looked like a red chili pepper.

"Let me go get Sarah," I said, practically running out of the room, up the stairs, and into the bathroom.

I was right. My cheeks were red, as though I had applied too much blush and not stopped. After turning the faucet on, I ran my hands under the cold water and splashed my face. What I really needed was a cold shower.

It seemed as though I needed one frequently around Charles. I might as well prune up and stand under the cold water indefinitely.

⸻

That night, it wasn't my cries that woke me; it was that of a young girl. My nightmare hadn't taken me under because I wasn't fully asleep yet. When I registered Mary crying, I jolted from my bed and ran to her room. Usually, Brad would be in there, consoling her, as his room was closest to Mary's, but he'd gone out, and he wasn't home yet.

I opened her room, and the night-light shone on her face. "Mary ... did you wet your bed?"

Her answer was a muffled, "No."

When she stretched her arm toward me, I padded over and sat at the edge of her bed. Pushing her hair from her face, I said, "What's the matter?"

"There was this ghost, and he had teeth and a wand and a crown." Her words came out in short, broken puffs.

"Aww ... come here." I crawled on the bed, resting my back against the headboard, and pulled her against my chest, rocking her in my arms. "I know all about night-mares." My fingers threaded through her light-blonde locks. "But this is the thing—nightmares aren't real."

She peered up at me with her electric-blue eyes, eyes that were Natalie's. The rest of the Briskens held dominant brown ones.

"But, Becky ... they seemed so real."

I pulled her closer and cupped her cheek. "They always do, honey." I knew this statement on a personal level, more than anyone. "When I was younger, you know what I did when I was scared?"

Her curious eyes met mine. "What?"

"I hid under the bed."

"Why?"

"Because I felt like the monsters wouldn't get me there."

When my mother had come home drunk, I'd hide, so she wouldn't find me and yell at me. Under the bed was my regular hiding spot. It eventually became my comfort place.

I adjusted myself, so I was lying on the bed with her right beside me. "Why don't you sleep? I'll stay right here." I pushed her hair away from her face and tucked an escaping strand behind her ear.

Both her hands lay under her cheek, and when she peered up at me, I could see Natalie in her. I'd obviously never met Natalie, but the house was filled with her pictures. In the main dining room, in the girls' rooms.

She must have been a good person, maybe even feisty and stubborn at times. But no doubt, she was kind and full of love. I knew this because her children and Charles exuded those qualities, and she must have had a hand in that.

"Mary?" Charles peered in her room. His eyes widened, taking me in as I lay on Mary's bed. "Her door was open."

"Daddy, I had a nightmare." She wiggled her fingers, her arm outstretched.

When he walked toward the bed and squeezed Mary's outstretched hand, she tugged him toward the other side of the bed. "Sleep here, Daddy."

When I inched away, getting ready to scoot off, Mary snuggled against my chest. "No, you too."

"Mary." My face was heating again as discomfort washed through me. "Your dad is here."

"No. You. Too." She peered up at her father. "Daddy, please. Sleep here." Her voice was sweet, soft, sad from the nightmare.

The bed dipped when he lay on the other side, Mary now sandwiched between us.

My breathing accelerated, and I didn't know what to do. *Should I leave?* But I didn't want Mary to start crying again.

"Mary?" I whispered.

"Shh," she said, all snuggled against my chest, her eyes pressed closed. "I'm sleeping."

Charles laughed softly at her bossiness until she took his

hand and wrapped it fully around her waist, his fingertips brushing against my waist.

"Closer, Daddy. I want to be in a bubble."

Bubble of love.

He complied and moved closer, his hand fully on my hip. His touch was light, but I felt his touch everywhere. Pure heat rushed through me. It was so wrong, given that Mary was between us, yet I couldn't stop my body from reacting.

I swallowed and counted the glow-in-the-dark stars on her ceiling. I could count a thousand sheep backward and forward or do breathing techniques, but I knew it would all be for nothing because there was no sleep happening tonight.

———

But I had been wrong.

The next morning, I awoke, drool down the side of my face. And alarmingly, I was in Charles's arms, lying on his chest, still in Mary's bed, sans Mary.

Goodness gracious, great balls of Zeus.

Because Charles's erection was massive and pushing against my stomach.

My nipples pebbled against my thin white tank top and pushed against his chest. I hadn't really noticed how thin it was when the only light in the room last night was Mary's princess night-light.

I lifted my head, and with one hand, I swiped the dried drool from my mouth. On his shirt, I'd formed a small pool large enough for twenty ants to party in.

Gross.

I pushed my head off of his chest, and the slight movement had his one arm snaking along my lower back, locking me against him. I cringed. *Now what?* I'd rather not wake him, morning wood and embarrassing situation and all.

I tried again, slowly lifting my chest off of him. His sleepy eyes fluttered open before flying open. His eyes flew to my cleavage squished together at the position I was in, and instantly, his dick hardened even more.

I thought he was already hard. Good Lord!

I swallowed, and our eyes both moved to the tip of his dick peeking out from his boxers, wanting to make a statement.

"Fuck," he grunted.

At that moment, Brad popped his head in. "Shit, please not in Mary's room. Can't you get *water* somewhere else? Damn it."

After Brad slammed the door shut, I lifted myself off of Charles, but when he scooted out from under me, he fell off the bed.

He jumped to a standing position, his erection still pushing against the edge of his shorts. Our eyes both flew to his hard-on.

"Uh, Becky." He covered his package with both of his hands.

When his face turned all shades of pink, I started laughing.

He shook his head and turned to the door, but he swiveled around to face me again. "It's a natural morning reaction in men. It would have happened even if I wasn't attracted to you ... um ... yeah." His eyebrows scrunched together before he walked out. "I mean ... I know you already know this." The color from his cheeks moved to his ears before he about-faced and walked out the door.

When he left, I fell back in a fit of laughter because

hellooooo, uncomfortable. I'd just woken up in bed with my boss, where he'd sported a *so huge that I'm afraid it won't fit* erection.

The laughter ceased when I realized one thing. In Charles's arms last night, I hadn't had a nightmare. It was the first time since the accident that I hadn't had one.

CHAPTER 17

CHARLES

Walking downstairs that morning and facing Becky at breakfast was awkward, to say the least. I made the girls breakfast and ignored Brad's snickers and straight-on smirks, as though he knew something was up, when he obviously didn't.

I couldn't even look her in the face, given what had happened earlier.

When I sat at the table with my morning coffee, Sarah tilted her head, assessing me. "You're late this morning. You're never late."

Of course, she was the most attentive.

"Daddy probably had to poop," Mary said, head deep into her cereal, analyzing the marshmallows. "Sometimes, his poop takes a long time."

My gaze flickered around the table—to Brad and Sarah laughing and to Becky, whose smile widened, stare focused on her plate.

"There's no poop talk at the table, Mary," Brad said.

I sighed. There was no way this day could get any more embarrassing.

"But it's true. Daddy sits on the toilet for a long time." She giggled. "While his long vagina just sits there with him."

Brad laughed so hard that he coughed up his coffee, and it was coming out of his nose.

"Mary," I cautioned her. "Eat your food. Stop talking until your food is eaten."

She giggled. "I'm just telling the truth, Daddy."

I swallowed and downed all my coffee, taking the cup to the sink. "Mary, that's enough. If you don't finish your breakfast, you'll be late to school." My face warmed, and I didn't dare look in Becky's direction, not wanting to take this embarrassment to the next level.

That was what happened when you had three men raising all girls. I never kept my bedroom or the bathroom locked. When I showered, they would come in and some-times take their Barbies in there to play. When I wasn't working, they always wanted to be with me—understand-ably so.

"Charles," Brad called out, forcing me to look at him. If he spouted out with a smart-aleck comment, I might have to hit him. "Don't forget, I have the photo shoot for that maga-zine spread today. Just keep the long vagina covered." He barked out a laugh and stood from his seat, meeting me at the sink, placing his mug in the dishwasher.

"It's for that *single and ready to mingle* bachelor billion-aires under thirty." His smile was smug. "The girls and everyone should be there. It'll be an impromptu shoot." He shot Becky a look. "Can you make sure the girls will be ready after school? The photographers will be coming to the house."

"Sure thing."

My eyes swung her way. "Becky, I'll take the girls to school today." My gaze flickered back to the door. "Girls, meet me in the car."

We had a good five minutes before we needed to be out the door, but with all the talks of poop and swinging long ones, I'd had enough embarrassment today. I didn't do well with situations I wasn't in control of, and the situation with Becky and me was out of my control. I couldn't rein in my feelings toward her. I couldn't control how my body reacted to her. I couldn't control what I was going to do next around her.

So, right now, I headed to the car.

———

Throughout the day, Becky filtered through every one of my thoughts. Her citrus scent followed me everywhere I went. Maybe I was conjuring up the smell of her shampoo. All I knew was that I was going a little bit crazy.

Fuck, it is going to be such a long, awful day.

And now that the embarrassment of waking up with a hard-on next to her and the poop situation had died down, I wanted to see her again—be in her presence, drown in her laughter. Yes, it would be awkward, seeing her again, but the need to see her trumped that.

"Charles?" Selena said, shifting in her seat to get my attention.

My head flipped up to our head of marketing sitting in the chair in front of me in my office.

I straightened in my seat and swallowed, unsure of how to answer because I hadn't heard the damn question.

"What do you think, Charles?"

I cleared my throat and tapped my fingers against my desk.

She tilted her head, assessing me. She lifted her mock-ups and waved them in my direction. "You don't like it, do you?"

I released a silent breath of relief, noting the mock-ups were of the packaging for the Colby Chocolate endeavor, one of the contracts we had with the biggest chocolate and candy factory in the nation.

"I like it. Seriously, it's clean, and the branding is on point. Email it to Connor. Have him approve it, and then we can start printing their labels at the end of the month."

Selena smiled, and her shoulders relaxed, fully satisfied with my answer. She stood and playfully saluted me. "Sounds like a plan, boss."

As soon as she left and the door shut behind her, I rubbed at my brow.

Get a grip, Charles.

The door swung open, and Brad sauntered in like he owned my office. In typical Brad fashion, there had been no knock on the door. He sat in the seat that Selena had just vacated.

"You like my tie?" He unbuttoned his suit jacket and lifted his tie. "It's new. It's for tonight's shoot. When I asked Sonia, she ignored me. Seriously, I can't get an answer from that woman when it's not about work."

Which is exactly why Mason and I'd brought her on.

"It's fine," I said.

"This is the thing. I need a great tie, not just an *it's fine* tie."

My face was steady, my mouth slipping into a grimace. I had work to do, and given that my thoughts were on Becky, there was not enough time in the day to finish all I needed to do.

"It's a great tie," I deadpanned.

"Now, you're lying." He dropped his tie and rested his elbows on his thighs, leaning in. "Did you know that Mason is bringing Janice tonight?" His face scrunched, as though he had eaten something sour.

"You did say the whole family has to be there," I pointed out.

He glared at me. "She's not family."

I threw my hands up. "They've been together for years. She's on the way to being—"

He shot up on his feet. "Don't say it. I mean, can we just be in denial and hope for the best for a little bit? Seriously, do you want that thing to be part of our family?"

I threw him a pointed look. "Be nice, Brad."

He huffed like he was two. "All right, all right. Fine. Anyway, see you at the house later." He stood and was almost to the door when he turned around and held out his tie again. "Fine tie or great tie? Tell the truth. This tie might be the difference between wife or death."

I couldn't help myself; I laughed, raising an eyebrow. "Wife or death?"

"Yeah. Finally finding myself a wife I can spend the rest of my life with or dying a lonely death by myself." His eyes flickered to behind me, focusing on the skyline beyond my floor-to-ceiling windows.

With Brad, I never knew if he was serious or kidding. But in the brief silence, there was this look in his eye, a vulnerability that I never saw.

"At least I have the girls," he said, erasing all the vulnerability I'd just seen moments ago. He smiled then. "They can change my Depends diapers. I changed their diapers for years, cleaning up poop and puke and all other bodily fluids a man of my age should not have to deal with yet." With a wave of his hand, he was out the door. "Payback is a bitch, baby."

When the door shut behind him, I rested my ankle on the opposite knee, my eyes traveling the length of my office, the bookshelves holding all the awards that our company had won throughout the years, gifts from clients and from suppliers. I swiveled my chair and stood, staring out the window, at the buildings as high as ours in the horizon, some even higher. At this height, it would seem as though I were on top of the world, a king on his throne. But as I rested my forehead against the glass, looking at the people, like tiny ants moving across the streets, Brad's words rang loudly in my head.

"Wife or death."

It was crazy, downright silly, but also true. What was the point in having it all when you didn't have someone to spend it with?

If there was a difference between wife or death, I'd pick wife.

CHAPTER 18

Becky

"Mary, honey, get in the tub." I had fifteen minutes to get this poor child dressed and changed and downstairs, ready for pictures.

Talk about dilemma.

When Mary had gotten home, she had decided that while I was doing laundry and while Sarah was calmly helping me neatly fold clothes, she would bake a cake ... all by herself ... and melt the chocolate in the microwave.

I hadn't even known that the kid could use a microwave.

But no doubt, she was a genius, and she'd hoisted herself up onto the counter all by herself, shoved the chocolate morsels for chocolate chip cookies in the microwave, and pressed the minute button multiple times.

Too bad the chocolate morsels were still in the Nestlé bag. Too bad it almost caught on fire after the bag exploded.

Bless Mary's heart as she tried to clean up everything with the dishrag, only to drop the chocolate morsels and get it all on the floor. Then, the smart kid had used her hands to clean it up and licked her hands clean in the process.

Now, not only was chocolate on her, but it was all over the house, and since I'd carried her upstairs, it was all over me.

Goodness gracious.

"Becky?" Sarah said, walking into the bathroom, me on my knees as I tried to get the water to run faster.

The smarter thing to do would have been to give her a shower and wash her clean, but Mary hated showers, as she said the water got in her eyes.

"Mary, Uncle Brad will be here soon. He called to see if we were ready."

Mary licked her fingers. Chocolate was on her face, on each cheek, on her nose, and just above her brow where she had probably scratched an itch with her chocolate-smeared fingers.

In any other situation, this would have been comical. But not when photographers would be here any minute to shoot this family, and my one job was to get these kids ready, which they were not.

"Honeys, I'm home!" Brad said, calling from downstairs.

Anxiety spiked within me as I quickly undressed Mary and gently placed her in the tub.

Mary had no sense of urgency. I guessed no kid did really.

"What the hell?" Brad said, stepping into the bathroom. "What happened? You guys are supposed to be ready. The photogs are here and setting up downstairs." He ran one hand through his hair and made it stand on end. In the next second, he was in front of the mirror, fixing it.

"There was a little accident," I said, exasperated. "Mary decided to bake a cake while I was doing laundry."

I poured some shampoo in my hands and ran it through

Mary's locks. She continued playing with her Barbies in the water.

"The chocolate was yummy!"

Brad slapped his head. "Sweet Mary, why today?"

"They're already here and set up downstairs," Charles announced, walking in. His expression pinched as he took in the scene. "What happened?"

Sarah filled her father in as I continued working in fast mode.

"Stand up, baby girl. Let's get you rinsed."

"Let me help you. What do you need?" Charles asked, unbuttoning the sleeves of his dress shirt and rolling them up.

"What is going on here?" Mason said, stepping into the bathroom.

Even though the bathroom was pretty big, having the whole family inside was excessive.

"Oh. My. God." A high-pitched voice sounded behind him. A tall look-alike Barbie figure scrunched her face. This must be Janice. "All right, it seems like you all have this handled. I'll make sure the team downstairs has everything they need." She about-faced and walked out of the bathroom, leaving the Brisken men and Sarah in with me and Mary.

"Look at my pool," Mary exclaimed, getting back into the bubbles and filling her Barbie pool in the tub with more water.

I lifted the drain. "You're done. Let's get you changed."

She visibly pouted and splashed around, getting water all over me. "I'm still playing."

"Okay, you guys handle this. I need to go downstairs to check on the crew," Brad said, finally leaving, followed by Mason.

Honestly, we didn't need that many people in the bathroom. I had this handled.

"Mary, you're done. Get out." Charles's voice was stern, brooking no argument, but it was as though Mary hadn't heard him. "Mary," Charles said, voice heightened.

I couldn't even rinse the girl because she had the bucket and she kept filling up her mini pool for her Barbies.

"Mary, honey. We have to get going, so we can continue making your cake." Yes, I was bribing her and playing her game, but right now, she was on top of the leaderboard.

"You guys ready soon?" Brad yelled from the bottom of the stairs.

"It's been literally one minute since he left," I deadpanned, my annoyance showing through my tone.

"Mary, out." Charles stepped around me and bent down to lift her.

I placed a wet palm against his shirt. A bad move since he was dry but, considering he was going to chuck a *fully soaked and not rinsed* Mary out of the water, I needed to stop him.

"You're going to get wet," I said, standing. I used my elbow to push the hair out of my face. I was already fully wet, so there was no need for the both of us to get ourselves soaked.

"It's fine. Mary ..." He sidestepped me and turned on the faucet, running the clean water into the tub.

"I'll do it. Mary, can I have that little bucket, so I can rinse you?"

Mary was being extremely difficult today as she continued filling up her pool.

"You're not listening!" Charles growled, making me jump. "You're grounded." He yanked the bucket out of her hands and tried to lift her from the tub, grabbing under her one arm.

"I'm not done, Daddy." Her pout was on full display.

Charles gritted his teeth, and the muscle in his jaw jumped. When he spoke, it was like the earth shook with the authority in his tone. "You're done when I say you're done, and you're done now."

Mary's tears streamed down her face as he rinsed her, dumping water over her head and over her body. There was no doubt that Charles would need to get changed before the shoot because he wasn't only a little wet; he was a lot wet.

"I have it, Charles."

"No, it's fine." He plucked her out of the tub, but because she didn't release her Barbie pool, she took the pool full of water with her, tipping it over and all over the floor.

"Fuck."

"Oh no."

"What's going on here?" Brad rushed into the bathroom.

I was about to warn him to be careful until he stepped into the bathroom and wiped out, slipping and falling to the ground.

"Great," Charles grumbled, wrapping a crying Mary in a towel. "Now, we all have to get changed."

"Why me? Why now?" Brad lay there for a few seconds, staring at the ceiling, and then he began to laugh.

Charles placed Mary on her feet and grabbed a few towels, layering them on the floor. I assisted but stepped on a puddle and slipped. Strong arms wrapped around my waist, twisting toward the tub, steadying me, but too bad we both fell in a heap over the towels, me on top of Charles.

My breath caught as I felt every inch of him against me —his chest against my chest, his hip by my hip. I pushed at his chest but ended up getting tangled up and head-butting him.

Ow ...

I expected more anger, more frustration from him, but out of nowhere, he let out a deep rumble of laughter that eased my insides.

Then, I started laughing. Brad was laughing. All the adults were laughing.

What a day. And there was no way it could get worse, right?

Wrong.

Suddenly, from the door, a bright light caught us all off guard as the flashes from the photographers began.

CHAPTER 19

CHARLES

Every king, even the powerful, almighty ones, fell.

And I fell.

Hard.

For the first time in a very long time, I was sick. Not just a little cold, but a full-on type A flu. It had been confirmed by the doctor. It had also been confirmed that since I had gone too late, I couldn't take Tamiflu.

Good God. My only saving grace was that it was the weekend, but I felt like utter shit.

Knock. Knock. Knock.

"Daddy," Mary said. "I made you something, but Uncle Brad said I can't come in there."

I grunted, unable to move because every muscle hurt, as though I'd just worked out. "Thanks, baby."

"I'm just going to slip it under the door." There was a long pause before she continued, "And don't die, okay? 'Cause I love you."

I laughed. Then, I realized it hurt to laugh.

"Dad?" It was Sarah this time. "Brad and Uncle Mason

are going to take us out. We might sleep at their place in the city since you're ... sick and stuff."

Good. Even better.

I didn't want to contaminate anyone with this virus, let alone my children, who had perfect attendance thus far this year.

I lifted my head and peered over at the tall glass of water at the side table. Stretching my hand, I tried to reach for it. I could have tried harder, but I plopped back down and threw one arm over my eyes.

Fuck it.

I was going to sleep instead.

———

Becky

I'd been knocking on Charles's door for the last few minutes, but he hadn't responded, so I turned the knob and walked in, bringing a tray of soup, crackers, tea, and medicine.

I'd never been in his room before, and I was surprised it was so bland. Where the rest of the house was filled with color, Charles's room was gray, from his sheets to his walls, and there was nothing hanging up. Not a speck of art or a single frame.

I'd suspected he'd have a picture of Natalie somewhere, anywhere, or maybe even of the children, but his dresser and side table were empty. I didn't know if I found this interesting or incredibly sad.

The blinds were all shut, but little shadows of light still filtered through the slits of the blinds.

"Charles?" I padded to the bed and placed the tray on the floor.

Half the sheets were off the bed. He had one arm thrown over his head, and he was breathing heavily. I could hear the congestion in his chest. He was in the middle of his California-king bed, so I had to slide onto it to feel his forehead and his cheeks.

"Oh, Charles, you're burning up."

He needed some Tylenol to get his fever under control. And he needed a change of clothes because his white shirt was damp.

I decided to tend to him first, then feed him, and then medicate him.

In nurse mode, I went into action, walking to his master bathroom made for a king. A tub the size of a small swimming pool was situated in the far corner, and every crevice of the white marbled bathroom sparkled.

Interestingly enough, his bathroom was not as bare as his bedroom. For instance, Natalie's side of the double sink was untouched. Her makeup and her jewelry case were there. Even her toothbrush was in its holder. She'd died almost four years ago, yet all of her belongings were still here in the bathroom, as though she'd never left.

In the middle, on the counter, was a mini ceramic dish, and as I walked closer, I realized it held their wedding rings.

I paused as I thought about it.

No, he'd placed it here. This was originally his parents' house.

My heart clenched at the enormity of his heartache. He'd moved her stuff in, after she'd passed away, because he'd wanted her still with him.

My heart ached for Charles and for a woman that I didn't even know. Just the fact that her life had been cut so short, that she was not able to enjoy her children, love them, love and take care of Charles.

Take care of Charles.

I shook my head into focus and went to the linen cabinet to grab some washcloths. Finding everything I needed wasn't that hard; it just consisted of opening drawers and rummaging through some of Charles belongings.

After a good few minutes, I had washcloths, a bowl, and a clean T-shirt.

"Charles?" I approached the bed. I dipped the washcloth in the water and wrung it out. After climbing onto the bed, I placed the damp cloth across his forehead before dabbing it down his cheek and around his neck.

His eyes fluttered open. "Becky? What are you doing here?" he croaked out. "You need to stay away." He coughed. "Whatever I have, I swear you don't want it."

I ignored him, swiping at his cheek and his neck, repeating the motion.

He grabbed my wrist, his skin on fire. "Becky, I'm fine." His voice was low, rough, as though there were sand in his throat.

"You're far from fine," I said gently. "Your fever is through the roof."

"I probably look like death and smell like death, so please ... let me keep my dignity here." His fingers moved from my wrist to my hand, placing it on top of his chest. "I'm sure I'll be fine."

"You will be because I'm here now," I said, maternal determination in my voice.

He lost his argument at that, and his eyes fell shut. His lips tipped upward, and it made my heart pitter-patter. Why couldn't he smile more often, not when he was in an utter state of delirium caused by a high temperature?

"I'm supposed to be taking care of you," he slurred, his

eyes still shut. "That's my job. Why I was born. It's my purpose in life. I take care of people."

I paused, just staring at him, at the light stubble forming at his chin, at the length of his eyelashes with his eyes shut. It wasn't fair, was it? All the responsibility set on his shoulders.

"Maybe you should let people take care of you sometimes," I whispered.

I watched the even rise and fall of his chest, wanting to hug him for no other reason than for taking on that role, for being a good guy. He could have left the company to his brothers, he could have chosen to be less, but he hadn't. He took on the world and refused to let it crush him.

I admired that more than he'd ever know.

"First things first." I placed the washcloth in the small basin and got closer, on my knees. *I am going to need all my strength for this one.* "Let's get you into a fresh, clean shirt. This one is damp."

My arms went to the upper part of his chest, right underneath his armpits, and I lifted him.

"Becky," he said groggily.

"Just help me a little here. Can you sit up?"

He grunted as I helped him to a sitting position. Grabbing the edge of his shirt, I lifted it to his neck. And then I just ... stared. I couldn't help myself. Because damn ...

I knew Charles worked out on his lunch break at work, and for the most part, he ate clean, which paid off because holy washboard abs.

"Are you taking advantage of me, Becky?" Charles tried to joke, his eyes still closed.

I pushed his shirt over his neck and pulled it up his arms before throwing it on the floor.

"And about the other day ... about Mr. Woody."

Mr. Woody?

I smiled because he was cute, making jokes.

"That's a natural reaction in the morning for men." He coughed a few times. "But let me tell you a secret." He coughed again. "Mr. Woody is almost always at attention whenever you're around."

Oh goodness. High-fever delirium.

My cheeks heated. Thank goodness his eyes were still closed, so he wouldn't witness my flaming hot cheeks.

As hard as I tried, I couldn't help but be flattered because there was no way I couldn't be. *Did he like me?* I truly hoped and wished he did.

I shook my head, dimming the thoughts. Wanting him, wanting him to like me, would complicate things—this job, my relationship with the kids. He couldn't like me. He wouldn't like me if he knew about my broken past.

I focused on the task at hand and pushed the clean shirt over his head and down his stomach. With a lot of effort, I helped him slide down to lie flat again.

It was fine until I fell on top of him in the process in a big *oomph.*

"Taking advantage now, are we? You don't even have to ask." In that moment, he sounded like Brad.

I would have laughed if my pulse wasn't in overdrive. I pushed myself off of him and groaned when I spotted the Tylenol on the tray on the floor.

Mother-pluckers.

I stared back at my patient, who was now snoring soundly.

One of my greatest qualities, in addition to staying hidden, was my persistence.

I hopped off the bed, grabbed the Tylenol, then climbed

back on, and straddled his waist. I bent down and lifted his chin. "Charles." I shook him a little. "Charles!"

"Hmm?" One eye opened and shut.

I needed his fever to go down. I placed the little pill on his pillow and reached for his full glass of water at his side table. Then, I dipped a few fingers in his water and splashed some water on his face. "Charles!"

He didn't move. Stupid me, it probably felt good. If I were raging with fever, I'd probably love some cool sprinkles to the face.

With a sigh, I repeated the motion until he stirred, and both sleepy eyes opened. I pulled at his shirt until he was elevated a little higher on his pillow. If he started choking, we'd have a different problem.

"Open your mouth." When he didn't comply, I pulled at his chin and stuffed the pill in his mouth. Then, I put the glass on his lips.

His eyes fell shut again, and I slapped at his cheek. "Hey, you. Come on. Come on. Come on." Slap. Slap. Slap. "Come on. Swallow."

"Do you swallow?"

This guy. I couldn't dim my smile even if I tried.

I tipped back the glass, cupping the back of his head to guide him.

When the pill went down with a gulp of water, I almost laughed out my next words. "I always swallow."

His eyes slowly opened, and a drunken smile surfaced before I let him fall to his pillow.

Gah!

If I wasn't careful, I could fall in love with this guy.

⊏⊐

Charles.

Who knew what time it was or what day it was? All I knew was that I had to take a real bad piss.

I stepped off of my bed and almost tripped on the comforter on the floor.

"Becky?" I asked, my throat as dry as a desert.

She yawned and slowly pushed herself to a sitting position.

"What are you doing here?" I shook my head, confused, and did a once-over of my surroundings. Yeah, I was still in my room. "Becky, I'm sick, so you really shouldn't be here."

She stretched, and her voice was heavy with sleep when she spoke, "But I had to check on you and make sure you were okay." She pushed the covers off and stood. "I'm glad I did. Your fever was through the roof."

After she stepped into me, she placed the cool back of her hand on my forehead and then my neck.

She exhaled a sigh of relief and smiled. "I think your fever broke."

I stood there in silence for a good whole three seconds, taking her in. Her messy blonde hair, the green in her eyes that seemed to sparkle against the light in my room. And in that moment, something broke in me.

My heart warmed, and that tough demeanor that I always displayed cracked. She'd taken care of me—me! The guy who had been taking care of himself for the last four years. The last time I'd gotten really sick, I'd had the stomach flu. I had woken up in sweat and thrown up, but I'd peeled myself out of bed, showered, gone to bed, and repeated the process until the virus was gone. All by myself.

So, taking in her blanket on the floor, the tray with Tylenol, some soup, a washcloth and basin ... well, shit. This touched me on a deeper level, a level that caught me off guard. I blew out a long, slow breath, and my eyebrows pulled together as I took her one hand and squeezed it. "Thank you, Becky."

She smiled a sweet smile. Then, it hit like a train coming at me full force, knocking the breath out of me. Just like I had known many years ago, when I was in high school, I knew now. It had only happened one time before. I wasn't only drawn to Becky's beauty. I was falling for this girl. Deep, hard, and completely.

The shock of realization had me dropping her hand and turning toward the bathroom, almost sprinting. "Sorry. I have to piss."

I shut the bathroom door and leaned against it, running one shaky hand down my face.

My bladder was about to explode, but I was paralyzed in my spot because I couldn't deny it. I liked the nanny. I knew this. I had admitted this to Natalie.

Problem was ... what was I going to do about it?

No, that wasn't the problem.

The problem was, how was I going to get her to fall for me?

CHAPTER 20

CHARLES

The moment I realized I was going to pursue Becky, everything changed. But not in a good way.

It was as though my life had been turned upside down and inside out.

That Monday morning, I'd woken up late. I'd forgotten my tie at home and a belt, too, for that matter. I'd missed an important vendor meeting at work. I had been spacing out when people were talking to me because I couldn't stop thinking about her.

I was a damn lovesick puppy again, as though I were living my high school years all over again.

I sat at the boardroom table, but everyone else had already cleared out. Monday mornings, I led our company meetings with all of the VPs and above to get an update on what everyone was doing. My job was to give them an overview from an upper-management perspective on our projections and upcoming projects we had planned.

My fingers tapped on my knee, then on my untouched coffee, and then tip-tapped on the long mahogany table that took up the room. Problem was, I liked her, and I didn't know what I was going to do about it.

Like the CEO I was, I started listing all the pros and cons of dating her in my head.

The major con was that if we didn't work out, it wouldn't be the same in the household, and I'd have to terminate her employment. Because how could we possibly go from seriously dating to her just going back to her regular job as the nanny? We couldn't.

I wasn't going to pretend that was even an option.

Also, the kids. I'd never even thought I'd be contemplating this—dating again.

How will I break it to them? How will they take it?

And will she want to date me? Am I even her type?

A knock sounded from the door, and I lifted my head from my daze.

"Hey, are you okay?" It was Mason. His eyebrows scrunched together before he walked in.

"Yeah. Why?" My voice croaked out like a teenage boy going through puberty.

"Well, you've been sort of out of it lately. I mean, I've read that, sometimes, there can be delirium because of the flu, but that's because of the high fevers. I don't think that usually lingers."

I rubbed at my brow, feeling guilt wash over me. "Yeah. About that meeting ... I'm sorry about that. I ..." I tilted my head from side to side, feeling tension rise to my shoulders.

"Hey." Brad walked in. "Are we going to lunch?"

He took it upon himself to make an already-awkward situation more intense. Of course, this was his MO.

"Serious conversation?" He plopped down and reached for my coffee, taking a sip.

I glared at him. *This guy.*

Mason took the seat next to him, his face filling with concern. "Yeah. I was just going to say that I think you should see a doctor. You never get sick, and I think there might be lingering effects from your flu."

Brad laughed beside him.

Mason threw Brad one of his annoyed looks but continued, "I'm serious, Charles. You haven't been yourself lately, and I'm concerned."

Brad interlocked his fingers behind his head and leaned back. "I know exactly what the problem is. It's too much *water*." He winked at me like the devilish bastard that he was.

I rubbed at my temple, an ongoing migraine about to start.

"What the hell is that supposed to mean? I'm being serious, and like always, you're fucking around," Mason snapped.

Brad tsked beside him. "It's true. Tell him, big bro," he said, shooting me a conspiratorial grin.

I let out a long sigh. Where Mason looked at the analytical aspects of things to come to a conclusion, Brad called things out exactly how he saw them.

But I wasn't ready to expand yet when I hadn't figured out what I was going to do about my current situation.

We shared a knowing look, one Mason wasn't a part of.

Mason stood, crossing his arms over his chest, visibly agitated. His gaze ping-ponged from Brad to me and back again. "Listen, can someone fill me in on what's going on?"

"Getting water"—Brad cleared his throat in an exaggerated effect—"means banging the nanny."

Mason reeled back. "What?"

"I'm not banging the nanny," I insisted.

Brad pointed his hand like a gun. "But you want to, don't you?"

I groaned.

"Don't deny it, Charles. I've seen how you are with her, and I caught you ... in Mary's bed."

"You had sex on Mary's bed?" Mason jerked back, and his face scrunched up, disgusted. His voice hitched up, hitting a high soprano note. "Mary's bed?"

"No, Mason," I grumbled. "And I have not had sex with Becky."

Brad leaned in, getting in my face, his words firm, sure. "But you want to."

We were locked in this staring contest. I was never one to give in. Even when we had been younger, I had been the stronger one of the three of them, born bigger, born first, more reserved but the one with the most restraint.

But I was at a loss this time, so I dropped my gaze to the table and let out a long sigh. "I like her. Yes." It wasn't a direct answer to his question, but if I had my way, hopefully, it would eventually lead that way. I dropped my head in my hands, running my fingers through my hair over and over again.

Mason gawked at me. "You can't. You know nothing about her."

"Dumbass," Brad scoffed. "You don't have to be dating someone forever to know that you're in love with them. Just because you and Janice are like that doesn't mean that's how every relationship works."

"It's not love," I said, shooting my head up.

How could it be? We hadn't known each other all that long. With Nat, I'd known her for years before I knew I was in love with her.

My brothers completely ignored me.

"Says the guy who can't hold a relationship," Mason shot back.

"This is all premature. This might not even go anywhere," I said, mostly talking to myself.

"Or this might go on everywhere. My room is off-limits though, 'kay?" Brad smirked.

"For once, can you be serious? We don't even know her," Mason repeated.

"There's no *we* in *their* equation. And that's an easy fix, Charles." Brad leveled me with a stare. "Get to know her." He stood. "I have to get lunch. My stomach is eating its lining, and I don't do well without food." He placed a heavy hand on my shoulder and squeezed. "This is good for you, Charles. More than that, Becky is good for you. Trust me." And then the devilish bastard winked once more before he walked out with Mason who hadn't said a word.

CHAPTER 21

Becky

I woke up on my birthday like I did any other day—because no one was supposed to know. I thought no one did, but when I opened my bedroom door, a dozen pink balloons hit me in the face. On the floor lay multiple paintings and cards. There were three animal paintings—one of a llama, the other two of unicorns—all displaying two words: *Happy birthday*.

My heart expanded as I picked them all up and brought them to my chest. After pulling the balloons into my room and placing the paintings and cards on my desk, I skipped downstairs to get the girls' breakfast ready.

As always, Charles was there, with my coffee ready, another balloon floating above his head. After handing me my coffee, he pulled the balloon over by its string and gave it to me. "Happy birthday."

I was cheesing so hard that my cheeks hurt. "Who told you?"

"Patty told us. And you ..." He playfully narrowed his eyes. "Don't even try it. We make the birthdays big and grand for the girls. And they like to make it big and grand for each of us. So, we're celebrating today. Two years ago, the girls wanted to take Patty to Disney World, so we did."

When my eyes widened, he said, "Don't worry. Patty said you wouldn't enjoy that too much. You're more low-key."

I nodded. "I am." Though I'd love to go to Disney World one day. The day I wasn't afraid to go out of my house in general.

"But we'll be doing dinner tonight. All of us. Mary has picked where we're going."

My excitement could not be dimmed, and there was a little hop in my step.

We fell into our normal morning routine, me getting breakfast ready and him getting the girls' lunch ready at the kitchen island.

"What was your most memorable birthday?" Charles slapped some mayo on a piece of bread.

I inhaled and exhaled as memories came back. There were some memorable ones but only ones that I wanted to forget.

I thought he sensed my reluctance to answer because Charles rephrased his question. "Your happiest birthday."

"Hmm." I laughed without humor. "My mother did actually remember my birthday one year." I swallowed down through the pain of the memory. "I forget how old I was, probably a little older than Mary. But I remember it was also the same day that social services had a scheduled visit." I flipped the pancake on the pan. "I don't know how I remember that, but I do." A heaviness spread throughout my body, and I forced myself to focus on the task at hand before the hurt and pain from my past came rushing back and crippled me into a state of sadness.

Silence followed my response, so I peered over my shoulder and forced a smile on my face. "It's okay though." I pushed out the words, trying to focus on the positive before the negative took me under. "There are so many other memories, happier ones that replace that." None of them when I was younger, but more with the families who had adopted me, like Patty's family.

"I'm sorry you had to go through all of that, Becky. I am." There was true sincerity in his tone.

I shrugged. " 'Tis what it is." I let my past slip from my memory, forced it back down into a box I hardly ever opened anymore. I continued with the pancakes, placing the cooked one on the plate and pouring more batter on the pan. "It isn't any different from how you function. You haven't been dealt the best cards either, but you don't just lie down and die."

I watched a flash of pain cross over his face.

"I wanted to. Trust me. If it wasn't for the girls, I would have," he admitted. "Didn't your boyfriend ever celebrate your birthday?"

My whole body stiffened. My mind went into panic mode, searching through all the things I'd told him. *When did I ever mentioned my ex-boyfriend?*

"You mentioned dating a guy for a while. Someone who kind of enjoyed gambling." His voice was light, but I knew he was fishing.

I flipped the pancake while my heartbeat thrashed in my ears. *How much did I want to share without sharing too much?*

"He must have celebrated your birthday. What kind of boyfriend doesn't celebrate his girlfriend's birthday?" His voice was softer this time, more cautious.

"My ex-boyfriend." I turned off the stove and walked

straight to the kitchen table with my stack of pancakes. "Let's just say, he wasn't the best boyfriend."

When I passed him to get the milk and orange juice from the fridge, he reached for my forearm. "Becky ..."

My breath caught at the intensity of his stare, the concern in them.

"Is that who you're running from?"

His words were like a dose of cold water in my face, a slap against my cheek. I jerked back, unprepared.

I wanted to tell Charles everything. After keeping my secret to myself for so long, he was the person I wanted to tell the most because I wanted him to know me—all of me. He knew snippets of my life, but for once, I wanted to give someone the whole picture.

He squeezed my forearm, leaning in to get in my line of sight. "You can trust me, Becky. I'll protect you."

I squeezed my eyes tight. What a lovely thought, letting Charles protect me. Valiant of him. But he had no idea. He couldn't protect me from Paul. He had no idea what kind of monster Paul was. If anything, this family, Charles included, would be collateral damage, and I couldn't let that happen. I would never forgive myself. I couldn't even fathom accidentally bringing that devil anywhere close to this perfect family.

I slowly extracted myself from him and ignored his question, opening the fridge and avoiding eye contact.

"Becky ..." Desperation. There was desperation in his voice.

Charles was never desperate, and it tugged at my heart. Tugged so hard that I almost ...

No!

My ears burned. I needed a minute to myself, but

everyone would be down soon, and I had to get breakfast ready.

Task at hand.

Focus on the task at hand.

Glasses out. Juice for Mary. Milk for Sarah.

"Becky!" he whispered fiercely.

Cut the pancakes up for Mary. Tiny pieces. She likes tinier pieces.

"Becky ..." He gently yanked me to face him, his face tormented. "I just want to get to know you more."

There was a long, pregnant pause, and our eyes locked. I could see the confusion and sincerity in his eyes, questions he had for me, questions I couldn't answer because it would reveal too much.

I trusted him. I did. But not with this. My mother was harmless. She could no longer hurt me or this family. So, while talking about her was painful, it didn't bring imminent danger.

Still, I could feel this pressure cooker building inside of me, wanting to tell him, but I was also curious as to why he wanted to know so badly. "Why?" The word flew from my lips before I had a chance to stop it. I should have stayed silent. It didn't matter why he wanted to get to know me more because I wasn't going to bring up things I wanted to forget.

A small breath escaped him before he leaned into me. "Because ... because I like you, Becky." His words flew out effortlessly, straightforward, honest—all qualities signature to Charles, the CEO.

And I knew what he meant—that he *liked* me. Not just as a person, but he was also attracted to me. I guessed I should've known with the couple of hints he'd dropped, especially when he was sick, but I'd just assumed he was delirious.

My heart melted, and I wanted to cry because I liked him too. Good God, did I like him.

His fingers trailed from my wrist, intertwining our fingers. "And I'm kind of wondering ... if you like me too."

His intense concern shifted into the sweetest, most vulnerable smile. Something I'd never thought I'd see when I first started here. He'd been so stoic then, but he had been melting these last several weeks. Maybe I hadn't wanted to see it because it would mean too much. But now, here he was, revealing his emotions and looking at me like a boy and begging me not to break his heart.

I bit my lip, feeling shy all of a sudden.

He exhaled through his nose. "Becky ... I'm trying here."

I stared at our intertwined fingers, feeling a little lost, out of control, out of my depth. We were so different, alike but different.

"I do like you," I admitted softly because I knew in my gut that what I felt for this man went above the boss-nanny relationship. It went above my physical attraction toward him. I was attracted to him wholly—his personality, his physical appearance, his heart. "But you want to know things that I've buried. I'm not about to go digging them up again." I peered up at him, practically begging him with my eyes. "I just can't go there."

Our intense moment was abruptly broken by the sound of the girls' voices.

"*Happy birthday to you! Happy birthday to you!*" the girls sang.

Sarah walked in, carrying a box with the biggest polka-dot bow on the top, and Charles and I took one healthy step away from each other. I took a huge breath to cleanse me from these roller-coaster emotions and put on a brave face for the girls.

Mary charged toward me, practically jumping me in the process. "Happy birthday, Becky! We love you."

I pulled her higher, wrapping my arms around her waist and kissing her forehead. Tears welled up behind my eyes. I'd never felt so needed, so appreciated, so loved by a whole family.

Sarah hugged me next. "Thanks, Becky. For helping me yesterday with my homework."

I pulled her against me. Mason, the usual math guru, had been out with his girlfriend yesterday, therefore unavailable to help Sarah. To be honest, I'd had to YouTube some tutorials for fifth-grade math. It wasn't an easy feat.

As we sat at the table, it felt so surreal that, over the last month, I'd grown so close to this family. Where Patty and Eleanor had always made me feel like family, this felt different—because I was an integral part of the family, even in the very short time that I'd spent here.

It was so big, so important to me. This feeling of belonging.

I leaned against the chair, thinking that this had to be, hands down, the best birthday that I'd ever had. I exhaled a long sigh of contentment. Experiencing this immense joy, I paused, my gaze flickering to Charles.

I liked things how they were, so I had to think about this budding thing happening between Charles and me.

I wasn't sure I was willing to risk it.

Charles

We were at Pete's Pizza Palace. Sarah and Mary had

suggested it, and when had I ever denied my girls something that was reasonable and within my means? When Mary had asked for a unicorn when she turned three, I couldn't exactly buy her one. When she cried and cried, Brad had dressed up as one, horn and all. That year, for Halloween, he had worn the unicorn costume out to a party, but the horn was on his penis that time. Classy.

I had reserved us two corner booths, and I was watching my girls play Skee Ball with Becky when Brad strolled in, holding a medium-sized box wrapped in pink.

He slid into the booth, opposite me. "Hey. Sorry I'm late. Where are the girls?"

I tipped my chin toward the other side of the room, where Becky was roaring with laughter from who knew what. It made me smile to watch her be so happy. I hated that she had such shitty memories as a child, and I hoped we were creating memories of the best birthday for her.

"I can't believe she wanted to spend her birthday at Pete's Pizza Palace." Brad lifted the box he'd brought in, giving it a little shake. "I didn't know what to get her, so I got her Beats by Dre. You know ... so she can block out the noise when the kids are annoying yet still be present." He tapped a finger against his temple. "Smart, eh?"

I laughed. My brother, ladies and gentlemen.

Leaning in, he asked, "So, how's it going between you two?"

My eyes found her again, and I sighed with longing. Actual longing. The first time I'd ever felt longing for anyone other than Natalie. "I don't know. Normal." I wanted it to be the opposite of normal between us. I raised an eyebrow at him. "And don't think I haven't noticed you and Mason spending more time in the city lately."

He raised both eyebrows in innocence. "It's only

because we feel like you need time to get to know her when we're not all up in the house."

I shook my head. "It doesn't matter anyway ..."

He frowned. "What is that supposed to mean?"

"She's not letting me in. It's like she shuts me down every time I try to get to know her a little more."

He leaned in and his eyebrows pulled together. "What is she hiding from?"

"I don't know." It was a lie because from what I had gathered, she was hiding from an ex-boyfriend. A possibly dangerous ex from how tightly she kept a lid on him. I peered back to where she was standing, assisting Mary with the Skee Ball, making her swing higher. "I told her how I feel. And this won't work if she doesn't let me in."

He looked back toward the girls. "Maybe you need to give it some time."

I nodded. "I'd be okay with that if only I thought time would help our situation."

We both peered up when Mason strolled in with Janice on his arm. She wore four-inch heels, dark-washed jeans, and a fitted white halter top. Her hair was pulled up into a high ponytail. Swung over her arm was her Hermès bag that Mason had gotten her for her last birthday.

"Oh God. Here comes Barbie," Brad whispered under his breath.

"Hey, guys!" Janice leaned into me and touched my cheek against hers, doing the same to Brad right after. "Where's the birthday girl?"

I greeted Mason and answered Janice at the same time, "Over there. They were playing Skee Ball, but they've moved on to shooting hoops."

Janice made a face. "Yeah, I'm not really good at

games." She lifted up a gift bag that said *Burberry*. "I picked her up a gift. I got her a scarf." She beamed.

Whenever Janice was around, Brad's eye would twitch, as if he had a tic. And when he smiled, it was so forced that it looked like it hurt.

I hated it, hated that Mason looked so unhappy despite his insistence on remaining loyal to her, but I wasn't as vocal as Brad about it. Mason already knew how I felt. I'd told him in not so many words that he deserved better, but at the end of the day, he was a grown man. I wouldn't want to be told what to do with my life, and I trusted that Mason could make his own decisions even if we didn't agree with some of those choices.

"Uncle Brad," Mary called out, rushing toward him, jumping in his arms.

Sarah strolled over with a roll of red tickets, waving them in the air. Becky trailed right behind her.

"Sarah made a killing at that ticket machine over there. She hit the jackpot." Becky was smiling with such pride that you would've thought she'd won the tickets.

"Happy birthday, Becky," Mason greeted her, followed by Janice, who went in for a hug.

"Here's your gift! I think you'll like it." Janice handed her the gift bag.

Becky's face flushed prettily. "Aww, you guys didn't have to. Thank you." Her smile was genuine and drop-dead beautiful.

"And hey, kiddos." Janice awkwardly waved at the kids and then patted Sarah's head, like she always did.

Sarah threw me a look, and I knew what she was thinking. *Why does she keep patting me like I'm a dog or something?*

"I've never actually been to this establishment before,"

Janice said, turning her nose up as she examined our surroundings.

Mason slipped his arm around Janice's waist. "I think you have. Weren't you here for Mary's second birthday? I'm pretty sure her birthday was here."

She tilted her head. "No. I'd remember if I was somewhere like this before, Mason."

Brad's eye twitched again, and in about two seconds, he would say something that was undercover mean—like the times he played Kanye West's "Gold Digger" every time Janice walked into the room.

"Let's order the pizza." I stood. "Come on, Becky. Birthday girl's choice."

I slipped my arm over her shoulders and pulled her toward me. Then, I stilled because we hadn't spoken since this morning about my confession. I waited a moment to see if she'd pull away, but when she let me lead us to the front of the pizza joint, I smiled.

"Are you having fun?" I asked her, getting close to her ear and noticing the little shiver that went through her. I tried not to get too excited or hopeful.

Her smile was infectious. "Yeah. The girls are just so funny. I didn't realize how competitive Mary could be at such a young age, and Sarah, she's very meticulous about games. I swear she thinks there is a method to hit each game and maximize how many tickets you get." She leaned into me, and my heart started racing like a teenager. "She's a genius, Charles. Very bright. You should be proud."

I nodded. There was no doubt that I'd hit the jackpot with my kids. Above being good students, they were kind. My kids were part of the future generation who were going to change the world.

"So, I know this is a nontraditional birthday party for a

sophisticated woman like yourself," I said with a chuckle. "But the girls wanted to give you the royal treatment, so thanks for going along with it."

Becky laughed. "Please, this is great. I'd rather do this than go out for a fancy dress-up dinner any day." She motioned to what she was wearing. "If you haven't noticed already, I'm a *jeans and gym shoes* kind of girl."

I'd already known this about her, which was one of the reasons I was attracted to her. She wasn't the type of woman who tried so hard, which made me wonder why the hell I had engaged with Vivian for so long.

"So, taking you out to a nice dinner is out of the question?" I wasn't the nervous type, not usually, but shit ... I held my breath, waiting for her answer.

She visibly stiffened in my hold. "Charles ... about earlier."

I automatically went on the defense. "I get it. I pushed too hard and surprised you way too fast. That's one of my faults. I can be a little aggressive sometimes. It's the no-bull-shit CEO in me, and I'm sorry." *Please don't say no.*

Her gaze went to the floor.

Which wasn't a no ... so I tried again. "We still have a lot of things to discuss and sort out, but first things first. Will you go out to dinner with me?"

Her eyes met mine, and I read her reluctance in her features. "Charles, there are things about me, about my past, that I don't want to revisit, which means they're off-limits."

I swallowed. I didn't like that answer. Normally, it would be a dead deal right here. But she was being honest, up front, telling me what she needed from me before she moved forward. The ball was in my court now, and I still had hope. We could revisit her past when she trusted me more.

I put on my most confident smile. "Dinner. This weekend. Just say yes."

She glanced at me for a long moment, a slow smile spreading across her face. "Is it my birthday or your birthday, Charles?" she joked.

I shook my head and chuckled. "Well, it could essentially be an early birthday present from you. Mine isn't too far off."

It felt like forever, standing there, staring at each other until, finally, she nodded. "Okay. Dinner. One condition."

I reined in the victorious full-on grin that wanted to take over my face. "What?"

"I still get to wear my favorite jeans."

The grin broke through anyway. "It's a deal."

⌷

Twenty minutes later, our pizza came. I sat back and watched the interaction of my family. I was amazed at how Becky just fit. And so easily too. She was laughing with Sarah while Mary played with the toy she had just won with the tickets. Mason was quietly annoyed with Janice. Again.

And Brad was on his phone, laughing.

"Who are you texting?" Mason asked, narrowing his eyes at him.

Brad cleared his throat, looking a bit guilty. "Sonia."

Mason's nostrils flared. "Why are you texting your secretary after hours?"

Brad hadn't looked up from his phone, still smiling. "Because I told her we were going here, to Pete's Pizza Palace, and she didn't believe me. So, I sent her a picture of me and Pete the Pizza. The picture is pretty ridiculous." He lifted his head, smiling bigger, showing us a photo of him and the guy in the pizza outfit.

"Are you dating her?" Janice asked.

"He's not dating her," Mason snapped. "Sonia is his secretary."

"I was just asking," Janice snapped back, turning her nose away from Mason and crossing her arms over her chest.

"No, I'm not dating her." Brad dropped his gaze back to his phone. There was a long pause, where he stared blankly at his phone, and then he added sullenly, "She has a boyfriend."

Mason tone hardened. "I hope you're not planning on doing anything stupid."

He shut his phone and gave Mason a pointed look. "I'm not dating her, okay? I'm not planning to date her. I just like to annoy her because she makes me laugh. It's refreshing. When I'm not home or out, I'm at work, and so it makes sense that we're friends since we see each other all the time."

Mason finally chilled, and he smirked. "I'm pretty sure she hates you."

"She only acts like she hates me because she secretly loves me." Brad winked.

"I think I want to meet this Sonia girl," Becky said, smiling.

As their conversation continued, I slipped out of the booth. I took out the candles from my back pocket and split the candles between Mary and Sarah.

The cake was a princess cake, which the girls had picked out for Becky. I positioned the chocolate cake with pink letters spelling out *happy birthday* on top in front of her.

Becky clasped her hands together and smiled so big that it warmed me from the inside out. "I love it."

We all sang a loud, slightly out-of-tune rendition of "Happy Birthday," after which Mary scooted onto Becky's lap.

"Make a wish," Sarah exclaimed.

After Becky closed her eyes tightly, she blew out her candles.

And as I gathered everyone for a family photo behind Becky, Sarah pointed to the cake. "Do you like it, the decorations? It's an angel." She pointed to the little pink figurine on top of the chocolate frosting.

At a closer glance, I realized the figurine had wings, so I'd been wrong about it being a princess, or maybe there was such a thing as a princess with wings.

My thoughts were brought back to the last time I'd visited Natalie at the graveyard. On that desperate day, I'd asked Nat, *"Please ... send us an angel."*

And just as I wondered what Becky had wished for, I wondered if this was my wish come true.

CHAPTER 22

CHARLES

By the time we put the girls to bed, it was almost ten in the evening.

I headed downstairs to give Becky her present.

I rubbed the back of my neck and cleared my throat. I'd racked my brain, trying to think of the perfect gift to give her, and I just hoped and prayed that she liked it.

"Hey," I said, strolling in to the kitchen.

She wore her hair up in a sexy bun and her pink plaid pajama pants that I'd grown to love. No matter what she wore, she looked beautiful. She took out the cake from its plastic container and proceeded to put it in Tupperware.

"Did you have fun?"

She smiled up at me, and I swore everything else around me dulled to a buzz. Remember the lovesick-puppy syndrome? It was getting bad.

"I had an amazing time. It's weird, but I don't remember a birthday where I was celebrated by so many." Her chin dipped down to her neck with almost-self-conscious gratitude. "Thank you, Charles."

"You're welcome." I cleared my throat. "I realized I never gave you your gift."

She peered up at me with amusement. Her cheeks turned a rosy pink, and she averted her gaze. "Charles, you don't have to give me anything. You just don't understand how much you guys have given me so far."

I shook my head and approached her. Within my hands, I held an envelope. I didn't know if she would take my gift, but I knew it was what she wanted.

I reached for her hand, and for a moment, I just halted, looking at her, noting how, earlier, she'd had on some eye shadow that highlighted her eyes. But now, she was barefaced and still astonishingly beautiful.

I opened her palm and placed the paper within her hands. Her eyebrows pulled in together, and her smile widened. "What's this?" Her eyes squinted and lit with an inner glow. "Are you the sadistic type to take me out on my birthday and then fire me on my birthday? Is this a termination letter?"

I smirked because I couldn't help it. "Just open it."

She opened it gently, savoring it like it was already precious to her, and pulled out the single sheet of paper. Her eyes widened, and her mouth slipped ajar. Then, she folded the paper back up, her green eyes sparkling. "Charles ... I can't take this."

I was already prepared for this. "Wrong answer. Your response should be ... *thank you.*" What I had given her was a full ride to any nursing school, tuition paid. "You can go part-time. You can go to the university or the local community college. There's no expiration to that. You said that you always wanted to finish nursing school."

She opened the paper again, looking astonished, as though she couldn't believe it. And maybe she wasn't used to people taking care of her, being spoiled, but she'd better get used to it because I wasn't holding back.

Her eyes met mine again. There was a hopeless glint in them, clear and compelling, and it had me smiling. "Charles ..."

"Just say thank you," I said, gently prodding her to accept it.

Her bottom lip quivered, and she nodded slowly before propelling herself into my arms. I was unprepared, my body tensing up.

Eventually, my arms folded around her waist, and I brought her into me, breathing her in, sighing against her neck because she fit perfectly in my arms. "You're welcome."

She laughed against my shoulder, and it warmed me from the inside out. If this was what she really wanted, I wondered if money was the only issue that had stopped her before.

"Why did you quit nursing school?"

It was the wrong question to ask because she stiffened in my arms. A moment later, she stepped back, her face unreadable, the joy I'd put there gone, as though it'd never happened.

I ground my teeth together. I'd meant it as such a simple question, but now, by her reaction, I needed to know more. "I know money must have been tight for you ..." I was fishing because my regular up-front tactics would get me shut down.

She took a step back. "It wasn't the money." Her fingers were wrapped tightly around the envelope.

I closed my eyes and exhaled a long breath. And when I opened them, I couldn't take it anymore. It was like I had no control anymore, too much of me was involved now. "It was just a question, but when you freeze like that, I know it's not a simple answer."

I dipped my head, getting directly into her line of sight. Her face scrunched, and she closed her eyes tightly, shaking her head, as though she was trying to shake off a memory.

"What happened, Becky?" I urged, wanting desperately to fix it for her.

Whatever it was, I would fix it. That was my job. I was the fixer, and I'd be damned if I couldn't do it for her.

When she opened her eyes, they were resolute. "I can't take this, Charles." She placed the envelope on the kitchen counter.

I gripped her wrist, not letting her leave me just yet. She could only get so far in my house. "Stop. It's yours, no strings attached."

She jerked back and let out a shaky sigh. I could read all the emotions on her face, unshielded to me now. Raw, unfiltered pain fired behind her eyes, and all of me wanted to erase the distance between us and hold her and take it away.

"You say that ... but there are. There are always strings attached, and in this instance, what you want ... I can't give it to you." Her breathing accelerated. "Because where you want me to go is somewhere it took me a long time to bury. It's a place I don't want to visit anymore when I'm awake because, as you know ... it already haunts me in my sleep." She shook her head. "So, no, Charles. I know you mean well. But no. I'm sorry." Then, she stormed out of the kitchen, leaving me speechless and hurt.

My head dropped to my hands, and I rubbed at my brow, frustrated and sad and disappointed.

This was never going to work. None of it. Because she was right; there were strings attached. I wanted more, which meant I had to know her to love her. The woman who had stormed out of here had secrets buried deep, and although I wanted to know her, she was not letting me in. Maybe she never would.

So, any hope in a future together had disappeared the moment she shut me out and walked out of the room.

CHAPTER 23

Becky

I hated this. The silence, the distance, the unnatural way we floated around each other. For the past few days, we would go about our routine, but in separate headspaces, no longer connected, no longer enjoying each other's company. It was misery. I was starting to question everything. But I couldn't be forthcoming with Charles. I just couldn't. Which meant this silence might continue forever.

I can do this, right? Stay here, with this tension in my chest every time I saw him?

I shook my head, watching the girls swim in their Olympic-sized pool.

I had to do this. This was my job. Now, all I had to do was keep things strictly professional between Charles and me, and I'd be fine.

I walked closer to the edge of the pool, seeing my reflection in the ripple of water. Just being this close made a hollow pit in my stomach. I hated the water. It held so much of my fears, brought back so many unwanted memories.

Paul.

I squeezed my eyes shut to dispel his name, his face, his memory. I wanted no part of him in my life, not even a sliver.

After school, the girls had asked if they could go swimming, and I wanted to tell them no. I wanted to take them anywhere else. I wanted to offer them ice cream instead or take them to the local fudge shop.

The first thing I asked was if they could swim, to which they both replied, "Yes."

So, even though I didn't know how to swim, I'd told them as long as they stayed in the shallow part, then I would allow it.

It was an unusually warm fall day. What I'd learned in the short time I'd lived in Illinois was that the temperature could change twenty degrees within a span of a few days. Today, it was eighty-five degrees, so the kids wanted to take advantage of the warmer weather. I guessed it really didn't matter, as the pool was heated.

So, as the sun beat down fiercely on the exposed skin of my one-piece, I slathered Mary and Sarah with sunscreen and then myself and watched them swim back and forth, splashing, enjoying each other and the water, as they should.

I stood at the side, arms crossed like a lifeguard, knowing that if anything were to happen to the girls, I'd most likely die, trying to save them.

Sarah was on her swim team, so I wasn't worried about her, and even though Mary had said she could swim, I wasn't risking it and had her wearing floaties.

"Becky, get in," Sarah tried to coax me, eyes alight, floating on her back.

"I think I'm okay here." I lifted my hair and secured it to the top of my head in a high bun. It was a muggy day, and if I actually knew how to swim, jumping in would have been a good idea.

"Look at me! I can hold my breath underwater." Mary stuck her head under the surface, and I walked farther down to where she was, anxiety prickling my skin.

"Mary, how about we swim normal and closer to this side?" Although she had floaties on, I wanted to see her face.

I peered around me and noticed various flotation devices, even a large unicorn. If it came down to it, I'd get on the unicorn and jump right in.

"Becky, do you have a coin? I want you to throw it in the water, and I'll dive for it," Sarah said, her slick dark brown locks sticking to the side of her face.

I shook my head. "I don't. And I don't want to leave you guys out here."

My eyes searched the vicinity and landed on some pebbles on the outskirts of the backyard by the tree house that could rival a small house.

I pointed to Sarah. "Watch Mary for two seconds."

I ran toward the grass, bent down, and picked up the biggest pebble I could find. I raced back to the edge of the pool.

And panic seized my chest because in the next second, Mary was gone.

"Sarah! Where's Mary?"

Her floaties were up at the surface, but she was nowhere. Sarah dived and swam to the deep end of the pool, and my feet could not get to the end fast enough.

Mary was lying facedown, floating, arms and legs stretched.

I didn't think.
I reacted.
I jumped in.

CHAPTER 24

CHARLES

I heard the frantic screams coming from the backyard, and I dropped my briefcase and ran. Ran so damn fast that I almost tripped on my own two feet.

Mary was sitting at the edge of the pool, extending a life preserver, while Sarah struggled at the end of the pool, her head bobbing up and down ... wait. Not Sarah. Becky.

It took a second to analyze the situation.

Sarah was trying to save Becky, who bobbed up and down and was taking my eldest under in the process.

Sarah spat up water, going under again, coming up for air and reaching for Becky, who was flailing and splashing, her body and hands erratic.

My instincts kicked in, and I jumped in, fully clothed.

"Sarah, I have her," I shouted, motioning for Sarah to get to the side, to safety.

I treaded to Becky, reaching for her waist, but she struggled and pushed at my chest and went underwater. I pulled her up by her swimsuit, but she slapped at my hands.

"Becky ... stop!"

I spit out the water that had been splashed in my face and reached for her waist again—with force this time. In the process, her hands pushed down my shoulders as she tried to elevate herself above me to cough out the water in her lungs.

I closed my eyes and held my breath as my head was submerged. Then, I popped back up, and determination set deep in my skin. With one hand wrapped tightly around her, I swam us both to the side. I lifted her out of the water, where she dropped on all fours, coughing and choking up water.

My body felt twenty pounds heavier, as my polo shirt and pants were weighted down with water. A second later, I bent down, heart still racing but knowing that my kids were okay. I had to assess Becky. Who knew if she needed medical attention? The fact that she was coughing meant she was breathing, which was good.

"You're okay," I repeated to her, but I felt as though it was mostly for me.

When the coughing ceased, she took big, deep, breaths.

"Hey ..." I said, my voice hoarse.

She stood and jumped on me, startling me. Arms around my neck, legs wrapped around my waist, sobbing uncontrollably into my neck.

I was surprised at the contact.

And my heart broke, hearing her endless cries.

My arms went around her, and I squeezed her tightly against me. "You're fine. I have you, Becky. You're fine."

Her sobs accelerated, and she ducked her head into the crook of my neck.

I backed up and sat on the lounge chair behind me. "Sarah, get me a towel."

When Becky's cries heightened, she was practically convulsing, but my grip only tightened.

"Becky ... everything will be okay."

I wrapped the towel around her, around the both of us, and tucked her in closer. Words flew out of my mouth, fast and furious. I didn't know if it was my adrenaline talking or what, but when my hand made it to the crook of her neck, keeping her in place, I knew in that moment that I never wanted her to leave, that in my arms was where she belonged.

"I'll take care of you. You'll be okay." Because she would be. I'd make sure of it.

Her body molded into mine, and I gripped at the wet fabric of her swimsuit, digging my fingers into her waist.

Suddenly, an overwhelming emotion washed over me, making my breathing rampant, and a lump formed in my throat.

Relief.

Yes. That was what it was. Undeniable, full-on relief that she was safe.

Fuck, if I had lost her ...

I couldn't even let my mind go there. It was too impossible, too overwhelming.

Brad walked out, eyes wide, a moment later. "What happened?"

Panic struck his features, but I shook my head.

"Everything is okay. Can you get Sarah and Mary inside? Sarah can fill you in." I pointed back to the house.

He picked up my shell-shocked Mary, still very wet, and carried her inside. She soaked Brad's clothes, but he didn't care. Sarah followed him in, giving us concerned glances as she went.

Once we were alone, I kissed Becky's forehead,

brushing her hair from her face. I let the relief flood me and just reminded myself that she was still here. Still breathing, heart still beating, blood still pumping. Still beautiful, still perfect, and still in my arms.

But I couldn't dispel the idea of losing her. I wouldn't be able to survive another loss ... and not any loss—her.

And that was when I knew ... I loved her. With my whole heart. Even with her secrets and my fears and the unknown, that love only burned brighter, stronger inside of me.

There was no going back from these feelings. I'd been in love before. And when I was in love, I loved fully and completely. It was how I was built.

She pulled back and struggled to get up, swiping at her eyes. "Where's Mary?"

"Becky. Stop." I readjusted, so I had a better hold on her. I wasn't ready to let her go. "Mary's fine."

As soon as the words left my mouth, she cowered into me, tucking her neck into my shoulder, sobbing again.

"I'm sorry. I don't know how to swim, and it was stupid of me ... I'll go. If you want to fire me ... I'll leave."

She was talking nonsense now. *Fire her?* I didn't want her to leave—ever. I wanted to hold her, keep her, care for her.

I held her for minutes that felt like hours. Eventually, I stood, tightened my hold on her, and marched into the house, past the kids and Brad, whose eyes widened as I proceeded up the stairs and into my room, dropping my ass on the edge of the bed.

Who knew how long I held her? But I held her until her sobs subsided. Until those cries eventually ceased. Until the sun set through the blinds in my window.

I kicked off my shoes and backed us into the headboard

of my bed, pulling her into me, her head still tucked in the crook of my neck. We were both soaking wet, so I pulled the blanket over us.

As I took in my room, I realized this was the second time she'd been in this room, and the thought brought me back to Natalie's death. The feeling of unbelievable heartbreak hit me in the gut, and I pulled Becky tighter to me. She was comforting me now, without even knowing it.

I listened to the even sounds of her breathing. Though I couldn't see her face, I knew she was still awake.

"He tried to drown me," she finally said, her voice a light croak.

Every muscle in my body tensed. My breathing slowed, and I needed to know that I'd heard her correctly. "What?" My fingers went to the base of her neck, massaging.

"When I tried to leave him the second time, he tried to drown me in the lake. He took me to the place I feared the most, and I was helpless." A sob escaped her, and I held her tighter. "That day, I thought I was going to die. And I almost did. I was almost there ... until he hit me so hard, punched my back to get the water out." She paused again and then uttered, "I wanted to die."

The fury almost choked me, and my temper flared. I gritted my teeth as I squeezed her against me. My lips thinned into a straight line, and my body numbed with increasing rage and shock.

"I was with him when I left foster care. He was the first guy to come into my life and love me. At least, I thought it was love ... it was the only love I knew."

I swallowed the bile in the back of my throat.

I want to kill the bastard.

"The first time he hit me, I was in shock. He apologized and cried and begged me up and down that he didn't mean it. And the cycle would repeat again. Where love and fear were distorted in my head."

My body battled to stay still. I had an uncontrollable urge to get up and find this guy and teach him a lesson for ever touching a woman this way.

"The first time I left, he stabbed me in the ankle. Third try was a charm though. I got away. But I had to. I knew I would never live to see a fourth."

I pulled back, unable to take any more, framing her face in my hands. "No one will hurt you again. Ever." I leaned in, our faces a breath apart. "I never want you to be scared, okay? I never want you to worry if he'll find you 'cause he won't. He won't." My thumbs brushed across the apples of her cheeks.

"He said he'd find me." Tears fell from her cheeks again, harder this time. "And I'm just afraid that ... that the people around me, the people I love, will be collateral damage."

Love.

"He won't. I live my life to protect my family." Out of all my qualities, this was my strength. My innate need to take care of the people around me. It was what I loved to do; it was what I had been born to do. "My loved ones." I swiped at her tears escaping her eyes. "Don't be afraid ... I'm here. And I'll make sure everything is okay."

Our eyes locked, and something passed between us. I didn't know when she'd decided to trust me. All I knew was that she did because a moment later, her arms went around my neck in a tight vise, her soft body crushing against my hard one.

I held her in the silence, knowing I'd never let anything happen to her. I made that promise to her tonight, but I also made a promise to myself. I couldn't help what had happened to Nat, though I'd blamed myself for years. In the end, there was nothing I could do.

With Becky, I would use all my resources to keep her safe. This I was capable of.

I eventually adjusted us, laying her head on my chest, brushing my fingers through her damp hair.

"Thank you for telling me."

I knew how much she had given of herself tonight, and she had to know she was in safe hands.

Her fingers made tiny circles on my chest. "I wanted to tell you. For the first time ... I want to let someone in. I want to be happy."

My lips made it to her forehead. "I'm glad. Everyone deserves to be happy." Myself included.

━━━

Sleep took us both eventually, but when I woke up hours later, it was late in the evening. My gaze traveled to the clock on the far wall, noting that it was two in the morning. The worry and concern from earlier disappeared and was replaced with something utterly different.

Desire.

There was no way I couldn't be aroused. I tried to think of anything else because now was not the moment to get horny.

But it was hard not to when her body was pressed firmly against mine, her soft breasts against my hard chest. Her swimsuit had dried, but it was like Saran Wrap against her body, and I could feel every inch of her body against mine.

If I slipped her swimsuit to the side, I could feel if she was wet.

She lifted her chin the moment the thought filtered through, her eyes fluttering open from her heavy slumber.

And now, I was hard.

I was sure she could feel my bulging erection against her stomach. It pulsed and prodded and wanted to be released.

My eyes flickered to her lips and then back to meet her eyes.

I gritted my teeth, grinding my molars. *Not now, asshole.* Now was not the time to think about how her body fit perfectly against mine. How we were in a right position to ...

"I'm sorry," she said, her face falling again.

For what? Making me hard? She couldn't control how my body reacted to her.

She added, "I don't know how to swim."

Ah, okay.

"It was stupid of me to let the girls be in the pool, but Mary was so happy and excited, and Sarah said it would be fine, but I'm the adult—"

I pinched her chin. "Stop crying." My voice was whisper soft against her skin.

She kept on, so disappointed in herself, "If you want to fire me, I understand. I take full responsibility."

What absurdity is this woman talking about? Fire her? Not likely.

"The girls are fine," I insisted. "You're fine."

"No ..." She shook her head, her eyes pained.

And then I kissed her to shut her up but mostly because I wanted to.

There was a shift in the air. A shift in the mood. My lips froze against hers, tentatively asking permission. I was shocked that I'd even made the move. I breathed through the next seconds, and when her lips moved against mine, I took that as an invitation.

If anything, she hit the accelerator. My body followed her direction, though my mind told me to slow down, but I couldn't. She was too soft in my arms, too pliable, too warm, too sexy. One of my hands moved to cup her ass while the other threaded fingers through her hair, and I tugged lightly, exposing her neck.

My lips dragged a path up the creamy span of skin to her mouth.

I devoured her lips, flicking my tongue to taste and savor her mouth. Becky tasted exquisite, and I wanted to taste all of her, every inch of her body.

She rubbed against me, riding my length behind my clothes, our lips never breaking contact. I groaned. My breathing quickened, but so did hers.

My fingers slipped under her suit to the bare skin of her ass, pushing it against my hardness.

Becky let out a longing moan, and I almost lost it.

"Charles ... I need you."

I moaned against her mouth as my name fell from her lips.

She tugged my hair, getting up on her knees and inching closer against me, where there was no span of space between us. The towel slipped off her shoulders to her waist, and suddenly, all I wanted was to see her undone.

My fingers moved from her ass to the front of her swimsuit, slipping between the folds.

Oh fuck.

She was soaked.

"Shit ..." I groaned.

When I slipped another finger in, she gripped my shoulders, our lips losing contact as she sucked in a breath. I pushed in and out of her faster, harder, watching her chest rise and fall with her quick breaths, and tiny moans left her body.

She was glorious, eyes at half-mast, lips slightly parted, breathing rampant and shallow. She bit her lip to prevent her moans from escaping, resting her forehead against mine. "Charles ..."

I grinned. I'd never get tired of her calling my name. I wanted her to scream it louder. "Baby, take it. I want to see you come apart."

I knew when I hit her sweet spot because her head fell back and her eyes clenched shut.

It didn't take long for her breathing to accelerate and for her to spasm against my fingers, finding that climax that sent her soaring.

And what a damn glorious sight to see. She was beautiful, head lifted, neck stretched to the ceiling. Her fingers dug roughly into my back, and there was no doubt I'd have marks tomorrow.

When she was finished, she collapsed into me, head tucked into my neck, panting. I decided that was the sexiest sound she'd ever made, and I wanted to hear her make it often.

When her heartbeat slowed to a normal pace, she pulled back, bit her bottom lip, and smiled. "What's happening?" she whispered, shy all of a sudden.

We were happening.

She stared down between us, my painful erection pushing against the seam of my pants. "Your turn." She reached for the buckle of my pants, but I stilled her.

"Not now." I tipped my head back against the headboard and pulled at her hand.

"Oh." Her eyes went wide.

Then, I knew the moment that she thought I was rejecting her because her face fell, and she got up, taking the towel with her.

I gently pulled her down. I wasn't like her ex. I imagined he was a take, take, take kind of guy. I wasn't going to take her here. I wanted to wine and dine and romance her first.

"Can I just hold you? Just hold you for tonight?"

Her smile was small but sweet, her eyes lighting up. After a tip of her chin, her cheek rested against my chest, and I held her through the night, our breathing in sync.

I couldn't remember a time I'd slept so soundly.

CHAPTER 25

Becky

Three days had passed since I'd snuck out of Charles's room before the girls got up for school. Since then, we had been doing the same routine every day. Same but different because Charles's hands were on me every chance he got. When he handed me my coffee in the morning, he pulled me in and nuzzled my cheek. It always sent my heart into crazed flutters, but it was the best good morning a girl could ask for.

This switch in our relationship was welcome but scary, beautiful and unnerving. I felt like I was going to turn into a puddle of goo on the floor from his affection. Like when he kissed me while I scrambled eggs, or every time I went to the fridge, he'd reach for my waist and pinched my side. He was playful and loving, and I couldn't wait until our date tonight.

What hadn't been discussed fully was how we would tell Sarah and Mary about us.

We'd touched on it briefly, but we hadn't gone into detail. That was something that Charles would have to take on. We already knew that Mary would be adaptable, given that she was so young. But Sarah ... we both worried about Sarah.

As I was frying the bacon, Charles grabbed me, hugging me from behind. "I just love how my mornings have changed. I don't want to go to work."

He kissed my neck and held me close. At one point, he took my hand holding the spatula, and we fried the eggs together.

"I can't wait for our date tonight," he said, causing goose bumps to form against my skin.

His lips went from my neck to my shoulder, and I exhaled a heavy sigh. Being with him, our new day-to-day was a dream I never wanted to wake up from.

"My brothers will be over at six thirty. So, we'll leave by then."

I turned to face him, curious now about what he had told them. "What did you say?"

"Nothing." He smiled. "Yet. But I'm gonna tell them at work today. I'm going to tell them that we're dating. Because"—his smile widened—"that's how I roll." Then, he winked, which was so unlike Charles. "I just told them that I had plans and I needed either of them to watch the girls. They both volunteered."

"Dad?"

Charles jumped two steps away from me, and I dropped the spatula on the floor when Sarah entered the kitchen. She raised an eyebrow, taking us in as though she knew something was up.

Charles always said she was an old soul, even at the tender age of ten. And I knew she'd seen us. A part of me wondered how long she'd been standing there.

"Mary's crying," she said. "I have no idea what it is this

time. She's just whiny. And she's asking for you."

Charles was almost out of the kitchen when he said, "Okay. I'll take care of it."

Studying me with curious, narrowed eyes, Sarah sat down at her regular spot at the table.

"Bacon and eggs. That's what we're having this morning." My voice sounded nervous. How could it not?

Tonight was our first date, and the girls still had no idea.

Charles

I tapped my pencil against the boardroom table, unable to stop this nervous tic I had. We were going over next quarter's projections, and I couldn't keep my head in the game.

Mason sat next to me, head deep in his financial statements. We were waiting on Brad.

I'd always been up front with my brothers. So, why the hell was I so nervous right now?

"What time do you need us there tonight?" Mason asked, flipping through the financials. "Where is Becky going? Why isn't she available again?"

I peered down at my watch. I didn't want to say this twice. "Where is Brad?"

And right on cue, he strolled into the boardroom with that easy stride. He plopped down in his regular spot, to the right of me, laughing, slapping a magazine on the table.

"What's so funny?" Mason asked.

"Sonia."

Mason glared at him. "What now?"

"Nothing. She's just funny." He waved a hand toward the magazine, knocked on the table twice, and placed his ankle on his knee. "Check out page forty-four. It's hot off the press, not even on the stands yet."

I picked up the magazine and flipped through the pages. Opening to the page Brad had mentioned, I laid the magazine flat on the table. Brad's smile was small yet charming, his elbows on his knees, as if he were sitting against our black leather recliner at home. He looked relaxed, at ease, and—though I'd never admit it to him out loud because his ego was already bigger than life itself—very sharp.

"Brad Brisken leads the company at Brisken Printing Corporation as VP of acquisitions and sales by day, but by night, this single man is helping his widowed brother raise two little girls. When he's not working, he's playing Barbies or watching princess movies." My eyes flipped to Brad.

"What?" He cheesed. "I know. It sounds insensitive. I guess it's a way for them to sell papers. It's a great picture of me, isn't it? The tie is fine, but that"—he pointed to the table for emphasis—"that is a great photo."

"It is." I flipped to the next page, which showcased a mirage of photos. Brad laughing with Mary. Us in the bathroom, cleaning up the mess that Mary had caused. Becky laughing beside me. Brad drying off Mary and getting her changed. Downstairs by the swings, all of us playing in the yard.

The collage made me gulp. I loved this picture of us, the idea of this being our future. Becky just fit. She molded nicely into our family.

"The pictures turned out great." *Wife or death.* Brad would definitely be getting prospects for the wife part after this magazine when into circulation.

Brad reached for the magazine and tucked it into his side. "Okay, let's go. Projections. I still gotta take off a little early to pick up the Frozen Monopoly game for the girls tonight. Where are you going anyway? Is Becky not available?"

I swallowed and readjusted my tie. "Uh, I'm taking Becky on a date tonight."

"Wait, what?" Mason blinked at me.

His mouth opened again, and I shot his next question down with a stare.

Brad smirked. "What happened between you guys? You can share it with me. After that little accident, I saw you carry her, wet swimsuit and all, up to your room."

"Nothing happened." Then, I shook my head.

I'd asked Brad what he'd told the girls on why we'd disappeared. He'd told them that I took Becky to the hospital to check if she was okay. I'd let that lie slide since he had put the girls to bed that night.

"What accident?" Mason's voice heightened.

Brad pursed his lips. "We forgot to tell you about all the drama on Tuesday. Becky thought Mary had drowned when Mary was only floating like Superman underwater."

Mason's mouth slipped agape.

"Becky jumped in the pool. Too bad the girl doesn't know how to swim." Brad threw Mason an all-knowing smirk, most likely amused that Mason didn't know this. Mason did always want to be in the know.

His mouth slipped open even wider.

"Worst day to be sleeping over at your girlfriend's house, little bro." Brad sported a cocky smirk. "Someone got action. Satisfaction."

I rolled my neck from side to side, breathing out my annoyance. "Nothing happened. I haven't even taken her out on a date."

"Yes, but you've been living together for a bit now, so this dating action doesn't matter," Brad said.

I groaned. "It does." It did to me.

Mason rubbed at his brow, as if the whole thing was

exhausting him. "We still know nothing about her."

"That's not true," I said, my voice hard.

Maybe they didn't know her, but I did. I knew her heart, I knew how well she fit in my arms, and I knew I was in love with her.

Brad cocked an eyebrow. "Are you saying that she talked to you?" He placed both elbows on the table. "Really talked to you?" He leaned in, leveling me with a stare.

My jaw tightened. *Nosy bastards.* "Yes, she did. And, yes, she has a past. And, no, you guys are not privy to it unless she wants to tell you herself."

Mason ground his molars. "Who is she running from?"

"Mason ..." I warned coolly.

But he wasn't backing down. "Who? If that person is crazy, we have a right to know."

My fist pounded against the table, my patience thin. "One, I won't let anything happen to my family, and two, what you get is what Becky herself decides to share with you. Period. The end." I grabbed my copy of the projections, flipping to the first page balance sheet, challenging them to say one more word.

Brad nodded slowly. "Got it." He flipped to the first page of his copy. "And I've decided. Frozen Monopoly is happening at my place in the city. I'll bring the girls back on Sunday."

I sighed. "Brad, you don't have to do that."

He shrugged. "I know. But I'm the better brother, so ..." He winked.

If he wasn't helping me out, I'd slap him.

There was no comeback from Mason. Silently brooding, he flipped to the first page of the financials.

Basking in Mason's silence, Brad grinned. "Let's get this over with. Someone has a big date to get ready for."

CHAPTER 26

Becky

"Where are we going?" I couldn't hide this giddy smile on my face. I slung my bag over my shoulder as Charles led me to the car. My hair swished against my back in a low ponytail, and I sported these dangling earrings. My silk yellow shirt, which reminded me of sunshine, hugged my frame, and I wore the stonewashed jeans he had promised I could wear.

So, as we walked to the car, I was on edge with curiosity.

When he opened the door to his Porsche, I stepped inside, and before he shut it, he said, "Where we're going is a surprise."

I tried not to frown. Surprises were not my favorite because, in my lifetime, most of my surprises had been tragic, hurtful, and caused me pain. As soon as this thought registered, I pushed it away and peered up at Charles in his light-blue polo shirt and casual jeans. Then, I decided this was my happy place—in this car, with him.

Charles held my hand as he drove us to our destination

—wherever that was. It felt strange, holding this man's hand, our fingers intertwined, because I hadn't held anyone's hand intimately in this way in a long time. His hold was strong, his fingers firm, as though he was sure, so sure of this day, so sure of us.

Charles embodied strength in his stance, in the power of his walk, and now, even his hand-holding. When we pulled up to a park reserve, I already knew what we were up to.

I turned to face him. "Are we going on a picnic?" I beamed. "Just so you know, I've never been on a picnic before."

"Will you stop spoiling my surprise?" That small smile he rarely showed popped up on his face, making me sigh silently.

We passed the park district farther down a gravel road and to an empty field, except for a large truck towing a trailer behind it.

Odd. If we were having a picnic, I'd guess it would be at a lake, at the park, somewhere scenic, except for a lone truck on an open field.

He placed his car in park and stepped out. I heard the trunk open before he stepped around to open my door. "Let's go." His one hand went to mine, like magnets meant to unite, and in his other hand, he held a cute wicker picnic basket. It had frilly red-and-white plaid fabric that outlined the top, which seemed way too girlie for someone of his height and stature.

"Are we having picnic on that truck?" I said, being cheeky, squeezing his hand harder.

"You're funny." Then, he tugged me faster toward the truck, and the closer I approached, the more my heart sped up in my chest because on the back of the truck was a life-sized wicker basket.

Three burly guys jumped from the truck and greeted us. "Hey, Charles."

"Hey, guys." He tugged me against him, slipping his arms over my shoulders. "Noah, James, Tony ... this is Becky."

After I shook their hands, Noah, the taller one with a full-on beard, said, "Today is a good day to fly."

I blinked up at him. "Fly?"

"Yeah, fly." Charles sported a full-on smile this time, and I paused for a moment, ignoring his words and simply just took it in.

Fly?

The two men carrying the basket from the trailer broke me from my momentary staring. After they placed it on the ground, I realized that the basket was meant to be ridden.

My eyes widened, and I jumped. "Charles!"

His voice was a low rumble directly behind me. "Have you ever experienced a hot air balloon ride?"

"Yeah." My voice was breathless, dazed.

He reeled back. "You have?"

"I mean, kinda. If you mean, experience it as in watching it on television. I watched a romantic comedy once where the hero surprised the woman and took her on a hot air balloon ride on their first date. I think you must've watched it."

"Are you saying this is cliché?" His eyes followed Noah and James, who pulled out the balloon from the bag and unwrapped it on the field. "I guess it's not really original."

My gaze traveled back to him. Is *he pouting?* Good God, it was the beginning of a pout. I doubted that word was even in his vocabulary.

"I'm kidding, Charles. It's perfect." I turned to face him

fully. "Seriously, it's perfect that it's in the movies. I always dreamed about being that girl, wined and dined."

He nodded, but he wasn't convinced. "It's not original. I mean, the last time I went on a first date was in high school. The first date I ever took Nat on was to the movies and to the local Steak 'n Shake. It's been a while, so I"—he averted his stare, looking almost bashful—"I googled romantic first dates."

The corners of my lips turned down, trying to keep in my smile. Now, wasn't he the cutest? "I love it. It's perfect." I snuggled next to his side, and my arms wrapped around his waist.

A hint of a smile surfaced. "And I did bring the wine, if you were wondering." He lifted up his picnic basket.

Ahead of us, the two men had spread the balloon flat across the field. The nylon was an array of bright colors of the rainbow—vibrant yellows, oranges, reds, greens, purples and blues.

"Can both of you assist us?" James called out.

They positioned us at the bottom of the balloon, at the opening, which was called the mouth.

James placed the edge of the balloon in my hands. "All you have to do is hold on tight. We're going to get the burners started and fill this baby up. Whatever you do, don't let go."

I nodded, but my heart was beating like crazy.

Charles was on the other end, mirroring holding the mouth of the balloon. He staggered his stance, and so did I. When Noah ignited the burners, hot air blasted in my face, but then the balloon inflated, getting wider. The bigger the balloon got, the harder it was to hold the nylon. It felt as though I was being pulled. I planted my feet firmly on the ground and took in the multitude of colors in front of me. I almost felt like I was inside the balloon; watching it blow up to its full capacity was beyond amazing.

There went my cute ponytail. Escaping strands were everywhere. But it didn't matter because as I got whipped by my hair, I was smiling like a loon. I peered over at Charles, and he was beaming, a full-on, all-out smile. It was beautiful. It lit up his face.

They tilted the wicker basket to its side and positioned it at the opening of the mouth. I stepped back, watching as they tied the balloon to the basket. And then James and Noah tipped it over until it was standing up.

One hand flew to my mouth as I tilted my chin all the way back, taking in the height and mass of the vibrant balloon.

"Ready?" Charles yelled above the burners blowing.

I nodded, and he ushered me to the basket. It was tall, the top resting right underneath my breast line.

"You're going to have to hop up on the lip, and we'll help you inside," Noah said. "Like this." With his arms, he used the lip of the basket to lift his butt to the edge and swing his legs inside the basket in one swift movement. "Easy."

I laughed. "Sure. Says the man who's a good head taller than me."

"I'll help you up," Charles said, dropping the picnic basket on the floor.

"No, I'm pretty sure I can ..." I was struggling when, without warning, Charles lifted me like I was a feather, his body close to mine, his hands at my sides. My breath hitched when my feet came off the ground. I was supposed to grab the lip of the basket and use my arms to get me on the edge, but I failed, falling into him.

Heat rushed my body everywhere we were connected,

my breasts crushing against his hard chest, hip to hip, thigh to thigh. And when I peered up at him, I saw the mirrored heat in his eyes.

"Let me help you up, Becky," Noah said, oblivious to the fireworks going off between us.

Charles flashed him a not-so-happy look, and his eyes met mine again. "Listen, use your arms to pull yourself up and anchor your butt on the edge." He tipped his chin toward Noah. "And then you can help her when she swings her legs into the basket."

I smirked. *Is he jealous?* There was a definite fiery spark in his eyes as he stared Noah down. I think he is.

"Ready?" he asked.

I used my arms to pull myself up with all the strength I had. When I was at the edge of the basket, I lifted my knees to my chest and fell in backward.

I yelped before Noah caught me, and then I stood and pushed my hair out of my face. I looked over at Charles, who handed the picnic basket to James, and then he hopped in gracefully, as though he'd done this a million times before.

He had asked me, but I'd never asked him.

"Have you ever ridden in one of these?"

"No. I always wanted to. I wanted to take the girls, but they're not tall enough to see over this basket, so what's the point?"

Our attention was back on Noah as he said, "Okay, we're going to take off soon. Sky is clear, and there is no sign of rain. Let's go."

Tony unhooked the anchors, and we were off. I leaned over the edge of the basket, watching Tony and his truck shrink into a little figure below. We brushed against some tree branches as we were lifted higher. We were flying. Really flying. Above the houses, above the trees.

It felt unbelievable. I felt free and, at this height, like I could breathe freely. I inhaled deeply, taking in the fresh air.

"This is amazing," I breathed. "Isn't it beautiful up here?"

Charles's arm brushed against mine as we took in the scene below us. "I couldn't agree more." But he was staring at me, his brown eyes intently on me, and my cheeks warmed.

We rose higher into the clouds. As the city disappeared below us, all we could see were the whites and blues of the sky and clouds around us, caging us in, as though we were in the heavens.

"I can't believe we're flying." I inhaled deeply again, letting the air fill my lungs.

He slung an arm around my lower back, and butterflies fluttered in my belly, as though I were a teenager. As I peered up at him, smiling freely, I realized one thing. "You didn't have to google first dates."

His stare met mine.

"Any date you picked would have been perfect because I'm with you." I playfully nudged my shoulder against his.

"Cornball," he said.

"I know, right? And I didn't even have to google that line."

CHAPTER 27

CHARLES

I didn't want the night to end. After the balloon ride, we'd gone to dinner at this restaurant overlooking Lake Michigan. It was quiet, romantic—something I'd also searched online. The day so far had gone perfectly, as planned, and as I drove us home, I was already thinking of our next date in my head.

In a normal first date, I would have been driving her home, to her own place, but this was far from a normal situation. Instead, I was driving to my home, where she also lived.

I stepped out of the car, reaching for her hand. I walked us through the garage, into the house, and through the kitchen. It was eerily quiet, which never happened in my house. No laughter. No bickering children. Just complete silence.

"What time are the kids getting home?" Becky asked as she strolled to the cupboard to grab two glasses, and then she walked to the fridge.

My throat felt tight all of a sudden. I had to clear it. "They're not."

Her hand stilled on the fridge as she turned to face me.

"The girls wanted to sleep over at Brad's. They haven't been over there in a while." *Could she tell I was lying?* It was just a tiny one. Could she blame me?

"Oh." She poured us some water, and we sat at the table. When she gazed up at me, her eyes were thoughtful. "Doesn't it feel like we've known each other forever?"

Yes, I thought. But I wanted to hear what she had to say. "How so?"

Her fingertips lightly tapped on the glass. "Maybe it just feels like that for me because you're the only one who knows me truly. Because there's no present without one's past, and I've never told anyone about my past."

My fingers met hers across the table. They were long and delicate, and by looking at her, one would never know she'd been through so much. She looked so perfect, untouched by life. I hated that she'd been through so much.

"I feel like everything between us is moving at lightning speed yet not fast enough," I said. "I don't only want to know the things that hurt you in the past. I also want to know the good things, too, what makes you, *you*, what makes you smile. What's your favorite color? Favorite foods? I already know you make the best pancakes I've ever tasted." I smirked as I played with her fingers.

She flipped my hand over and traced the lines on the inside of my palm, nodding. "I totally get it. It's the little things, the everyday things that makes us, *us*. What is your favorite color?"

I narrowed my eyes in thought. "I don't really remember. For the longest time, I saw things only in black and white. Yes or no."

I thought about how I'd lived every day after Nat passed away—getting up, going to work, taking care of the kids. And now, more recently, since I'd decided to live more for myself, that life that had been a muted gray was slowly becoming more ... vibrant.

I intertwined our fingers again, pressing my palm to hers. "I don't know what my favorite color was before, but I know what it is now. Green."

Her sparkling emerald eyes shone, and she averted her gaze, blushing. "You, Charles ... have the best lines."

I laughed because no one would ever pay me that compliment. I'd been out of the dating game for so long. "Those lines only come out when you're around."

And I was officially turning into a cheeseball. Who knew I had it in me?

We talked for hours, sitting at the table where we'd originally bonded over nightmares. I found out the minuscule things. Her favorite Disney flick was *The Little Mermaid*. Spaghetti was her favorite meal. And she loved anything chocolate and with ice cream.

Hours later, I finally walked her up the stairs, dropping her off in front of her bedroom door.

She pushed her toe into the plush carpet, nervous all of a sudden. "I had a great time tonight. As all first dates go, this has been the best one I've ever gone on."

"Have you been on a ton of first dates before?"

She shook her head. "No. But if I had, I imagine nothing would top this."

I nodded, swallowing, assessing my next move. We had reached that awkward moment right before you said good-bye at the door, that moment when you decided to kiss her, to try, to see if she'd let you.

I swallowed again.

I should kiss her.

No hesitation.

We stared at each other for a good few seconds before she laughed, pulled me in by the shirt, and kissed me. My arms wrapped around her lower back, bringing her in, and I deepened our kiss. She felt like heaven in my arms, my lips on hers. She pushed against me, crushing her breasts against my hard chest. My body was on high alert, wanting, needing. I gripped the back of her shirt, bringing her closer yet it wasn't close enough.

We went from zero to one hundred in a nanosecond, my hands in her hair, her back against the door. After a beat, she placed a hand on my chest, and both of us were breathless.

I rested my forehead against hers, pressing on the brakes, not wanting to rush anything. "Sorry. I ..."

"Do you want to come in?" she whispered.

"Uh ..." *Shit ... I really shouldn't. Not on the first date at least.*

Was this rushing things? I knew that once we crossed this line, there would be no turning back, and I was well on board with that—with all of her in my life.

I just wanted *her* to be sure because I'd never been more certain that I wanted to be with her.

Her hand was already on the knob of her door, leading me in.

"Okay," I said.

As soon as her door shut, I lifted her in my arms, and she wrapped her legs around my waist, grinding into me. I groaned, barely able to guide her to her bed, where I laid her out on her back. We made out like teenagers, kissing and groping until we were both breathless and naked over her comforter.

But then I stopped cold. "I don't have a condom. Not with me. Not here," I said, pulling back to meet her eyes.

She stroked my cock up and down, and I groaned, dropping my head against her neck.

"Well then, get one," she whispered, her voice husky soft against my skin.

I pushed myself off the bed, reached for her, and pulled her into my arms, carrying her down the hall, both of us buck naked. In my room, I kicked the door shut behind me. Gently, I placed her on the bed, her hair a mess of blonde splayed out on my gray comforter. The green in her eyes sparkled with want, with lust, and with a deep emotion I was familiar with because I was sure my eyes mirrored hers.

"I'll be back."

I rushed to the bathroom, seeing my reflection in the mirror above the double sinks. My cock was hard, needy, and it wanted one thing—to be inside of Becky. Dropping to my knees, I opened the cabinet, searching for the box of condoms. After finding it, I pulled out the string of condoms and tore off one.

I stood but stopped, stoic and still because something had caught my eye.

Nat's and my wedding rings sat in a small ceramic dish that we had painted together when we went to Mexico. I swallowed as a slew of emotions bombarded me at once.

This is me moving on ... and that's okay.

Nat would be okay with this.

As long as I am okay.

But as I repeated the mantra over and over in my head, I knew it wasn't true.

That I wasn't fully healed because, if I was, why did I place her belongings on that side of the sink? It wasn't even her side of the sink. This was my parents' house. I'd moved her in even though she was no longer physically here. In the beginning, after she'd passed, seeing her belongings had given me comfort. Now, it just reminded me of everything I'd lost.

I closed my eyes, and the only thing I saw behind my eyes was Nat—her smile that Sarah had inherited, the blonde in her hair that was so much like Mary's. Our wedding day, filled with love, our families and both of our parents surrounding us.

The birth of Sarah.

Her first birthday.

Her first day of school.

Me taking over as CEO of Brisken Printing Corporation.

Then, the endless sorrow that hit after.

I rested my palms on the sink, staring at my reflection in the mirror.

Maybe I'd been lying to myself all this time, thinking I was over it. That I'd healed and moved on. I'd been with Vivian, hadn't I?

But that was different, purely physical. She didn't share a place in my heart.

And I was making room for Becky, in a place that Natalie had once taken residence.

Problem was, Natalie was still very much present even though I'd thought I'd closed that chapter years ago.

CHAPTER 28

Becky

I was staring at the ceiling, wondering how much time had passed. It wasn't hours, but it felt like it. The door to the bathroom was still shut. And now, as I lay naked and waiting in his bed, I wondered what was going on.

When he finally emerged, he had boxers on and one hand on his hip, his gaze toward the ground. I pushed myself to my elbows.

"So ..." He scratched his head, still not meeting my eyes. "This is embarrassing. But ..." He was no longer hard.

While my lady parts wept, I sat up, meeting his stare, smiling because I didn't want to make an awkward situation more awkward. "Too much excitement for one day? Maybe we should just call it a night." I moved further up the bed to the headboard and patted the spot beside me.

His eyebrows pulled together, and his gaze teetered back to the ground.

Well, shit. This can't be good.

Maybe I was reading this situation all wrong. I shouldn't have assumed that I was allowed in his bed, right?

My jaw locked. Talk about throwing me all kinds of weird, crazy, mixed signals. My cheeks flamed as I moved off of the bed, taking the sheet with me, remembering that I was naked.

"Where are you going?" The worry was heavy in his tone.

"To my room."

I exhaled loudly, but just as I made it to the door, he advanced toward me and gripped my wrist, forcing me to face him.

"Don't go." His shoulders slumped as he stepped into me, his eyes downturned.

I sighed and tugged my arm back so that I could readjust my sheet and hold it against myself. I suddenly felt too exposed. "What's wrong, Charles? One minute, you're hot and heavy, and the next, you're icy cold."

I tried to read the emotion behind his eyes, but they were guarded, unreadable.

My voice quivered as I asked, "Did I do something wrong?"

"Of course not." Panic settled in his features.

"Is this happening way too fast?"

His hands went to my waist, pulling me in. It was then, as I met his chocolate eyes, that I read the emotion swimming in them. He was scared. And here I'd thought, I was the only one afraid of this new relationship.

My fingers brushed the light stubble at his chin. "What's wrong? You can tell me."

"Nothing." His voice trailed off, his gaze drifting to somewhere over my shoulder. "I don't think it's happening too fast. Or maybe it is." He laughed without humor. "Now, I'm not making any sense." He shook his head and pulled me further into the room until we were both sitting on the edge of his bed. "I'm not used to this, Becky. Sharing my thoughts, my kids, my life with someone else who isn't"—he exhaled heavily—"Natalie."

In that moment, I understood him, where he was coming from. We were both scared but for totally different reasons. I was scared of getting hurt again, and he was scared of letting go.

I wrapped both hands firmly around his neck. "We're both afraid of what's happening between us. Maybe because it seems like it's too good to be true. But"—I exhaled, deeply, meeting his eyes firmly—"I'd like to believe that we deserve happiness. That everything we've gone through was enough trauma for one person in a lifetime of lifetimes and that we can finally be happy."

His arms wrapped around my waist, and he bent down and placed a chaste kiss on my lips. Then, he pulled me in tightly against him. We held each other in silence, comforting each other without words, until he finally pulled us to the bed, and I found myself lying on his chest while his fingers rustled through my hair.

After a few long, quiet moments, he stilled. "When I moved into this house, I moved her stuff in too. Her clothes are still in the basement. Her toothbrush and our wedding rings are on her supposed side of the bathroom." His voice was soft, and it was as if he was talking mostly to himself. "What crazy man moves his dead wife's belongings into his parents' house?"

His breathing turned shallow beneath my cheek, and I could hear his heart pounding faster.

"In the beginning, the insane part of me thought maybe she'd come back. But ..." He held his breath for a few seconds before getting the next words out. "She can't. She's dead."

Tears formed behind my eyes, and I bit my lip, willing myself not to cry. I'd suffered tragedy and heartache and pain during my lifetime, but so had he on a different level. He'd lost his other half, his wife, the mother of his children. The thought gutted me. To have it all and then, in a split second, have that taken away.

"And I think of putting it away." His voice choked with sadness. "I tried to once. But then it seemed like ... I was erasing her memory. It felt ... wrong."

All my restraint was weakened by the sound of his voice, and the tears fell, streaming down my cheeks. I lifted up higher on his chest and kissed him, wanting to comfort him—or more so, needing him to comfort me. "It's not like that. You can't think of it like that."

He visibly swallowed. I couldn't help but think of how we were opposite on this. I had lived my life, trying to forget my past. He was afraid he wouldn't remember it anymore.

"Everything happens for a reason. Every single thing," I said. "I wholeheartedly believe that. Every heartache, every-thing that has happened in my life, every hurt—it's made me who I am today. Stronger ... more resilient." I paused, framing my own thoughts in my head. "I'm ashamed of my past. More than that, I'm trying to forget what has happened because I hate reliving those memories." I touched his cheek, staring at the newly formed stubble. "But you've helped me get over that."

He had. I wasn't healed from everything that had happened to me, but telling him had been a huge hurdle to overcome and one more step to me getting where I wanted to be—healed and whole and new.

"Moving on for me means something different for you. You have happy memories with Natalie, joyful ones." I touched his cheek as a shudder ran through him. He had one hand thrown over his eyes, and then I knew. I knew he was crying. "Moving on doesn't mean forgetting. Moving on means remembering. Remembering how she impacted your life, how she showed you love, shaped you to be the father and CEO you are today."

My tears fell down my cheeks because it was true. There was no doubt that she'd played a major part in shaping this man—this kind and thoughtful man in front of me. They had known each other since high school.

I pulled his arm away from his eyes, forcing him to look up at me. "Her love is shown through you—how you love your kids, how you lead the company, how you have compassion in everything you do. And I ..." I inhaled deeply. "One day, I want to be the recipient of that same love." I lifted myself higher on his chest. "It's okay to remember because if there wasn't Natalie, there wouldn't be the you that you are today."

CHAPTER 29

CHARLES

I didn't get an ounce of sleep that night, my mind rampant with thoughts of Natalie and Becky, my past and future meshing.

But the longer I held Becky in my arms, peace filled me. There were a lot of things said yesterday, in the early morning. Things that we needed to deal with, but we both realized we had come a long way already from where we had been with emotionally healing from the past.

I slipped out of my bed, careful not to wake Becky, and walked to the bathroom, staring at Natalie's belongings on her side of the sink. I could almost hear her voice as though she were in the room, her nose wrinkling when she didn't agree with something that I had done.

What are you doing, Charles? This is ridiculous.

It was me holding on, and in my heart, I knew that she wouldn't want me to do that. With a huge breath for courage, I took a duffel bag from my closet and carefully packed up her side of the sink. As I placed her makeup brushes and her perfumes and her toiletries into the duffel bag, surprisingly, the tightness in my chest lightened.

Letting go is not forgetting, I could practically hear her saying.

And I knew that Natalie, my angel, was watching over me.

It didn't take long to get her side of the sink cleaned up, and as I bent down to zip up the duffel bag, that same voice whispered in my head, *Keep on going.*

And so I did.

The clock said three in the morning, but I headed to the basement to go through all her belongings. It would have been easier to just walk the bins straight to my car and take them to the donation center, but I opened each bin and allowed myself to reminisce, grieve as I folded the clothes and placed them back in the bin. I kept certain items, ones I knew that Sarah and Mary would want when they were older—her favorite sweater; the shawl she'd always worn while she was reading; the shirt that said, *Today's not the day to get on my nerves;* the shirt I'd bought her that read, *Best Mother Ever* because she had been. The girls were the luckiest to have had Natalie Mary Brisken as their mother.

I kept going, stopping only to hold certain pieces that reminded me of an occasion—our date at the theater, Sarah's Christmas recital, Christmas with my parents, where the theme was ugly sweaters.

I brought the sweater to my nose and inhaled deeply, seeing if there was any trace of her left on the clothing, a light scent of her perfume, anything ... but it was gone. The only traces of her left were the items themselves that had once belonged to her.

Who knew what time it was? I was head deep into the

bins when I peered up to see Becky by the bottom of the stairs.

"Hey." She waved a hand, her eyes still drowsy from sleep. She was fully changed into a T-shirt and running shorts. I figured she'd gone back to her room to change. "I was looking for you."

"What time is it?" I asked.

She yawned. "It's around ten."

"Oh."

Well, shit. I hadn't realized I'd been going for so long. I was three quarters of the way done and kind of on a roll.

"Did you sleep?" she asked.

I sat on my heels. "Not really." I scratched at my temple. "You had me thinking a lot about things, Nat, us."

"You didn't have to do this because of me," she said softly, her eyebrows pulling together, her gorgeous green eyes soft and gentle. She leaned against the doorframe, crossing her ankles.

"I didn't. I did it for me. I did it for Nat."

Because there was that little voice of hers that had kept telling me to move on. I'd tried to mute it for too long. It was time. Time for me to take a path without her ghost walking alongside me and time for Natalie to have peace, knowing I was happy again and no longer living in the misery of losing her.

I placed the Disney T-shirt that I had within my hands in the box and stood. "Let's get breakfast."

"Are you done?"

I looked at the boxes still left to go. "Almost but not quite."

A sweet smile popped onto her face. "Well, let me help you, then."

Before I could protest, she got down on her knees and rummaged through the box closest to her.

"Becky ... you don't have to do this."

Immense guilt hit me in the chest because she didn't have to do this, didn't have to help me go through my deceased wife's belongings. I didn't want her to feel uncomfortable with the situation.

She paused, her hands stopping at the edge of the box. "Unless you don't want me to. If this makes you uncomfortable—"

"No," I protested, frowning as I assessed her. "I'm just surprised that you're not."

Her tone softened, and she tilted her head. "I just want to help you, Charles."

With Becky, I was too much in my head. I never used to be that guy. I never assumed things. Here I was, assuming she wouldn't feel comfortable, putting away all my dead wife's belongings, that it would be too much for her.

"Thank you." I plopped down next to her and continued to place things that I would donate in a big garbage bag.

"This shirt though." She lifted it up, so I could read the front. *I'm going to do nothing all day.* "You know Mary will wear this."

I shook my head and laughed. Wasn't it the truth though? Mary had won this family over with her cuteness, and I wondered if she'd keep pushing the same envelope when she was older.

Most definitely, came the voice again, and I smiled to myself.

An hour and a half later, we were done. I stood there, hands on my hips, taking in the bags that were all ready to be sent off to Goodwill. Natalie's clothes and belongings that I would keep for the girls all placed in bins and labeled.

A weight lifted from my shoulders, and even though we were in the basement, in the dim lighting of the storage area, I felt as though Natalie's light was shining down on me, showering me with warmth.

I exhaled deeply and turned to Becky. "Mission accomplished. Now, let's go out to eat."

Becky's smile was soft, beautiful, something I could get used to every day, going forward.

"You don't want to make breakfast?"

"No, let's go out. We have the whole day together since the girls are with Brad till tomorrow."

She extended her hand and nodded. "Let's go, then."

I pulled her in and dropped my head to the crook of her neck, breathing in her natural scent of citrus, most likely from her shampoo.

My new favorite scent.

Becky

We were seated at an outside patio that overlooked the lake. The scent of the crisp fall air, the breeze against our faces, the sun beating down against my skin had me giddy. I ordered blueberry crepes. Figuring that I could have made pancakes, bacon, and eggs at home, I wanted something different.

"So, what do you want to do today?" Charles asked above his chicken and waffles.

He wore a Cubs baseball cap today and a regular white T-shirt, dressed down, unlike his usual professional attire.

"I'll do whatever you have planned."

He laughed, taking a sip of his coffee. "I'm not much of a planner. Every vacation or dinner reservation is made by Mason. I'm thankful for him because he makes an itinerary for the girls when we have to go out." The way he talked about his brothers made my heart full. "But, yeah, I'm pretty proud of my planning abilities yesterday even though I had to google *best first dates*." His mouth twitched with amusement.

I laughed. "It was perfect." I finished the last of my crepe, slipping the fork in my mouth. "How about we take a bike ride and then go grocery shopping for what we want to cook for dinner? Then, we can rent a movie and watch it back home."

The corner of his mouth tipped upward. "Home." The smile played on his lips, and then his gaze dropped to the table before meeting my eyes again. "I like the sound of that." He reached for my hand and intertwined our fingers. "And biking, grocery shopping, making dinner, and renting a movie sounds like every other night, no?" He pulled me in, angling closer. "Not like I have a problem with that."

"But this time, there will be no kids around." I suggestively wiggled my eyebrows as I closed the gap between us and kissed him.

After breakfast, we walked farther up the lake, hand in hand, to rent bikes. I wanted to ride one of those tandem bikes, where I rode up front and Charles rode on the back. I almost skipped down the sidewalk while I spotted the multitude of bikes ahead of us, but something—or more so, *someone*—caught my eye.

I stopped mid-step, and my stomach dropped to the ground and kept on going.

It was impossible.

Impossible!

Bile crept up my throat as my whole body trembled.

"Becky? What's wrong?" Charles asked beside me. His grip tensed around my fingers, sensing my stress.

I shook my head, seeing him in the distance, up the hill —his profile, the sharp lines of his jaw, the bridge of his nose.

Panic threatened to choke me.

Paul.

Fear clouded my vision. Not for me. But for Charles. For Sarah. For sweet Mary.

But I didn't want to run and hide today. I didn't know what took over me today, but I wanted to fucking take him down.

I ran at a full sprint up the hill, arms pumping, legs moving. He turned and walked in the other direction, ignorant to me fast approaching him, and I ran even faster, hearing Charles call after me.

He wasn't going to hurt the people around me, be a threat to their lives like he'd done with mine. I wasn't leaving because of him. I had found my place on this earth, where I was needed, where I was wanted. He wasn't going to take that away from me. He'd already taken too much.

I was almost up the hill when Charles gripped my arm, stilling me.

"Becky, what's wrong?" He was breathing fast from having to chase after me.

I flipped around, but Paul was gone.

Instantly, I tore myself from his grasp and raced down the street, doing a three-sixty, trying to find him.

Where is he?

Where the hell did he go?

Then, I saw him. By the stoplight. And I took off running again like my life depended on it. He'd know today that he couldn't scare me anymore. That I had someone who loved me, someone who cared and would stay by me this time. I wouldn't hide anymore. I'd fight him back and confront him.

The light changed to red, allowing the pedestrians to walk, and I charged toward him, whipping him around by tugging at his shirt.

"Shit." I dropped my hand as soon as I realized it wasn't Paul.

From the side view, he was unmistakably Paul, but this wasn't the Paul who haunted my nightmares.

"Sorry." I raised both hands as he stared at me, thoroughly pissed, in the middle of a busy road.

The light changed, causing oncoming traffic to press on their horns, and I tipped my chin, my eyes apologetic. "I'm so sorry."

"Becky." Charles reached me again and grabbed my hand, dragging me back across the street to safety. When we were on the sidewalk, he gripped both of my forearms, bringing me in. "What's going on with you?" His eyes were full of worry.

"I thought ..." My eyes went back to the stranger crossing to the other side of the road. "I thought I knew him."

His eyes followed mine across the street. "You thought that was your ex?"

I nodded, still not taking my gaze from the man I'd almost assaulted.

Without warning, Charles pulled me into him until my cheek planted against his chest. "I promise you, nothing and no one will ever hurt you again. Ever."

I snuggled against him as he kissed my forehead. I wasn't worried about Paul hurting me anymore. This new realization pushed through while I was in Charles's arms. He couldn't do anything to me that he hadn't done already. I was more scared of Paul hurting the people around me, the people I'd grown to love.

But no, never again.

CHAPTER 30

CHARLES

Becky's nerves were shot after that encounter with the stranger that she'd thought was her ex. The bike ride down the lake did not ease her anxiety, and when we went grocery shopping, I noticed how her eyes searched the vicinity, as though he would pop up from the condiments aisle.

That was when I made a decision for the safety of my kids and Becky. I would legally find this son of a bitch and serve him a restraining order.

I'd hire a private investigator to find him and enlist my legal team to serve him the papers.

We were seated at the kitchen table with our steak and potato meal that we had cooked together. There had been times through the night, after the laughter and short make-out sessions, that she zoned out, and I had known she was in deep thought.

As she sat there, poking at her steak, I knew this was one of those times.

"Hey."

No answer.

I toed her foot under the table.

Still nothing.

I pulled at her plate, forcing her head up from wherever she had gone to a minute ago. "What's in that beautiful mind of yours?"

She shook her head, her eyes gaining focus. "Stuff."

When I threw her a pointed look, she laughed. "What happened earlier. How I'm so on edge. I wonder if that paranoid feeling will ever go away."

I reached for her hand over the table, placing my hand over her fist. "I was thinking." I paused, knowing how I phrased things was important. It was how I handled my business, my household. It was all about the approach. "I don't want you to be paranoid anymore. I don't want you to keep looking behind you at the grocery store or when we're out at the park with the girls. So"—I leveled her with a stare —"I want you to think about getting a restraining order."

"What?" She reeled back as all these questions played behind her eyes.

I continued before she had a chance to deny my request, "If we find him and file a restraining order against him, he can't hurt you anymore. I don't want you to live a life where you're afraid."

Her gaze dropped to the table, and I squeezed her hand tighter. "Let me do this." I paused, needing her to really listen to me. "I care about you, Becky." My thumb brushed against the top of her fist.

Her eyes focused on the table, her eyebrows pulling in. "I can't." When her gaze met mine, her decision was made. "If I believed for one second that a restraining order would stop him, I'd do it. But it won't. I know him. Paul Clark is one of a kind. He won't stop until he has me under his control."

Her words seared through me, and I wanted to protest and argue with her that I had all the means to keep him away. Even if I had to hire round-the-clock security for her, I'd do it.

She smiled then. "I can only imagine what's playing in that mind of yours. Just don't go there, Charles."

I swallowed hard. "It's impossible for me to not take care of the people I care about the most."

Her fingers came to my fisted hand on the top of the table. I hadn't even realized that my body had gone stiff, my muscles tightening at this conversation.

"How do you know?" I pressed. "How do you know we can't get this guy in jail if he tries to come at you? Not like I'm willing to risk it, but I want you to no longer be afraid."

Her eyebrows pulled together, and her gaze dropped to the table. "I'll be more afraid if he knows where I am."

When her eyes flickered toward mine, I read the fear clearly, forcing me to pull her from her seat and into my lap.

I held her close, and my lips found their way to her forehead. "Okay," I said, knowing I wouldn't be at ease but wanting to please her, do what she was comfortable with. "I'll let it go."

I cupped her face, forcing her to look up at me. Her eyes were a blazing green, as fierce as a newly watered lawn.

A deep emotion settled in my gut. "You don't have to be afraid anymore. You know that, right?" My voice was strong, firm. I'd protect her and everyone close to me with my own life. "Because I am here—to serve and protect." My smile surfaced, waiting to erase the fear in her eyes.

After a beat, she kissed my lips with a sweet peck and pulled back, smiling. "That's good to know."

Becky

The weekend seemed to speed up. Didn't it always when you were having the time of your life? In a span of a short day and a half, I'd learned so much about Charles, about Natalie, about his little quirks.

I always knew what motivated him, and I knew some of his favorite things from living with his family, but finding out little tidbits while it was just the two of us was different. Charles was a hand-holder. Though his outward appearance would make him seem rough and tough around the edges, his hand-holding or little brushes against my waist showed a different side of him that others never saw, and I got to experience it firsthand without little eyes in the house.

I was sitting on his lap, watching the most recent Jason Bourne movie. Barely watching really because his fingers were threaded through my hair, his tongue was down my throat, and more accurately, I was not sitting on his lap. I was straddling him.

I hadn't been kissed like this in ... never. I'd never been kissed like this, slow and sensually yet where every flick of his tongue sent shivers straight through me.

My heart raced. My pulse thrummed rapidly against the inside of my wrist. I wanted him, no doubt, but I wanted him to be ready, to go at his pace.

Sure felt as though he was ready now, given that his one hand was on my ass.

When he pulled back, I was allowed to breathe. I thought it was game over until he lifted me, both hands on my ass.

I wrapped my arms around his neck. "Where are we going?"

"My bedroom."

My heart almost jumped out of my throat. I didn't know what I had expected, but I for sure hadn't expected that.

His lips peppered kisses against my collarbone as he ascended the stairs two at a time, sending a jolt of tingles through me. His kisses accelerated from zero to one hundred in a matter of seconds. He moved his tongue against mine with unrelenting passion, flicking and sucking my lips, moving to my neck, nibbling my ear. Before I knew what was happening, he guided me to my back on top of his bed. Our make-out session was heating up my body to immeasurable temperatures, causing the ache between my legs to intensify.

He fisted his shirt and lifted it above his head in one swift movement, and then it was chucked to the side.

Holy two hundred miles per hour.

When he met my lips again and he crushed his bare chest against mine, I placed a hand against one of his pecs. Meeting his eyes, I said, "Are you sure?"

His eyebrows pulled together then, and his expression filled with worry. "Why? Are you not sure?"

I shook my head and laughed at the pinched expression on his face. "I'm sure. But last night ..."

His hand traveled up and down my side. "I like you, Becky. There's a part of me that's still scared and nervous, but right now, here, what I can't fight is how much I want you."

I understood him. I knew where he was coming from. We were both reluctant for different reasons. But, yes, above all my insecurities of jumping in with Charles, passion outran those doubts.

"Question is"—I threw him my sexiest, most seductive look—"do you have a condom?"

"Yes." His smile was blinding and sexy and all the things that made my lady parts weep.

His lips descended on mine in a mess of fiery lust. Slowly, he stripped me bare, as though he was unwrapping me like a present. First, my jeans. Then, my shirt. Finally, my undergarments.

The look of awe and reverence in his eyes made my heart pump harder and faster in my chest. But more than that ... I couldn't breathe. He looked at me as though I were the only woman in the world.

He pushed himself up and knelt above me. The crinkle of the condom and the anticipation of what was coming next had me wriggling beneath him, wanting and needing him. His body was glorious, an Adonis in the flesh, a man to be worshipped and adored.

A second later, his lips were on mine again, his chest crushed against my chest, his hard length pressing against my stomach. The unbearable ache in between my legs was too much for me to bear, so I rubbed my core against his hardness. His breath came out in big, broken puffs.

"You keep touching me like that, and I'm not going to last long. And I want to last a very ... very ... long time."

He took the lead, taking his length and guiding it to my entrance. With one thrust, he entered me, and the feeling was glorious. I cried out in pleasure. I hadn't been with a man in years and never with a man of this strength and stature.

I moved beneath him, meeting every pull and push of his body. Wrapping my legs around his waist, I angled closer, wanting him deeper, nearer, when we were already flushed skin to skin.

His movements were slow and sensual at first, his hands cupping my face and then threading through my hair. My body adjusted to him, but more than that, my heart did too. Because as our eyes locked, I saw him open and bare and scared, mirroring the emotions I felt inside.

With every push and pull of his body, my heart opened a little more.

The pinch in the deepest part of my belly indicated that I was close. "Charles ..." I moaned out.

"I know, baby."

His movements became harder, faster, pumping in and out of me. And I knew he was close too.

"Let go, Becky. I want to see you come apart."

The buildup of sensation was all too much to take, and I did as he'd said ... I let go.

We came together with him calling out my name and me tightening my hold around him as my body was sent through a wave of sensations everywhere.

And it was ecstasy.

CHAPTER 31

CHARLES

"Daddy!"

Knock. Knock. Knock.

It was Mary.

I jolted to a sitting position and stared at Becky, whose eyes widened. Immediately, she sat up and pulled the sheets over her breasts.

I glanced at the clock. It was three in the afternoon. We hadn't gotten a lot of sleep the night before.

"Daddy! Open the door. I want to show you something."

Maybe if we stayed silent, she'd leave.

"Daddy?"

It was quiet, and my shoulders relaxed for a bit—until I heard the jiggle of the doorknob.

Fuck.

"She knows how to unlock the door with a Q-tip," I said, already getting up and slipping on my boxers.

"Shit," Becky hissed.

Just when the door opened, Becky rolled off the bed,

taking the sheet to wrap up her body, and slipped underneath the bed.

Her clothes.

Shit. They were on the floor.

I jumped off the bed and kicked her clothes under the bed as I walked toward the door.

"Daddy!" Mary held up a pink unicorn in the air. The tips of her horns were covered in glitter. "Look what I got. Uncle Brad took us to Game Arcade. Don't you love her?" She squeezed the unicorn against her chest so tightly that I swore the stuffing would burst from the seams.

"She's cute," I answered.

"Hey, Dad." Sarah walked in, holding some pens and a journal in her hand.

"Hi. Is that what you won at Game Arcade?" My voice hitched up, as though someone had kicked me in the balls.

"Yeah. I killed it in Skee Ball." She frowned at me, sensing something was up. "Were you working out or something?"

"N-no," I stuttered, feeling my throat close up.

She tilted her head. "Oh, 'cause it looks like you're about to work out."

Of course it did. I was in boxer shorts and shirtless. "I'm about to take a shower."

It wasn't like the girls hadn't seen me naked before. They were everywhere, playing with toys in my bathroom when I took a shower. Mary would walk in on me, taking a shit, wanting me to read her a book.

This happened to Mason and Brad too. We'd realized long ago that there was no privacy when we were raising girls.

"Where's Becky?" Sarah asked.

I cricked my neck from side to side, trying to get the

kinks out. My stomach tightened at her question because I hardly ever lied to the girls. There'd been no need to ... until now.

I swallowed. "She must be in her room or ... downstairs ... maybe outside." My voice was pinched, not even sounding like my normal self.

"Yay! I wanna show her my unicorn," Mary said, hopping like a bunny on Easter morning.

Oh, great.

"Hey, girls." Brad strolled in, his eyes panicked for a second before scouring the room. "I was looking for you guys."

"Hey, Charles." Mason walked in next, holding a pint of ice cream. "Girls, Janice has the cones ready downstairs."

Well, damn. We had the whole darn family in the room now while Becky was underneath my bed, buck-ass naked.

I swallowed as every inch of me sweated profusely.

Mason's eyebrows scrunched, and he sported a very disappointed gaze. "Did you just wake up? It's practically three in the afternoon."

I wanted to tell them Becky and I were tired from having nonstop sex last night and into the morning. That we had eaten breakfast, watched a reality TV show in bed, had sex again, eaten lunch, and repeated the process.

"I ... I was about to take a shower," I stuttered.

"Where's Becky?" Mason asked, still clueless.

God help this man.

I gritted my teeth and shuffled from one foot to the other, running my hands through my hair.

"She might be in her room. Come on, Uncle Mason. Let's look for her." Mary took Mason's hand. Sarah followed behind them.

As soon as they left, I released a heavy breath. Brad

smirked, placing both hands on his hips. *Why the hell is he still in my room, standing there, smiling like an idiot?*

"Get out," I snapped.

"Purple?"

I quirked an eyebrow. He tipped his chin toward my bed, and I turned to see what he was motioning toward—Becky's bra.

"I didn't know you were cross-dressing now."

"Shut up," I growled.

He turned around but not before saying, "Hey, Becky."

I groaned. "You could have called before you came home."

He threw me a look as though I'd said something stupid. "I did. Multiple times. But I figured you were preoccupied."

Bastard had the audacity to full-on grin.

I glared at him. "Get out."

He smirked. "You go shower. And if you need more showering time, we'll be having ice cream outside by the pool. It's nice out. I'll be waiting for my Best Brother Award later."

I didn't have time to retort before he shut the door behind him.

I went on my knees and ducked under the bed. "Hey."

"Hey." Becky's soft voice was shaky.

I assisted her out from under the bed, and when she stood, her hand trembled.

"Hey ..." I pulled her into me, and my fingers threaded through her hair, bringing her head against my chest. "You're shaking." My arms fully wrapped around her lower back, pulling her in closer.

"That was a close call," she said, her voice muffled against my chest.

"Yeah. Feels a little like we're teenagers and I snuck you

into my room." I noted every inch of her body against mine, her soft breasts against my hard chest, her little patch of hair against my side. My mind was thinking one thing, but my body wanted her.

Brad's words reined in my head.

"We should get ready and go downstairs. Showering together will save time."

She lifted her chin and rested it against my chest. Emerald-green eyes bore into mine. "Nice one."

She pinched my side, and I jumped, unprepared. When she went in again to pinch me, I grabbed her hand and kissed it.

"Mary is looking for me. I should go." She inched away, and my shoulders slumped just at the immediate absence of her.

Our eyes locked, and she placed one light hand on my chest. Her eyes flittered to the ground and back to meet my eyes. "What happens now, Charles?"

Such a loaded question, and there was such intensity in her tone that it stilled me for a second, making it seem like a hesitation but it wasn't because I already knew that I wanted this, a relationship with her.

But she read it as hesitation. "I ... I mean ... we can talk about this later."

When she took another step back, I gripped her hand and squeezed. "Hey."

Her eyes met mine, and I read the slew of emotions swimming in her green irises, the fear.

"I know what this is. This is different for me too." I swallowed. "Because I haven't had feelings for anyone like this since ... since Nat." As soon as the words left my mouth, there was no guilt behind them, like there had been with Vivian. And that was how I knew whatever this was, was real, was good. "What happens now is that I tell my brothers, and then *we* tell the girls that we're together."

It'd be an adjustment, but I knew in my heart that Sarah and Mary had grown to love Becky. Hopefully, us together would be a good thing.

Becky smiled, her whole face lighting up. "Okay." She nodded.

She turned to walk toward the bed and ducked down to reach for her clothes, giving me a perfect view of her ass.

"Are you sure you don't want to save time by showering together?"

She smirked, then slipped on her underwear and pants. "Mary is already looking for me."

She plucked her bra from my bed and slipped it on, followed by her shirt. She went on her tiptoes and sweetly pecked my lips. It wasn't nearly enough, cut short as she turned on her heels. She opened the door slightly to see if anyone was in the hall and slipped out.

I rested one hand on my hip. The conversation with the girls had to happen sooner than later because then I'd be able to have Becky in my life openly, holding her, hugging her, and having her in my bed.

I peered down at the major hard-on I was sporting.

Yep. A shower was definitely needed. A very cold one.

CHAPTER 32

CHARLES

Mason looked expectedly at me from in front of my desk. "So, I see that Becky and you ..." His voice trailed off.

He was fishing, no doubt for information about us since we'd been close ever since our date. At times, I wished he was like Brad, straight up and honest.

I lifted my head from my computer and leveled him with a stare. "If you have to ask me something, just ask me, Mason. And Becky and I are becoming more serious."

His gaze flickered to the side, to his iPad in his lap, to the corner of my desk. "So, yeah ... since you've gotten more serious with her, are you going to tell the girls soon?"

I nodded, rubbing at my brow. "Yeah. I'm thinking this weekend." The tension was back in my tone. I didn't know what I was nervous about. I was a grown man, but it felt as though I were bringing a girl home for the first time to introduce her to my parents, which was absurd because my parents were dead.

This was different. Harder in a way. The stakes were higher. Any person I brought into my life and into my heart romantically would involve the girls. If by chance we didn't work out, I didn't want my girls to suffer through another heartbreak that I could have prevented.

Problem was, I couldn't predict the future. Right now, I was sure of us, so sure that I wanted to take a chance on us —together.

"Before you do that though"—his eyes met mine firmly —"don't you want to find out more about her to be sure?"

"I know everything I need to know," I said, my tone unwavering.

I knew almost everything about her now that she had shared her past. The issue was protecting her now, keeping her safe. The irrational part of me wanted to take her abusive ex-boyfriend and beat him until he was unconscious. The reasonable part of me knew there was a process with these things.

"I'm happy for you. I am." Mason rested his elbows on his knees, leaning in. "No one can deny that if anyone deserves the world, it's you, Charles. You've been through a lot, and I just want to make sure you're with the perfect girl —one who loves you for you and is not with you because of who you are, what you own, and—"

I held up a hand. "She's not like that," I said. I knew his heart was coming from the right place, but couldn't he see that Becky's character didn't care even the slightest about money? Not more than it took to survive anyway. "For heaven's sake, Mason, the girl wanted to wear jeans on our first date. If she's a gold digger, she's the worst one I've ever seen."

And he was one to talk. Janice was blatant in her mission—land the biggest fish—and so far, she was managing that.

"I get that. I don't doubt it, but still ..." Mason rubbed at his jaw, and his words came out softer this time. "I just want to be sure. Don't be mad or hate me for wanting the best for you."

I sighed. There wasn't an evil bone in Mason's body, so I couldn't fault him just because he was concerned.

A few stretches of silent beats spanned between us.

When he spoke, his voice was barely above a whisper, "She wouldn't even have to know we're doing a background check. I have a private investigator who can just do a little digging."

I laughed. "Why doesn't that surprise me?"

"Oh. Yeah, well"—his cheeks flushed—"I've run them before."

"On who?" My eyebrows flew to my hairline.

"On the numerous nannies that we interviewed. And I ran one on Janice because I had all her information. With Becky, I don't," he said defensively. "Janice and I were in college, so it wasn't anything new, but she seemed too good to be true. I had to check her out if I was going to invest in a long-term relationship with her."

Invest.

The chuckle that came from my mouth was uncontainable. Of course he had. It was almost comical how he was methodical in all aspects of life.

"So, should I contact the PI, then? Is that a yes?" Mason asked.

He carefully kept his face neutral, so he didn't come off too anxious, but I could see right through him.

I leaned back in my chair, steepling my fingers by my lips. Slowly but surely, I was moving on, but there was no way Becky could move on, not when she had to constantly watch her back, worried that bastard would show up one day and hurt her again.

Over my dead body.

She'd said she didn't want to file a restraining order. I had to respect her wishes about that, but she didn't say anything about me digging around a little, finding out where this bastard was. If I knew he lived halfway across the nation, I'd feel better. Or maybe the bastard was in another country altogether. Even better yet.

I tipped my chin toward Mason. "Give me his number. I'll do the digging."

Mason smiled, and his facial features relaxed. "I think this is your smartest decision yet."

Shit. I sure hoped so. I hoped this wouldn't come back to bite me in the ass later.

CHAPTER 33

Becky

Out of the both of us, I had more self-control than Charles. There were many times, even when the girls were in the room, he'd steal a quick kiss on the lips, which would render me stupid and speechless for at least a good fifteen seconds.

Standing in the kitchen, making cupcakes with the girls ... this was one of those times. I stood and noted Charles's smile heavy on his face.

"Becky, can you pass me the powdered sugar for the frosting?"

I blinked at him and then stared at Sarah and Mary, who were busy mixing the cake batter. I shook my head through my hazy thoughts. My cheeks felt impossibly hot.

"Here." My fingers brushed against Charles's.

When his sexy smile widened, I realized that I'd never seen him smile as much as he had in the last few days, and I liked to think it was because of me.

"Where are the cookies?" Brad strolled in, walking over to Mary and Sarah and dipping his finger in the batter.

"Hey," Sarah complained, shoving his hand away. "And we're making cupcakes, not cookies."

"Well, let me help you."

When Brad tipped his pinkie again in the batter, Mary lifted the mixing spoon and slapped it against Brad's shirt.

"No cheat eating!" Her adorable pout was signature Mary.

"Hey! I like this shirt." Brad peered down at the white batter smeared against his navy-blue polo.

In response, Mary stuck her spoon back in the bowl and began to mix it again.

"That'll teach you to cheat eat," Charles said, laughing.

Being the rebel Brad was, he dipped his pointer finger into the bowl and licked his finger clean.

Mary's mouth slipped ajar in a visible O, and in retaliation, Sarah dipped three fingers in the bowl and rubbed it against Brad's shirt.

"You guys," I scolded.

But it was all for nothing because as Mary got in on the action and dipped her hand in the batter, Brad was faster and smeared some white batter on Mary's cheek.

"Guys, stop!" Charles commanded.

There wasn't a second round because, with his words, they all stilled, all eyes wide and fingers full of batter—Brad included.

"Mary ... Sarah ... get changed." He pointed to the door. "Brad, you should know better."

"She started it." He pointed to Sarah, going for cute, but Charles tipped his chin to the door. "Get them changed."

When the culprits filed out of the room, I laughed. "It's amazing how a few words from you shuts them down quick."

He advanced toward me, pulling me into him so fast

that I almost stumbled back. Automatically, my arms wrapped around his neck.

"Kiss," he said with heated affection. "There's one word for you."

I sighed. "You can be bossy with everyone else, but your tactics don't work on me, mister."

"Kiss me." His voice was sharp, meaning business, but there was a lightness in his eyes that made my stomach flip.

I closed the gap between us and met his lips. He smelled of mint from his toothpaste, and the masculine scent of his aftershave filled my nose.

He pushed me against the counter, and the edge of the island dug into my side. My body tingled with anticipation. It had been days since we'd last been together, and besides stolen kisses here and there, there were no other opportunities other than this weekend—when Brad had promised to take the girls again.

When he pushed his hips into me, I could feel how much he wanted me. When he flicked his tongue over the seam of my lips, I opened my mouth to let him in. This felt dangerous, as though I were at the edge of a cliff, about to fall, but what a wonderful fall it would be.

"Daddy?"

We separated as fast as we'd come together. Chests heaving. Breathing hard. My hand flew to my mouth in utter horror.

Her face was shell-shocked.

"Sarah." Charles's features crumpled.

"I'm sorry," I whispered, but he didn't hear me because Sarah had darted out of the room and Charles had gone after her.

Charles

Sarah ran, and I followed her outside, past our pool. I watched her climb up the tree house that Brad and Mason had bought the girls.

"Sarah!" I called out, but she'd already shut the door.

I gritted my teeth and kicked the ground, lifting a piece of grass from the roots.

That had been reckless; I should have known better.

Fuck.

"Sarah," I called out again.

"I wanna be alone right now." Her voice was soft, shaky, and I wondered if she was crying.

Fuck, fuck. Me and my stupidity.

I one hundred percent blamed myself. There was excitement in stealing kisses from Becky when the girls weren't looking, skirting the edge, watching the flush in her cheeks, but I hadn't thought I'd get caught before telling them.

I should've told them sooner. Fear had been pushing this conversation off. *Stupid.* I shouldn't have put it off. Well, cat was out of the bag now.

"Sarah, honey ... we need to talk."

Silence.

I knew my daughters individually, their strengths, what motivated them, what they were into, what they wanted for their birthdays, and also what made them angry. Sarah ... she'd need time to process, simmer. Time alone.

I touched the base of the tree house, placing my hand on the bark of the maple tree, and released a silent breath, peering up at the house that held part of my world.

Sarah was old enough to remember Natalie. They'd been two peas in their mismatched pods in looks, but in personality, they were similar. Sarah had a bond with

Natalie that I could never touch, and when Nat passed away, I spent thousands of dollars on counseling as a family and her individually to make sure she was processing Nat's death in a healthy manner.

It had been years since her last crying-fest, her blowups, her shutting down.

And in one instant ... my one moment of carelessness, I'd taken her back years.

Brad jogged toward me from a distance, and I met him halfway.

"Becky told me what happened." There was no humor on his features and no witty comment, which I was glad for because I couldn't take it right now. "Is she okay?" he asked, peering behind me, his gaze traveling toward the tree house.

"No." I rubbed at my forehead. "I'm so fucking stupid."

"It happens," Brad said, sighing and shrugging, knowing I was going to be in the doghouse with Sarah but also knowing we couldn't rewind.

I dropped my head and ran one heavy hand through my hair.

He placed a hand on my shoulder. "But mistakes don't normally happen with you though."

I groaned. "You're supposed to make me feel better."

Brad lifted a shoulder. "That's your job, too, so I'm out of my element here."

I threw him a look, and he offered me a small smile.

"Listen, big bro, we all know how Natalie's death affected Sarah hugely. But she's strong, resilient. She's older now. She can handle it. You just need to talk to her ... when she's ready."

I nodded and swallowed. I knew that too. She needed time. I just didn't want to give it to her. The father in me wanted to fix it *now*.

In the beginning, we'd talked about how much we both missed Natalie; we'd reminisced and watched old home videos. It was a way of healing rather than pretending it'd never happened. But as time had passed and we got busy, watching our old life on the screen had stopped, and so had reminiscing. I wasn't naive to believe her wounds were not still there because my wounds still weren't healed. When someone died—someone you loved dearly, maybe even more than yourself—that pain never really went away. It might dim, but I knew from experience, you never fully forgot.

"Just talk to her," Brad repeated.

I nodded, my eyes going shut. "I was going to, but it looks like that talk is going to happen sooner than expected."

I peered up at the door she'd shut on me and knew there was no way I'd fit in that small space with her. And knowing her, she wanted to be alone right now. But I'd wait by this tree house all night if I had to, wait till she was ready to talk to me, wait until she was ready to forgive me.

CHAPTER 34

CHARLES

My gaze dropped to the ground, the grass, to the area of dirt where I'd uprooted a patch of grass. I whispered, "Nat, do a Hail Mary, will you? You know your daughter more than I do. Show me how to handle this situation."

A small laugh escaped my lips. I could picture her shaking her head, giving me that look that said, *Charles, you should have known better.* She'd never utter those words, but with that one look, I knew what she was thinking.

It was a whole two hours later when Sarah descended the steps from the tree house, and I was right there, butt on the grass, leaning against the tree, waiting for her.

She wrung her hands in front of her, and her eyes were noticeably red.

I stood and brought her into a hug, grateful she didn't push me away. As soon as she nuzzled her head into my chest, I released a breath of relief. And then she melted into my arms, her body going limp.

"I miss Mom." Her voice was muffled against my shirt, and I pulled her in tighter against me.

My chest seized, and I swallowed the lump in the back of my throat. "I know. I do too, honey. I do too."

I pulled her up then and lifted her into my arms. At ten, her legs dangled. She wasn't a little girl anymore, but she'd always be my little girl.

When she tucked her chin into my neck, I lifted my eyes to the sky—searching for a cloud, the sun, some sort of sign. Sometimes, I'd pick a cloud in the sky and picture Nat, sitting there, watching me.

In that moment, I thanked her, like I'd done so many times before. I thanked her for these girls, my most precious gifts. One she'd even died for.

"I'm sorry." My voice was choked with emotion.

Sarah shouldn't have found out about Becky and me that way. I'd never been sloppy before. With my girls, there was no room for mistakes, but with Becky, as I had quickly learned, all those rules were out the window.

Sarah shook her head and pushed her face further in my neck. My fingers went to her hair, and I turned my face to meet her cheek, planting a kiss there.

Why did every little thing have to be so damn hard? Letting go, moving on, learning to live without someone, and then figuring out how to fold someone new into our lives ...

I hadn't thought Sarah would be ready for me to date again. And as I gritted my teeth, I realized that accelerating my relationship with Becky without telling my girls first was the most selfish thing I'd ever done with my girls, and it was the first time I hadn't put their emotions and their needs above mine.

If they weren't okay, what was I going to do?

The thought hadn't even crossed my mind, but my girls were young, and there'd be time for me later, right? To date, to love again, when they were grown and had lives of their own.

I swallowed as sadness hit me directly in the chest. The thought of ending this new thing with Becky already gutted me.

For a brief moment, I closed my eyes, my breaths matching Sarah's, and I decided whatever my girls wanted, whatever they needed, it was my job to provide that. If, in the end, they weren't ready, I'd have to accept that. That was something Becky would have to accept to, right? Would she wait?

Slowly, a breath escaped me. That wasn't my priority now. My priority was the little girl in my arms.

When she pulled back, she swiped at her tears, and grief tore at my heart.

"I just miss her." She sobbed, her tears falling relentlessly down her cheeks.

Good God, I hated seeing my girls cry. It took me a moment to speak. "I know. I miss her too. Every day."

"And Becky ..." Her voice trailed off.

I swiped each of her cheeks with my thumbs. "I know. I'm sorry ..."

She placed her small, fragile hands on my cheeks, and her words stunned me. "I want you to be happy, Daddy." Her eyes shone with tears, with heartbreak, and yet a maturity I'd never seen before. "I know you miss Mommy, and I know you're sad about her and you have been, but I just want you to be happy, Daddy. I just want you to be happy."

I tried to swallow past the giant lump in my throat, but I couldn't.

This kid. My awesome, wonderfully made kid.

I didn't deserve her.

Now, it was my turn as tears outlined my eyes. I pulled

her in close, holding her with one arm and lifting the edge of my shirt to wipe my eyes with the other.

Thank you, baby girl.

But I couldn't even get the words out. It took a good few minutes to pull myself together and place her back on her feet.

We walked in silence to the lounge chairs by the pool, and I sat down and pulled her into my lap.

I pushed her hair out of her face and smiled. "You know I love you, right?"

She nodded, her smile matching mine.

"And you know that everything I do, have ever done, is always with your best interest in mind. You know that, right, Sarah?"

"I do." She reached for my hand and squeezed, turning over my fingers in hers.

"And above all ... I want to make sure you guys are happy. Not only that you have the things you need and want, but that you're happy too." I blew out a long breath, wishing I were better prepared for this conversation. "When you say you want Daddy happy"—that same lump formed in the back of my throat—"you don't know"—I swallowed—"how much that means to me because"—I lifted my eyes to hers—"I feel like I've been so busy, making sure you're happy, that I forget about myself sometimes. By you saying that"—I cupped her cheek—"that means a lot to Daddy."

She nodded, and it looked like she was going to cry again. "I know ..." Her lip quivered as she stared at our hands. "I see you, Daddy. I see you when you're not looking, and I know you're sad. I keep thinking ... maybe if I get better grades ... maybe if I don't fight as much with Mary, then maybe you'll be happier. But now"—a small smile surfaced—"you're different. Even when you're sitting by yourself, you're smiling, and now, I know why."

"Oh, honey." My thumb swiped at her tears. "You make me happy, just by being you."

She nodded.

"But, yes ... Becky makes me happy too." I ducked into her line of sight because I needed her to believe me, to understand. "I love your mom. I think about her every single day ..." It was the truth. Every time I looked at Mary, I saw her spitting image, or when Sarah said something witty, it would remind me of Nat. "No one can or ever will replace her."

One warm hand patted my cheek. "I know. You don't have to tell me or worry about me anymore because I'm a big girl." She sat straighter in my lap as proof. "I know no one will ever replace Mommy, but I want you to know ... I like Becky. She's kind and fun, and she ..." She looked like she was searching for the words when she said, "I dunno. She just fits."

I blew out a breath of relief, of happiness, of gratitude for this child in front of me. "That she does, baby girl. That she does."

CHAPTER 35

Becky

By the time Charles and Sarah entered the house, I was making dinner. Heat flushed my cheeks as I tried to make eye contact with Sarah and smile, but she hadn't lifted her head, only skipped out of the room.

My eyes immediately met Charles's as I took the cupcakes out of the oven.

"How is she?" My muscles tightened as I waited for his answer.

"Good." He leaned against the counter and shook his head. "That girl ... old soul, that one. She's beyond her years."

"She's been through a lot."

I knew from experience, as I'd also grown up fast, experienced a lot of hardships, heartache. The difference was, Sarah had a great support system around her. I'd had to fend for myself.

"Yeah, that's true. First, losing Nat and then her grandparents." His eyes traveled beyond me, somewhere over my shoulder.

"I'm glad she's okay. What did she say about me and you and catching us ..." My voice trailed off. "Charles ..." I took a step toward him. While they'd been outside, in between making crafts with Mary, I'd decided that I would not cause drama in this house or any more heartache than they'd already gone through. When I'd moved in here, my job had been to make it easier for the Briskens, not fall for my boss. "Whatever is happening here ... between us ... I don't want that to cause a disruption in this household. Maybe we need to take—"

He didn't even give me a chance to finish my sentence because he was right in front of me, arms around my lower waist. He lowered his forehead against mine. "You don't understand how much you saying that means to me. That you'd put the girls' wants and needs above your own even though they're not yours."

I swallowed hard, feeling weak with him so near. "Of course. I care about them deeply. I love them."

He took in a deep breath through his nose and then asked me, "Do you love me?"

His question was unexpected, and it caught me by surprise. *Love?* I breathed through the next few seconds, careful with my words. I placed one hand on his chest, flattening the collar of his shirt. Oh, how I wanted to say yes, but I'd said yes before and realized later that it was only a facade. So many people had left me or treated me badly, and though I knew Charles would never be that person, it was still difficult to tell if what I felt was real. It was difficult to trust my own emotions and thoughts because they were all jumbled anyway whenever I was around him. And maybe a big part of me didn't want to jinx this—this epic happiness I'd been feeling simply by being with him.

"We're new, and it's amazing, but all that might not matter if the girls—"

"Sarah wants me to be happy." He smiled. "I told you she was mature beyond her age. And what makes me happy is you, Becky." His eyes shone with an inner glow, a surety of us that I didn't have. "I know we're new. I know this is going super fast. We just had our first date last weekend, but ... I know what this is because I've been here before."

He cupped my cheek, and I felt his touch everywhere.

"I love you, Becky. I love your strength, your kindness, your patience. I know this is love because I wouldn't incorporate you into my life and in the girls' lives if I wasn't sure, and I'm sure. I'm sure of you, of us and ..." He shook his head. "You don't have to say it or feel it right now. I'm okay. One of my best qualities is patience. I'll wait, okay? Until you're ready."

I nodded, feeling too close to tears. I closed the gap and kissed him. I had no words. I wasn't ready to proclaim that I loved him even though I knew in my heart and in my gut that I probably did.

I pulled back, not wanting to be caught in the act again by the children. "Now, you have to tell Mary."

He nodded. "Yeah." His sigh was deep, and it seemed endless. "Hopefully, she'll take it just as well as Sarah did."

"Well?" I let out a shaky chuckle. "Sarah couldn't even look at me when she walked in."

He tenderly brushed the back of his knuckles against my cheek. "She just needs time. Plus, I'm assuming she's a little embarrassed. She walked in on me mauling your face." He felt playful enough to add a smirk.

I pressed one heavy hand against his chest, feeling like I was about to let him maul me again if I wasn't careful.

"Well, no more mauling until we have all of this out in the open, okay?"

His gaze turned serious, sweet, and full of so much love that I felt weak in the knees. "Sounds good."

—————

Dinner could be summed up in one word—*uncomfortable*. Brad had ditched us, thankfully. I didn't know if Charles had talked to him, maybe asking him to leave so we could talk to the girls by ourselves. All I knew was, one minute, Brad had been excited for my chicken potpie, and the next, he was saying his good-byes with an evident frown on his face.

The only person who spoke during dinner was Mary. It was like she was having a one-way conversation with herself, talking about her stuffed animals and school and the teacher who loved her, though she believed all her teachers loved her.

Sarah only moved food around the plate, her head down, her eyes never meeting mine.

My stomach churned with anxiety.

"After dinner, we're going out for ice cream," Charles announced cheerily, breaking up Mary's story about the worm on the playground that the kids had bullied. Yes, they'd bullied a worm.

Immediately, Mary's smile slipped, and she dropped her fork. "Last time we went out for ice cream, you told us Nana was leaving." Her sparkling blue eyes flipped to mine. "Are you leaving, Becky?"

A nervous laugh escaped my lips, and I met Charles's eyes. "I hope not."

"No. Becky is staying," he said firmly, holding a secret smile that had my stomach lurching forward.

Sarah's gaze flicked upward, her face unreadable, and immediately, my stomach dropped for a different reason now.

After dinner, I stood, ready to clean up. Sarah picked up all the plates, discarded the uneaten food into the garbage, and handed me the plates, so I could rinse them and place them in the dishwasher. Mary wiped down the table with the dishcloth while Charles put the leftovers in the fridge.

I loved these moments—the togetherness, the simplicity of everyday, mundane tasks. I craved them. Craved the normalcy. These small things were what made me feel like we were all a family.

I had never wanted acceptance as much as I did right now. I'd never belonged anywhere, bouncing from foster family to foster family, but I wanted to belong here. I wanted them to claim me and love me because I already loved them—Mary, Sarah, and inevitably, Charles.

Charles

Sweat beads pebbled the back of my neck, and I adjusted my T-shirt to get myself to cool down. Even though I was eating rocky road ice cream on a cone, I sat utterly still in our booth, sweating profusely.

Thank God for Mary because there wasn't a silent beat between us, therefore making it seem like it was a normal day out for ice cream, though I had to talk about serious topics. But in essence, Mary was right. Now, she was going to think I was always going to take them out for ice cream to reveal shocking revelations.

Becky's eyes focused on her bowl of cookies and cream, and she slipped the spoon in her mouth. It was her favorite flavor next to mint chocolate chip.

Every day, I filed away little tidbits on her favorite things in a Rolodex in my head. She preferred her coffee black and her chicken parm lightly coated, not fully breaded. Her absolute favorite movie was *You've Got Mail*.

She was a hopeless romantic at heart even though she didn't believe she deserved or would receive that romance in her life, but I was about to change all of that. I'd use everything in my arsenal to romance her because I was determined to give her everything she desired and wished for, just like I did for the rest of my family.

Now, I only needed them on board with the plan.

After finishing the last of my treat, I straightened and awkwardly smiled at my children. "So ... girls ..." I cleared my throat, smiling so hard that my cheeks hurt.

Mary tilted her head and double-blinked at me. "Uh-oh. Now comes the bad news, doesn't it, Daddy?"

Sarah and Becky laughed, and the sound was music to my ears because it loosened some of the tension in my shoulders.

"No bad news. Not this time." I blew out a breath. "So, you know that Daddy's never really ..." I fumbled with my fingers, my gaze teetering from the table to my children and back again. "What I'm trying to say is that in the past, I've been too busy to ..." Which was a lie. I was still busy, but now, I'd found someone I wanted to make more time for. I scratched at my temple. "What I'm really trying to say is that recent events have happened where ..."

My gaze flicked up to Becky, but she bit her bottom lip and tore her stare away from me, equally nervous. This was unlike me. I never fumbled with words. I was concise and articulate when I was in front of the boardroom or on a pedestal at the Hilton at our annual convention, but today, I was at a loss. But I needed the words out, so I could move on with my life, make myself happy for once.

"Recent events have happened between Becky and me and ..." I choked, stopping mid-sentence. *Damn it.*

Mary chewed at the edge of her spoon, peering up at me with the bluest eyes.

I gazed at Sarah helplessly, and she sighed, saying, "Daddy and Becky are dating now."

Mary scrunched her nose, and I wondered if she didn't agree or didn't know what that meant.

"Daddy and Becky are a couple now," Sarah added. "Like Janice and Uncle Mason."

It took a few seconds, but as soon as Mary registered her sister's words, she screamed and jumped from her chair. She clapped her hands and ran to me, hugging my middle. "Yay, Daddy! I'm so happy." Then, she jumped into Becky's lap, wrapping her arms around Becky's neck, and kissed her tenderly on the cheek. "Now, I won't be the only kid without a mom on Muffins for Moms day."

"Oh, honey." Becky pulled Mary flush against her, and my heart hurt.

Even though I gave them everything they possibly needed and wanted and I took time to be with them at school events, there were things I could never give them, just by being me. Year after year, I was the only dad at Muffins for Moms with Mary. Patty had always gone with me, and I thought by us both being there, she'd get two for the price of one, but it was never the same.

Mary pulled back and cupped Becky's cheeks in her small hands. "I'm so happy." She spread her arms wide, beckoning me forward. "Bubble of love, Daddy."

I stood and moved over to them, grinning.

"You too, Sarah." Mary waved her hands, getting Sarah to stand from her chair.

I encased the four of us in our new little bubble, feeling my heart expand to an immeasurable size.

Sarah peered up at me, and for the first time since we'd sat down, a genuine smile surfaced on her face. "I'm so happy for you, Daddy." Then, she sidled up next to Becky. "Happy for all of us."

And so was I.

So. Damn. Happy.

CHAPTER 36

Becky

"That's why Daddy doesn't want us in the bathroom," Mary said from the back of the car as I drove them to school.

I laughed. The things these girls had witnessed, seen, and heard, just by being brought up by three men.

"Mary, just stop talking about Daddy's private parts," Sarah groaned.

I could see Mary's pouty face from the rearview mirror.

"That's why I was late. I had to wait for Daddy to finish taking a shower."

"Mary, you have your own bathroom," Sarah said.

"But there was a spider in there the other day," she whined.

I laughed.

Mary had screamed so hard that I thought she'd slipped, fallen, and broken a bone. I'd never, ever experienced such fear for a child before. This was all so new to me, and my imagination was taking me for a ride.

After the incident, I'd disinfected and cleaned her bathroom, to the point where you could basically eat off the floor, but the girl was traumatized. She wouldn't be using her bathroom again anytime soon.

Mary flipped to other topics. At times, she'd go into full-on question mode, asking me about things I didn't want to talk about—mainly about me and her father.

"You think you'll get married soon?" Mary asked.

"Stop with your questions, Mary. You can't be asking those types of things," Sarah responded.

"But I wanna know when I can start calling her mom. Is she still our babysitter? What do I tell my friends?"

"You tell them it's none of their business."

Thank goodness for Sarah because I didn't have to answer the difficult questions.

I pulled into the school parking lot, noting the bustling parents trying to get their kids off to school. Usually, I'd drive through the drop-off line, but this time, I had to go down to submit Mary's preschool field trip form, so she could go to the pumpkin patch today.

When I stepped out of the car, two small hands filled mine—Sarah on my right side, Mary to my left—and we crossed the parking lot as a threesome. My heart filled so high that I thought it'd spill over.

I swung their hands between us as we entered the building. Before I had the chance to tell them to have a great day, tiny arms wrapped around my waist, and a body crushed into my side.

"Thanks, Becky. See you later," Mary said, squeezing me tight before skipping down the hall to her classroom.

Sarah side-hugged me before scurrying off. I watched her walk leisurely down the hall, her strides long and confident and with purpose. And then I smiled.

This was my life now.

My mornings were filled with breakfast with the family,

whom I'd grown to love, and my nights were filled with me being in Charles's arms. Some days, I had to pinch myself to make sure it was all real.

I entered the office, and my high suddenly deflated. Carol, the principal, was at the front desk, talking to her office assistant. Maybe it was childish, but I still couldn't get over how she'd dealt with the whole bullying situation with Sarah and that other little girl. I was sure Charles had taken care of it with the parents, but I was still sour about it.

When Carol's eyes met mine, I focused on the task at hand and placed the signed permission slip on top of the table. I wasn't going to get into it with this woman today and ruin my mood.

I turned my attention to the secretary. "I'm just dropping this off for Mary Brisken. It's her permission slip for the pumpkin patch. It's late, so I wanted to turn it in directly to ensure that she can go today." I offered a small smile.

"She'll be able to go. Thanks for dropping it off." Carol smiled.

I tipped my chin in farewell. I was about to turn and face the door when she approached.

"About the other day," Carol began, "I'm sorry. I didn't want to escalate the situation and have both girls in the room. I know that the Brisken girls have been through a lot, but that doesn't mean that Sarah's actions should be overlooked."

My whole body tensed. "Did I ever say that?" My voice came out low, barely controlled.

Carol raised her hands, already on the defense. "I'm not saying you said that."

"If you know Sarah, you'd know she wouldn't do something unless she was provoked. I'm not excusing her either, but that other girl should have held some sort of responsibility in the situation."

Carol's face softened. "I know. What I wanted to say is that I'm sorry how it came across. Jennifer and her parents have been talked to. Sarah and Mary are great girls. It was very out of the ordinary, what happened, and I admit that I could've handled it in a calmer and more collective way. For that, I apologize."

A low breath escaped my lips. I was being stubborn, overly emotional maybe because of my strong feelings for Sarah. Maybe I needed to forgive and forget.

"Thank you," I said. "I'm sorry too. For maybe getting a little too heated that day."

She blinked, and her smile widened. "No need to apologize. I'm just glad the Briskens have another person in their lives who will always be in their corner."

I smiled, giving a nod of acknowledgment, and then made my way back to the car. I had a list of things to do—mostly laundry and groceries. But I wanted those menial tasks done before tonight because we were having a Harry Potter marathon.

The sun was shining brightly overhead, and I inhaled the crisp fall air. I stepped into the car, mentally making a note, prioritizing where I needed to go first. *Post office. Drugstore. Grocery store.*

After I placed my key into the ignition, I screamed. My blood thrashed in my ears, and my whole body went on high alert, tensing and quivering and heating.

I see you live the cushy life now, huh? Does that mean you don't need me?

I shoved the door open, ripping the Post-it Note from the dash. Outside, I searched the vicinity, looking past the cars, the school, doing a three-sixty to find him—Paul.

I knew he was here. Around this school, lurking in the shadows because I couldn't see him anywhere. The only ones walking around were a few women congregated by their cars.

I hopped in the car and circled the school three times, but he was nowhere to be found, so I did what I knew I had to do to keep my girls safe—I drove to Brisken Printing Corporation.

I knew they'd be fine at the school. They had a security system and a guard on the premises and adults accompanying them to the pumpkin patch. They would not allow the girls to leave without a signed confirmation.

All these thoughts played in my mind as I tried not to panic but think straight. But the shock was too great. *How the hell did he find me?* I'd been so careful. And even though I thought I'd seen Paul on the street that one day, this was different. He knew where the girls went to school. He knew my car. He knew where we lived.

This was a nightmare. My literal nightmare come to life.

When I pulled into the parking garage, my brakes squealed to a stop. My feet could not move fast enough out of the car, into the high-rise, and toward the security desk, where I was stopped by a turnstile.

Shit, I didn't have a badge to swipe.

I told one of the guards, "Hi, I'm Becky Summers, Charles Brisken's children's nanny. I need to see Charles."

The stocky over-six-foot male with the burly beard towered over me. "Do you have an appointment?"

My arms crossed over my chest, and I peered up at him, straight on, unblinking and agitated. "I don't, but it's an emergency."

Before he tried to deny me entry again, I plucked out

my phone from my purse and called Charles.

He picked up on the second ring. "Hey, Becky."

"Charles, I'm down here at security, but they won't let me up." I tried to keep the panic out, but I couldn't.

There was a note of worry in his voice. "I'll come get you."

And then he hung up.

"He's coming to get me."

The security guard's tough-looking demeanor wavered. Minutes later, Charles was down at the security desk.

He swiped his card to let me pass through the turnstile. Then, he turned to the stocky male. "Becky Summers. She gets a permanent all-access pass. Make sure she has it before she leaves today."

Charles surprised me by taking my hand and leading us toward the elevators.

A few bystanders paused to gawk at us. If there was any doubt that we were together, it was squashed by Charles's proximity to me.

We entered the far elevators, where it was less busy.

As soon as the doors shut, his face clouded with concern. "What brings you to the office?"

I trembled with unrelenting fear and placed a heavy hand on his chest. "Charles. I ..." Sheer black fright swept through me, clouding my vision, swallowing up my words. My gaze dropped to the ground as I visibly shook. "I'm not here for a friendly visit."

Both hands framed my shoulders, and Charles ducked to get in my line of sight. Tense lines of anxiety formed on his features.

Icy fear twisted around my heart, and my face crumpled.

I swallowed hard. "He's found me. Paul has found me."

CHAPTER 37

CHARLES

Becky paced the room while I stayed utterly still.

How the hell did he find her? What does this guy do for a living that he had the means to come find her?

I'd tried to search for this guy, and I'd hired the private investigator, but without knowing a lot about him, and with so many searches of Paul Clark coming up, there was no way to pinpoint whether I had the right guy.

"Where's the note?" I shot out.

She plucked a three-by-three-inch yellow Post-it Note out of her purse.

My body tensed when I read the words. I had the sudden urge to punch something. Crushing it in my hand wasn't enough. This man had to be found.

"I need you to find him." She ran both hands through her hair and pulled at the ends. She shook her head back and forth. "Ignore everything I said before. All of it. Find him." Her voice trembled. "Put a restraining order on him. I don't care. Keep him away from the girls, from you, from your life here. Once I know you're all safe, I'll go."

"You're not going anywhere," I said, my voice firm.

When she dropped her face into her hands, I went to her and brought her into me, needing to comfort her and feel her—alive, heart beating, in my arms—as much as she needed comfort from me. I hated that she was feeling this way. Hated that I was helpless to do anything about it.

"You're shaking." I rested my chin against the top of her head and tightened my arms around her, whispering into her hair, "He's never going to hurt you again."

"I don't care about me," she said softly, her voice cracking with heartbreak. "It's the girls I'm worried about. He'll use me working for you as leverage. He knows you have money. What I need to do is leave. I need to go and stay far away from—"

I didn't let her get the next words out because I pulled back and gripped her chin to force her to look at me. "You're not going anywhere." My voice was strong with conviction. "Especially because you're scared. I swear to you, I will never let anything happen to you or my girls. I swear it."

Her face crumpled. "You don't know what this guy is capable of."

I read the fear and anxiety in the span of green staring up at me, and it gutted me. I tilted her chin further up. "Do you know who I am?" I said with a sly smirk, trying to break the sullen look in her eye. "Do you know what I'm capable of?"

"Charles ..." She wasn't convinced.

I cupped her face, brushing my thumb tenderly down her cheek. "I'm Superman, don't you know? I can lead a whole company even though the world is falling apart around me." Wasn't it the truth though? I'd still had to show a brave face when Natalie died, showing up to work every day. "Above that, I'm a man raising two girls. Girls who have turned out pretty all right by my definition."

"They're great." A small smile surfaced, and I took it as an opportunity to kiss her.

"They're more than great. They're perfect."

She blew out one shallow breath. "I'm scared."

"Do you trust me?"

She nodded.

"Then, trust me when I say, I will protect you and my girls till the very end."

She let out a long sigh and buried her head into my chest.

I rubbed a hand along her back. "First things first. I need more information on Paul and anything you have on him, so we can identify him and track him down."

"Okay," she said, her voice shaky.

After I took all of Paul's information down, I canceled all my meetings, called the school and my security team, and led Becky to the conference room, where we had lunch as I made plans to protect her and my family.

Action was key. I could freak out, worry about the future, about the unknown, but nothing had happened, and there was not going to be a *yet* at the end of that sentence.

Her mind was filled with anxiety. It was evident in the little crease between her brows and the frown heavy on her face.

"I've hired a private investigator, and he'll find out where this guy is."

She nodded as she took another bite of her sandwich, her eyes focused on the table. "I hate this. Absolutely hate this."

I placed my hand on hers on the table.

"Why didn't I think? How could I have possibly led him here?"

"It's not your fault," I assured her, as I had only minutes before.

"How can it not be? If it wasn't for me, he wouldn't be here. I wouldn't have led him to the girls." She placed her sandwich down, and her gaze traveled past my shoulder. "I wish I'd never come here." Her voice was a breathless whisper, but it gutted me.

"Don't say that." In the next second, I reached for her hand, pulling her into my lap. "I don't want to think of my life without you in it." I tenderly kissed her forehead. "Everything is going to be fine. I've already contacted the school and my private investigator again today. I've already informed my security team to go to the house and make sure it's secure. Tomorrow, you'll have an escort to and from the school. It will be fine."

She sighed into me, not truly believing—I could tell. Either way, I held her tighter, knowing there was no way in hell I'd ever let her go.

Becky

The cool breeze prickled my skin as I walked to my car from Brisken Printing Corporation.

I'd spent the last few hours with Charles trying to convince me that everything was gonna be okay and me delving into my past, giving out as much information as I could about Paul so Charles could find him.

But as I pushed the key in the ignition and turned the engine on, anxiety deep inside of me lit up like a ball of fire ready to explode. I started to hyperventilate, so I took a moment and rested my head against the steering wheel, taking in deep, long breaths.

Everything will be okay, right?

In a matter of minutes, security would be at our house, surveying the area to make sure it was secure. Charles would have someone meet me at the school today to accompany me and the girls home. And tomorrow, I'd have an entourage of two security guards who would take us to and from school until Paul was found.

Everything will be okay.

As I drove to the school, flashbacks of everything that Paul had put me through bombarded my mind, bringing up the immense pain that came with that relationship.

As hard as I'd tried to erase the memories from my mind, I couldn't.

All that occupied my thoughts was the violence, the verbal abuse, all the things that I didn't want for my newfound family.

I drove to the school in a rush, needing to get to them, needing to bring them home safely. Typically, I would have stayed in the car and gone through the carpool line, but today, I didn't. I placed the car in park, surveyed my surroundings, and rushed to the front doors, waiting for the bell to ring to dismiss my girls.

I debated on waiting for the security guard that Charles had hired to meet me here, but I didn't. Anxiety and anxiousness in having the girls safe in my arms won out.

Minutes seemed like hours as I stared at my watch and back at the door again. My foot tapped against the concrete, and I bit anxiously at my pinkie nail.

When will the bell ring?

I waited and waited and waited.

Finally, when the bell rang, I rushed toward the doors,

and when the teacher opened the door, I almost crossed the border to go inside. She raised a hand, as though I were new to the proceedings of dismissal but I wasn't. I was to wait outside, but my anxiousness got the best of me.

Other parents were congregated by the door. My eyes swept over the crowd, teetering between my car, the surrounding areas, and back to the school again. *Could he be here now?*

I watched every single kid leave the building. Minutes felt like years, and I paced a path in front of the door, waiting for Sarah and Mary to emerge. Usually, it was Sarah who would come out first, but she was three minutes late. In about a hot second, I would charge in, not caring about the consequences.

I came closer, telling the teacher on duty, "I'm sorry, but my two girls haven't come out yet. Can I just go grab them? I'm kind of in a hurry."

"I'm sorry. For security reasons, we can't let you inside right now." Her face was apologetic, but it didn't help the unease inside of me.

My mind was playing that negative game again, envisioning worst-case scenarios. Like Paul in the school with my girls.

My heart pumped and thrashed within my chest. Just the thought threatened a heart attack.

I took one step forward, about to cross the line, consequences be damned, when a swoosh of air released from my lungs as Sarah came toward me, smiling. Genevieve, one of her friends, was with her.

After a quick hug of farewell to her friend, Sarah walked toward me. The second she crossed the threshold of the front door, I erased the gap between us and pulled her into my chest. I was sure I was embarrassing her, but I didn't care. I crushed her into me, as though we hadn't seen each other in years, pressing a desperate kiss to the top of her head.

"Becky?" she said, her voice muffled against me. "Are you okay?"

I was shaking. Visibly shaking. But relieved—almost. Because I had one last child to pick up.

I pulled back. "Have you seen Mary?"

"No." She was giving me a look like I'd gone crazy. And maybe I had, but it was for good reason.

I took a step away from her. Both of us glanced toward the door, and I kept a hand on Sarah's backpack for peace of mind.

Five minutes passed. Little girls who looked like Mary exited the building, but Mary was nowhere in sight. I walked up to the teacher again because she was about to shut the doors, but I didn't have my child.

"Did you dismiss the preschoolers?"

Her eyes widened just a tad. "They were dismissed at the south entrance, where the school buses are. They had their field trip at the pumpkin patch."

"Wait. What?" I was already running with Sarah before the teacher got her next words out.

I ran like my life depended on it, arms pumping, legs making long strides. Sarah could barely keep up with me, so I slowed my pace because there was no way I was losing two kids in one day.

The buses were empty, and there was no one in the south entrance. No kids could be seen. When I saw a bus driver, I rushed toward her as she got back on the bus, and before the doors closed, I waved my hands like a lunatic to get her attention.

"Um, hi there," I said to her as she frowned at me from her high seat. "When were the preschoolers dismissed?"

She blinked at me. "Yeah, they were just dismissed at the regular dismissal time."

"What?" I barked.

She reeled back at the sharpness in my tone. "After the buses dropped them off, parents were supposed to pick them up from here. There were a few kids that went inside to go to the main entrance for pickup."

I about-faced and hurried back to the main entrance, gripping Sarah's hand so she stayed with me.

"Becky, where are we going?" Sarah whined, but I could hear the note of concern.

"We have to find Mary. She's probably inside." My voice was frantic.

Even though I knew it wouldn't help the situation to freak out, I couldn't help it. But it couldn't be. She wasn't gone. She wasn't lost. She was inside. Where else could she be?

"Don't worry, Becky. Since she didn't come out, she's in her class for sure, or if not, she's at the main office. We'll find her." Sarah's calm voice was meant to ease the tension in my gut, but it didn't.

I smiled down at her for her benefit. "We will."

I hurried into the school, no longer being guarded by the teacher, and into Mary's classroom, which was empty, and then I charged toward the main office. "Did the preschoolers in Mrs. Cininski's class get dismissed yet?"

Brenda, the school secretary, peered up. "Yes, they were dismissed with all the other kids." She glanced at the clock behind her desk. "That was fifteen minutes ago."

"I can't find Mary Brisken," I said, my hands beginning

to shake as much as my voice. "Would there be a dismissal without someone signing her out?"

She stared at me as though it was a stupid question to ask, and I admitted it was. Because this school's number one priority was safety. Problem was, how did I not have my kid in front of me?

Brenda was trying to be patient with me. "They were dismissed how they usually are—in the carpool line."

I blinked furiously, my nostrils beginning to flare. "She's missing."

Brenda's eyebrows shot to her hairline. "What do you mean?"

"I went to the south entrance, and there are no more cars there, and my kid ... she's missing." *Please, please, please ... please no.*

Brenda picked up the phone and dialed security. "Can you search the area and school for a preschooler, Class 304, blonde hair, blue eyes?" Then, she hung up and dialed the principal's office. "Ms. Klein, we have a situation in the front."

CHAPTER 38

CHARLES

After I had explained the situation to my brothers, my anxiety heightened.

Brad was calmly seated at the long boardroom table while Mason paced the conference room.

"So, he's here. In town?" Mason asked.

"I'm assuming so," I answered. "Who else would've left her the note?"

Brad steepled his fingers by his lips.

"I've called our security team. They're at the house now, and tomorrow, they'll accompany Becky to drop off the girls and during all her errands if she needs to do any."

The security company I'd hired, we also used at Brisken Printing Corporation and at any outside company event or if we needed personal security, which we typically didn't. Normally, we were three grown men who could handle our own business.

"It'll be fine," Brad said, though his calm was receding.

"Fine?" Mason threw up both hands, already giving in to panic and rage. "We got a crazy man on the loose, following around our nanny and stalking our girls' school. I wanna say I told you so, but I won't."

"Don't," I said, not wanting to hear it. My hands went to my hips as I stared outside at the other high-rises in the horizon.

"Did you contact the PI?" Mason asked, pacing a hole in the industrial carpet.

"Yeah. I gave him everything he needed to do a thorough search." Now that I had complete information on this guy, I'm sure something would come up. "I paid an expedited fee, so we should be able to find out about him before today's over."

I needed this guy in jail. Stat.

She wouldn't go into hiding anymore, and she wouldn't feel the compulsion to run away. Whatever this was, whatever was happening now, it had been meant to be. I had been meant to find her and meet her and love her.

Mason dropped to the nearest chair. "How did we get here? What could we have done to prevent this?"

I shook my head. "Nothing."

Because if this asshole wanted to find her, there was nothing I could have done to stop him.

I wanted this confrontation. This would only lead to legal ramifications, where I could keep this guy far away from Becky and the kids, where she wouldn't be scared anymore to do the normal things I knew she loved to do—go biking, go out to a restaurant by herself without watching her back, and take the girls to a park, unafraid of who she might see there.

I reached for my phone and texted my security team to tell me when Kenzo, one of the head guys, arrived at the school. He texted back immediately and was only a few minutes away.

Brad kicked up his feet on the conference table. "They'll be fine. Today, we are securing the house. Tomorrow, they'll roll up at the school with security, like they're famous. Then, we'll find this guy, and we'll have a good talk with him." He ran one hand through his hair. "All will be fine. You guys are freaking out about a note."

I texted Becky next, but she didn't answer.

Kenzo will be there any second, I told myself. *She's probably getting the girls settled in the car, or Mary is keeping her preoccupied with her stories of the pumpkin patch.*

Panicking would not help me right now.

The phone ringing from my back pocket broke up my random thoughts, and I plucked out my cell and answered. "Hey, Becky."

"Charles"—her voice was a garbled sob—"Mary is missing."

Her four words had my heart stopping in my chest.

It was an out-of-body experience, hearing the words but not knowing what to do with them.

I stood utterly still, unmoving, barely breathing.

There were a few other times where I'd had this sort of panic attack, not sure how to react, unable to connect my brain to my body.

For instance, when the doctors had told me that Natalie was dead. When Mason had called me at work, sobbing that my parents had been in an accident. And now ... when Becky told me that my sweet Mary was missing.

"Charles?" She had repeated my name a few times before I responded.

"Mary's missing? Where are you?"

Brad jumped off his chair, and both he and Mason faced me directly, their looks of complete shock most likely mirroring mine.

"I'm at the school. She didn't go out of her normal door because they had a field trip. They dismissed from the south entrance and..." Her sobs heightened.

I was slow to respond, even slower to react. I should have been out of the corporate office and in my car by now.

"Don't move. I'll be there."

"Cops are here. Kenzo just got here. They're searching the vicinity for her."

I hung up the phone and turned to the door, putting my body into action.

"What happened? Mary's missing?" Brad said, the fear in his eyes evident.

"Yeah." I pointed to Mason. "You get in contact with that PI and find out all we need to know about Paul. Tell him we need the info in the next hour. It doesn't matter how much it costs to speed it up."

"I'm going with you," Brad said before I could give him a directive. "You don't need the PI because I will personally find this guy and fuck him up if he has her."

I couldn't even let my mind go there.

I'm coming, baby girl.

We were both out the door in no time.

"Let's go together because I want to drive Becky's car home."

Her nerves had been shot earlier. And so were mine now. Where could she have possibly gone? Warning spasms erupted within me, and it felt as though a hand were wrapped around my throat, preventing any air from getting in my lungs. *Did he have her?*

I gritted my teeth. I didn't want my thoughts to swerve in that direction because it wouldn't do me any good now.

"Give me the keys," Brad said as we both approached my car.

I threw him a look, at him wanting to drive *my* car.

"Charles, you know me. I don't do good sitting still, especially when some son of a bitch has my niece."

"Don't say that. We don't know that right now." *But where else would she be?*

A chill black silence surrounded us, but I didn't have time to argue, so I threw the keys at him, and he caught them midair.

"Plus, instead of thirty, I can get us there in twenty."

"We need to make it there alive to be of any help." All of my muscles tensed beneath my suit.

He didn't say a word, which was so unlike him, as he drove over ninety miles per hour toward the school. Right before we got there, my phone rang again. It was Mason.

"Did you call the PI?" I asked.

"Yeah."

"So, he's here," I said, wanting Mason to confirm what I already knew.

"Charles ..." The way he uttered my name was the same way he'd uttered it when he called me years ago, telling me that our parents had died in an accident.

"What!" I found myself screaming into the phone as all of the muscles in my body tensed.

"Charles ..." His voice shook with full sullen emotion.

"What? Just tell me, Mason."

I couldn't take any more bad news. I'd had enough bad news to last me a lifetime. We all had. Any more would break me.

"Paul's dead."

Impossible.

The ringing in my ears intensified.

"They did a search on him, and he'd died of a self-inflicted gunshot wound."

"How can he be dead?" I breathed. Goose bumps prickled the back of my neck. "Then, who the hell has my Mary?"

It happened in a split second as Brad registered my words. His eyes flipped to mine, but in that nanosecond, he didn't brake fast enough, rear-ending the guy in front of us.

CHAPTER 39

Becky

"We found her backpack." A police officer approached me, handing me Mary's *Little Mermaid* backpack.

I rubbed Sarah's back, who was sobbing beside me as we sat at the bench overlooking the swing set and slides in the back of the school. I'd never seen Sarah shed a tear, even when she fought with her sister, yet now, she was inconsolable.

"Why would she wander off? Do you think someone took her?" Sarah's questions came at me, at the officer, at the teachers and principal, who had all tried to look for Mary. When we couldn't give her the answer she wanted, she burst into tears again.

I rubbed her back and held her close as I glanced up at the officer. He was a taller male with a dust of red hair and sharp blue eyes. "Where did you find it?"

"In the playground."

"But we went there," Sarah cried out. "I would have seen it there for sure."

The officer offered Sarah a small, apologetic smile and

motioned toward me. "We are searching the vicinity, outside of the school perimeter too."

I visibly shook. "Thank you." I wanted to throw up from the shock of everything happening around me. The guilt I felt was overwhelming, and it left me immobile. Ice spread through my stomach, and I shriveled into myself.

Sarah hugged the backpack, the top pressing against her chin. "Mary, please be okay. I promise to never fight with you again. I promise to let you play with my American Girl doll whenever you want. I promise you can sleep in my bed when you're scared."

My eyes became wet with tears. I pulled the bag out of her hands and brought her to my chest, kissing the top of her head. She shuddered against me as Kenzo watched us, only a few steps away.

"Mary will be just fine. She's probably out somewhere, playing with a lost dog." I uttered those words even though I wasn't sure if they were true. I needed them to be true. I needed my Mary to be okay. I needed Paul far, far, far away from the family I'd grown to care for.

I reached for Mary's backpack and dumped all the items onto the concrete, searching her belongings—her pencil case, her folder of assignments, her notebook, her lunch bag stuffed inside. I picked up every piece on the ground, as though something would give me a clue as to where she'd gone but I came up with nothing.

When my phone rang, my heart leaped in my chest. I checked the screen and answered immediately. "Charles?"

His voice was frantic and out of breath. "I'm running toward the school right now. I'm a good eight blocks away."

"Running?" I said, my mind muddled and not computing. "What happened?"

"Brad got into an accident, a fender bender. Either way

... Becky, I have to tell you something. The PI came back with some information."

My hands stilled on the notebook that I had been about to stuff back into the bag.

"Paul is dead."

Dead.

The word just sat there in my mind.

Dead.

Then, it started chugging like a train, loud and clear and deafening ...

Dead, dead, dead ...

Fear knotted my insides.

"What do you mean?" I swallowed the bile that had crept up my throat.

Charles's breath was coming out in chugs as he relayed grimly, "He died two years ago from an apparent suicide."

I wasn't sad, of course. But I wasn't relieved either. I was numb. In shock. And confused. So confused.

But ...

"I don't understand ..." My voice trailed off as other negative thoughts filtered through my head.

If Paul hadn't taken Mary, then who had? At least with Paul, we could put a face to a name; we could track him down.

"Just stay there," Charles ordered. "Don't move. I'll be there soon." And then he hung up.

I frantically searching the front pockets of Mary's backpack when my fingers found a yellow Post-it Note. My whole body prickled when I read the words.

My eyes focused on Kenzo talking to a police officer who had approached, and then my attention fixed on the paper within my fingertips.

I have exactly what you are looking for.

The number on the Post-it pulsed on the paper, causing my adrenaline to spike. I jumped to a standing position, thinking of my next actions.

If I handed this newfound information to the authorities, they'd take me out of the picture. But I had this inner need to find her myself. To get to Mary.

I waved at Kenzo, getting his attention. "I'm going to the washroom, but I'll be right back. Can you keep an eye on Sarah?"

After he nodded, I kissed the top of her forehead. "Stay right here. I'll be back." *With your sister. I promise.*

When I was a good distance away, I dialed the number on the Post-it Note.

"Hello?" I said, my voice small and desperate.

"Hello, Becky." Her tone was low and gravelly, a direct consequence of excessive smoking. I could almost smell the stench of cigarettes wafting from her mouth. "Long time no talk, honey."

The voice that greeted me was familiar. And female.

It had been a long time but apparently not long enough.

I was more confused now than when Charles had told me Paul was dead.

My voice croaked out, "Mom?"

Charles

I was running as though my life depended on it—because it did. My children were my life. Sweat coated my neck and my back through my suit, but I didn't let it deter me as my arms pumped harder and faster.

The sound of a car horn honking behind me had me turning. I only stopped when I realized it was Brad.

"Get in."

I hopped in the car and chucked my suit jacket to the back. "What happened?" I asked, trying to take a full breath into my lungs.

"I told the lady we couldn't find my niece, told her we'd pay for all damages and insurance wouldn't have to get involved. I gave her my number." His face was stoic and still.

On any other day, Brad giving a woman his number would be a family joke. Not today. No jokes today.

No, we are going to fucking find my daughter, and then we're all going to laugh about it later, I told myself to try to keep calm. I reminded myself that today was going to have a good outcome.

We are going to find her. Everything is going to be okay. I repeated the words in my head over and over again.

"Nothing had better have happened to her," he ground out.

"Don't go there, Brad," I warned him. I didn't need his panic spouting out scenarios. "If Paul's dead, there's hope to believe there is a reasonable explanation for all of this," I said.

But he kept going, "Life is a shitty, shitty game. We've been dealt bad hand after bad hand. I'm done with this shit, man. If someone hurt my baby, I'm going to jail. Guaranteed."

I pushed his words out and cleared my head. I needed all my faculties to make sure this thing came to an end and that Mary was found safe and sound. We double-parked in the emergency lane, jumped out of the car, and ran into the school. In the main office, my eyes connected with Sarah's, and my whole body relaxed. Immediately, I dropped to the ground and pulled her into my arms, breathing her in, holding her close.

Tears fell down her face as her small arms wrapped around my waist.

"Did you find her?" I asked, pulling back to swipe the tears that had fallen down her cheeks.

She shook her head. "No, Daddy." She sobbed uncontrollably.

I gulped. "Where's Becky?"

"She told me to stay here with Kenzo."

A prickle of goose bumps trailed up my arm. *What? Where the hell did she go?*

When I released Sarah, Brad lifted her in his arms, her legs dangling above the ground. He kissed her cheek over and over again. "I'm homeschooling you from now on," he growled, his normal vibrancy gone.

I stood at full height, turning my attention to Kenzo. "You let her leave?"

"She said she was going to the washroom and didn't come back."

Two more officers approached me, followed by the principal right behind them.

I didn't want to talk to any of them right now. I wanted to take things into my own hands. I needed to find Becky and Mary.

A tall male officer with light-brownish hair came closer. "Mr. Brisken, hello. We have a few questions, and we will brief you on our search efforts."

"One second." I turned the other way, not wanting to be rude but needing to speak to Becky. Something wasn't right.

Why would she just leave? And without Sarah?

I plucked my phone from my back pocket and called her. It kept ringing and ringing. The longer it rang, the more my lungs constricted. For the first time in a long time, I couldn't get the next breath in my lungs.

When I called a second time, she finally picked up.

"Where are you?" I asked, beyond panicked.

"I'm going to get Mary." She sounded out of breath as her sobs escalated, harder, faster.

I strained my ears to hear her.

"Who has her?" Because at this point, with the way Becky sounded out of her mind, I knew it was a *who* and that she wasn't just simply looking somewhere.

"My mother has her, Charles. My mom has Mary."

The hairs on the back of my neck rose.

Her mom? I was so shocked that I couldn't even say the words aloud.

I shook my head, flipped around, and locked eyes with Brad and Sarah. They were staring back at me expectantly.

I didn't get a chance to ask my next question.

There was determination and anger and fear in Becky's voice. "I promise I'll get her back, Charles. If that's the last thing I do."

And then the line went dead.

CHAPTER 40

Becky

All my mother wanted was money. All she ever needed was money. It was her motivation. What drove her. It wasn't love. There was no love in her heart.

If I'd been old enough to work, only then, maybe ... just maybe, she would have kept me. Growing up, I'd only been a burden to her, a drain to her penniless situation, so she gave me up. It didn't help that she'd been in and out of jail for petty crimes. She'd never fought to keep me, looked to find me—until now, and I knew why.

While I knew my mom to be a cunning, conniving person, she wasn't violent. Not to me anyway. She could've changed in all her years, I wouldn't know, but I thought—at least, I hoped and prayed with all my heart—that even though she had Mary, she wouldn't hurt her. And I definitely knew she wouldn't keep her. But what I didn't know was whether she had a partner or if she was working alone. And if she had a partner, then all bets were off. I had no idea what I was going headlong into.

I swiped at my cheeks, driving faster toward a destination she had texted me. Guilt plagued my insides. If I hadn't come here to nanny for the Briskens, Mary would be at home, safe in Charles's arms.

The realization that I'd put them—an innocent family—in this situation had me shaking uncontrollably.

Please. Please. Please let Mary be okay.

I rubbed at my brow, biting my lip as I pulled into the parking lot. Nothing would calm my nerves. I couldn't count anything out, not when it came to Mary's safety. Desperation made people do stupid things. I should know. I'd lived half my existence watching my mother wreck her life into pieces.

There was only one car in the parking lot of the high school, and before I knew it, I was gunning toward the vehicle, not sure of what awaited me.

Automatically, I took the make and model of the car, and when I slowed to approach, I memorized the license plate. Then, she stepped out of the car, and I swallowed hard as my breaths came out in shallow puffs. It was her, my mother. She looked different now. Her hair was dyed a dark brown, her white roots showing like she'd been too lazy to redo it—or more likely, she couldn't afford it. Her green eyes—the one thing I'd inherited from her that I didn't hate—met my gaze with a coolness that chilled me to the bone.

My eyes flickered from her to the car, searching for my girl and any sign that she was in there. I was about to jump my mother if she didn't tell me when, suddenly, sweet Mary waved at me from inside the car, her face pushing up against the window in the backseat, her smile bright and shining like the sun, as though it were a perfect day.

I couldn't even describe what it felt like, seeing her in that moment. Like my world had shattered and come back together in one swift second.

"Mary ..." My word whooshed out in one big rush.

I waved at her and approached slowly, assessing the situation to see if my mother had a gun on her. She'd carried firearms before, and I knew better than to think that she wouldn't have one on her now.

As though she could read my mind, my mother tipped her chin down and nodded. I followed her gaze to see a bulge in the front pocket of her worn jeans. My whole world bottomed out because, now, she had leverage.

Then, she nodded toward the car. "Get in, Becky." Her voice was cheery, which didn't match this disconnected look in her eye.

I debated on what I should do, but Mary was in the car.

"What do you want?" I snapped, slowly heading for the car.

I'd never felt so helpless. Living in foster care didn't hold a candle to how helpless I felt in this moment. There was nothing I could do. There was only one choice I could make. If I wanted to keep Mary safe, I had to go with her.

"I'll tell you once you get in the car," she snapped, fake cheer all gone.

I shivered as I opened the backseat door of the car, and once inside, I pulled Mary into my lap. I crushed her into me, and she giggled as if she didn't have a clue that everyone who loved her was searching the city. Her laughter was rich, a glorious sound, the best sound, like the symphony playing at the opera house, like the church bell ringing right before mass.

My lips pressed to the softness of her hair, and I shuddered against her, relief washing over me. Not full, total relief, but a fraction of it. I was with her, my Mary, my girl.

Because she is mine, and I'm never letting her out of my sight again.

"You missed me. I can tell." She laughed, completely oblivious.

Tears outlined my eyes as I held her close. I didn't want to show fear, to show relief that she was safe, to show her the desperation I felt, the need to get her away from here. I tried to hide that anything was wrong. I wanted to shield her from it all.

But she knew because Mary pulled back, and her eyebrows scrunched together. "What's wrong?"

I cupped her cheek. "Nothing, baby girl."

The sweet smile was back on her face. "Your mama got me ice cream."

I nodded, securing her in, buckling her seat belt. "That's great, baby girl."

Mary told me about her day, rambling on as though nothing was wrong. She told me she had left the little pumpkin that she got from the pumpkin patch on her desk at the school.

It was as if this were a regular day, as though we were on our way home and she was recounting the day's events, but this could not have been more different.

Kate, my mother, drove, to who knows where.

While we drove, I scrambled to come up with a plan to get Mary as far away as possible from this situation. When I took out my phone, Kate stepped on her brakes so fast that Mary and I jerked forward.

"No phones," she barked out.

Mary's eyes widened, and I patted her knee. "I'm not calling anyone. I'm going to play a show for Mary, so she doesn't have to listen to any adult conversations."

My mother eyed me for a second, and I took out my AirPods from my bag. "Mary, do you want to watch *Peppa Pig* or *Sofia the First*?"

"*Sofia!*" she exclaimed, throwing her little arms in the air.

I pushed the earbuds in her ears and played a YouTube video of one of her favorite shows.

When Kate faced the road and continued to drive and I knew that Mary was occupied, I finally spoke, "How much do you need this time?"

Her laugh was cynical. "How do you know that I just didn't want to see you?"

My laugh was more cynical than hers. "See me? When have you ever in my whole life wanted to see me just because?" My jaw locked. Anger clouded my vision, and I spat out my next words, "Just tell me why you're doing this."

The car turned silent, so silent that I could hear Mary's show playing on my phone.

"There are some people I owe money to, Becky. And they're not nice people." Her voice had that manipulative quality to it, like she knew she could make me feel for her.

But I couldn't feel anything but contempt for her. I'd lost all compassion for my mother long ago. And I didn't care what she did to me, but I wasn't going to let the people I cared about be collateral damage.

I wasn't going to let this woman use an innocent child as leverage to get what she wanted. This woman had to go to jail, and I swore she would if it was the last thing I did on this earth. I needed her locked up, so she couldn't hurt the people around me any longer. Once I had Mary safe, I'd lead the cops to her, find authorities to take her. She couldn't get far. I had her license plate memorized by now.

"How much?" I repeated, working hard to keep the anger out of my voice.

She was silent for a beat. "Ten. Ten thousand to get me back on my feet."

I released a long, jagged sigh.

"It's only money, Becky." She rolled her eyes. "And looking at the Briskens, it looks like this would be nothing for them."

A sudden reality hit me that this had been my life with this woman. Each and every time she had needed money, she'd come to me. And she clearly knew the Briskens had the means. Not like I was surprised. But still, my fear only heightened at this new reality—that she'd gone to a great extent to research them. That only meant that her desperation ran deep.

Now that she had connected the two, she would always use me as leverage against them. If there was a bounty on my head, Charles would pay whatever it was to keep me safe. I knew that much.

I swallowed down the bile that had crept up my throat. "Let Mary go, and I'll get you what you need." *And get you in jail.*

She laughed again as she pulled off the highway. "Do you think I'm stupid, Becky? You know your mother better than that."

I gritted my teeth. *How dare she!* My blood was beginning to boil. "There are cops swarming the school. Mary's father has a whole security team scouring the vicinity. There's no way this will end well, Kate, so just let her go."

She shook her head, slow and patient. "That's not going to happen, and you know that."

I did know that. I knew how she was, how greed drove her, but still ... I had to try. There was no way I was going to allow her to get away with this. If anything, she'd come back again. I knew that much. She'd use the Briskens as her personal ATM, and I wouldn't allow that.

She pulled in front of a run-down house. It was as if we

had stepped into a different world altogether—boarded-up houses, unkempt lawns, bars on windows of the surrounding residences.

The phone ringing had me glancing up. Kate reached over and ripped the phone from Mary's hand with such force that Mary cowered into me, her face flipping to a state of shock.

"Helloooo," Kate cooed. "Hi, Charles."

I felt disgusted with her. Her voice, her motives, her character. She knew who these men were. She knew that Charles was Mary's father.

My stomach dropped, and I surveyed my area again. She hadn't blindfolded me. If only I could talk to him and tell him where we were, but a bigger part of me knew that he was already tracking my phone.

"So, we can make this really easy. I'll tell you the location where you can pick up Becky and Mary, but first things first. I need you to drop a pickup fee. No cops. No funny business. I'll text you the information once we get settled."

I gaped at her from the backseat. She wasn't this dumb. Of course there would be cops. Kate would be in jail, no doubt, before her hands touched the green.

"They're fine," she said into the phone, like she was talking about her own children and this was just another day. "I told you, I'll text you where to drop the money."

She wasn't thinking clearly. But I knew my mother wasn't the smartest. With her, the execution was the hardest; finishing anything was not her strong suit. Maybe she'd conjured this crazy plan in her head and researched how to get to this point, but she'd never take this to the end.

Confidence filled my shoulders because I could do this.

I broke up my plan in steps.

First step. Get Mary out of this situation.

Then, call the authorities and give them all the information to catch this woman.

I strained my ears to hear Charles's voice on the other line, but I could barely hear him.

"No cops," she repeated. "No crazy shit or else ..." Her voice lowered. "You don't want me to finish that sentence." She extended the phone to me. "He wants to talk to the girl."

"Mary. Her name is Mary." I seethed.

The fury I felt toward this woman almost choked me. My mood veered sharply to anger. I couldn't believe she had put Mary in this danger. I breathed through the next seconds, and that few moments only solidified my resolve to put this woman in jail.

When Mary placed the phone on her ear, her voice quivered, her tone changing, most likely because she'd overheard the conversation. "Daddy?" Hearing her father's voice had her smiling. "I'm okay, Daddy. Yeah, Miss Kate and I had ice cream." Her voice lowered. "Yeah, we're in the car."

I grabbed the phone before Mary could give away more information, causing my mother's evil to come out in full force.

I spoke desperately into the phone, "Charles, we'll call you. I'll get Mary back to you. I promise."

I hung up and then threw the phone in my purse. It was his phone, the phone he'd given me. There was no doubt he was tracking it right now. And to my advantage, I knew that wasn't on the forefront of Kate's mind. If she were smart, she would have confiscated our phone already.

"Out," Kate said, opening the back door of the car so I could slide out.

Mary followed. As soon as her eyes met my mother's

and the surrounding area, she hugged my center. "I don't feel safe," Mary whimpered.

My heart broke in that instant because my job was to ultimately make her feel safe, to make her feel loved and happy, and I was failing on every level.

I'd brought this upon her. I'd brought this fear and heartache upon this family that had only taken me in. I swallowed hard, holding my chin higher. The guilt would cripple me if I let it, but I couldn't let that happen right now, so I forced that guilt to amplify the anger within me.

I lifted Mary up in my arms, and her legs wrapped around my waist. "You'll be fine." Then, a thought pushed through, a breadcrumb of a plan that would get Mary to safety.

I walked behind Kate as we ascended the creaky wooden steps to what looked like an abandoned house.

I spoke so softly against Mary's cheek, so Kate wouldn't hear, "I'm going to tell you a secret. Do you remember where I used to hide when I got scared?"

Mary lifted her eyes to mine and nodded. "Under the bed," she whispered.

I nodded. "When we go inside and when I give you a signal, I want you to go there. Can you do that for me? And if there isn't a bed, I want you to play the best game of hide-and-go-seek there is. I want you to imagine that at the end of the game, there is a trip to the toy store, and you can get whatever you want to get."

She shivered against me. "But why?"

"Just do it, Mary," I whispered. "And I know Daddy will find you. I'll wink at you, okay? That's our signal for you to hide."

When we walked up the stairs and into the house, her face crumpled. "But I'm scared."

My mother's back was toward us. I could have made a run for it with Mary, but I couldn't risk it. I wouldn't be able to outrun a bullet, and I wouldn't put Mary in danger if I couldn't guarantee her safety.

My voice stayed at a whisper. "Don't be. You're brave. When you're scared, you hide. Somewhere the monsters can't get you."

She didn't seem convinced, so I held her gaze and prayed to the heavens that she would listen and go with the plan.

"Just do it, okay, Mary? For me. For Daddy." *For yourself.*

When she finally nodded, I kissed her cheek.

Thank you. Thank you. Thank you.

"You're so brave, my sweet Mary."

The house was small, dusty, and smelled like mildew. From the front door, I could see the living room and outdated, disgusting kitchen. The lights in the house were dim, and the one light in the kitchen flickered, giving the ambience of a horror movie.

The only furniture in the house was a floral old couch, and the color had faded over the years. A kitchen table was at the far end of the room with a few folding chairs.

I surveyed the room, noting where all the exits were.

I'd risk myself to ensure Mary's safety. I didn't know what was going to go down today, but I knew that much.

"Sit down, but don't get too comfortable." She pulled out the gun and waved it in our direction.

I pushed Mary's head into my shoulder, trying to shield her from what was happening.

"I'm thinking of the closest location that he can drop off the cash."

I almost balked. You'd think she'd planned and plotted

all this out, but she hadn't, which only meant that she was reckless.

When I stood there, unmoving, she jerked the gun straight at me. "I said, sit down."

I sat on the couch, securing Mary in my lap as I discreetly took in my surroundings. I didn't want to ask questions on how she'd ended up in here or if she'd lived here all her life. I'd grown up in Tennessee and moved to Florida, and now, we were here, in Illinois. I doubted her existence here in this state was a coincidence.

The whole area, kitchen and living room, was one big square. You could see everything by standing in the middle of the room. I found the closest exits to be the back door by the kitchen and the front, where we'd just walked in.

"I'm renting this place. It's an Airbnb." Her voice was light, almost friendly.

I could almost pretend that we were having a cordial conversation if she didn't have a gun in her hand.

I nodded vaguely. It was as though she could read my thoughts through the dimly lit room.

She went to the fridge and grabbed a water. She opened it up and chugged it down without offering us any. "So, what have you been up to lately? You're a nanny now. How long have you been with this family?"

Small talk? Is she serious?

I stared at her, pulling Mary closer into my chest, and stayed silent, my shock turning to fury. I bit my tongue hard because if I lost my temper, this would not end well.

We weren't going to pretend that everything was normal when it was far from it. I wasn't going to play catch-up when I knew she didn't care about me and she was using useless words to occupy time.

My eyes flew to the window, to the door, and back to

meet her face. It was only a matter of time before Charles showed up.

"Don't try it, Becky," she snapped. A sudden chill hung on the edge of her words. "I need this money, and I'll do everything I can to get it."

The danger she was in was evident from her tone. These loan sharks, whoever she owed money to, owned her life. There was no doubt there was a bounty on her head.

"There is only one way everyone is going to get out of this safely. That's if everybody does what I say and follows directions." Cold eyes narrowed at me.

Mary's eyes teetered between Kate and mine, and then tiny tears fell down her cheeks. "I want to go home. I want to go home right now. Call my daddy." Her cries heightened, and I pulled her against me.

Kate's voice was cold when she asked, "Can't you get the brat to shut up?"

Mary's cries were uncontrollable then, and my voice was equally as harsh back. "If you would be quiet, then I might be able to."

She narrowed evil eyes on me. "I'm going out for a smoke. Give me your phone. The back door is bolted shut. There's only one way to escape, and it's through that front door." She waved the gun in the air. "Don't try it. I won't refrain from doing what I need to do." She tipped her chin. "Your phone."

I didn't hesitate. I knew my phone was one of my lifelines, but in this moment, I had to calm Mary down first. I plucked it out of my purse and slid it on the hardwood toward her.

After she was out the door, I took Mary's heart-shaped face in my hands. "Don't cry. You know I can't stand to see you cry."

She pushed out her lip. "That's what Uncle Brad says. But this time, it's real tears."

I tried to smile. "Why are they not real sometimes? Can my little actress force out fake tears?"

She nodded and then laughed. "Yeah, sometimes in front of Uncle Brad."

Man, oh man, she really knew how to work her uncles. My heart ached again, and I hoped we could both get out of this together and in one piece.

"Why is she doing this?" Mary asked.

I swallowed hard. There was so much I could tell her, but she wouldn't understand. More than that, I wanted to keep her safe and sane and not have her worry about this crazy world around us.

This was temporary.

It was only a matter of time until Charles arrived; I could feel it. He'd have the police here, and Kate would freak. I couldn't predict her reaction, what she'd do. But I had a plan. I just needed to execute it.

"I want to go home," Mary repeated, her eyes filling with tears again.

The guilt was overwhelming—so much so that tears lined my own eyes. Looking at the innocence of her features, I knew what I had to do. I had to get Mary to safety and go with this woman and get her the money she needed. And make sure that my mother was put away, so she could not hurt anyone else in the future.

"You will get home. I promise." My thumb brushed against an escaping tear. "Just remember what I told you, Mary. You can do this. Because you're the bravest little girl I know."

But even though I was telling Mary this ... it was my turn to be brave.

CHAPTER 41

CHARLES

"Maybe we should wait for their call," Mason said from the backseat of the car. "Not make any rash decisions."

"Screw that. This psycho has Mary," Brad shot out, doing ninety on the highway.

My security was tailing us to our destination, and the cops would be right behind them. I couldn't wait for them, and since I was tracking Becky's phone, I knew exactly where they were.

Part of me, the rational part of me, wanted to give this crazy woman the money she needed. It was the most certain way to ensure their safety—both Mary's and Becky's. But who knew when it would stop? If I paid her fee now, what was to say she wouldn't come back and take Sarah next time and ask for more money then?

My phone pinged with a text, and I immediately swiped up to read it. I'd been holding on to my phone like it held my life. Which it did. My family was my life.

The cops had been trying to call the phone, but no one was picking up. Becky was smart though; she hadn't turned off the phone, merely silenced it. Her mother wasn't too smart. That was the first thing that she should have confiscated.

We were five minutes away, and my heart pounded hard in the chambers of my chest.

"She says to put ten grand in an envelope inside a bag and drop the money at Monroe and Lexington." My voice shook as I spoke, my normal confidence not there.

"Let's go there. Going to where Becky is will cause trouble. How do we even know Mary is with her and this crazy woman hasn't taken her to a different location?" Mason said, his voice full of stress.

"Shut up. The only way to get this done is to go there and get Mary ourselves," Brad snapped, eyes solely focused on the road while his hands were wrapped tightly around the steering wheel at ten and two.

I closed my eyes. Fear and adrenaline were a dangerous mix. For once, I didn't know what to do. *Did we just give this woman the money? Would that ensure the safe return of Mary and Becky? Would there forever be a bounty on my kids' heads if she wasn't caught?*

What if she had a gun or other people working with her?

I knew nothing.

"Text her back, Charles," Mason ordered.

I tried to focus on the task at hand, but my brain was mush.

"Charles!"

My eyes blinked open, and I texted four words back.

We'll get your money.

"Did you text her?" Mason asked.

"I did."

"So, where are we headed now?" he asked, frantic.

"What do you mean, where, Mason?" Brad griped. "We're going to get Mary."

"That's stupid," Mason ground out. "She gave us an alternate location. We still have to get the money. Right now, the banks are closed. The max that we can withdraw is three thousand."

"Well, there's three of us, so ..." Brad tipped his chin. "We'll get the money just in case, but we're not going by her terms."

"What do you mean? She has our kid," Mason said.

I couldn't think. I inhaled deeply, held my breath, and then counted to five.

"Charles ..." Mason demanded.

Exhale.

"We get the money and head to where this phone is tracking their location."

When he piped up, I shot him a look. I wasn't in the mood to argue. And I was done trying to figure this all out.

I was fucking getting my girls back.

This ended today. I wouldn't live in fear, and neither would Becky. This was the one thing I could do for her.

Becky

Kate slammed the door shut, making Mary and me jump when she returned from her smoke.

"I texted them a location. Let's go."

I stood and couldn't breathe for a second as anxiety spiked within me. "Mary, go to the bathroom."

She widened her eyes, about to speak, until I winked at her.

"Come on. You can go. Or else you'll go in the car."

Her eyes wavered until I tipped her chin.

"You wouldn't want to go in the car, would you?"

"Go, then! If you are going to take a piss, go now," Kate shot out, making Mary still.

I gave Mary's hand a squeeze, and reluctantly, she released my hand. I prayed with all my might that she would go through with this, that she would hide like I'd told her to.

The best thing I could do in this situation was get Mary as far away from the threat as possible.

Kate was watching Mary leave with narrowed eyes, and I took this as an opportunity to play fake catch-up.

"Where are you living now?" I couldn't have cared less, but I needed Kate distracted.

My mother laughed, both a deadly and uncivilized sound. "Wouldn't you like to know? Not here—that's for sure. Or anywhere in your surrounding area." She ran a hand through her oily, mid-length, dyed hair. "So, you don't have to worry about me coming back." Her eyes teetered to somewhere behind me, her look going blank. "I'm desperate this time, Becky."

I'd seen her desperate. If this topped those times, I knew she was in trouble—most likely the six-feet-under kind.

You'd think I'd feel some sort of pity for this woman, but no. All I felt was this utter resentment that had been caused from years of neglect and mental abuse from my childhood. There was no empathy in my emotional jar left for this woman.

"Where are we going now? Where are you going to go after this?" I asked, not really caring but making conversation to stall for time, to get Mary to safety.

"I'm going to have to stay low for a while. A long while." A flicker of apprehension passed through her features.

I studied her for a moment, her shoulders lax, her

mouth downturned, and the lines permanently etched on her face. Did she owe more people? Was her debt more than the ten grand she was asking for? It didn't matter though. I didn't believe anything she said. She'd always been full of lies. Watching her pace the room, I knew she'd come back. And each and every time, I'd be her only way out.

The thought only solidified my decision to leave.

A flash of light caused us to peer at the front window behind me. Her face registered shock, and we both rushed toward the front.

We were surrounded.

She turned to face me, and I felt the whoosh of air before I felt the impact of her hand against my cheek.

"You bitch," she growled. Such betrayal in her tone, as though it were my fault. As though I had called the cops myself.

I held my cheek and greeted her gaze with narrowed eyes. She'd lost. And she knew it.

"There's nowhere to go now."

We were only inches apart, and she yanked her gun out of her pocket and waved it in my face before shoving it in my chest. "That's what you think. You think that either of you have outsmarted me?" Her eyes held danger now, desperate danger. "We're leaving now. Get the brat. Now."

Panic instantly hit me. I hoped that Mary had gone into a secure hiding spot. When I didn't make a move, Kate took off running toward the back of the house, and I sprinted after her, making sure that she never caught my girl.

Kate headed to the bathroom and pushed open the door. "Where is she? Where did she go?" Her eyes turned wide as she stormed through the house, and I heard the closets opening and slamming shut. A few seconds later, she stalked toward me. "Where did she go?"

I raised both hands as relief flooded me. "I have no idea."

That was when Kate raised her gun from her side and pointed it directly in between my eyes.

I blinked. In a flash, my life played like scenes from a movie in front of me.

This was it. This was how I would die.

I hadn't experienced true happiness before Charles and this family that I'd grown to love. In every sense of the word, I loved them. Each of them individually—the children, Mary and Sarah, and Charles.

Tears lined my eyes. Because this was the story of my life. I should have known better. For me, happiness always was temporary. It never lasted. It was never in my cards to live without fear, without violence, without hating myself.

My only regret would be that I was never allowed a chance to tell him. There was no amount of time or measurement for when or how long it took for a person to fall in love. I knew that now because looking in the face of my death sentence, I knew that I loved him. And I wanted to thank him. Thank him for showing me what true, unconditional love was. Thank him for giving me the experience of being a mother, even for a short while. Thank him for making me feel important and worthy and valued.

For that, I would be forever grateful.

"Where did she go?" my mother seethed.

Her words broke me from this trance, and I straightened. An internal shift happened—one where the sadness and fear was overtaken by determination.

Mary was still not in the clear. The threat was here, present, in this house, pointing a gun at me that could be pointed at Mary next.

What I needed to do was take Kate far away from Mary,

and then I could think through my next course of action, which would get her permanently in jail.

"I have no idea where she went." All my muscles tensed with fire and fight because I wasn't going down without one. "But I have what you are looking for. I can get you the ten thousand dollars you need." My voice was even, exuding a confidence I didn't feel.

"Liar." She saw right through me, but I didn't care.

I lifted my hands to the ceiling and then slowly motioned to my purse, so she wouldn't feel threatened. Then, I plucked out an ATM card.

"I have their card. I can get you cash but only to the max. Then, we can think of another way to get you more. But the longer we wait here, the more likely you'll go to jail than get your money."

Voices sounded from the front.

Indecision played on her features, and I held my breath for what seemed like forever until she waved her gun toward the door.

"Let's go. I know how to get out of here."

Charles

I sat in silence, forced by authorities to stay in the car. Brad was so aggressive that he'd been put in the back of a car and ordered to calm down.

The only thing that could be heard in the car was Brad's heavy breathing. Mason had gone utterly silent, his eyes glued to the front of the run-down house.

I had stopped breathing altogether. I closed my eyes and finally broke down. The silence and the not knowing and thinking about the worst-case scenarios broke me.

I rested my head against the steering wheel, and for the

first time in forever, I prayed. I asked my parents and Natalie and all the forces that might be to help my child, to help Becky.

One strong hand rested on my shoulder. "It'll be fine." Mason's words broke through.

"When has it not been okay?" Brad added.

My eyes slammed shut. I didn't have the energy to breathe, let alone talk.

"What Brad means is that in the end, everything turns out all right."

"Yes. Because you have to believe that we wouldn't have made it this far without some sort of help. Mary is fine." Brad didn't sound too convinced, but he kept going, "Dad and Mom are looking out for us. And Nat. Nat will pull through. She's not going to let anything happen to her baby girl."

My body trembled, and I exhaled a shaky sigh.

One breath.

Two.

Three.

"When will it end?" I didn't have to explain. My brothers understood.

"Maybe it never will," Mason admitted quietly. Brad laughed, sarcastic and snarky, and Mason added, "Life is never going to get easy. We've lived through so much, and we continue to live through events that shake our world. But maybe it's meant to be this way ... in order to shape us, make us wiser, make sure we never take anything for granted. Make sure we know what's important, and that's family."

"Okay, Vincent van Gogh," Brad griped.

"You mean, Socrates?" Mason snapped back. "Vincent was a painter."

I lifted my head, staring at these two. *What the fuck?*

We were at the height of the most hostile situation, yet these two somehow found the time to bicker.

Brad smiled then, meeting my eyes. "Big bro, at the end of the day, at the end of it all and all we've been through"—he cupped the back of my neck, bringing me closer—"we've got each other."

My eyes shone with tears. Wasn't that the truth though? They had been my constant through it all.

I nodded.

And if I was being honest with myself, tragedy had brought us closer. I hated to admit it, and I wasn't accepting that any tragedy was happening today, but it was still the truth.

When life had been perfect and we'd been relatively untouched, going about our day-to-day, we hardly saw each other. After work, before Natalie's death and our parents' deaths, we would only see each other at work. As crazy as it seemed—and though I would not wish tragedy on anyone—we were only closer now because of everything we'd gone through.

The commotion at the front of the house forced my head up as fresh panic had my heart beating frantically. First, three officers emerged and then two more, one carrying a small child.

All at once, we stormed out of the car, *stay put* warning be damned.

There was a barricade between the house and the sidewalk, so we couldn't pass.

"Mary!" Brad shouted.

The officer crossed the barrier, and in the next second, he placed her in my arms. The relief I felt was so overwhelming that it choked me into silence. All I could do was kiss her and hold her tighter. I couldn't even offer consoling words without the risk of breaking down.

She peered up at me with the bluest of eyes. "I'm hungry, Daddy."

Then, I laughed. "I'm going to feed you whatever you want, little girl. Whatever you want, it's yours." I kissed her forehead again and pulled back. "Are you okay?"

She nodded, seeming shaken but in one piece.

"Where's Becky?" I asked her, not sure if she'd know but needing details.

Mary's face became sad. "She left with that mean lady. Her mom is so mean, Daddy. She's so mean. We have to make sure we don't let Becky live with her."

I peered up at the house, the tattered shutters, the worn-down wooden front porch. Through the windows, I could see a dozen officers congregated inside.

Gone? What does she mean, gone?

"Stay with your uncles. I'll be right back."

When I placed Mary in Brad's arms, he wrapped her in his embrace and dropped to his knees, dipping his head in her neck, visibly shook. "Thank God you're okay."

Mason followed me to the front of the house, where I waved at the officer guarding the barricade. "Is there no one inside? What happened to the woman, Becky Summers— the one who was kidnapped with the child?"

He teetered back on his heels. "You'll have to talk to the detective."

"Then, call the detective down here. Now," I snapped out.

Maybe Mary had misconstrued things. Maybe Becky was inside, but they were interviewing her. I took a step past the barricade, but Mason pulled me back, tugging at my shirt.

I broke free from his grasp.

"Charles ..."

"Who is in charge?" I ground out.

I needed self-control, and for the most part, I had a limitless amount. But not today.

Not in this instant.

Not when I didn't know if Becky was with her psycho mother.

I was one second from going to jail when a tall, broad male with a beard approached. "John, it's fine. Let him pass." He extended his hand, and I reluctantly took it. "I'm Detective Timson."

I tried to keep the panic out of my voice and spoke rationally, "Where is Becky Summers, the woman who was with my daughter?"

He peered back behind him, toward the house swarmed by authorities. "That's what we are trying to find out. There is no one in the house."

"Her phone." My tone was harder than I'd expected it to be. "We tracked her phone here."

I was already getting out my phone to track hers when he told us, "We found the phone, but there was no one but the child inside."

A pang so hard hit me in the chest, causing me to shiver. Momentarily, I was frozen, and every muscle tightened. "She's gone?"

I felt impaled by his steady gaze. "Yes, sir. She's gone."

The relief I'd felt moments ago with Mary in my arms disappeared and was replaced with a feeling I had become used to more recently—fear.

CHAPTER 42

Becky

I stood by the ATM, purposely looking at the camera as I slipped the card in. Kate was steady by my side, her hand in her pocket, heavy on the trigger. I should know; she had cocked the gun in the car and ushered me right to the machine.

I was about to withdraw three thousand dollars. It wasn't the total she needed, but she'd said she had a secondary plan on where to go, how to bridge the gap.

I felt nauseous as I slid the card into the slot.

It's okay.

It's fine.

Mary is safe.

I just couldn't get past all this. I'd caused problems and tragedy for this family, and now, I was going to essentially steal from them too. I could possibly deny Kate, refuse to give in to her demands, end the cycle here, but then the survival part of me wanted this done, so I could call the authorities, tip them off on her plates, and run as far away from this woman and state as possible. I needed to keep her close before then.

I would no longer have a tie to the Briskens. She could no longer use them as leverage against me to get whatever she wanted because this was going to be the last time I would be used as a walking ATM.

After this, I'd disappear somewhere, a place where I couldn't hurt the people I loved any longer.

The money spat out of the machine, and I plucked an envelope from the open slot and slipped all the bills inside. My breathing became rampant, and my stomach churned with unease.

Kate's eyes widened beside me, at the amount of cash I held within my fingertips.

This is the last time.

The last time I hurt them. I swore it.

She yanked the envelope from me, shoved at my side with the gun in her pocket, and tipped her chin toward the car.

After I slipped back in the passenger seat, she opened the envelope and started counting the money inside. The gun stayed planted on her lap. I eyed it and debated if I could grab it and make a run for it.

My life was inevitably going to end in tragedy. It was as though my cards had already been written when I was born to a deadbeat mother like Kate Summers. Why couldn't it have played differently for me? I stared at her profile, the line of her jaw and nose, the green in her eyes that I'd inherited.

A raw and primitive grief overwhelmed me at the lack of a mother figure that I had. When I had been younger, when I'd been in bed, crying at the circumstance of my situation, at another night with my mother not coming home,

I'd tell myself that I would be a better mother—that I couldn't control my own mother, but I could control the kind of mother I wanted to be.

Now, I knew I'd never get that chance.

"Good job, baby girl," she uttered with a sick sort of pride. She stuffed the envelope in her right pocket.

She hadn't called me baby girl since I was a teenager. The endearment was like tiny spiders crawling up my skin.

When she placed the car in drive, I turned to face her fully. "Where are we going?" I had tapped the cash advance on the credit card. Where else could she take me where I could charge and she could flip the product and get cash back?

She smirked. "We're going to buy some jewelry."

I frowned at her. Everything was closed right now. It was nine in the evening. "Where?"

"The pawn shop."

I rubbed at my brow, irritation prickling my skin. *When will this nightmare be over?* I'd given her everything she needed. Now, I had to make my escape.

"This is it," I said, my voice defeated. "This is the last time, Kate."

"Yeah, yeah. For sure. I'm not greedy."

I didn't know if that was meant to be sarcastic or if she really believed that. I didn't want to overanalyze this woman I would no longer see, so I stared out the window instead, hoping and wishing that Mary was okay—that she was safely in Charles's arms right now, tucked securely in her bed.

I closed my eyes, resting my head against the window, wishing so hard for it to be true. I pictured her bedroom, her glow-in-the-dark stars on the ceiling, and I drowned in the memories of Charles and me in that bed, as bread to the

Mary sandwich. Agony and an acute sense of loss flooded my senses, and I squeezed my eyes tighter to prevent full-blown emotional tears to fall.

Not only did I wish that Mary were soundly sleeping in her bed, but I also wished that Charles were right next to her. I wished he could move on from this, from me, even though I knew in my heart that I would never move on from him.

—

Twenty minutes later, we were in front of Al's Jewelry and Pawn. Reluctantly, I got out of the car. The sooner this was done and over, the sooner I could close in on my plan to get this woman in jail.

The door chimed as we entered, and I took in a row of televisions against the far wall. Guitars hung from the ceiling. PlayStations and radios sat on shelves.

In the center were large display cases, holding everything from watches to rings to necklaces.

My shoulders slumped, and exhaustion hit me straight in the face, but I trekked through, forcing myself to relive the past few hours, which only emboldened my purpose—to make sure Kate would go to a place she could not hurt other people.

"Hey, lovely ladies." A taller male with a darkish blond buzz cut emerged from behind the bulletproof glass. "How are you guys doing?"

I swayed a little and then rested one hand on the glass to steady myself. I hadn't eaten anything or drunk anything in hours, and the adrenaline and emotional overload were making me light-headed.

"Looking for anything in particular? My name is Ben.

Just let me know if you need anything."

Kate ran one hand through her hair and smiled at the younger male who was half her age. "We're looking for earrings or rings or anything big you got."

He grinned. "Well, you came to the right place. We got a few pieces in this morning. What are you looking for?"

"Do you have anything two carats or higher?" Kate asked, leaning against the glass to look at the inventory.

"Oh, big spender, are we?" His grin turned flirty.

She motioned in my direction. "My daughter here is a big spender. I'm more the woman who carries all her jewelry."

I sent her a look. *Did this man believe this?* I didn't have one ring on, and I wore tiny hoop earrings that weren't even gold. They were gold-plated.

After he unlocked the display cases, he pulled out a black tray that showcased an array of jewelry, all mismatched. Some were rings with gemstones, some had diamonds, and some were earrings.

He took out a ring that was a lion's head made of diamonds. It was ridiculously gaudy and just plain horrid, but it was no doubt a custom piece because who would take a bunch of diamonds and set it into an over-the-top lion's head?

"How much is that?" Kate asked.

He lifted an eyebrow, his eyes sharp, ready to bargain. "Twenty-three hundred. It's approximately one and a half total carats."

Kate pursed her lips. "Do you have anything else that's a little bit fancier?"

He nodded and then pointed his thumb toward the back of the store. "Yeah, I actually do. I'll be right back." Then, he disappeared through the door.

Kate paced the length of the display cases, hands behind her back, eyes scanning the merchandise. Her hand was in her pocket, and from the outline of her jacket, her finger was still very much on the trigger.

I leaned against the glass, wrapping my arms around my center to keep me steady.

When Ben emerged, he had four stacked black trays. He came to the front and set them on the counter, laying them in a vertical row. "Whatever you want, we have it."

Kate picked up the biggest ring on the tray—a round solitaire stone. "How much is this?" The greed shone bright in her eyes.

"You're going for the big one, huh?"

She tipped her chin in agreement.

"Twenty-three thousand," Ben said, his tone smooth. "That's three carats, internally flawless. The woman who sold it is going through a messy divorce. Her husband was basically the millionaire who cheated on her with his secretary. She took all his money and even sold his ring for more."

Kate joined Ben in laughter, but I had no energy to laugh.

"I'll take it," Kate said, her cold eyes turning to me.

I gaped at her. I'd already given her three thousand, and she was going to get another twenty-three more?

"That's too much," I said, my voice firm but wobbly.

"I don't think it is. It's a steal, right, Ben?" She flipped to face him. "How much is this really worth?"

He pursed his lips and shrugged. "It's probably worth thirty. If you can find a buyer. I mean, it's internally flawless. The woman just wanted to get rid of it."

"It's too much," I said, my voice louder and bordering on hysteria.

This woman was pushing it, and I was about to break.

She turned to face me, both hands on her hips. "Too much? All right then." She waved her hand, and her voice was hoarse with frustration. "Do you have smaller jewelry that I can buy? I guess this is too much for my daughter's blood." She drawled out the words with distinct mockery.

And because my mother was immature and petty and all the things a mother should not be, she had him take out all the small chains and rings and made him charge them separately with separate receipts.

It was an hour later when my mother had a bag of jewelry. I was thoroughly annoyed and spent and sick of this woman.

After I showed the guy my ID, I charged the lot of jewelry. My mother was surveying the jewelry that she'd just bought, and I took the opportunity to pluck a piece of paper and pen from the pile when Ben turned to help my mother wrap up her belongings.

My fingers shook as I made out the words.

Need help.

Please call the cops.

I printed her license plate number in neat, legible letters and numbers underneath my dire plea. Then, I turned to leave with her.

When we were in the parking lot, it hit me.

I was leaving.

For good.

I had nothing on me other than the clothes on my back. I did have some savings, but all my physical belongings were at the Briskens' house, and there was no way I was going back.

"I guess this is where we say our good-byes and I say thank you."

Kate had the audacity to smile after that statement, and I wanted to throat-punch her.

"Take care, honey. I'm sure I'll see you around." She about-faced and walked toward the car.

And with every step she took away from me, you'd think that relief would flood me. Instead, her words lit me on fire like a house sprinkled with gasoline. My blood began to boil. Then, my arms and legs were on fire, then my hair and my face, and then all of me was freaking. On. Fire.

"Stop!" I ordered, forcing her to turn. My hands fisted at my sides, and I was visibly shaking. "You are never to contact me again. And don't worry about the Briskens because I won't be under their employment after today. So, you and me? We're done. You hear me?"

Her face was hard, like stone, a statue, unmoving. "I was desperate this time." She said it as though I should understand, as though I should forgive her for everything she'd put Mary, the Briskens, and me through.

I threw up both hands. "You're desperate all the time. You live in despair and desperation. That's your middle name." I took a step forward, meeting green eyes so similar to mine. "You want to live that life? You go ahead. But I've lived my whole life trying to *not* turn out like you. And I was doing fine until you came along."

"Becky!" The voice wasn't my mother's. It was male and enraged, just like I felt at the moment.

My eyes shot to my left, and I squinted to see someone approaching closer.

No. No. No.

"Stay right there," Kate shouted. "Don't you dare come closer." She had her gun out.

The scene played out in slow motion. The flicker of the

lights from the lamppost highlighted the dimly lit parking lot, accenting his approaching figure.

My mother erased the gap between us, standing directly beside me.

She had both hands on the gun.

It was cocked, ready, loaded.

And directly pointed at Charles.

Might as well have been straight at my heart. Because he was my heart. Those girls and Charles owned my heart.

Watching my mother point that gun at him, at my heart, I knew I was done. I wasn't playing nice anymore. I went apeshit crazy.

Charles

Shit.

This had to be the stupidest move I'd made to date. Coming here and not telling anyone.

I hadn't known what to expect or what I'd find. The cops were out, looking for Becky, and my brothers were home with the kids. But when I received notification that there was a big withdrawal from the bank, I drove to that location. Then, I had my credit card company notify me when there was another transaction.

It was farfetched that I would find her. I mean, by the time I got to the bank, they were gone. But I was on high alert and jetting to the pawn shop when I got another notice.

And then I had seen Becky and couldn't stay quiet. Now, her mother was pointing a gun at me. My pulse pounded hard in my ears, and I raised both hands up. Adrenaline pumped through my veins as I approached. I wasn't being held back, not anymore.

"Stop." The woman shook the gun in my direction, her eyes wild and dangerous.

"Kate. Just put the gun down," Becky said, her face a state of hysteria.

I gulped, wanting to hold her, wanting to take her home. I'd give this woman whatever she wanted just to have Becky right beside me.

"What do you need? What is it you want?" I tipped my chin in Kate's direction. "More money?" Because that was nothing in the grand scheme of things. Not when Kate could obliterate my world with a shot of her gun.

"It's yours," I said, my voice firm and confident, bred and learned from years of negotiation from being Brisken Printing Corporation's CEO.

She smiled then, her eyes crinkling at the sides. Besides the color of her eyes, there was no resemblance between Becky and her mother.

"Well, since you offered and all."

"No!" Becky snapped, forcing Kate to tighten the hold on her weapon. "You're going to leave. That's what you're going to do."

"But"—she shrugged, unaffected—"since your boyfriend here is offering to give me a little cushion, then it would be rude not to take him up on his offer, no?"

"No!" Becky repeated, advancing toward Kate. "You are not involving them anymore. I refuse to let you take more from them. You've already taken too much."

The hairs on the back of my neck rose because Becky was undeterred by the gun that Kate held in her hands. Reading her, how she was positioned in front of Kate and the look in her eye, I knew she had one goal in mind—to protect me.

And that scared me shitless.

"Becky, stop!" Before I knew what I was doing, I erased the gap between us.

And the next few seconds happened in slow motion.

Kate pointed the gun in my direction. Becky reached for the gun and forced it upward. They struggled, fighting for it.

I couldn't get to them fast enough.

A shot rang out.

And then silence.

CHAPTER 43

Becky

The sound was deafening. Ear-splitting.

All I could hear was the ringing in my ears. All I could feel was the pain in my side as I tumbled to the ground.

But for the first time all day, relief flooded me.

Because I had the gun.

It was a toy, which I now had in my hand. It had never been real. The fear of this inanimate object was almost comical—*almost* because it wasn't real.

The ear-splitting gunshot had come from Ben. He'd emerged from the store, seen us struggling, and shot his gun into the air to stop our fight.

My head fell to the right, to the cold concrete rough against my back. For a brief second, my focus was on the clear night sky and the stars twinkling above me. I took a breath and exhaled slowly. The grandeur of the expansive sky could almost give off the feeling as though this were a normal night, but it was far from it as I sat up and witnessed Ben and Charles pinning a struggling Kate to the ground.

They'd used rope to tie her hands, and once Ben had her pinned against the wall, Charles ran toward me.

In the next second, I was in Charles's arms. He'd dropped to the ground and pulled me into his lap and buried his head into my neck, shuddering as though the adrenaline was dying down at a rapid rate and he couldn't control his emotions.

"I'm sorry." My tears flowed like a river down my face. I was saying sorry for so many things. I was sorry for putting his children's lives in danger. First, the pool incident and now with Kate. I was sorry for putting him in this situation, almost putting his life in danger too.

My life had been a string of unfortunate events, and now, those events had trickled into Charles's life.

A wetness touched my neck, and I knew he was sobbing too. And it broke me because he was so strong and brave, and now, he was breaking down because of me.

I'd caused his pain and misery.

I needed to leave. Leave and never come back. That was the only way to ensure that Charles would live the full and happy life that he was meant to have.

"I-I hate that I put you in this situation." I'd never loathed myself more than I did right now in his arms. "It's all my fault. It's all my fault," I repeated on a loop, in an utter state of shock. Because here he was, comforting me, grateful that I was alive. "When I think of what could have happened ..." I shook my head and breathed in and out to calm myself. I couldn't go there.

Everything was fine now, and everything would be in the future because I would ensure it.

He held me in silence, as the world around us erupted in chaos. The cops had been called in, and within minutes, the parking lot was filled with police vehicles and flashing red and blue lights.

Full-body shakes took over me as it all sank in, and Charles lifted his head, his eyes lined with tears. And then he kissed me. Hard and desperate.

I didn't deserve any of this. His affection. His love. None of it. But I melted into his kiss anyway because if this was the last time I was ever going to kiss this man, I would greedily take it and savor it and commit it to memory.

When he pulled back, his hand cupped my cheek, and he stared deeply into my eyes and uttered the words I was unworthy of, "I love you, Becky Summers."

The tears gushed out harder, his figure a blur behind the waterfall trailing down my cheeks. "You can't."

"What do you mean, I can't? It's too late. I already do."

The smile that surfaced should have made me feel better, but it did the opposite.

"I hate myself, Charles. I hate what I did to you, to Mary, for putting you in this situation."

He rested his forehead against mine. "It's not your fault."

"How can you possibly say that?" I pulled his hand down, giving me space to breathe and think clearly. "It is my fault. All of it. I'm bad luck. I'm jinxed. Everyone who comes in contact with me—"

He kissed me again to stop the words from flowing. Then, he pulled back, such gentleness in his eyes as he continuously swiped at my endless tears. "Everyone who comes in contact with you falls in love with you."

I shook my head, but the sincerity in his eyes stilled me.

"It's true. My brothers. The girls ... me. I thought I'd never love again, and"—his voice hitched—"you changed that. You changed me."

He cupped my chin, bringing me even closer, and I couldn't look away this time. I was transfixed.

"I lived my life by going through the motions, living for others, not myself. But for the first time since Nat died, I feel like I can finally live for myself, be in love, be loved without the guilt. Growing up, seeing how my parents were, I thought there was only one person for everyone. You would spend eternity with them, and that one person for me was Nat. And when she died"—he shuddered—"I thought I would never find a love like that, but I was wrong. So wrong. Because I love you, Becky Summers, and for once, I'm going to do what my brothers and Sarah and everyone else have told me to do. They want me to be happy, and I'm the happiest with you."

"I don't deserve you," I croaked out. Because I didn't.

He was everything good in the world—provider, light— and my past dimmed in his presence.

"Says who?" he asked, his voice tender.

"Me!" I crumpled against him, my eyes downturned as all the emotions from the day rained down on me like a tsunami.

He let out a slow breath and lifted my chin with the lightness of his fingertips. "If you feel like you don't deserve me, then I most definitely don't deserve you—your kindness, your patience." He stood then, taking me with him. "We're done."

"Where are we going?"

"Home," he said, pulling me to his side. "You don't think you deserve me. I don't think I deserve you. We can both live undeserving lives ... but together."

"Charles ..."

Charles's take-charge attitude was coming out. "Becky, I'm not taking any more of this nonsense. You've been through a lot. And I'm going to do what I know—I'm going to take care of you, okay? I'm going to run you a bath, feed you a good meal, and tuck you in next to me so that you can't leave. Ever," he added at the end like he was reading my mind.

There was a fierce determination in his eyes, the same look I'd witnessed so many times before.

"I mean, if you really hate me and don't want to stay, that's another story, but you're not going to leave us because you're scared or you feel guilty because that's all bullshit. Everything is going to be okay." He paused then, his fingers tightly intertwined with mine.

"I know how that sounds. After Nat died, after my parents died, everyone told me that it was going to be okay. It was repeated over and over again like a broken record. I never believed them because that's what people said when something tragic happened in someone's life. But for the first time, I believe them. Life might throw other curveballs, but I'll be able to handle them because I have another person on my team who's playing catcher." Playing for cute, he tapped the tip of my nose with his fingertip. "We're on the same team, Becky—Team Brisken. And you're going to be okay. Maybe you won't feel like it tomorrow or the day after that, but once everything turns back to normal and you're not worrying about the stress of the past, you're going to be okay."

The cops had my mother handcuffed and were ushering her into the back of the cop car. There was no doubt I'd spend hours being questioned. I watched the car pull away until it was a blurry figure down the street.

Finally.

She would spend her time in jail, away from me, away from the people that I was close to. And not only for a few months, but because of what she'd done today, it would be years. She was no longer a threat to Charles and his family, and Kate could never use them for money ever again.

Charles's tender hand brushed against my cheek. Peering up into his chestnut-brown eyes, I believed him. It was in the strength behind his voice, the intense look in his stare. That hope bloomed in my chest because I believed him, believed that everything would be okay.

So, for once, I gave in to him, in to his light. I went on my toes and framed his face with both of my hands. "I love you, Charles." Then, I erased the gap between us and kissed his lips. "Forever, until you won't have me anymore, I'm Team Brisken."

CHAPTER 44

CHARLES

Eight Months Later

As I held Becky's hand and we watched our girls run to the park ahead of us, I wondered how I'd gotten so damn lucky.

I would never have predicted that I would get a second chance at love. I'd thought the love that Nat and I had was a once-in-a-lifetime love, but love had struck me twice and in the best, unpredictable way. Not only had it struck me, but it'd also struck my girls.

Becky loved them like they were her own flesh and blood, and the girls—*our* girls now—adored Becky.

Tragedy could teach you things, and one thing it had taught me was to never take things for granted, to enjoy every moment, to live your life to the fullest. And that was what I did day in and day out—with the girls and with Becky.

Every Friday, after work, we went to the park to have a picnic. I planned this event like I planned my meetings, putting it in the calendar and making sure I set the time to go.

Becky stopped mid-step and turned around, peering at something behind her. My eyes followed her line of sight.

"What are you looking for?" I asked.

She squinted and narrowed her eyes at something in the far vicinity.

"What is it?"

The inclination to give in to panic was still there, even after all these months. Even though we knew Paul was dead and her mother would be in jail for a long while. I had hired the best lawyers who were relentless in their pursuit in making Kate serve the maximum time in jail for her crimes. She'd gotten twenty years for aggravated kidnapping.

Becky released my hand and took two steps toward where she was focused, which was away from the park. "It's crazy, but I feel like we're being watched." She pointed to someone past the trees.

I squinted against the sun. I couldn't make out who it was, only that the person was tall, broad, and male. I reached for her hand, shoving that panic back down. "He's just taking a walk."

She didn't budge. "He isn't. He's been watching us walk here for the last ten minutes. Look, he's right by that black SUV. It's the same one that followed us here."

Then, realization hit. "Shit," I said under my breath, rolling my eyes. *Seriously? Not again.* I plucked my phone from my back pocket and dialed my brother. "Mason," I shot out, "are you having someone tail us?"

"Oh, hey. Uh ... well—"

My jaw tightened. "Call them and stop the tail, all right?"

"I'm sorry," he said, not at all apologetic. "There has

been a string of robberies around the neighborhood, and I wanted to make sure—"

"Call them off, Mason."

He sighed. "Okay. I will."

I shook my head, and Becky laughed. This wasn't the first time that Mason had had our security guards tail Becky or the girls. After Mary and Becky had been kidnapped, Mason had had a tail on them for a month. It was only when Becky had gone head-to-head with the security personnel following them that we discovered that Mason had hired them.

Becky was cautious, still always aware of her surroundings, still getting spooked from time to time when she heard loud noises. I guessed that was a good thing to a point, as long as fear didn't own her.

"Your brothers ..." she said, laughing and cuddling close.

"Are over the top," I finished for her.

"In the best possible way," she added.

We sat at the bench. I'd liked to call it our bench now because it was where we sat every time we came here. We'd watch the girls jump from the monkey bars, run up the slide, and rush to the swing.

"I can't believe how time is flying," Becky said absently as I rubbed her shoulder. "The school year is over, and now, summer is here." She pushed her hair out of her face, but the wind blew it forward, causing her to huff and push it back again.

"Here." I pulled back her hair and tucked it in the back of her shirt, which caused her to laugh.

She threw me a look—her playful, annoyed look—which made me pull her closer and into my lap.

"I'm going to have to secure you right here so that your hair doesn't fly everywhere."

She was in my lap, facing the front.

I leaned in closer, whispering in her ear, "Let's get away. Me and you." I had a secret plan on proposing to Becky, but we hadn't had the opportunity to get away, just the two of us.

A small smirk tugged at her lips. "Where?"

"Anywhere. I haven't planned anything, and it's about time we got away, just us."

Her eyes shone with an inner glow. "What about the girls?"

I shrugged. "The guys can watch them for a week."

She sat up straighter, facing me fully this time. "But I want to take them. I want our first trip to be as a family, all of us—Brad and Mason and Janice if they want to go too."

I held back my grimace at the mention of Janice. And the idea of my brothers tagging along didn't appeal to me, not when I wanted to be alone with my girl for once.

Becky's stare flickered back to the girls, now on the seesaw, and then back to meet my eyes. "We'll have so many opportunities to take trips with just the two of us. But, I'm still getting to know the girls. My first vacation ... I really want it to be all of us."

I sighed, feeling myself giving in to her even though I wanted her all to myself.

This woman. I didn't think I could love her any more than I already did.

I raised a dubious eyebrow. "You know where they'll want to go, right?"

We both responded at the same time, "Disney World."

She sighed into me. "I've never been even though I lived in Florida." Her smile widened. "We can even take Patty. She doesn't live far from Disney."

I took her chin and angled it closer to me, kissing her.

"Disney it is." Because I couldn't help but give in to her. Her hold over me was powerful in the best possible way, and I vowed to give her whatever she wanted for the rest of our lives together.

She jumped out of my arms, as though the news were a burst of caffeine in her veins. "Girls! We're going to Disney!"

Mary stilled mid-climb up the slide. Sarah dropped her feet, stopping the swing. And then they both screeched with excitement and ran at warp speed toward us, hugging Becky and jumping and cheering as though they'd won a real, live unicorn.

I shook my head. The girls had been four times already, but they clearly never got sick of it.

Mary bum-rushed me, and I bent down and took her in my arms. Her small hands squished my cheeks, forcing me to make a fishy face. "Thank you, Daddy!" Then, she kissed my lips.

Mary motioned for Becky and Sarah to come closer. "Bubble. I want my bubble."

"Dad," Sarah said, her cheeks red with excitement, "are we really going to Disney for summer break?"

I smiled down at her. "Yep."

"Well, it is the happiest place on earth," Becky added, her own glow spreading over her beautiful face.

I held out my free arm, bringing the rest of my family in. I was now surrounded with everything I would ever need in life. "No, this, right here"—I pulled them into our bubble of love—"is the happiest place on earth."

EPILOGUE

SWEAT LINED the top of my brow, and as I swiped my forehead with the handkerchief Mason handed me, I knew it wasn't the summer weather that was causing my perspiration. Plus I was inside, seated in the dining room, watching the waitstaff I'd hired move about the house, getting the food ready for the reception.

I was afraid to move, let alone undo my bow tie.

"You look nervous." Mason laughed, standing right beside me.

"Me? Nervous?" I shifted, placing my elbows on my thighs. I hadn't done this in a while. And if it was up to me, it would be the last time I ever did.

"This is what you wanted, Charles. This is what you need," Mason said.

"Yeah, I'm just excited to get all the formalities over. I need to get to the kiss-the-bride part, then the drinking part." I smiled, though nothing could calm my nerves.

Standing in front of the boardroom was different than standing in front of three dozen people, with them watching you proclaim your love to the woman you were going to spend the rest of your life with.

I should have nixed the idea of inviting more than a handful of people, but I relinquished all wedding planning to Mason, who was more than up for it with his type A, organized ways.

"It'll be fine." One strong hand landed on my shoulder. "It's a quick ceremony by Minister McKinnley. No more than fifteen minutes. I've timed his recorded ceremonies on line." He squeezed my shoulder. "Give or take a few minutes."

Mason glanced at his watch. "Speaking of the minister, he's five minutes late." He plucked his phone from his back pocket, then dialed. He walked away, with one hand on his hip.

"Hey, groom-to-be. Again." Brad strolled in with a bacon-wrapped asparagus, half hanging from his mouth and another in a napkin in his hand. "I'm here to tell you that the girls are ready and waiting upstairs. Twenty minutes till go time."

"I specifically told the waitstaff to keep the food from you until after the ceremony," I said.

He laughed. "That would only work if your staff wasn't predominantly female." Brad wiggled his eyebrows in a playful manner. "Let's just say, I have my ways."

"What?" Mason's heightened tone had us turning in his direction. "This is bullshit. You couldn't find a replacement? This is your one job. Whatever. I'm done." Then he ended the call and turned to face us, eyes wide.

"Minister McKinnley is sick."

I jolted up and stood. "What?" I swallowed, then ran both hands through my hair. Bad idea, since my hairstylist was one of the guests invited. No officiant. Shit. Shit. Shit. Now what?

Mason rubbed at the back of his neck and glanced at his watch again. "I don't know why I didn't think of this. I had a backup for the food, a secondary waitstaff on call. Not once did I think the officiant wouldn't show up." When Mason let out a jagged sigh, Brad laughed.

And the look on Mason's face told me, now was not the time to mess with him. He was out for blood at Brad's simple reaction. "You think this is funny?" Mason said, his tone menacingly low.

"Yes."

When he took a step forward, I placed myself between them.

Brad shrugged his shoulders, unaffected. "I wouldn't be laughing if I didn't already have a solution."

Mason scoffed. "Do you have an officiant up your sleeve that's readily available? Do you? Do you!"

Mason's voice turned frantic.

Brad's smiled widened. "Actually I do. Up my sleeve. In my pants. In this tux."

I couldn't read between the lines. I needed it spelled out. "What have you got, Brad?"

"I'm an ordained minister."

"What! When?" Mason and I spoke at the same time.

"Remember when Jimmy got married a few years back?"

His question was returned with blank faces. Jimmy was his high school friend, but I had no clue the guy was even married.

"Anyways, Jimmy had to get married a few years back. He needed a shotgun wedding." Brad patted his chest. "It took an hour to get legally ordained online."

My mouth slipped ajar. I could hug him but it was too late, Mason had jump-hugged him first. "For once, I thank God for your crazy antics."

Brad was so shell-shocked into surprise, his arms stayed glued to his side. "You're welcome."

Mason cleared his throat, without looking at any of us, obviously embarrassed. "I'll make sure everything else is running smoothly. Got to check on the waitstaff and the guests ... and the girls." His voice trailed off as he continued listing who he needed to check in with.

"Well, that was awkward," Brad said.

"You liked it. I could tell," I joked.

"So, should I print something out and read it or just wing the whole thing."

He asked the question as though he hadn't already made a solid decision.

He slipped an arm over my shoulders. "Ready to get married?"

After flattening out my disheveled hair, I nodded. I was still in disbelief that Brad, of all people, would be the one officiating the wedding.

Becky:

The dress was a slinky stretch slip white gown with baguette-encrusted halter straps that led to a low back. The gown hugged my hips and accentuated my slim figure. It was simple, yet flattering and perfectly me.

When Mason had set me up with one of the wedding planners to look for a dress, I'd felt like Cinderella. They'd picked me up from the Brisken estate in a limo, whisked me away for high tea at the Peninsula to discuss my perfect wedding dress and then off to designer bridal boutiques to pick the dress of my dreams.

The lights flashing from the photographers could not have caught a more perfect picture.

As I peered at myself through the floor-length mirror with my two girls beside me, holding my hands, my throat closed up and I blinked back tears, afraid to ruin my makeup.

I couldn't believe that this was my life now. I'd come from nothing, hadn't known my father and had lived with my deadbeat mother until she went to jail, I was in and out of foster care. Just thinking of my life before and my life now had the first tear falling down my cheek.

"Becky, your makeup." Linda, one of the wedding planners, approached with a pressed compact, ready to touch up my cheeks but I raised a hand to stop her.

"I'm fine."

"I'm sure you are, but your makeup is not." Her voice was stern, her eyebrows narrowed.

Mary squeezed my hand and in the next second she tugged me forward, placing both of her tiny hands on my cheeks. "Why are you crying? Aren't you happy?"

"Mary, careful of Becky's makeup."

I didn't appreciate the tone in Linda's voice and I shot her a look. "Can you please give me and my girls a few minutes?"

There must have been something on my face that told this woman there was only one correct answer to my question, because without another word, Linda and her team of five—yes five—were out the door.

My attention was back on Mary as soon as the doors shut and I bent down and rested my elbows on my knees to get into her line of sight. "I am happy. These are happy tears. I promise you." I turned my attention to Sarah who had this blinding smile that lit up my insides. I cupped her cheek. "You just don't understand. From someone who didn't have much of a family before to having you girls ..." My words got stuck in my throat from all the emotions running through me.

Sarah placed her hand on top of mine on her cheek. "And Daddy."

More tears.

"And Daddy," I repeated, my voice soft and full of emotion.

"And don't forget Uncle Brad and Uncle Mason," Mary added, wrapping her arms around my center.

"I love you, Becky." Mary full-on crushed me, followed by Sarah.

I couldn't get out the words I repeated before bedtime, before we hung up on the phone, before I dropped them off for school. Not because they weren't true anymore or that I didn't mean them with every fiber of my being. Simply because the emotions of uttering those words were so overwhelmingly powerful that I was a nanosecond from washing away all of my makeup with even more tears. "You girls ..." I swallowed and tried hard to make the tears cease. "Are my whole world." Now and forever, I silently promised them.

The knock on the door had us peering up to see a not-so-happy Linda. "It's showtime."

After we all stood from—as Mary would call it—our bubble of love, Linda came over and fluffed out the girls' white tulle bridesmaid dresses. They seemed more like flower girl dresses to me, but Sarah noted that they were my bridesmaids since I didn't have anyone else standing up.

After Linda retouched my makeup, my fingers intertwined with my two little girls. Because they were mine now. Today I would claim them in front of an audience, even though I'd already claimed them long ago in my heart.

We walked hand in hand down the stairs, passing some of the waitstaff and other coordinators. They oohed and aahed at my dress, at my hair done up in a ponytail of flowing curls. I felt like a queen, but more than that, my heart was so filled to the brim with joy that I'd thought it would burst.

I closed my eyes briefly, lifting my face to the skies, taking in the summer sun on my cheeks, the breeze from the light wind against my skin. When I opened them and walked further into the backyard, I took in the decor, the flowers, the guests.

Long tables were set at the outskirts of the pool and the pool? For tonight, it was a lit dance floor. Mason had hired someone to place a covering on top of the pool so we could dance on it. It still freaked me out to think that at any moment we could fall, but Mason assured everyone that we'd be fine. Knowing him, he'd done the research on the reputability of the company that had installed it.

The Brisken brothers went above and beyond to make this the wedding of the century. A champagne wall was set up to the right of the pool. A donut wall right next to it. Candles were everywhere. On pedestals in every corner. On top of the tables. On top of the highboy tables toward the far end of the backyard. And the flowers were intense. Pillars of pink and purple roses and hydrangeas were stationed every few feet and scattered throughout the backyard.

Mary practically pulled me past the pool, where there were rows of white chairs. I knew when we'd reached our destination when not too far past the tree house, I spotted a wall of roses with our initials.

With all the guests standing on either side of me and holding my girls' hands, I walked down the aisle, over the rose petals that were made into a swirly pattern, toward my forever and final destination—Charles. He stood tall, powerful, and insanely handsome in his classic tuxedo. Right beside him stood his brothers, the ones who took me in as their own, the ones I knew I could count on.

And when our eyes locked, my breath caught because I could read all the emotion and love swimming through his chocolate-brown irises.

It was only after Sarah and Mary had hugged their father and he took my hand in his hand that I realized I'd been crying.

He cupped my face and leaned in, brushing my tears with his thumbs. "Don't do that, beautiful. I hate it when you cry."

I pulled his hands down and smiled. "It's happy tears, I promise."

"Good." He angled closer, his lips a millimeter from mine, when Brad placed his mic in between us.

"Not yet, big bro. I didn't say kiss the bride." He cleared his throat and motioned with his hands behind us.

In the heat of the moment and run by emotions, I almost forgot that we had an audience.

Most of the guests were the Brisken family's friends but front and center and seated next to Mary and Sarah was Patty, all dressed in an elegant summery floral chiffon dress.

Brad tapped the mic to get everyone's attention. "Hear ye. Hear ye."

My eyes flew to Charles who was grinning.

"The minister didn't show up, so guess who is officiating

this wedding?" He tapped his chest with a light hand. "The one and only—me." He took an overexaggerated bow.

My eyes widened and I expected Brad to drop the mic with those mic-dropping words, but he continued.

"Don't worry, I've done this once before and the couple is still married." He laughed at his own joke, while the guests were still in awe. I knew the feeling.

Mason rubbed at his brow, then his hair, then his arm, then repeated the motion again.

"So I tried to pick a quote to begin this ceremony. Well, that's what Google told me to do, so I did. I was searching for the perfect line and the first that popped up was, 'Marriage is like a walk in the park ...' " He paused for a dramatic effect. "Jurassic Park."

The audience laughed. "The Jurassic crazy part happened before today, so technically they weren't married yet." He blew out a long breath and the smile slipped from his face as he eyed the room, his gaze landing on Mary before sweeping back to ours. "We've seen enough craziness for a lifetime. Although Becky and Charles's start was a rocky one—one plucked straight from a horror film—that's okay, because right here, right now ... this is their new beginning." His eyes grew soft and he pressed his free hand to his chest. "And I see years and years of happiness, of joy and lots of nieces and nephews in my immediate future." He focused all his attention on Charles, then. "You deserve this, this love. Because you are one of the greatest men I know. And you deserve an epic love story made for the movies because you have given up everything for this family and now it's your turn to be happy."

Then his attention turned to me. "Becky. Becky. Becky." The way he uttered my name had me smiling. "What did you put in that water he was drinking?"

I laughed because it was our inside joke.

"Whatever it was, you have him hooked for life. 1 you, Becky. Thank you for coming into his life, for ma him smile, for making him happy. What I don't thank you for is tipping the scales. We were evenly matched before. Now there is more estrogen in our household and I don't know how I feel about that." His voice softened, but was still loud enough for everyone to hear. "Besides coming into his life, thank you for coming into ours—into the girls'. Not only does he need you, but *we* need you." He bit his bottom lip and I assumed he was getting emotional then because he called Mary to bring up the rings.

We said our vows under the perfect summer sun, as though we were the only two people in the room, promising to love each other, for better, for worse, for richer, for poorer, in sickness and in health, to love and to cherish, till death us do part. There was comfort in taking the original vows, vows said by so many before us and that will be said by so many after us.

And when Brad pronounced us as man and wife and Charles's lips connected with mine, I thanked the heavens above and fate and all the forces that may be that we both— finally after experiencing heartache—got our very own happily ever after—with each other.

———

Did you love this story? Do you want to see what kind of crazy antics Brad is up to? Keep reading in BOSS I LOVE TO HATE to see if Brad gets his own happily ever after?

Here is a sample of Mia Kayla's bestselling novel, BOSS I LOVE TO HATE.

BOSS I LOVE TO HATE

SONIA

"Her boobs can't possibly be real."

My best friend, Ava, always tried to make me feel better. Too bad I knew she was lying. Lying through her teeth.

With my forefinger, I pushed my glasses farther up my nose and leaned closer to the computer screen, so close that I nearly went cross-eyed. The scent of coffee hit me directly in the nostrils. The sound of paper spat out of the printer. The chatter of my coworkers rang loudly behind me. But I ignored it all and concentrated on my computer screen—her —my replacement. Jeff's replacement for me.

"She's not that pretty," Ava continued.

I scrolled through my ex-boyfriend's Facebook feed again, fixated on their endless pictures together, laughing, hugging, smiling, eating. And her ... I couldn't get over her. The replacement was beautiful, her body built like those mannequins at the store, tall and perfectly proportional. Blonde hair. Blue eyes. High cheekbones contoured like those stupid tutorials Ava always watched on YouTube.

"I hate her." Venom dripped from my tone. Not only because she was beautiful, but also because she had him.

Already tired of looking at my computer screen, I leaned back against my chair and straightened my pens, separated by color in their cup-like containers.

"I'm telling you, she's not that ..." She coughed. "But do you think her boobs are real?"

"They can't be." My eyes level with the screen. "Who has a perfect face, body, and boobs, too?"

Why must life be so unfair?

"Sonia!"

I jerked back at the sound of my boss's voice and knocked over my coffee in the process, causing me to jump back and drop the phone. "Damn it!"

Liquid spilled everywhere—on the desk, on my keyboard, on my skirt.

Fisting a handful of Kleenex from my tissue box, I cleaned up my desk. The light-brown liquid soaked the tissues. I grabbed more, repeated the process, patted my damp skirt down, and glared at his office door.

I had ordered his breakfast, picked up his dry cleaning, and gone over his schedule for today. *What the hell did he want now? Couldn't I get some peace for five freaking minutes?*

I reached for the phone dangling off my desk and placed it to my ear. "Gotta go, Ava. The crass hole is beckoning."

She sighed overly loud. "Tall, dark, and oh-so fine. Give my love to your BILF."

Boss I'd Like to—yeah, right.

How about Boss I'd Like to Kill?

"I'll tell the BILK you said hello. Bye." I reached for my iPad, adjusted my glasses, and skittered to his office, my two-inch turquoise Mary Janes clicking against the black marble floor. After I pulled down my plaid knee-length skirt, I entered his fishbowl office.

Floor-to-ceiling windows outlined every single wall. His eyes focused on the screen in front of him, his backdrop was worthy of a picture frame—the Chicago skyline.

Brad Sebastian Brisken had the face of a Hollywood heartthrob, the jawline of a *GQ* model, and the body of someone who lived at the gym all the time. His suit was always perfectly pressed, and the lines in his sleek slacks always hugged his firm thighs. There was never a dark strand of hair out of place. He looked like a Greek god—tall, fit, and fine.

"Took you long enough."

"Sorry, was on the phone with my mom." *Jerkface.* I didn't sound sorry.

And this was how our two-year working relationship had been going. Him being a jerk, me snapping back or blatantly not caring.

Who cared if Brad was a millionaire? Who cared that he was seriously one good-looking, fine specimen of a man with his chestnut hair and dark brown eyes? Every woman fawned over him. Every male wanted to be him.

Me? Sometimes, he drove me to the point of insanity where I wanted to wrap my arms around his neck and choke hold him, WWE-style, until he turned blue.

After working for him for over two years, there was one thing I had come to realize: good looks and all the money in the world did not make up for his jerk-like attitude.

He motioned to the chair in front of his desk, and I sat down. And, as I swiped at my iPad, his phone rang.

"Hey, Jimmy." He leaned back on his chair, resting his ankle on the opposite knee, and with a flick of his hand, he waved me off as though I were a fly on his shoulder.

I stood, about-faced, and was almost to my desk when he called out to me as though he had a permanent megaphone attached to his mouth, "Sonia!"

I pivoted and walked back into his office. When I sat down, his phone rang. He picked it up, and with a flick of his hand, he waved me off—*again.*

"Yeah, yeah. But did you get the tickets?" His boisterous laughter grated on my nerves. He swiveled in his chair and faced his floor-to-ceiling windows, his back toward me.

This guy!

I glared at him, stomped back to my desk, and was about to sit down when he called out again.

For the love of all that is holy.

My eyes fell shut, and I inhaled deeply. I took out my essential oils and rubbed one at my temples and my wrists. Lavender was supposed to alleviate stress, and I debated on dumping the whole bottle on myself to speed up the process.

Breathe. Or go postal and lose your job.

I counted backwards and walked into his office at a normal pace, purposely taking my time.

"Did you spill coffee on yourself?" He lifted a perfect eyebrow and eyed the brown stain on the front of my skirt. "That's a first."

Of course, it was a freaking first. I prided myself on being organized and neat, and I was—before stalking Jeff and his new girlfriend. Seeing them together and being so in love had officially screwed with my head.

Brad's head ducked back to his computer screen where he tapped away. "Dry cleaning is on the couch. Where're my other clothes?"

I peered over at the far corner of the room where a pile of pants, suit jackets, and shirts were stuffed into an over-flowing bag.

"Last week's dry cleaning is in your closet." That was the first thing I had told him when I saw him this morning.

Maybe I needed to slip him some of that earwax solution, leave it on his desk with a little courtesy note.

"I've also made reservations at Alessi's Restaurant for your date tonight."

He lifted his head from the screen. "I said Carlucci."

"You said Alessi." My eyes widened, and I double-blinked. I'd chased this reservation down for the past few weeks and called every day to check if there was a cancellation. I'd finally snagged a reservation yesterday. *Is this man serious?*

"I'm pretty sure I didn't."

This coming from the guy who couldn't read his schedule. Despite that I kept it organized, yesterday, he had met with the wrong Mr. Wilson.

Boss, really quick, can I borrow your desk because it's closer than mine so I can bang my head against it?

"Did you book the hotel?"

"Yes." I clenched my teeth in a tight smile and ground my molars. "I also ordered flowers, and they will be delivered to your table."

I'd basically set the plans for him to get laid tonight. Who knew what poor soul he had his sights on?

I had tried to warn off the countless interns and account officers who walked through Brisken Printing Corporation, but they still wanted him. Brad threw them one look, and they were all a forgone without-a-job conclusion.

Because canoodling between the sheets with the boss could turn the most professional women into the jealous and crazy stalker types, which usually ended up with them quitting and heading to the back of the unemployment line.

"What kind of flowers did you buy?" He leaned back on his chair and steepled his fingers by his lips.

"Roses, the kind I always order."

"I want to change it up this time. Order me some peenees."

My brow wrinkled, and I leaned in, clutching the iPad against my chest. "What?"

"Peenees. Remember, I told you about them the other day. The front desk had an arrangement of peenees."

My boss loved to hear himself talk, and I was on the

receiving end of that one-way dialogue, but I filtered out all things not work-related, and that didn't require my attention.

What the hell is he even saying?

"What kind of flowers?"

"*Peenees,*" he drawled out the word as though elongating the E would make me understand him. He sounded like he was saying penises.

Why will I have to order that? Isn't she going to get that later?

He almost looked annoyed, so I made him repeat it again.

"Sorry, what was that again?"

I bit my lip and schooled my features. If he was going to make my life hell, I could at least have a little laugh of my own.

"Peenees." His voice was softer this time as though he were unsure. "Oh, for shit's sake, come here."

He began typing on his keyboard, and when I approached behind his desk, I expected to see a bunch of penises on his screen, but he typed *peenees* flowers in his search engine, and peonies came up.

Like a smart-ass, I pointed to the screen. "There's an O there. It's pronounced as pee-O-nees."

He visibly frowned. "Real funny," he deadpanned. "Do I look like a florist to you? Just add those flowers to the order."

"Okay, will do." I smirked, stepping around his desk.

He waved a hand, dismissing me. "Thanks. Wish me luck tonight."

Brad didn't need luck. He'd get laid, and he'd lose interest. It was his MO. And I'd hear about it all the next day because he was a sharer—but only to me, it seemed.

"Make sure you pick up my lunch at Klypso," he added.

"Already ordered. Is that it?" I lifted an eyebrow.

The sounds of him typing on his keyboard echoed through the room.

"Yeah." He didn't even lift his head from the computer.

He was in fine form today. I tried not to roll my eyes as I slowly shut the door and made my way back to my desk.

This is just a job, I reminded myself.

Charles—his brother, the CEO of Brisken Printing Corp.—and Mason—his younger brother and the VP of finance—had hired me over two years prior. They had interviewed me, and I had been told that the job had two main functions. One: keep Brad's schedule organized and on track. And two: do not sleep with him. It was two requirements that I had to adhere to.

Before me, Brad had gone through six secretaries within six-months. But his inability to keep it professional and their inability to say no were affecting their work, and his schedule was disorganized. It didn't help that some of those secretaries had gone on a warpath when Brad decided to move on. And he always moved on.

He changed women like he changed the channel—quick and wanting to know if there was something better.

I had been in a serious relationship with Jeff, so that number two rule was a no-brainer. It would not happen. Following rules was built into my DNA, and organization was one of my strong points.

And, although super fine, Brad was not my type.

I was kinda geeky. I embraced the romantic nerd in me. I loved playing Pokémon Go, I read a dangerous amount of romance novels, and I was the biggest Harry Potter Head.

I couldn't exactly picture Brad watching a marathon of

everything on the Hallmark Channel or all seven Harry Potter flicks.

Brad tended to like the girls with the A, B, Cs—ass, boobs, and curves.

And I was five-two, petite, and flat-chested with dark brown hair and glasses because I couldn't function without them.

It was a match made in secretary-boss heaven. Purely platonic.

No secretary in the whole Chicagoland area made as much as I did. Seriously. I was overpaid but under-laid, which was fine by me. And it was worth it. My friends who had full-time jobs worked a part-time job to make ends meet. Me? I had a one-bedroom condo in walking distance from work in downtown Chicago, and I could only afford it because of my job. Every year, I got a substantial raise and a bonus. It was as if they were increasing my pay exponentially every year I continued to keep my legs closed.

The Brisken brothers paid their employees well, and keeping my panties on meant it would stay like that.

Brad

Maybe Charles was right. I was already tired of the dating game.

Looking at myself in the hotel bathroom mirror, I ran one hand through the top of my dark hair and let out a tired sigh. Tired dark brown eyes stared back at me.

My younger brother, Mason, was in a five-year-long relationship with the epitome of a gold-digging she-devil. When I thought of their relationship, it only confirmed what I never wanted in one of my own.

But my older brother lived in romantic bliss with his second wife, reminding me again how a good relationship should be. Seeing Charles and Becky together changed my mind about relationships.

I wanted what they had and what my parents had—a real relationship with someone I could connect with.

"Come back to bed, baby," Olivia cooed when I stepped from the bathroom. Her tone increased in pitch, the way women tried to sound cute but weren't.

I toweled off my wet hair and body, slipped on my black pants, and worked to button my shirt. I stared at her long and hard, trying to force a connection between us, but it simply wasn't there. "I'm sorry. I have to go. Early morning meeting."

She'd seemed prettier earlier, but maybe that was because I'd been drinking.

That wasn't true. I hadn't had too much to drink. I had purposely remembered to pace myself.

I averted my gaze, disappointment seeping deep into my skin. I had known this night would come. I was hoping it wouldn't, but it had with the previous girls I dated. Like clockwork, after sex, I lost interest. Not because the sex was bad. It was good, as all orgasms were, but that closeness I had been hoping for—that familiarity—wasn't there.

This was our sixth date. I'd thought dragging it on would be sweeter, and we'd have more of a connection, but I guessed not.

It wasn't only Olivia's red hair and deep brown eyes that had caught my attention; it was also her sharp wit and intelligent, investment banker self. Now, her red hair had lost its sparkle, and her brown eyes, which had once seemed endless and deep, were now shallow. I'd spent time getting to know her, wanting to know her, yet something else was missing.

She pulled the sheets to cover her breasts and sat up straighter on the bed. "Are you really doing this right now, Brad?" Her once-strong tone turned whiny.

This was the part I hated, but honesty was better than leading her on.

"I really do have to get to work early." I walked closer to the bed and sat at the edge, finishing off the last button. "You are welcome to stay till the morning. Breakfast will be delivered." I took in her tousled red hair, her once-piercing brown eyes ... but there was nothing. No spark. No sudden urge to kiss her. Only an unbearable itch underneath my skin to get up, leave, and shower again at home.

"You're not going to call me." Her tone was resolute, soft, her high-pitched, trying-to-be-cute voice gone.

This was better than the previous psycho woman who had destroyed the hotel room when I left, but it still sucked.

I sighed resolutely, trying to add some feeling into it. "You're way too good for me, Olivia. I'm too busy, I would never pay you any attention, and I'm an asshole."

All of this was true, but really, she wasn't the right girl for me. Maybe I was looking for something that didn't exist. My parents had been married thirty-five years, and when my father had met my mother, he said he had known. It was in the way she'd made him laugh. He'd just known that she was it for him. I knew Olivia wasn't it. And the woman before her hadn't been it and the woman before that.

Will I eventually find someone I want to be with? What if it isn't in the cards for me—to have what Charles or my parents had?

My gut clenched at the thought.

She leaned into me and rested her head on my shoulder, and I resisted the urge to cringe.

"But, if you change your mind, you will call me, right?"

"Of course." I forced an even smoothness in my tone, knowing I wouldn't, and I kissed her forehead one last time before standing up to leave. Relief flooded me once I was out of the hotel.

I hopped into my Aston Martin and headed home to the suburbs. I didn't want to sleep alone tonight, not at my condo in the city. That wasn't where I called home anyway.

As I drove and the city lights disappeared behind me, my shoulders slumped. I should've felt energized. Olivia was a freak in the bedroom, but all I felt was fatigue in my bones and an undeniable desire to knock out on my bed. All this work when dating—the wining and dining and the sex —was tiring. I didn't mind the sex, but it seemed as though I were on the hamster wheel of dating. I'd pick a girl, repeat the cycle, and hope that it was different this time, that I'd like a girl long enough to keep her. But finding *her* hasn't happened yet and round and round the cycle I went.

I hated when my brothers were right, and they were; I was already tired of the game.

I waved at the guard at our palatial estate to open the gates and drove up the winding road to the mansion that my parents had built and expanded over the years.

Thinking of not having them here anymore always sent an ache to my chest, an unbearable tightness in my lungs. It was almost four years ago, and it seemed as though tragedy had hit us one after the other during that time.

Charles's wife, Natalie, had died when giving birth, leaving him to raise two girls by himself. And my parents asked Charles to move in so they could help with their grandchildren. Charles was an absolute wreck during that time, unable to go to work or properly care for the girls. It was one of the hardest times we'd gone through; we were all afraid he wouldn't break out of his depression.

And, just when life had gotten back to normal, a drunk driver had taken my parents' lives. It had gutted us, and we'd never been the same since.

But family was of the utmost importance, so we all tried. Mason and I had moved in to help Charles raise the kids. Though Mason and I had our places in the city, we were sleeping in our Barrington suburban house we'd grown up in because family always came first in the Brisken household.

As I entered our house and stepped into the silence, an agonizing sadness took over me. I took the stairs two at a time and slowly opened Sarah's door. I could see the moonlight shine a light over my niece's small twelve-year-old frame, and I released a soft sigh, knowing she was safe.

Next, I tiptoed into Mary's room. The night-light on the wall illuminated her room in a faint amber glow. The princess decals on her walls smiled down on my sweet niece. I walked closer and took in her petite features, the way she hugged the elephant that I had given to her when she was three, and the way she slept with her mouth slightly ajar. *Damn precious.* I kissed the top of her head and brushed the back of my hand against her cheek.

Dads weren't supposed to play favorites, but no one ever said anything about uncles.

Go to www.authormiakayla.com to see where you can purchase this book.

STAY IN TOUCH

Thank you so much for reading. There are a ton of books to read out there, but you have chosen to spend your time with mine.

And for that...I appreciate you.

Here's where you can find me. Join my reader group to stay in the loop about my most recent books.

JOIN MY READER GROUP
https://www.facebook.com/groups/miakaylabooks/
WEBPAGE
http://www.authormiakayla.com
FACEBOOK
http://www.facebook.com/authormiakayla

ALSO BY MIA KAYLA

Let me help you find your next read...

Go to www.authormiakayla.com to find out more about her books.

THE BRISKEN BROTHERS

Boss I Love to Hate - An Office Romance

Teacher I Want to Date - An Opposite Attract Romance

THE TORN DUET - ROCKSTAR ANYONE?

Torn Between Two - Book 1

Choosing Forever - Book 2

THE FOREVER AFTER SERIES

Marry Me for Money - Forever After Book 1

Love After Marriage - Forever After Book 2

The Scheme - Brian's book - Forever After Book 3

Naughty Not Nice - Forever After Book 4

BILLIONAIRE BROTHERS

Unraveled - The Tattooed Bartender

Undone - The Actor

STAND ALONE

Everything Has Changed - The Football Player

Sweet Love - An Office Romance

ACKNOWLEDGMENTS

This book was so hard to write because of 2020 and all it entails. Through it all, one thing I've done is I've forced myself to be grateful for all the things—big and small.

It's crazy that I have to force myself to do what would seem like a normal thing to do, right?

But given the state of the economy, politics, the pandemic and our world turned upside down and inside out, it has been a little difficult to stay positive.

But... I got us gratitude journals.

And each morning, I get up and before I even brush my teeth I give thanks. Then I do my morning devotional. And all of these things has helped tremendously.

As always, I thank God, for leading me to this path—to write, to provide escapism for people that need it, to show others that despite peoples' faults and shortcomings everyone deserves to be happy and to be loved.

To the husband, who is and has always been my number one supporter, thank you so much for all you do.

To my girls—I took a lot of these adult and children

interactions from you. I can only write a toddler and almost teen because I've been through those phases, raising my own kids.

It takes a team to get this done and I want to thank everyone that has helped me make this book the best it can be.

To my writer friends who listen to me vent daily and help me promote — To Michelle, El, Tracey, Danielle, Suzanne, Erica, Jenny and to all those in the Office. True loyal writer friends are hard to find. I only have a few and I'm keeping you close and never letting go.

To my beta readers—To Megan, Elizabeth, Johana, Melanie, Melai and Sarah. Thank you for your honest feed back and helping me in strengthening the story. You guys spent the time out of your day to read, analyze and answer all my questions and I appreciate you.

To Gel for doing my amazing teasers. I heart you.

To my PA—Elizabeth, you keep me organized and sane and happy. I appreciate everything you do for me.

To my developmental editor—Kristy, thank you for reading this and helping me get this to tip top shape. I know you're probably tired of hearing me vent, but you do it anyways and I appreciate you for it.

Megan—you are *my* person. Now and forever and until the end of time. Thanks for simply getting me and my characters.

To my cover designer—Juliana, you've got talent and so much patience. Thank you for putting up with me and for my stunning cover.

To the bloggers that have consistently supported me from my very first book to now. I heart you! Thank you for following me on this journey.

Last but not least to my readers— From those who have followed me from my very first book and to the new readers, thank you! thank you! thank you! Thank you for reading my words.

Made in the USA
Las Vegas, NV
15 December 2020

13135739R00218